WE BOTH SHALL ROW,
MY LOVE AND I

Mark G. Turner

◆ FriesenPress

Suite 300 - 990 Fort St
Victoria, BC, V8V 3K2
Canada

www.friesenpress.com

Copyright © 2019 by Mark G. Turner
First Edition — 2019

All rights reserved.

This story is a work of fiction. All characters and events are the product of the author's imagination. Any resemblance to any person, living or dead, is coincidental.

Stock imagery within this book is provided by Thinkstock. Certain stock imagery © Thinkstock.
Scripture quotations taken from the King James Version of the Holy Bible. www.biblegateway.com.
Public domain.

No part of this publication may be reproduced in any form, or by any means, electronic or mechanical, including photocopying, recording, or any information browsing, storage, or retrieval system, without permission in writing from FriesenPress.

ISBN
978-1-5255-3635-9 (Hardcover)
978-1-5255-3636-6 (Paperback)
978-1-5255-3637-3 (eBook)

1. FICTION, ROMANCE, HISTORICAL

Distributed to the trade by The Ingram Book Company

Table of Contents

Dedication	vii
Acknowledgements	ix
Preface	xi

Book One **1**

The Valley Trail	3
Cumberland, Northwest England May 1789	
Midway Bridge	25
Oak Harbor	37
The Brigand's Camp	53
The Royal Stag	65
Warrington Hall	73
The Pedestal	91
The Harbor Master's Office	111
Fair Havens Church	131
Blenheim Chapel	147
The Brigand's New Camp	159

Book Two **171**

The Parsonage	173
The Atwater Home	183
Edwyn's Porch	191

The Sea Wall	201
Edwyn's Workshop	217
Lord Warrington's Study	231
The Main Dock	253
The Harborside	271
The Cleared Lot	293
The Healer's House	307

Book Three **327**

Captain Henderson's Quarters	329
The Field Of Retribution	343
The Traveler's Studio	353

July 1789

The Brixton Home	369
Liverpool	383
Our Home	405

October 1789

Saint Bega's Priory	415
The Precipice	433
In The Midst Of Loved Ones	453
The Place of Remembrance	467
The Eleutheran Quest	479
A Closing Pastoral	501
About the Author	503

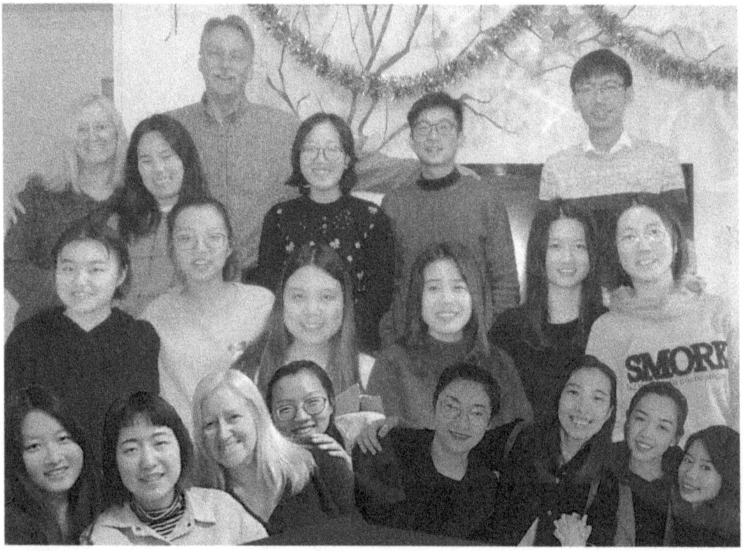
SMORE

Dedication

I am forever amazed by the way in which God works in the hearts and lives of people. This novel is dedicated to the **many** Chinese Christians that we have had opportunity to get to know and work with when we ministered in England and in the People's Republic of China.

In particular, this novel is dedicated to the members of the Biscuit Club in China that my wife and I had the opportunity to work with and lead.

The Lord has inspired me through each of you. It has been a tremendous source of joy to watch each of you blossom in the Lord Jesus. Your knowledge of the Scriptures has increased, your spiritual gifts have grown, and your service skills have developed. Continue to love and trust Him with your whole heart. You are truly His workmanship.

Ephesians 2:8-10 ESV

For by grace you have been saved through faith. And this is not your own doing; it is the gift of God, not a result of works, so that no one may boast. For we are his workmanship, created in Christ Jesus for good works, which God prepared beforehand, that we should walk in them.

Acknowledgements

With humble appreciation, I would like to recognize the assistance of my loving wife, Marie, and our always-supportive daughter, Anna Marie Dueck. Their assistance in the preparation of this novel was priceless. Their prayer support, proofreading, editorial advice, manuscript suggestions, and frequent encouragements have been a genuine source of strength.

Marie, thank you for your wonderful artistic work with many of the illustrations. Your sketches, drawings, and diagrams have served well to represent many significant features found in the novel.

Preface

Michael would have been content living out his days in the peacefulness of his quiet mountain hamlet in northwest England. The complexity of urban living and the activities of sinister criminals never reached their sleepy village. This would all change when an evil family, lacking a moral compass, challenged the peacefulness of their way of life.

Eighteenth century Georgian England was a dangerous spider's web of intricate social relationships, diverse communities, and compelling business interests. Confronted by the maliciousness of the wicked, Michael's conscience and sense of morality would serve as the battleground for his growth as a man.

Michael, a confident musician, would find himself thrust out upon the turbulence of a more challenging life by two things: the cancer of criminal intrigue and the consolation of tender romance with a woman who would bring out the best in him. They would explore what it would mean to have a deep and maturing relationship with one another. They would learn that love is so much more than romance.

For Michael, much like a ship, greatness wouldn't be discovered until it had weathered perilous storms and survived desperate battles.

MARK G. TURNER

> **The strength of a person's life
> is not easily determined until decisions are made,
> a course of action is pursued,
> and challenges are faced.**

Book One

The Valley Trail
Cumberland, Northwest England
May 1789

Quietly, I passed beneath the lofty green canopy of the forest. The earthy smell of the decaying vegetation that made up the moist woodland floor filled the air. The damp soil, the softness of the fallen leaves, and the pine needles beneath my feet caused my passing to be a silent one. The shadows of the forest embraced me and the absence of human activity along the path instilled tranquility within me.

I was comfortable here. It was where I belonged and the misty grey of early morning was always one of my favorite times of day. This peaceful place penetrated and calmed me.

A few birds—wrens, finches, and a nuthatch—had started their day, moving from branch to branch overhead. They sought seeds and insects, unconcerned about my passage beneath them. Their intermittent chirping and pleasing songs demonstrated an unhurried pace, and soothed me.

It wasn't the first time that I'd been asked to take a message to the leaders of the seaport, beyond the mountain valley far below. It was, however, the first time that I'd been asked to do so because of alarming and tragic circumstances.

Detaching myself from the awakening forest and seeking a few minutes of rest and refreshment, I eased my pack from my shoulders. Stretching my arms, my shoulder strain was relieved. *Oh, that feels so good.*

Being quite warm from the invigorating walk, I opened my coat, took a long drink of cool water from my leather-bound canteen, and ate a couple slices of delicious raisin bread. I felt rejuvenated.

I caught my breath at this spot where another trail met mine, and looked further down the path into the forest depths. I reflected carefully on the seriousness of the meeting the previous night.

~~~~~~~

Old Thomas, with two young men and a woman still in the flower of her youth, had come to my home long after darkness had fallen the previous night. He was, beyond a doubt, the wisest man in our settlement of Cliffside, and often came to visit me and discuss things that he had seen or heard. I enjoyed his friendship deeply, ever since I was young, and with the passing of my grandfather, he filled a void in my life. With my mother and sister having left many months earlier for Penrith, I was thrilled by the possibility of a stimulating visit when he arrived at my door.

The sleepiness of Cumberland's mountain district was like a warm bed on a cool night. It was much quieter than the industrial towns to the south or the bustling seaport to the west.

When the visitors arrived, I had been sitting in front of the last glowing embers in my fireplace, eating some cheese and enjoying a moist and delicious pear. I was reading several well-worn, yellowed manuscript pages, trying not to further damage them with my drippy fruit. The yellow glow of an old oil lamp barely provided the needed light to enjoy what was written.

Hearing some movement outside, I glanced towards the window beside my door and recognized Thomas, my dear old friend. He tapped on the door, mumbled something, and looked back at several companions that were standing just beyond him.

I stepped over to the window and peered out through the glass.

The two men with Thomas looked familiar. They may have passed through Cliffside, perhaps on their way to the village of Stone Ridge, further up the mountain, but I didn't remember ever having seen the woman before. She was beautiful. Her long dark brown hair cascaded over her shoulders and her expressive eyes were difficult to disregard. She was perhaps a few years younger than I was.

Opening the door, I invited them in. "Thomas, you and your friends come in and sit by the fire."

In a subdued tone he responded, "Only me for now, Michael. The others will wait outside."

He eased himself into a chair as I gently placed another log onto the glowing embers. I sat beside him as he opened his big rumpled coat and held his cold, weathered hands, towards the fire.

"I have something that I need you to take to the leaders of Oak Harbor." He reached into his coat and from his inside chest pocket took out a wax-sealed envelope and a small wrapped package. They were tied together with a faded tartan ribbon.

"What's this about, Thomas? Oak Harbor is several days away."

He looked at me thoughtfully, parted his lips, and inhaled. "I dislike speaking of this and I don't want any of the children of our villages to know of it. Keep it to yourself." He moved his chair closer to the fire. "There's been an abduction and a fatal fire up in Stone Ridge. That's where the others outside are from. They've come seeking what help they can find." He wet his lips with his tongue.

I grasped his uneasiness. "The men are familiar to me but not the woman. You speak of an abduction, who's missing? How do you know that it's an abduction and not merely someone lost in the mountains?"

Thomas gestured towards the door. "Lorena's little sister is missing—she's the woman outside—and there were signs of a struggle. We've been searching the area around Stone Ridge for several days and haven't found her."

"What were you doing up in Stone Ridge?" I asked.

"I was helping my cousin fell some trees and then one evening, the little girl was abducted."

"The abduction of a child, that's such a wicked crime." I looked at Thomas, my brows angrily furrowed. "Does anyone have any suspicions as to who may have done it?" I didn't wait for an answer. My eyes met his. "Tell me more about the fire. Someone died in it?"

"That's right, an itinerant merchant of glass and clay vessels. His name was Charles Hawthorne." Thomas leaned further back into his chair, causing it to creak. "The wagon that he lived in while traveling from town to town caught fire."

"*Hawthorne.* Sure, I've met him many times and I've purchased things from him for my mother." I paused. "The two horses that pulled his wagon, what happened to them?"

Thomas shifted in his chair. "They were found in a clearing quite a distance away."

"Were there any indications on his body that something other than the fire had killed him?"

He was quiet for a moment, staring at the floor. "I found his body myself." His eyes met mine. I grasped his pain. "There were no indications how he died other than the fire." He paused, broke eye contact, and slowly shook his head. "The body was terribly burned. I've never seen anything so horrid." He looked away. "I'll never forget it."

Hearing the tremor in his voice and seeing his great distress, I respectfully waited for a moment. "Was there a connection between Hawthorne's death and the abduction of Lorena's little sister?"

"Both things happened the same night," he responded. "The merchant and his wagon were consumed by fire this side of Stone Ridge and the little girl, Myra, went missing from her family's cabin, only a short walk away."

At length, he shared with me more details about the fire, the missing girl, and the fear that has gripped the village. Listening closely, I asked a few more questions until our discussion tapered off as we reflected on the seriousness of the double tragedy.

I shook my head and added another log to the crackling fire. "Such a tragic night for Myra's family and the little village." My gaze moved towards the door. "Why didn't the others come inside with you?"

"Lorena's desperately upset about her missing sister—an adopted sister, actually. They found her as a toddler, six or seven years ago, wandering in the forest—"

Interrupting him, my questions poured out. "Wandering in the forest? Was her family ever found? Did anyone ever come looking for her?"

He looked at me with surprise. "You've not heard of this?"

"No, Stone Ridge is quite a distance away and I've only been back at Cliffside for a year or so."

"That's true." He shifted in his chair again. "Lorena finished her crying as we arrived. If she was in here with us and heard me talking about Myra's disappearance, she would've started up again." Thomas shook his head and leaned in towards the fire. He wet his lips. "Make sure that the leaders down in the seaport give this their greatest consideration, but don't speak of it to anyone else until James Warrington, Earl of Cumberland, is consulted."

"What's in the package?" I gestured towards it.

Thomas fingered the little packet he'd been holding. "It's a small silver dagger, a highland dirk. It was found on the cabin floor from where Myra was taken." He paused, looked into the fire, and adjusted a log with the toe of his boot. "I want the leaders to see this, especially Edwyn."

"He's well-travelled, having spent so many years at sea before settling in Oak Harbor."

The fire snapped a few times and he scratched his chin. "Maybe he'll know something about the design on the handle. No one in Stone Ridge has ever seen the dagger or the design before."

"May I take a look at it?"

"Of course." He untied the tartan ribbon and opened the cloth.

I studied it intently. "Interesting ribbon, but the tartan doesn't look familiar."

"It was Myra's. Mrs. Wood, her mother, usually tied the little girl's hair back with it. It also was found on the cabin floor after the abduction."

"The design on the dirk certainly is unique. Was there a sheath with it?"

He shook his head. "No. Only the dirk, partially concealed beneath a big padded chair."

I inspected it more closely. "Hmm, a precision blade with a fine edge and an artistic pattern on the handle." Picking up a small piece of blank paper from beside the manuscript pages I'd been reading, I carefully copied the design.

He looked up from the fire and his tired eyes met mine.

"Describe Myra to me." I leaned back in my chair, straightened out my legs, and crossed my ankles.

"She's eleven years old, curly blonde hair, thin, and rather tall for her age. A bright child, loving the forest, and full of fun. Lorena says that Myra has a distinctive birthmark, a port wine stain, on her neck beneath her ear." He raised his hand to the right side of his neck and tapped it, and with his fingertip, traced the shape of the birthmark on his neck. "It's a backwards letter 'c'."

"I'll leave for Oak Harbor at first light." My eyes met his and I believe he understood my sense of duty. "I'll do my best." I rewrapped the dirk with the cloth and tied it and the sealed envelope together with the faded ribbon.

"I know you will. You're a man of integrity and learning. Tell the leaders what I've told you tonight and tell them that I'll be down to Oak Harbor in a few days." He coughed a couple times. "Think this through with them. Perhaps you and the leaders could decide on a course of action to locate little Myra."

"Certainly." I nodded. "Thomas, look again at the area where the fire occurred and also in and around Myra's home. Don't look for the obvious." I paused and leaning forward in my chair, rested my elbows on my knees. "Look for the subtle, the curious, the thought provoking. Anything that her family can't explain."

He nodded. "I will Michael. Ask the help of any other trusted people in the seaport. It's possible that someone might know something. There are ships and people coming and going all the time in the harbor."

"Thank you for trusting me with this, Thomas."

He gestured towards the door. "I'll invite the others in but let's not speak of this again. Lorena's sorrow is finally subsiding." He glanced over at the little three-legged table in the corner and my oboe laying upon it. "Perhaps you'd be willing to share a song with us."

He stepped towards the door as I leaned to the side and reached for my oboe. I laid it across my knees, resting one hand on it, while I lifted my mug to my lips. I drank the cool spring water, rinsing my mouth, and set the mug back down. The reed, which I had left in the instrument, was still damp, having been played earlier in the evening. I moistened it further and exercised my fingers on the keys as the others entered. The two men sat on the raised stone hearth and the young woman sat upon a small stool near my feet. Her beauty was astounding.

Thomas told the others that they could rely on me for help, and then he returned to his chair, which creaked beneath his weight.

We engaged in friendly conversation and when it ended, I started to play the slow lament that I had practiced earlier. It was a duet that I had composed for flute and oboe. The primary melody, written for flute, wasn't too high, and was therefore also suitable for oboe. They sat quietly and listened. The plaintive notes of the song, filling my cabin with their low throaty tones, created a sorrowful mood.

Part way through the repeated variation of the melody, Lorena, with tears filling her eyes, began to weep quietly for her sister.

I ended my playing. "I'm sorry. Perhaps I should've played something less sombre." I set my oboe back on the table.

Lorena, with heavy brows and quivering lips, whimpered, "Not at all. It was both beautiful and melancholy at the same time. Thank you for sharing your music with me." She tried to smile, looked at the others in the room, and corrected herself. "With *us*."

Thomas and his companions stood and moved towards the door. As they passed by me, I rested my hand on Lorena's shoulder and her long, soft, scented hair brushed over my bare arm. I wanted to reassure her. "We'll do all that we can. Let's trust that she'll be found soon, without harm." I held my breath, waiting for her response. She turned towards me and her tender tear-filled eyes met mine.

Lorena nodded solemnly. I brushed a tear from her cheek and she held my gaze for a moment. "Myra's alone in the world," she said, looking at me. Again, another tear ran down her cheek. "She's in harm's way. I know it for sure. I've lost hope."

Old Thomas sought to encourage her. "Have faith, Lorena. Hope deferred makes the heart sick." His voice lightened. "Let's cling to hope and pray that she'll be found unharmed."

She looked at the floor as she continued out the door.

Watching them disappear into the shadows of the trail, I heard a dog bark ominously in the distance. I returned inside and bolted the door for the night. Sitting in my chair, staring into the fire, I reflected on the events of the evening and what Thomas had shared.

~~~~~

Having considered what had been shared at the previous night's meeting, I thought that I should pray, but didn't. Instead, I left my thoughts of the night before, arose from the boulder where I'd been sitting, and took another long drink from my canteen. As I returned it to the bag at my side, I heard the voices of several men coming towards me on the path that met mine.

The wise old saying came back to me: '*A rabbit never seen, never sees the pot.*' I quietly slid down behind the boulder, concealing myself.

Three rough men with staves in their hands and blades on their belts walked passed my hiding place. The shortest of the three, muscular and carrying a leather backpack, was robust and seemed to be the leader. He had a sword at his side. The second man, even taller than I, was powerfully built. He had an impressive longbow over his shoulder, a quiver of arrows hanging from his belt on one side, and a knife on the other. The third man, an overweight fellow, clumsily followed.

They spoke with an unfamiliar accent and were talking about some ruler's banquet, describing enormous platters of food and endless tankards of ale. Laughing and talking, peppering their conversation with profanity, they were unaware that I was watching them.

Continuing on their way towards Oak Harbor, I decided to follow them. *Their profanity reflects their character. Who are they? Why are they heading towards the seaport?*

Descending the trail quietly, I snacked on some delicious bread and an apple while studying their boot prints and the poke marks from their staves. One of the men was missing part of the heal on his right boot, and its distinctiveness made it easy to follow. Soon the path would cross a mountain stream near a waterfall, and not wanting the sound of the waterfall to mask their talking, causing me to carelessly overtake them, I slowed my pace.

By the time I had finished my snack, I could hear the sound of the turbulent waterfall rising up through the valley. At a curve in the trail, I peered through the shadows and trees, looking for them.

There's no sight or sound of them, but their boot prints and staff pokings are easy to see.

I stepped a few paces into the forest bordering the path, listening and watching quietly, but could no longer hear them. As I pivoted to return to the trail, an imperial stag of fourteen points passed by upwind on the path. It paused, lowered its head, and began eating some low shrubs, only a dozen steps away. With quiet, shallow breathing and remaining motionless for a time, I was undetected. Eventually, the fatigue of maintaining such stillness caused me to shift my weight and, repositioning my foot, I made a slight noise. The beautiful reddish brown lord of the woodlands quickly lifted his head, froze for a moment, and then bolted, disappearing into the shadows.

Continuing on my way, I came alongside the stream below the waterfall and saw the place where they crossed. They had removed their boots and stockings to keep them dry, and would presumably put them back on when they reached the other side. I did likewise and crossed the cold mountain stream. Beside the log where I sat to put my stockings and boots back on, and where they must've done the same, I saw a small coil of fine twine with a fishhook on one end. Uncoiling it to check its length, I discovered it to be about forty feet long.

This will be useful. I put it in my backpack and returned to the trail after refilling my canteen.

A few hours later, with the shadows growing longer and the cool breeze rushing up the path from the valley before me, I realized that I should find a suitable campsite for the night. Leaving the trail for the security of concealment in the forest, I found a small clearing in a half circle of rocks about the height of my waist. The clearing, a stone's throw from the path, was further concealed from the trail by some bushes and a low earthen ridge.

Noticing that the wind was coming up the path from their direction, I concluded that they wouldn't be able to smell a campfire. I collected a handful of dead leaves for tinder and some dry twigs for kindling, and being far enough away from them that my flint and steel wouldn't be heard, I set about lighting a fire. In a few quick strokes, I had sparks, and a short time later, a set of glowing embers suitable for cooking.

In a glass jar full of water, I had sliced carrots, potatoes, and peppers, which I now dumped into a small dented pot from my backpack. I set the pot on the embers in my cooking fire, added some dried beef to the mix, and patiently cooked the mixture. With my knife, I sliced off and ate some cheese from a large wedge. Half an hour later, having eaten the delicious soup with a couple more slices of bread, I was content.

Playing my oboe, which I'd carefully packed for the journey, was out of the question. I didn't want to make any sounds that others might hear.

I don't know how far ahead of me they are. I don't want to be surprised while I'm asleep. I satisfied myself with some reading by the light of the fire.

I had borrowed a book from Edward Stewart, a friend in Oak Harbor. It was a set of weekly journal entries that spanned an entire year. The entries were lengthy, and at the end of the book were numerous pages of sketches, some of the author's personal reflections about his travels, and many hand-drawn maps. His name and the year of the journal were beautifully embossed on the leather cover.

Captain Edgar Fenton Bridger – 1764

We Both Shall Row, My Love And I

Interesting: 1764, the year that Mozart, at eight years of age, met Johann Christian Bach in London.

Captain Bridger, after serving in the king's army for twenty years and losing his wife to a riding accident, departed for continental Europe with three other men. When they arrived on the coast of Estonia, they set off on foot to search for an abandoned monastery in the Ural Mountains. The monastery was said to have hidden within it several chests of old scrolls and maps dating back to the time of Emperor Constantine. I read for almost an hour until it became too dark to continue, even by the light of the fire.

I doused the fire, removed my boots, and unrolled a large sheet of leather from my backpack. Stretching out on it, I covered myself with my woolen blanket. The night sounds of crickets and frogs from a nearby pond increased, as did the bothersome activity of the midges and mosquitos. They all had their place and their purpose; I simply wished that I were not a part of it. The air was growing cooler and I pulled my blanket, more hood-like, around the back of my neck. While thinking about little Myra's abduction and Hawthorne's death, it occurred to me that I hadn't asked what exactly was in the envelope. *I suppose there's a note in it. Is there something written there that I shouldn't see? I never asked Thomas about it and he never offered to share the contents with me.*

I listened quietly to the night breeze moving through the branches and the mysterious hooting of an owl. My breathing became deeper and slower. I dropped off to sleep.

～～～～～

The next morning I was awakened by the chirping and flitting about of birds in the branches above me. As I rolled over and then leaned up on one elbow, a small red squirrel, filled with terror, darted out of my backpack.

I hope the little raider didn't devour my bread and cheese.

Looking inside I saw that there were only nibbles missing here and there. I suppose that I startled him as I awoke and stirred.

Rolling up my wool blanket inside the leather ground sheet, and then looking intently at the envelope and package with which I had been entrusted, I wondered what might be written inside.

Are there details that I should know? Is there something in the envelope that Thomas forgot to tell me about? I fingered it, wanting to tear it open and read it, but my integrity restrained me. Part of me wished that it hadn't. I reluctantly returned it to my pack.

I tied my leather ground sheet and blanket across the top of my backpack and continued on my way down through the valley.

I hadn't been on the trail for more than half an hour when I came upon the place where the three men had spent the night. A wary badger was exploring the remains of their camp and sought refuge in the forest as I approached. The boot print, missing part of the heel, was as obvious as ever. They had taken time to eat some breakfast and their still smoldering fire meant that they were not far ahead. I looked around the campsite, gathered up and buried their debris, and carefully doused the fire. Once again, I found something they'd lost. It was an odd-looking green button, carved from bone, a little larger than my thumbnail, and having three holes. I slipped it into my pocket.

Returning to the path near the sleepy village of Little Town, I resumed my descent, winding my way through the trees and along the wall of a sheep enclosure. At a point where the path paralleled a small tumbling mountain stream, I refilled my canteen and drank of the refreshing and deliciously cool mountain water. I ate a hard-boiled egg and some more cheese.

There was less tree cover here and there were many places where sunlight broke through the canopy in generous bright swaths. The extent of deforestation because of heavy logging was alarming. The ugly stumps stood as eerie monuments of the forest's devastation and as helpless sentinels guarding what little remained. Men sought these great trees for timber and the less substantial growth for hearth and forge.

It was getting warm and my back was sweaty so I removed my coat and tied it to my wooden pack frame. My cotton shirt and tweed waistcoat would suffice.

The path ran along the rustic shoreline of Wainwright Lake, which glistened invitingly in the sunlight. I was amazed at the extraordinary schools of fish and the great number of waterfowl that could be observed, and as I sat upon a large shoreline rock and enjoyed the scene, I wished that I had time to camp and fish at this peaceful site.

A mother otter led her three young pups along the rocky shore towards me, and at one point, only ten to fifteen feet away, partially concealed by a fallen log, she nursed them. A few minutes later, they moved off and one of them still had a droplet of mother's milk on its mouth.

The trail left the edge of the lake and returned to the deep forest. Ahead, I could hear the three men arguing and cursing. *I'd better be careful. I must be getting dangerously close to them.*

My route descended more steeply now along the stream, and there were places where I turned about and climbed backwards down through small rocky crevices. There were wider parallel trails near these climbing points, but they were filled with mud.

The loud angry voices grew more distinct. After setting my pack behind a tree out of sight, I crouched low and peered through some cedar shrubbery between two boulders.

The tall man, with his longbow across his knees, sat on a rock watching the other two, and from time to time, he joined in their argument. The shortest but most robust man, the one with the sword, probably the leader, was ridiculing the big clumsy one. He had seen some fish in a pool of the stream, beneath a fallen tree, and wanted to catch them. The awkward fellow, unable to find the fishing line, was being blamed for his carelessness. The bowman silently pulled an arrow from his quiver and moved towards the pool. He stood upon a rock, perched like a voracious predator, scanning the chilly depths.

Stealthily, I moved a little closer to hear their conversation.

"Hurry up. Get us some fishes," said the swordsman.

"It's a stony stream. I don't want to break an arrowhead or a shaft," responded the bowman.

He cautiously positioned himself on the rocky shoreline, closer to the fallen tree. "Victor, you fool, if you hadn't lost the fishing line I wouldn't be risking my arrows. I only have nine left."

"You're a fine shot," said the swordsman. "If an arrow is damaged, Victor will owe you for it."

"Curse you Gavin, I will not."

Now I know a couple of their names.

"Victor, shut your mouth," whispered the bowman. "You're frightening the fish." He inhaled, held his breath, and let fly an arrow. Twang. "There we go, men. Victor, get the fish and be careful with my arrow."

Clumsy Victor stumbled into the water up to his knees as Gavin and the bowman laughed and mocked him.

The bowman sat on a rock beside the pool. "Mind that arrow, Victor. If you break it by stumbling around like a drunken fool, I'll put an arrow in you." He and Gavin laughed.

Victor climbed up out of the thigh deep water with mud on his boots and went over to the bowman, dripping on him. "The shaft is fine but the tip of the arrowhead is bent and needs sharpening." He handed him the arrow.

The bowman pulled a pair of pliers and a small file from a leather pouch. "You're dripping all over me and my gear, you clumsy oaf. Back off." He began straightening and sharpening the tip of the arrowhead.

Gavin had left the path to collect some tinder and wood for the fire and by the time he returned, Victor, quite adept with a knife, had already gutted and scaled the fish. He then inserted a green stick through its mouth, spread out the body with a few green twigs, and sat beside the place where Gavin was attempting to ignite the fire, ready to cook the fish.

"What do you think you're doing?" Gavin kicked clumsy Victor's thigh. "This fish is for me."

The bowman was back standing beside the water with his bow and the re-sharpened arrow. "There's another trout awaiting my arrow." Twang. He let fly again, piercing the fish.

"Victor, you clumsy hedgehog, grab that fish and bring the arrow to me."

"Why do I have to get wet again?" he responded. "What a bother. We passed some sheep back along the trail. I should've just grabbed a lamb and gutted it."

The bowman searched the pool with intense concentration. "Stop your complaining, you're still wet from before. Gavin made the fire, and I'm using my bow."

"Umph, you're both lazy and I'm doin' all the work," responded Victor. He stumbled, falling down onto one knee as he stepped into the stream. He reached into the water and grasping the arrow, still piercing the trout, turned, and climbed back up towards the fire. He handed the fish to Gavin and then stumbled over towards the bowman. Setting the arrow on a flat stone and sitting on a rotten stump, which collapsed sideways beneath his weight, he landed on his backside in some mud. "Cursed stump." He slowly got to his feet, passed wind, and jokingly said, "I didn't know that was in me!" Gavin and the bowman laughed scoffingly.

"Your deathly odor makes me want to wretch," exclaimed Gavin.

The bowman grinned and released another arrow. Twang. "There now, we have the third." Gavin was cooking the first two fish as Victor climbed up out of the water and stumbled up the embankment. He handed the arrow and the third trout to the bowman.

"Keep the fish, that one's for you. Gavin's cooking mine and his own."

"This is the smallest of the three," said Victor with derision. "I got all wet and muddy. Why do I get the smallest fish?"

The bowman glared at him. "The biggest fool always gets the smallest fish." He stepped towards him, staring and hoping for a fight, but Victor backed down.

"If you don't want it, bring it to me, I could eat two," said Gavin, as he and the bowman started laughing at wet and muddy Victor once more.

Victor finished cleaning his fish and sat by the fire.

"You stink somethin' awful," Gavin said, further berating Victor. "You smell like a privy."

He and the bowmen, cursing, moved upwind from Victor to eat their fish.

"I don't know what's worse," the bowman added, "your smell, your clumsiness, or your stupidity."

Victor, mocking with a screechy high woman's voice, mimicked the bowman. "I don't know what's worse, your smell, your clumsiness, or your stupidity."

Gavin threw a clod of mud at Victor. "Eat your fish and shut your mouth."

Victor returned to his usual voice. "I don't hear ya' complainin' when we're in a fight."

"That's true. Few fight better than you when it comes to wrestlin' and tuslin'," said Gavin. "That was a vicious end to the fight you had with that woodsman in Dumfries when you stabbed that broken bottle into his face."

"He's lucky he didn't lose an eye," added the bowman.

Victor winced and mimicked a stabbing motion. "He's lucky he didn't lose both of his eyes." Victor spit into the fire and drooled on himself. "He'll carry those scars all his days." He grimaced. "Those scars are my signature." He laughed again. "It's how I sign my name."

Laughter enveloped the three miscreants. They were having a good time remembering their depraved crimes at the expense of others.

"Good we left as fast as we did," Gavin added. "The townspeople would've sided with him and beat us mercilessly, or worse."

The three vile brigands sat there, chuckling and shaking their heads.

How do people get that way? I asked myself.

Gavin said, "We'll not be going back there anytime soon."

Victor, with chin up and chest out, bragged, "Brawlin' with that clay merchant up the mountain was almost as much fun as stompin' on a chicken and then when—" He stopped suddenly.

Gavin raised his palm towards them. Alerted, they listened.

Snorting horses and thudding hooves on the trail had captured their attention. A moment later, five enormous, mud-splattered horses cantered down the trail with heavily armed riders upon them. The lead horse was a huge grey Shire. The riders, probably Lord Warrington's men, exchanged menacing glances with Gavin and his companions.

After the horses and riders passed by, I remained there concealed, listening to their conversation about violence and crime, but the fight with the clay merchant wasn't mentioned again.

What was he going to say next before he was interrupted? It was obvious that Victor had abused Charles. How do people live like that? What kind of parents raise children that become brawlers and rogues?

I watched as they packed up their things and resumed their hike down the trail. Retrieving my backpack and going to the place where they'd eaten near the stream, I examined the area around their fire. The disarray and filth was a testament as to how they lived; fish guts, bones, rubbish, and the smoldering fire spoke volumes. I extinguished their fire with water from the stream and buried their rubbish.

In the mud, where the fish entrails had been, a glint of light caught my eye. It was a small pendant necklace, smudged with earth. I carefully rinsed it in the stream and the bits of mud fell away, sinking into the pool.

The pendant was a small but well-cut teal amethyst. Its unique teardrop shape added to its mystery. It was set in silver and suspended on a silver chain. Shards of sunlight pierced the forest canopy, and the glistening amethyst revealed its fine quality. I lifted it higher into the sunlight and noticed that on the back of the silver setting was an etched design much like the one on the dirk from Myra's abduction. I untied the ribbon and unwrapped the deadly little blade. The etchings were identical. *Is there a connection between the two, other than the shared design? Are the miscreants the connection?*

I rewrapped the dirk and tied it and the envelope together with the faded tartan ribbon, and returned them to my backpack. I slipped the pendant necklace into the left pocket of my tweed waistcoat along with the green button.

A few feet away, partially pressed down into the mud, I found the utility knife that Victor had used to gut and scale the fish. I rinsed it in the stream.

It would be amusing to see a list of the things he has lost over the length of his life.

I returned to the path and continued on my way, eating an apple and a slice of bread as I hiked. It was getting late and shadows were stretching deep into the forest. I followed them no further that day but set up camp a short distance from the trail.

Midway Bridge

A heavy damp fog filled the valley when my eyes squinted open, searching for the dawn the next day. The birds were silent and in the absence of any breeze, the trees were still. I hadn't been able to get a good night's sleep, but later I enjoyed a tasty trout for breakfast, caught with the fishing line I had found. Clearing my campsite in the thick and grey fog was a dismal experience, but returning to the trail, I was encouraged by the easy hiking on the gentle downward slope. A cool breeze rose up through the valley an hour or so later, and sweeping the fog away, brightened the morning. Sheep enclosures were more common now and the damp woolly creatures within them often stood and stared as I passed.

I arrived at Midway Bridge shortly before noon. It was known by such a name for being about half way between Wainwright Lake and the seaport of Oak Harbor, where this mountain stream, having become a notable river, empties into the sea.

From this point onward, the stream, now more substantial, was known as the River Westbrook because of its westward flow.

The beautiful arched bridge crossing it here in a single span was wide enough for a wagon pulled by a team of horses.

Years earlier, a famous artist and traveler, William Gilpin, also of Cumberland, had called it picturesque.

Midway Bridge, a peaceful village of twenty-five or thirty cottages, was nestled in a quiet forest glen not far from the bridge that gave it its name. It was where several trails met; mine from the high country to the east, a narrow path from the northwest, and a wide trail big enough for a wagon from the south.

As I got closer to the bridge, a playful grin emerged on my face, which grew to a broad smile when I became certain that an old acquaintance from Oak Harbor was up ahead. He was sitting on a stump beside the bridge with his fishing line and hook dangling from a crooked stick. Cleverly and patiently, he was tempting the fish in the river below. John Lyon was affectionately known by many as John 'The Rotund' for the obvious reason of his substantial girth.

"Michael, I've not seen you for a long time," said The Rotund as he reset the bait on his hook. "You enjoyed me stories, I remember well, when last we saw one another." He scratched his chin. "'as it been three years?"

"That sounds about right," I responded. "I heard that you went aboard a ship bound for the Baltic Sea."

"And I made me a pocketful o' guineas." He chuckled. "I was at sea for two full years. I saw me some unusual things and 'eard some strange stories."

Leaning against the stonework of the bridge beside him and thinking back to the journal I'd been reading, I asked him, "Have you ever heard of Captain Edgar Fenton Bridger? He spent a great deal of time on the Baltic."

"'ear 'bout him? I met 'im. 'e be no longer a young man. 'e be livin' in Riga now, writtin' books and drawin' maps."

Nodding and removing my backpack, I offered him a drink from my canteen. "I'm reading one of his adventurous journals, the one dated 1764." I stretched my shoulders, aching from carrying the pack. "His travels are fascinating."

The Rotund gave a little laugh and shook his head. "Michael, you be the most dedicated reader o' books that I ever be to knowin'. Why is that? What be your intentions with that?"

"I seek to learn." To emphasize my dedication, I repeated myself. "My desire is to learn all that I possibly can, for all the days of my life."

John skillfully adjusted his fishing line and smiled in agreement. "It be a fine intention."

"Tell me more about Captain Bridger," I requested.

Midway Bridge

"I met 'im, Captain Bridger, in a tavern in Riga two years ago and 'e was 'appy to be speakin' the king's English." John adjusted the position of his hook and line. "'e doesn't speak Latvian, the language o' Riga, but 'is Spanish an' 'is German, so I've 'eard, is fair."

"You know a little German, don't you John?"

He laughed with a twinkle in his eye. "Well now, Michael, I be knowin' a stunted barmaid in Berlin that'll sing all night long. Is that the little German you be speakin' of?"

I rolled my eyes, shook my head, and joined him in his laughter. "You know what I mean."

"Yes Michael, I be knowin' some German. Enough to buy and sell, and get along when I be travellin'. Anyway, Captain Bridger was 'appy to meet me but 'e spent much o' 'is time complainin' 'bout the cold. 'e says someday 'e'll be goin' to the Caribbean. 'e 'as a young brother in a place folks be callin' Spanish Wells, in the Bahama islands." John paused and put his pipe in his mouth. "Michael, what are you doin' 'ere 'bout?"

"I'm traveling down to Oak Harbor on serious business." *Old Thomas expects me to ask trusted people for help about Myra's abduction and Hawthorne's death. The Rotund is one of those people.* "I have a couple questions for you."

"Go on Michael, ask away."

"Are you aware that Charles Hawthorne was burned to death in his wagon?"

His jaw dropped. "No. That's tragic! Poor Charles, I knew 'im well."

"There's more. Have you heard about a missing child, a recent abduction, from Stone Ridge?"

He grimaced. "Oh no, dancin' demons. That's terrible. The abduction of a child is a monstrous crime."

"I'm following three rogues that may have had something to do with Charles' death and perhaps the abduction. Have you seen three men pass by?"

"I did." He looked at me with seriousness. "I saw three rough lookin' men earlier."

"Look at this." I withdrew the pendant necklace from my waistcoat pocket. "Have you ever seen a necklace like this or the design on its back?"

He looked closely at the necklace, squinting and trying to focus. "Me eyes aren't so good as they once be."

He reached into his coat pocket and pulled out a small velvet bag. Carefully opening the string at the top, he withdrew a pair of wire-rimmed spectacles. One of the lenses was cracked.

"Michael, I've never been seein' a beauty such as this before but I'm certain that I've seen this 'ere design on the back, or somethin' similar." He put his spectacles away.

"Where?"

"There be a jewelry man, a metal worker, who specializes in fine work such as this. Jewelry and blades mostly. Sometimes 'e uses this design. I'm not sure o' 'is name."

"Where's his shop?" I asked. "I don't remember anything like this in Oak Harbor."

"Oh, you're quite right. There be nothin' of this quality bein' made 'n our little seaport." John laughed and shook his head. "Edinburgh, I think. Yes, I'm sure of it. That be where I've been seein' it."

"What does this 'ave to do with the three men?" He looked at me with a grimace. "'ow'd you come to get this 'ere pendant?"

"I was watching those three men from a safe distance on the trail yesterday, and when they moved on, I found it at their campsite in the mud."

"Watch yourself, Michael." He shook his finger towards me. "Them rogues, they be a dodgy trio. They'd just as soon be sendin' a man off to eternity as swattin' a fly in a privy."

The Rotund passed the pendant necklace back to me. "I think you're right. They looked dangerous to me too." I slipped it into my waistcoat pocket. "So, they passed by here?"

"Yes. That be the truth, they did."

"How long ago?"

"I think I filled me pipe twice." He dramatically held up two fingers. "I was sittin' 'ere enjoyin' my pipe and some fine tobacco when they passed me by." Again, he adjusted his fishing line. "They were a mockin' me, an' the one they called Victor kicked this 'ere stump I be sittin' on. An' then 'e made some threatenin' comments."

"Tell me more."

"The one with the sword told 'im to make 'aste 'cause they didn't 'ave time for the likes o' me. The taller one, the one carryin' the bow, said, 'Leave the fat troll alone, 'e'll be puttin' a spell on you.' Then they started to laughin' and walked on."

"They're trouble and I'm glad that they didn't cause you any harm."

"I never seen 'em before. They be a rough lookin' bunch." He stopped speaking and looked at me seriously. "Michael, my friend." He pointed at me with the stem of his pipe and licked his lips. "Be careful. You be a tall man but the one carryin' a bow be even taller an' bigger. Like a great tree 'e was."

I scratched my chin. "I'd better be on my way. I'm going to see Edwyn and the other leaders of Oak Harbor about Charles' death and the missing girl—"

"I 'ear 'e might be leavin' in a few days," John interrupted. "To the town o' Douglas on the Isle o' Man."

"Edwyn's not going back to his life at sea, is he? I'm hoping that he might have some ideas about the abduction, and I'm taking a letter from old Thomas down to the leaders in the seaport." I pointed at some ripples on the water near his line. "Bye the way, why are you here at Midway Bridge, so far from your home?"

"I be waitin' for a load o' slate."

"Slate from Honister Pass, I imagine." I removed my tricorn hat and fanned myself with it. "I hear it's the best in England."

"'onister slate is the best but I'm not waitin' for 'onister slate. I'm waitin' for me cousin. 'e's drivin' a 'orse cart down from Cold Crow, that little rat 'ole o' a village. 'es got some slate for 'omes in Oak 'arbor."

"What's the slate like from there?" I asked.

"If a man can't get slate for 'is roof from 'onister Pass, then Cold Crow slate will 'ave to do." He coughed and spit into the water. "'e said 'e'd meet me 'ere at mid-day." He adjusted the location of his baited hook in the stream below. "Best o' luck to you, Michael, and be keepin' your distance from those three ruffians."

"Good luck with your load of slate. I'll see you when you get down to Oak Harbor." I swung my backpack up into position on my back and started to turn and walk away.

"There be one other thing." He broke eye contact with me and gestured down the trail. "There be a big family in a wagon that passed me by."

"When was that?" I asked.

"That be a time ago, when I first arrived 'ere at the bridge. Mid-mornin' I suppose."

"Describe them to me, John."

"Well, there be a young man with a short but deep scar, 'igh on his right cheekbone, about 'ere." He reached up and touched his upper cheekbone, directly below his right eye. "Sittin' up and drivin' the 'orse 'e was, an ugly sway back mare. There be a scrawny man a walkin' beside the wagon. That was all I be seein' 'til it passed me by. Then in the back, I saw an old woman but she be dressed rather well. When she saw me a lookin'," he mimed himself looking intently, "she leaned back into the shadows o' the wagon, lost to my sight. I 'eard voices an' laughin', deep-voiced adults an' a few youngsters talkin' inside the wagon. Those folks that I could see gave me the creepers. Suspicious I was."

"Bless you," I said. "I don't know if it means anything, but thank you for telling me. I'll pass it on to Lord Warrington and the leaders of Oak Harbor. Are you and your brother still living in the ruins of the old lighthouse?"

"We are, but ruins they are not. Fixed it up right proper we did with new windows an' a new roof. Say 'ello to me brother if you be seein' 'im."

"Yes, I will. Thank you."

"A good man you be, Michael. I 'ope you find the little missy."

I wished him well, crossed the bridge, and continued on my way down towards Oak Harbor. Both the trail and the waterway were more substantial now. The prints of the three brigands, with their stave pokings and the boot with its partially-missing heel, were still visible from time to time, but they were often ruined by the tracks of others.

As the shadows of late afternoon began filling the forest, I made camp for the night in a small clearing out of sight of the trail, which could now be called a road. After eating some bread and dried beef and then rinsing them down with cool water, I sat on a rock and took my oboe from its case. Selecting the best of my three remaining reeds, I practiced the difficult, triumphant section of *Newcastle March*. Then, having lost the light of day, I returned to the lament, by memory, that I'd played for Old Thomas and the others. The resonance of the valley added to the somber mood of the piece. Finally, having become quite melancholy, I returned my instrument to its case.

I unrolled my leather ground sheet and wool blanket but sleep didn't come easy. My mind wandered to Lorena with her scented hair and enticing eyes. I've seldom seen such a beautiful woman up here in the mountains. *Truly, a rare beauty. I thought of her soft, dark hair.* My warm blanket embraced me. My breathing slowed. Sleep found me.

~~~~~

Sunrise, much like the previous day, never fully emerged out of the darkness of night. I awoke to a wispy fog, which I could feel on my skin. I returned to the road and soon realized that the increasing wheel tracks, footprints of others, and horse's hooves made it almost impossible to discern the three men's boot prints or the poke marks of their staves.

Around noon, I approached a little community known as Bridgeton. It was so named for the bridge that crossed the river. In earlier years, the people of Oak Harbor, divided by both the river and the harbor itself, needed to travel this far upstream to cross over if they didn't want to pay a ferryman.

Beside the bridge stood the once thriving *Edgewater Inn*. Dilapidated it wasn't, but needing paint and repair it was. It had been a substantial business, but now, with people seldom staying there for the night, it struggled to pay its bills.

Edgewater Inn of Bridgeton

Half an hour downstream from Bridgeton, I passed by a quaint stone cottage near the trail, and a disturbance caught my attention. I stopped for a moment to watch what would shortly become a drama, both tragic and humorous.

In a clearing behind the cottage, a fox, having come out of the forest, had begun chasing a monstrously heavy white goose. There were some agitated chickens scurrying about as well, but the fox seemed to be of the opinion that one of those scrawny little birds wouldn't be able to satisfy its appetite. The fox, having determined that the great white bird, more than five times the size of even the largest chicken, would be a finer meal, continued its pursuit.

The goose, being not only intimidated but also angered by the fox, decided to stand its ground. It hissed and honked, flapped and poked at the little fox, trying desperately to penetrate its defenses. Finally, the fox, with ambition greater than its size, grabbed one of the great bird's legs in its jaws. The goose, being quite large and far too powerful to be taken down easily, continued its frenzied defense. It began circling backwards with feathers flying and clouds of dust being stirred into the air.

The determined fox refused to let go. The goose, honking, fighting for its life, and continuing its backward circles, began to drag the stubborn fox, who was no longer able to stay up on its paws.

After a few more minutes of this conflict, the fox eventually let go. It shook its head, grabbed a tiny chicken that was running past, and disappeared into the forest shadows. The goose began straightening its feathers, the garden around the cottage quieted down, and I continued on my way.

Oak Harbor

Nearing Oak Harbor several hours later in mid-afternoon, the smell of the sea filled the air. Being in the presence of so many people with their carts, barking dogs, running children, and animated conversations was disconcerting, almost alarming. It was so unlike Cliffside.

As I approached the actual harbor area, I passed Kline's warehouse, where several groups of men were busy unloading a shipment of building supplies. Warehouse customers and building contractors walked around the laboring men, and an intimidating dog on a rusty chain snapped at anyone who came too close.

I had heard that several thousand people lived in Oak Harbor now, and I realized that I hadn't been here for over a year. The new three arch bridge over the River Westbrook was complete and some young boys were climbing over the stone sidewalls and jumping into the water below. To the lads this bridge was the greatest fun, but to the townspeople, it vitally linked the two communities, one on each side of the harbor. To cross to the other community in earlier years meant traveling several miles upstream to Bridgeton or crossing here and paying a ferryman.

Oak Harbor was a hub of bustling activity, and knowing that I might be distracted from my task, I determined to go directly to the home of Edwyn and Louisa Brixton. Their home, and especially their front porch, often served as an informal meeting place.

Seven ships were tied up to the various docks, several were at anchor out in the harbor, and another one, a sturdy little two-masted schooner, was entering from the open sea.

There were a number of ships laden with coal at the docks, but the most prodigious coal carrier was at anchor out in the harbor. It was an impressive sight as it hauled up its great hook and prepared to leave the port. A coal carrier wouldn't ever be at anchor for loading but perhaps it was out there now, having left the dock, for a reason unknown to me.

Seamen were grunting and cursing under their breath as a demanding officer shouted orders at them. They secured the anchor and set sail with a slight breeze that would carry them through the harbor and out to the open sea. It was a newer ship with four masts reaching skyward. Loved ones were being left behind; some were waving, a young boy was crying, and a few laborers on the dock were pausing from their work to watch it depart.

Gulls flew aggressively amongst the boats and many more were on the shore, scavenging whatever they could find. A smaller number of terns, being more timid, soared high above the harbor, and further out.

I turned to the right and walked along the cobbled road passed St. Cecilia's with its impressive twin towers and quality brickwork. It had the largest Church of England congregation in the seaport. Farther along, after passing several small businesses and a few homes, I came to *The Royal Stag* tavern. It had new benches, one on each side of its solid, weather-beaten door but what impressed me most was the new sign above the entrance.

My walk towards the Brixton home took me next past the Harbor Master's office, with its pale blue paint. In front of it stood a slate board for shipping notices, and its conspicuous brass bell, which alerted the community of ship departures and dockside emergencies.

A short distance beyond the harbor master's office, likewise set back from the water's edge by the width of the street, I could see Edwyn and Louisa's comfortable home. With its broad porch and overlooking both the street and the harbor, it had always been one of my favorite places.

Beyond the Brixton home was the spectacular forest of oak trees that had given the harbor its name. The grove spread up the hillside with a well-kept road ascending through it. The stately trees, being protected by James Warrington, Earl of Cumberland, and his parents before him, had been left undisturbed from logging until recently. Now, from time to time, he would have some trees harvested, cut into timbers, and shipped to Bristol for the shipbuilding needs of the empire.

Stepping onto Edwyn's porch and stroking the head of his drowsy dog, an enormous English mastiff named Eutychus, I knocked on the Brixton's door. No one answered, so I knocked again, more deliberately. Eutychus lifted his head, looked at me, drooled, licked his lips, and then laid his big wrinkled head back down across his huge forepaws.

No use walking around the port looking for such a busy man. He could be anywhere.

I removed my sweat-stained pack and set it down beside Edwyn's big rocking chair at the far end of his porch. Clustered near it were several other chairs of varying types. When I was seated and enjoying the big rocker, Eutychus got up, walked towards me, laid down again beside me, and returned to his sleep.

"It's good to see you again, Eutychus." I patted his head and ruffled the thick folds of his muscular neck.

I sat there for a long time looking out into the busy harbor and enjoying some water from my canteen. Edwyn's porch had always served as a front row seat to the drama of life in this busy seaport.

Directly across the river on the south side was Scott's Chandlery, a sail loft company, some more homes and shops, and finally, Fair Havens Church. It was pastored by Reverend Martin Ekland, a caring and godly man. Behind the church and the buildings fronting the harbor's edge were many more back streets of homes and businesses.

Fair Havens Church, the home of an enthusiastic Baptist congregation, was a sturdy stone structure with a tall square tower in the center. To the right of it was the cemetery, and to the right of that, the parsonage. Further to the right, towards the sea along the harbor's edge, were still more shops and quite a few row houses.

To my extreme right was the opening to the sea with its low rocky barrier island, which served as a harbor guardian from the terrible storms that struck the coast. There was also a low tree-covered point on the far side of the harbor, and on this side, the north, there was a platform of natural stone and atop it stood the impressive new lighthouse. Behind it were a storage shack and the old lighthouse, less than half as high as the new one but sporting a new slate roof. It was the home of the Lyon brothers: Stephen the main lighthouse keeper and John 'The Rotund' that I had met at Midway Bridge.

Of course, I could only see the harbor area from where I sat but I was aware that there were countless back streets. Well back from the waterfront, there was the coal pit, a water powered lumber mill at a nearby stream, a stone cutter's workings, a stinking tannery, two small printing firms, a brickyard, an arrowsmith's shop, a gunsmith's shop, several foundries, and a couple blacksmith's shops. Unfortunately, in some respects, Oak Harbor was rapidly becoming merely another grimy, industrial northern town, but it hadn't yet sagged to that level.

It was a bustling seaport and there were always things to do, both purposeful and exciting. Life in Oak Harbor was neither mediocre nor mundane. It boasted a superb fencing club with expert swordsmen, and a fine brass band that had recently won a prestigious competition. They had performed a rousing march, *Brass Exultancy*, supremely well. It was intriguing, being written in 5/4 time.

The beautiful, little two-masted schooner I had seen earlier sailed by as it headed for the upstream end of the harbor. I could now read her name, *Serene Breeze*. Two young men were on the forward deck, one preparing a coiled line and the other adjusting the foot of the jib. A third man, older and keeping a close eye on the others, was in the wheelhouse directing the schooner's progress. A moment later, they dropped and set their anchor and furled their remaining sail. Several more men came up from below and then they gently set their tender for reaching the shore onto the water, and set a ladder into place for climbing down into it.

Oak Harbor

- Warrington Hall
- pedestal
- stream
- oak forest
- arrow smith
- Carolyn's home
- cleared lot
- Brixton home
- lighthouse
- main dock
- Harbor Master
- Charging Stag
- St. Cecilia's Church
- warehouse
- bridge
- river
- parsonage
- cemetery
- chandlery
- Fair Havens Church
- road to St. Begas

We Both Shall Row, My Love And I

My consideration of the harbor was interrupted by a young woman with poorly kept hair and missing several teeth. She approached the porch carrying some buns and other pastries on a large wooden tray. When I saw the delicious assortment, I spoke up without hesitation. "Excuse me, are you selling those?"

She rolled her eyes and dropped her jaw, revealing the many missing ivories of her piano keyboard. *How unfortunate. She's a young woman. I wonder if she lost her teeth through accident or by poor care.*

"Yes o' course, I'm not bakin' and walkin' to break the boredom. Would you be likin' one or two?" She chuckled as she rested the tray on the wide porch railing for me to take a closer look.

"Perhaps two. This one." I picked up a bun covered with cheese gratings. "And this one." I picked up another. "It looks delicious with its apple bits and sprinkled cinnamon. They both look so very satisfying."

She looked at me and grinned as she reached out her palm for a few coins. "Thank you sir, some tea would go well with those. My friend is followin' me with two full pots. We sell our pastries and tea to the merchants, passersby, and longshoremen at the docks."

I held both of the large buns in one hand, not an easy task, as I searched in my pocket and then dropped a few coins into her palm. "That's a wonderful idea. I'd fancy some tea."

She stepped back onto the street, looked off towards the oak forest, and shouted, "Madelyn, come along now, this woodsman on the Brixton porch is lookin' to bless you with a few coins."

Beautiful Madelyn, possessing all of her teeth in a great wide smile, and with her wavy auburn hair shining in the sun, arrived at the porch a moment later.

She wheeled a large wooden cart and upon it sat two great teapots, a box of assorted cups, a sugar bowl, and a pitcher of milk. She poured me a large clay cup of tea, and smiling asked, "Would you, sir, fancy a bit of sugar and perhaps some milk?" I responded that I would like a taste of sugar and she complied. Stirring the tea, she told me to leave the cup on the porch railing. She said that she'd get it when she passed by later. She was thankful for the coins and her green eyes sparkled even more when she noticed the attention I directed her way. Smiling at me over her shoulder she left, as she wheeled her cart along the cobbled street.

Such a beautiful and cheerful woman. She's sweeter than the sugar and more warming than the tea.

A few minutes later, a big barrel-chested man named David approached the porch carrying a large wooden crate on one shoulder. He slowed and looked at me. "Are you waiting for Edwyn?"

"Yes. As a matter of fact, I am."

"He's buying a telescope and a few other things at the chandlery. He's off to the Isle O' Man tomorrow. When I drop this here crate off at the barkentine on the dock," he pointed with his chin, "I'll go and tell him you're waiting."

"Thank you, but there's no hurry."

"Not to worry." He continued on his way towards the barkentine moored on the dock. I noticed that it took two big men to lift the crate from his muscular shoulder and a third to help set it down gently. David was, by far, the most powerful man in the harbor, and I remembered meeting him years earlier.

Finishing my tea and turning over the cup to examine the bottom, the initials "CH" were evident. Charles Hawthorne had made it. A small but lasting token to his having passed this way. *I remember purchasing some teacups for my mother and sister from him. He always had a kind word and a friendly smile.*

Half an hour later, Edwyn Brixton, past middle age but not looking it, being robustly active, stepped onto the porch from the street. His physical labor as a lumberman and builder had provided him with wide shoulders and a fearsome grip. People in the seaport knew him as a master cabinetmaker and skilled carver. He greeted me with a face full of joy and a firm handshake.

"Michael, I haven't seen you for quite some time. What brings you down to Oak Harbor?"

I got up and moved to a simple wooden chair beside his favored rocker. "It's been a year, maybe a little more."

He sat and got comfortable in his rocking chair, which I had just left. "It's fortunate you came today. I'll be leaving on the morning tide, bound for Douglas on the Isle of Man."

Eutychus stood, rested his head on Edwyn's knee to receive some attention, and then after several strokes laid back down, crossed his massive paws once again, and fell asleep.

"I heard about your intended trip from The Rotund. I was chatting with him at Midway Bridge while he waited for a load of slate coming down from Cold Crow."

"John the Rotund." Edwyn smiled. "An interesting character."

"He truly is."

Edwyn continued. "Cold Crow slate isn't too bad but Honister Pass is much better. My slate roof," he gestured overhead, "is from Cold Crow, but Reverend Ekland's splendid church roof is from Honister—"

"I'm glad to spend this time with you," I interrupted. "But I must bring our pleasant conversation to an end. There's a serious concern of great urgency."

He looked worried and inhaled pensively. "Go ahead, Michael. What's troubling you?"

"There's been a shocking tragedy that's happened up our way in Stone Ridge, but first I must give you something from Thomas Baumann."

"Thomas, I haven't seen him for quite some time."

"Look at this." I passed him the wrapped dagger and the envelope bound together with the tartan ribbon.

"This all sounds quite mysterious." He opened the package carefully and looked at the dirk first. He examined the blade, the handle, and the etched design thoroughly. "This is a little knife but of superior quality. The design looks Highland." Next, he opened the envelope and leaned back in his chair, taking time to read it. His facial expression devolved into a grimace. He shook his head several times, looked at me, and said, "Poor Charles, that's awful, and what a cursing for the little girl's family." He held up the letter. "Have you read this?"

"No. Thomas gave it to me in its sealed envelope. He didn't say what the specific contents were but he told me about little Myra's abduction and Hawthorne's grim death in the fire. Both were the same night. Oh, before I forget." I leaned forward. "I want to tell you about a distinctive mark that little Myra has directly below her ear. The shape of a backwards letter 'c'." I indicated its location on my neck.

Edwyn raised his eyebrows and nodded.

"The Rotund also told me about a family traveling in a wagon that looked and sounded suspicious. They should at least be questioned."

His winced and passed me the envelope. "Go ahead. Read this." He stroked his dog's head several times and sighed as he settled back into his chair. He examined the dagger more closely.

"Thank you. The more I can learn about Myra's disappearance and Charles' death, the better. I'm determined to stay with this responsibility and help any way I can." I licked my lips and looked out into the harbor. "Old Thomas, being the one to have found the burned body, is quite shaken." I took the final bite of my apple cinnamon bun and wished I still had some tea to wash it down. I read the letter that I had dutifully delivered for Thomas.

Rev. Ashcroft, Rev. Ekland, James, Nicholas, Edwyn + Louisa,

We need your help desperately. Stone Ridge has been struck with an evil tragedy. Michael probably told you about the abduction of Myra Wood and the death of Charles Hawthorne the glass and clay merchant.

We've searched for Myra and cannot find her. The dirk, we've sent along with this letter, was found on the floor of the Wood's cabin. No one in her family or the village has ever seen it before. There was chairs tipped over, the cabin door was open and there was tracks leading down the mountain. Myra's father and mom are filled with sorrow.

We have great confidence in each of you. Many people come and go through Oak Harbor. Maybe you'll hear of someone travelling with a young girl. Myra's eleven. If she's being held against her will she might be hard to handle or maybe kept out of sight. You might hear people talking about this sort of thing. You may hear rumours. Some people may have overheard upsetting conversations about something like this.

We don't know what to do. We are needing your help. Please go with Michael to ask the help of James Warrington, Earl of Cumberland. He's the representative of the Crown. He must be told about the problems in the area and we know he can help.

With Hope and Trust,
Thomas Baumann

After reading it a second time, I passed it back to Edwyn. "What do you think about the little dagger?" I asked.

"I've seen this style of dagger many times but I've never seen an intricate design quite like this. There's a tiny flower or perhaps a scotch thistle in the center of it."

"John the Rotund said he remembered a metal worker in Edinburgh who uses such a design on some of his work, but he couldn't remember the man's name."

Edwyn stood and called to a teenage lad walking past carrying a flattened tin teapot. He gave him a couple of coins. "Go to the chandlery and tell James Scott to get Mr. Kline from the warehouse, and tell them that they need to come and see me immediately. Then, go to Fair Havens Church or the parsonage and tell Reverend Ekland to come to my home right away. Tell him there's a crisis that must be dealt with." He leaned forward and gave the boy another coin. "Run, Tommy."

"Yes sir, Mr. Brixton sir." He ran down the street back towards the bridge.

"What about Reverend Ashcroft and Nicholas?" I asked.

"Reverend Ashcroft is ill and Nicholas left earlier on a ship with his eldest son. They're delivering some of their glassware to Belfast."

"Nicholas is an amazing glass working artist." I nodded. "When will they be back?"

"Perhaps a week, unless his son talks him into going to explore Fingal's Cave on Staffa."

"His son has been borrowing a lot of books from Edward Stewart. Last year he talked Nicholas into going and seeing the remains of Hadrian's Wall, beyond Carlisle."

"Mr. Stewart's a well-read and learned man."

Edwyn leaned back in his chair and began reading the letter again. He looked over at me and asked, "Do you think Myra can be found?"

"I cling to hope." I looked out into the harbor. "Lord Warrington must certainly assign some men."

"Sometimes, hope is all we have." He looked pensive. "With the seriousness of this, I'll put off going to the Isle of Man. A week or so won't matter."

Then I noticed the three men I had been following on the trail coming along the street towards Edwyn's porch. They were arguing and Eutychus raised his head and began a low, barely audible growl. The one named Victor dropped something and bent over to pick it up, as the bowmen stumbled into him. The bowmen straightening up, put his foot on Victor's rear, and angrily shoved him off his feet and onto the flagstone path at the base of Edwyn's steps. Eutychus leapt off the porch and onto the flagstone walkway, growling furiously at the meddlesome trio, as the clumsy rogue regained his footing. Victor froze before me. I could clearly see that the two remaining buttons on his waistcoat were a match to the unique one that I had found on the trail.

"Eutychus! Back here," shouted Edwyn. The mastiff remained where he was, with teeth bared. His growling, aggressive stance, and long canines were alarming. The bowman had already yanked an arrow from his quiver, nocked it on the bowstring, and had it fully pulled back. His aim at the alerted mastiff was deadly accurate.

Edwyn, now on his feet, shouted again, "Eutychus! Back here."

Gavin, putting his hand on the bowman's forearm to calm him, said to Edwyn in a deliberately mellow voice, "That's a cracking good monstrous guard dog you have there."

The bowman relaxed his posture, took a deep breath, and eased the tension on his bow.

Eutychus ended his aggressive growl, looked at Edwyn, and climbing back onto the porch, stood beside him.

Edwyn apologized for his dog's behavior and bid the three men good day. As they continued down the street, Gavin swatted Victor on the side of his head and called him a clumsy fool, as the bowman looked back over his shoulder and locked his gaze on me.

"That bowman is one of the tallest and most powerfully built men I've ever seen," said Edwyn.

"That he is," I responded. "Those are the three men that I followed down out of the mountains."

"I wondered if that might be them," added Edwyn. "They look dangerous."

I reached into my waistcoat pocket and took out the pendant necklace. "Edwyn, look at the design on this. I found it in the mud at the trio's campsite." I passed it to him. "Compare it with the design on the back of the dirk handle."

He examined them together. "The engravings are identical."

"That was obvious to me as well. I overheard Victor, that's the one that was sprawled out on your flagstone path, say something about fighting with a clay merchant, but he was interrupted and stopped speaking."

At that moment, Tommy returned to the porch. "They'll be 'ere shortly, but Mr. Kline..." He tried to catch his breath. "Mr. Kline will be 'ere a wee bit later."

"You're a fine lad, Tommy. I heard that today's a special day for you."

"Yes sir, Mr. Brixton sir. I be fifteen now."

"Fifteen, that's the edge of manhood. A special happy birthday to you." Edwyn tousled his hair and flipped him another coin. The lad pivoted on his heels and ran down the street.

Turning to me, Edwyn asked, "Would you be willing to follow those three men? Maybe you can find out where they're staying. I'll wait for the others and show them the letter."

"I'm on my way. I can catch up to them."

"Michael, keep out of harm's way."

"I hope that it doesn't come to this, but I only have my Sheffield Huntsman's knife. Might I borrow your heavy walking stick?"

"For Louisa's sake, I call it a walking stick," he whispered. "Although it's more of a long cudgel. I've two now, the oak one I showed you before and I've made a new one of blackthorn. It's inside the door on the right."

Reaching in through the door, I grabbed his new knobby walking stick. Feeling its weight and thinking about its strength, I started down the street. It was well made, recently oiled, and its heavy weighted head made me think that Edwyn had drilled it out and poured lead into it. It provided me with some confidence. *If this blackthorn cudgel passes sentence on any of the brigands, there shall be no appeal and no mercy.*

The Brigand's Camp

I hurried up the street in the direction of the three men, and seeing them going up a hill on a heavily treed side lane, I knew I'd have no difficulty shadowing them. When they left the lane for a narrow woodland path over a hilltop, I was closer to them but still following at a safe distance. They wound their way through a grove of trees, around some rocky outcroppings, and alongside a low sheep enclosure wall. Nearby there was a modest farm with a large chicken coop.

No sign of any dog to start barking and give me away. That's a relief.

An old woman exited her house and entered the chicken coop as I slipped behind some bushes. A few minutes later, grasping the feet of a dead chicken, she came back out, sat upon a stump, and after dropping the limp chicken into a basin of scalding water, began to pluck it furiously. Passing her by, I flanked the house and continued following the brigands.

The men, after pausing to scan the path from which they'd come, entered the ruins of a house, beneath an enormous oak. It was a shambles. One of the stone walls was missing entirely, and the other three walls were only half as high as they once had been. Presumably, the farmer with the chicken coop had taken many of the stones for their own building purposes.

I watched the rogues from the concealment of some trees skirted by low, thick bushes. They busied themselves setting up a permanent camp, moving stones, and blocking what used to be windows with broken boards and bramble.

Victor came out of the ruins, removed his tattered coat, and sat on a moss-covered stump to enjoy the warm sun against a stone wall. He ran his fingers through his oily hair several times and took a long drink from a whiskey bottle hidden in his coat. Concealing it once again, he looked off to one side and berated an imaginary companion, laughing and spitting as he did so. He then leaned back against the stone wall drowsily, and after snuffing and wiggling his nose, he began to intensely pick it.

Gavin came out of the ruins and sat on a weathered, back-broken chair. "This sunshine is like a warm woman on a cold night."

Victor didn't respond but continued picking his nose.

"Your nose picking is going to make me retch," said Gavin.

Victor still didn't respond but continued his filthy habit.

"I've never seen anything so putrid. You're in up to your wrist." He gagged several times. "Stop pickin' your nose! It'll be bleedin' soon."

Victor finally responded. "I'm no' pickin' it," he laughed. "I'm groomin' it."

Gavin stood and shook his head. "You make me sick. Wash your hands before you make our soup." He kicked the stump Victor was sitting on and went back inside the ruins.

Victor, mocking with a screechy high woman's voice, mimicked Gavin: "Wash your hands before you make our soup." He laughed and scowled. "I'll drop in a little o' my pickins especially for you, Gavin, my dear brother."

Hmm, they're brothers? I must get a look inside the ruins to see if they have Myra. I worked my way around their camp, peered in through a broken window and discovered that she was not within the ruins. *I need to get back to the others on Edwyn's porch.*

Assuming the brigands would stay for a lengthy time, I quietly returned to the path, and in a few minutes, I was back on the lane heading towards the harbor.

After a brisk walk, I found myself back on the porch listening to the leaders discussing what should be done next. Edwyn told me that I had just missed Louisa, his wife. When she heard I would be staying with them, she started a slow cooking roast of beef in her cast iron Dutch oven.

"Michael, it's wonderful to see you again," said Reverend Ekland. He placed his hand on my shoulder. "Did you find out where the three travelers are staying?"

"Yes, I thought they might be staying at one of the inns but I was wrong. I followed them to a campsite they've established up the fourth side lane that climbs the hill. It's not far from a little farm with a lot chickens, in the midst of some ruins, and beneath an impressively huge oak."

"I think I know the ruins," said Albert Kline. "My eldest son and I will look in on them before sunset and again at sunrise to make sure that they are staying put."

The group decided that Edwyn, Reverend Ekland, and I would go and speak to James Warrington, Earl of Cumberland, the next day.

Many more details were discussed, and perhaps an hour later they departed for their homes. I remained on the porch with Edwyn, and we continued discussing many of the pertinent details. Eutychus would occasionally lift his head, lick his lips, and glance at the people passing by on the busy street.

Madelyn, the cheerful young woman from whom I had purchased the tea earlier, arrived back at the porch. She left her cart on the street, came near where I was seated, and shared a radiant smile. With her elbows resting on the railing, not even glancing at Edwyn, she grinned and asked, "Was the tea to your liking, sir?"

I was lost for a moment in the warmth of her voice and the glow of her smile.

"Was the tea to your liking?" she repeated.

"Yes, it was delicious."

Edwyn, noticing our attention for one another, cleared his throat. "Your uncle, Pastor Ekland, was here earlier, but I believe he's returned to the parsonage."

"I'll be heading over there myself in a moment," she responded. "I came to collect the last of my cups."

I picked up the cup from the table beside me, and leaning forward, passed it to her. "Thank you. It was excellent tea, and tell your friend that the buns were likewise superb."

Again, she smiled, and as she took the cup from me, our eyes met and our hands touched at the exchange. Eutychus, still asleep, sighed. We both glanced at him, then back at each other, and Madelyn giggled like a young school girl.

"I didn't realize that Pastor Ekland was your uncle."

Her eyes sparkled like emerald gemstones as she toyed in her mind with an amusing response. "He's been my uncle my whole life and now, as a grown woman," she winked, "he remains my uncle."

We both laughed. "Have you been here in Oak Harbor for a long time?" I asked.

She glanced at Eutychus and then, still smiling, looked up at me. "Long enough to meet some interesting people and have a few friendly conversations." She adjusted the silver comb in her hair. "Do you live nearby?"

"Near enough to visit should the need arise," I responded with a grin.

Edwyn, sensing that short of setting himself on fire, he would not be noticed by either of us, quietly rose to his feet, concealed a wide smile, and stepped inside his home.

A moment later, Tommy, the lad that had been sent on the errand earlier, came running along the street, doing his best to carry several big old iron hinges. He was laughing heartily and being chased in succession by several shouting boys, a small yapping dog, and finally, a drunken man staggering and shouting, "A nip from the horse, a bridle for the ass, and a rod for the fool's backside." People passing by stopped to look and stare at the commotion. Eutychus stood, sniffed the air, walked in a tight circle, as dogs do, and then laid back down, crossing his forepaws.

"Prankish Tommy, he means no harm, but mischief does find him from time to time." She chuckled and shook her head. "That drunken man misquoted the Bible passage: 'A whip for the horse, a bridle for the ass, and a rod for the fool's back,' is the actual text."

"You know the Scriptures well." I looked at her approvingly. "By the way, I heard that today is Tommy's birthday. He might be fifteen but he's a bit short. He looks perhaps twelve or thirteen."

She looked at me with her hands on her hips. "He is short and often behaves as if he were younger, but I assure you, he is fifteen."

"He's not a big lad but he is brimming with energy."

"Indeed." She smiled radiantly. "I'd better get back to the parsonage to help my Aunt Muriel with the dinner preparations."

"I enjoyed spending time with you, Madelyn."

Again, Eutychus sighed, lifted his head, yawned, and then laid his head back down.

"And I with you." She brushed a wayward strand of hair aside. She left the porch railing, returned to her cart, pushed it a few steps, but abruptly stopped. Looking over at me she asked, "What's your name?"

"Michael Sterling. I live up in Cliffside."

I watched her amble down the street with her cart. I may have imagined that she paused in the distance to look back at me. Sitting there for a few minutes, I enjoyed the memory of my precious encounter with her. Her long flowing hair, shining in the sun; her captivating smile, drawing me in; her cheerful voice, distracting me from all else that was around me.

My daydream was broken when Edwyn came back out onto the porch with two large sausages. Sitting down on his rocker, he passed one to me.

"You made quite an impression on her, Michael."

"I'm disarmed and totally distracted from the seriousness of why I'm here." I bit off a tasty piece of sausage. "I'm completely at her mercy, but I wouldn't want to say 'like a rabbit in a snare'."

Edwyn started laughing and bit off a huge piece of sausage. Still laughing and starting to gag, he realized that he couldn't get his teeth together without drooling or choking. He removed the sausage from his mouth. He leaned back in his rocker, wiped some sweat from his forehead, and caught his breath.

"Are you alright? What time tomorrow should we leave for the Warrington's estate?" I asked.

"I'm alright. Let's leave shortly after breakfast, but not too early. The wealthy like to sleep late." He took a deep breath and regained his composure.

"Michael, do you have a suitable wig to wear when we speak to Lord Warrington in the morning? It is a formal interview."

"Mice ate my old one, so when I was in London last year, I purchased one of the most recent styles. It will be perfect for such an occasion. I have it in my backpack."

"Better mice than lice," said Edwyn.

I winced and chuckled.

The boys that had been chasing Tommy walked by, followed by the little dog. A small grey horse and squeaky wheeled cart also passed by, loaded with baskets of flowers and some vegetables.

"This harbor town is a busy place and there seems to be continual amusing delight right here at your porch."

Edwyn saw me glance across the harbor towards Fair Havens Church and the parsonage. Still eating his sausage, he reacted to my observation, and grasped that Madelyn was the amusing delight I had in mind. "Well now, is your 'amusing delight' to be found in the parsonage?" He started laughing again, with his eyes watering, and a moment later he was choking and fighting for air.

In an instant, I was at his side striking him on the back as Eutychus jumped to his feet and stared at his master. He coughed up a large piece of sausage, which shot the length of the porch. Eutychus lunged at it, sniffed it a couple times, and then ate it. Edwyn leaned back into his chair, wheezing, breathing heavily, and wiping sweat from his forehead. His huge mastiff was laying down beside his chair, licking his lips from the sausage.

"See what I mean?" I said. "There's never a moment of boredom here. In Cliffside you could collect a few coins for a chair on your porch, simply to witness the drama in this seaport."

Edwyn was still breathing heavily but we both chuckled.

I asked him, "Could I read the letter again, please?"

He passed it to me and I began reviewing it.

"Edwyn, I haven't seen your wife or daughter."

"They'll be home soon. They went over to help Elizabeth Harcourt with her household duties. She's widowed now."

"I remember her. What happened to her husband?"

"A fishing death about a month ago. He went out alone on the sea in questionable weather and his body was found on the shore a few days later. She's stricken with grief." He looked out across the harbor.

"A death such as this, with a young widow and a small child, is such a painful thing." I shifted in my chair. "Her future has been stolen from her."

Edwyn said nothing but scratched his chin. "It is difficult to comprehend but we mustn't exclude God's plan in this."

"Perhaps," I responded.

"Elizabeth is left alone to raise her one-year-old daughter. She has a younger brother, a soldier at Warrington Hall, but he isn't often at home."

"The sea takes many men as payment for the fish. That's what some people say."

"That's what the sluggards say. The ones that don't want to get up before dawn and go fishing. In the book of Proverbs, it records that some lazy people say there's a lion in the streets to get out of work. Am I right?"

"I think that I've heard it before, but you know that I'm not as much of a churchman as I should be." By my personal admission, I felt uncomfortable. I wanted to change the subject. Leaning over, I stroked Eutychus' head. "He's a fine old dog."

"That he is. Time's rolling by," he said. "You sit here on the porch. I'll go check the coals in the fire and the roast of beef that Louisa started earlier." He stepped inside.

Louisa and Brynne, their daughter, looking much older than I remembered her, arrived home half an hour later. They served a truly satisfying meal of roast beef, mashed potatoes, gravy, glazed carrots, bread from the bakery, and warmed apple pie.

Edwyn leaned back in his chair at their dining room table. "You ladies need to know the truth." He inhaled dramatically. "That meal was as fine as anything that might ever be served on the table of James Warrington, Earl of Cumberland."

"Far better, father." Brynne's expression of confident joy was broad, and her eyes appreciative. "We love cooking for you, Daddy." She leaned over and affectionately kissed her father, but her eyes were on me. "And you too, Michael."

Edwyn, having loosened his belt, declared, "Louisa, my love, it's a wonder that I'm not a much larger man." He saw me glance through the window towards the parsonage across the harbor.

I expressed my appreciation profusely to Louisa and Brynne and said, "The bachelor's life can be a lonely one. When it comes to a fine meal and friendly conversation, I often long for a more comfortable domestic life."

They all laughed and Edwyn added, "Not to mention a warm bed on a frosty night, and a kind word, should discouragement find you."

I joined in the laughter as well but Brynne, being a bit young, blushed a rosy pink at her father's mention of a warm bed.

I arose from the table. "I think that I'd like to go for a walk through the town."

Edwyn, with eyes twinkling and his teacup in hand, said, "For not being much of a churchman, it's curious that your walk will probably take you to the parsonage." Tears of laughter formed in his eyes. "Michael, would you be going over for a little prayer?"

Edwyn started to laugh uncontrollably. Tea erupted from his mouth, and a moment later from his nose. Brynne turned to look at her father in disbelief. Louisa stood and stared, jaw agape, and Eutychus scrambled to his feet and moved closer to Edwyn, ready for whatever might pop out of his master's mouth this time. To the mastiff's disappointment, Edwyn regained his composure and took a few deep breaths.

Brynne carried some dishes and cutlery to the kitchen from the dining area in the front room, and I, sheepish because of Edwyn's comments, stepped toward the door. "Louisa, thank you for a wonderful meal. I'll be stepping out to get some fresh air."

Louisa touched my arm. "I've prepared the back room behind the kitchen for you. It was your grandfather's room when he came here from Penrith. I've put a lantern on the table at the head of your cot." She passed a platter to Brynne, who had returned to continue clearing the table. "If you get hungry in the night we have apples stored near the foot of your bed. Help yourself."

"Thank you so much, Louisa, for your care of my grandfather and me."

As soon as I stepped out onto the porch, I heard her disciplining her husband. She had noticed Edwyn's hidden meanings. "What was all that about? Your badgering and poking fun at Michael was unseemly. He's a fine young man and if he has shown some interest in Madelyn. Why would you interfere and make sport of that? Madelyn Haversham, God bless her, has been through enough."

I glanced through the window beside the door, saw her give him a sour stare, and heard her final pronouncement. "Edwyn, you went too far!"

After her tirade, Louisa was quiet, probably still simmering. I hadn't heard Edwyn at all. To avoid more playful vexing from him, I decided against the walk. I sat on the porch in the darkness, enjoying the refreshing cool breeze and the harborside lights shimmering on the water.

An effectively trimmed two-masted schooner, having moments earlier cast off from the wharf near the tavern, was taking advantage of the offshore breeze. It was being carried gently through the harbor and would shortly be out past the rocky point. *He must know the harbor well. Most men of the sea dislike night sailing when moving through a harbor and out past a rocky point.*

Upon hearing robust laughter and exuberant song coming from the tavern, I stepped back inside and fetched my oboe. I wasn't a drinking man but I did enjoy music a great deal.

The tavern owner, a gifted guitarist named Fernando, known locally as The Spaniard, was a swarthy Mediterranean. His Irish wife, Shannon, with her fair complexion, was an enthusiastic singer who knew all of the local songs and many from Ireland as well. They were a dynamic couple and their tavern was the center of entertainment each evening. I headed for The Royal Stag.

The Royal Stag

When I was in Oak Harbor more than a year earlier, the tavern sign was a weathered wooden board and the name had faded with the passage of time. It had a small rack of lopsided antlers, missing several points, and overall it was disappointing. What greeted the patrons now was quite impressive.

The sign, bolted to the wall above the door displayed the head of a heroic stag with fiery eyes. It was carved out of a large block of hardwood and mounted atop the head, like a monarch's crown, was an actual majestic rack of antlers. Hunters would describe the rack as coming from a twelve point royal stag. Below this regal head was the tavern's name inscribed in deep grooves of forest green on a background of lemon yellow.

The Royal Stag

After pausing to admire the sign, a truly masterful work, I stepped inside. A sizable group of men enjoying the camaraderie of the tavern after a hard day's work talked, argued, laughed, and sang. They stood at the bar or sat at crowded undersized tables, and five or six time-worn souls clustered quietly near the fireplace. It was a jovial atmosphere and not too smoky. Two old men, one with an ancient border collie on the floor at his side, were trying to concentrate on a game of chess.

Immediately as I entered, Shannon called out, "Michael, someone said that they saw you over on Edwyn's porch, and here you are!"

Gavin and Victor, without the bowman, stepped into The Royal Stag immediately behind me.

"What did you say, Shannon?" It was hard to hear her with the noise that filled the tavern.

"Good evening, Michael!" she shouted with a winsome expression.

I was keeping one eye on Gavin and Victor, who had walked across the room and sat at a table in a shadowy back corner. Gavin, with his back to the wall, watched the door.

"Shannon, you know that I couldn't come to Oak Harbor without stopping in to see you and the Spaniard. Your new sign is the finest I've ever seen!"

"It was made by Edwyn," she said. "He did an amazing job carving the head."

She was carrying a tray with six tankards of ale to a group of fishermen who were talking to several flirty young women, who were themselves fishing for the men's attention.

"I had dinner with him and his family and not a word was said about it."

"He'd never brag about his work," she shouted. "You know that."

"That's true. Who brought down the stag?"

"John the Rotund. He went hunting with my Fernando last fall." She wiped the long, patron-filled counter with a wet cloth, and went on to say something else but I couldn't hear her clearly.

"Shannon, what did you say? I can't hear you!"

The music and revelry grew louder. I was amazed how loud a guitar, a fiddle, a penny whistle, and a hand drum can get in pubs like this when leading men in boisterous song.

Shannon shouted once again, "I said, John the Rotund brought it down with Fernando!"

"Did he bring it down with musket or bow?" I shouted, but lost eye contact with her when another server, a young plump woman, too big for her faded dress, stepped in between us.

"You like my bow?" the plump server asked. She shared a curious expression and tipped her head so that I could see the bow in her hair more easily.

"I wasn't talking about your bow." The server picked up some empty tankards and headed towards the back of the tavern.

I repeated my question more loudly to Shannon. "Did he bring it down with musket or bow?"

"An old Digbeth musket!" she shouted back.

Someone stepped on the border collie's tail. It yelped and jumped. His master turned towards him, and his elbow wiped most of the chess pieces off the board and onto the floor. His opponent raised a threatening fist and shouted, but then he simply pounded the table. The elderly man, apologizing to his angry opponent, rose from his chair, swung his sheepskin coat over his shoulder, and stepped away from the table. He and his old dog, each of them with their heads down, sauntered towards the door and left the tavern. The remaining chess player shook his head, swore profusely, and started picking up the pieces from the floor.

Sitting at a table near the door, I shouted to Shannon, "Bring me a tea please." A new song started in the tavern.

With loud singing, the Spaniard's guitar, a fiddle, a penny whistle, a hand drum, and the beating of time on the tabletops, conversation was impossible.

"Nothing stronger?" she asked.

"For now, a tea. Later, maybe a light mead."

"What about you?" she repeated with a shout. I think that she had heard "me" when I had said "mead." With her brows furrowed and looking puzzled, she shouted, "Tea it is."

A moment later, Shannon approached with a tray and a pot of tea, a large cup with a spoon in it, a little wooden sugar box and an ample bun, sliced in half and covered with jam.

"Bless you, Shannon. I'll take it out front."

"Some of you mountain men don't abide the revelry well, but others thrive on it."

I chuckled and Shannon, having set down the tray, put her hand on my shoulder. With a raised voice right at my ear, she said, "I've put some flowers on your grandfather's grave. He was a kind soul."

"Thank you. He enjoyed your lively singing, and you always had a cup of tea and a kind word for him." I gave her a couple of coins.

Her eyes brightened, and smiling, she moved off towards the counter.

Lifting the tray with my fingers through the oboe case handle, I stepped outside.

Atop the lighthouse, the newly installed Argand lamp, backed by its reflector, shone out to sea through the evening mist. I sat with the tray across my knees, set my oboe case beside me, and prepared my cup of tea. The cool breeze gently drifting out to sea and the stillness of the water were an appreciated relief after the stifling and clamorous tavern. *I'll join in and play with the musicians another time, when it's less boisterous.*

From time to time, new patrons would enter and a few people would leave. The elderly chess player from inside, having gone for a walk on the nearby dock and now returning, ambled by with his equally ancient dog. They were well suited to each other. I imagined them to be retired from a life of shepherding and the writings of the long past, John Caius, came to mind:

> 'Our shepherdes dogge is not huge, vaste, and bigge . . . it has not to deale with the bloudthyrsty wolf, since there be none in England .

> .. This dogge either at the hearing of his master's voyce or whisteling or signals of the hand ... bringeth the wandring and straying sheepe, into the selfe same place where his master wishe is to have them.'

A faithful pair, now in the late autumn of their days. I wonder if they still live in a little shepherd's hut, helping out at local farms. Did he receive his faithful four-footed friend as a pup? Did the old shepherd know my grandfather?

Turning back towards his companion, the old weather-worn soul clapped his hands together. "Come along, Pepper. Don't lag behind."

Pepper, having stopped to sniff a post and then sprinkle it, lifted his head and took a few quick steps to catch up to his master.

A large woman nearing middle age, scowling and shabbily dressed, approached the tavern with two small girls and stopped in front of the door. She asked a patron entering the Royal Stag to send out her husband.

A few minutes later, a disheveled man came staggering out and flopped down onto the bench on the other side of the door from myself. Slurring his speech, he abused her. "You ol' crone, I was on me way 'ome with some coin. I 'elped load a fine ship bound for the south."

"You lyin' pub crawler!" she yelled. "It sailed three hours ago."

As he lifted his chin and parted his lips to speak further, her fisted backhand struck him in the mouth and laid him out on the cobblestone. He moaned several times, rose unsteadily to his feet without a word, spit out some blood, and stumbled back into the tavern.

The mother, with a child by each wrist, turned and stomped away. "Well, little darlings," she said through clenched teeth, "we'll be off to the workhouse soon enough, your father's gone back into the tavern to drink your dinner." The older girl started to cry as they disappeared into the darkness.

I leaned back on the bench and tried to enjoy my tea, but the memory of what I'd witnessed was distressing.

It was getting late and now there were more patrons leaving the tavern than were entering. Men were returning to their homes—some to scolding wives and some to a quiet night's rest in an empty room. Staggering seamen were returning to their ships with their arms around each other's shoulders, supporting one another, as stuporous friends often do.

Half an hour later, Gavin and Victor, together with the man that the angry wife had struck, left the tavern. George, Albert Kline's son, stepped out behind them, turned, and gave me a secretive wink as he followed them up the cobbled street.

Warrington Hall

After a refreshing harbor swim in front of the lighthouse the next morning, away from the other homes and buildings, I was ready to proceed with the day. The memory of the previous night, when the angry wife had back-handed her husband, laying him out on the cobbles, still troubled me, but the cold water helped to clear my mind.

The new lighthouse, painted white and glistening in the sun, was crowned with a circle of windows. It was sixty feet tall and could easily be seen over the low barrier island at the mouth of the harbor. Boasting a modern Argand lamp, it was visible for many miles out to sea and had saved countless fishermen, merchants, and sailors. When out at sea, even on the darkest night, a ship following a compass heading of 50° towards the light would safely enter through the deep opening to the south of the barrier island. The northern entrance was never used at night.

I decided to spend some time with Stephen Lyon, who most of the locals called The Keeper. After my swim, I dried off, pulled my clothes back on, knocked on the lighthouse door, and was welcomed inside.

Giving him greetings from his brother and listening to him as he spoke of the comings and goings of various ships, he suggested that I stop in and speak to William Langley, the harbormaster. He reminded me that Langley was hard of hearing, and that I should speak up to be understood. I planned to see him later in the day.

On my return walk, I noticed a little hill protruding from the slope of the valley beside the road and not far from the water's edge. It was perhaps thirty feet high and thinking that it might provide an interesting view of the harbor, I climbed it.

The Argand Lamp Lighthouse

A perfect spot to build a house. Fair Havens Church is straight across the water and with a front porch like Edwyn's, a person could watch the ships as they came and went. It's odd that I didn't notice it on my way to the lighthouse. I suppose I was looking out into the harbor or at the small strand of beach that was directly below it.

I returned to Edwyn's porch a few minutes later and settled myself into his rocker. Eutychus came to me and laid down beside my chair as Edwyn came around the side of his house from his cabinetry shop at the back.

"Edwyn, I have a question. Something has been troubling me."

"And what might that be?"

"I know that truth," I hesitated, "absolute truth, is a noble virtue."

"That's right. Continue."

"If I relate to Lord Warrington the conversation that I overheard from the three miscreants about brawling with that clay merchant, he might believe it to be of little significance. Should I allow myself..." I broke eye contact with him and looked out into the harbor. I was embarrassed to ask the question. "Should I allow myself to embellish a little bit to strengthen the weight of what I'd heard?"

Edwyn leaned back in his chair. "I'm having difficulty hearing this from you." He paused. "Truth must be cherished. It must be taken for what it is worth. Our Father in heaven doesn't want our interfering lies. In fact, He detests them. Express yourself truthfully with what you've heard. Nothing more, nothing less." He leaned over towards me and lowered his voice. "If lying enters this righteous route we are taking—justice for Charles Hawthorne and the recovery of little Myra—then we would step away from the presence of God. We would find ourselves standing alone. Our fellowship with the Lord would be broken."

"You're quite right, Edwyn. Forgive me."

He looked at me with affection, as a father would look at a son. "Thank you for sharing your feelings with me, Michael. You trust my judgment, and you trust me with the musings of your heart. That speaks preciously to me." He smiled and bobbed his head, strengthening his words.

We sat there quietly for a few minutes, enjoying the view.

A caring man. He could've rebuked me angrily. He chose instead to encourage me and correct me gently. What if he had been silent? I would've stumbled into this wrong and found God's displeasure.

Edwyn continued. "Who is the father of lies?" I remained silent. "Who is the Way, the Truth, and the Life?"

I looked up at him and smiled. He smiled back, knowing that these two simple questions had introduced God's perspective into my thinking. He said no more; he didn't need to. *Someday, I hope that I will know God the way that Edwyn does. I don't fully understand what devout Christians mean when they speak of things like having fellowship with the Lord, but maybe someday I will.*

While waiting for Reverend Ekland, who would take us up to Warrington Hall, we could see John the Rotund driving his cousin's now empty wagon towards us. Presumably, he was heading back to the lighthouse after unloading the slate at Kline's warehouse. He stopped directly in front of us with a sly and curious grin. Clenching the stem of his pipe between his teeth, he laughed and bellowed, almost unintelligibly, "Well, praises be, two o' me favorite mountain men in one place."

Puzzled, being the only mountain man present, I shouted back, "John, fetch your spectacles. I'm the only mountain man here." John sat there laughing, then reaching into the back of the wagon, he dramatically flung aside a canvas tarp. Old Thomas suddenly sat up like a Jack-in-the-box.

The Rotund announced, "You're one and 'ere's the other."

Eutychus stood, licked his lips, and looked at the wagon.

Old Thomas, groggy from sleep and squinting, mumbled, "John, I'm weary from unloading all that slate. Where are we?"

"You did more watchin' and orderin' about than unloadin'," laughed The Rotund, setting the brake on the wagon.

Old Thomas crept to the back of the wagon box, and then carefully found his footing on the road. "Thank you for the ride from Midway Bridge."

"Thank you for 'elpin' with the slate." Then, removing his pipe from his teeth and pointing with it towards the lighthouse, he said, "Stop by at the light'ouse for a spot o' tea when it suits you."

"Bless you, John," said old Thomas.

The elderly gentleman stretched as he stepped onto the porch, and tired from his journey, he sighed deeply, licked his lips, and seated himself on an old well-used chair.

Eutychus also stretched, sighed, licked his lips, and laid back down.

Edwyn and I, noticing the similarities between Old Thomas and Eutychus, caught each other's eyes. We chuckled but then quietly stifled our mirth.

"We're glad you're here, Thomas." Edwyn continued, "We're waiting for Reverend Ekland to come by and drive us up to Warrington Hall to speak to the Earl of Cumberland."

Thomas looked me in the eye. "I went back and closely examined Charles' burned-out wagon and Myra's home like you suggested. Guess what I found?" He reached into his pocket, pulled out a button, and held it towards us. It was a perfect match to the one I had found on the trail and the ones remaining on Victor's tattered waistcoat.

"May I examine it closely?"

He passed it to me. "I found it under a book shelf near the door to their home. When I asked the family about it, no one had ever seen it before."

I showed Thomas the button that I'd found and described the ones on Victor's waistcoat. His eyes brightened. Edwyn leaned forward to examine them more closely.

As I looked up, I saw Madelyn and Reverend Ekland approaching in a new carriage. She was driving an impressive, well-matched team of horses. "The reverend has a splendid carriage and beautiful horses. I didn't know the pastorate was salaried so well."

"He's a godly pastor and cares dearly for the flock. His carriage isn't derived from his salary. His parents are landed gentry with substantial farmland near Leeds." Edwyn took a deep breath. "He's given up much of this world's wealth for the pastorate. His father sent the carriage to him as a gift when Madelyn came to stay."

"Madelyn's driving the team with tremendous skill. Did you see how she passed around that farm cart?"

"She's a fine young lady, but she drives too quickly for my liking," Edwyn responded.

The open Landau carriage wouldn't be described as lavish; it was pulled by a team of two, not four, but it was well made, and most of the other carriages in the seaport were smaller. Its two-tone green paint, brass side lanterns, and black trim, gave it an elegance seldom seen in Oak Harbor. It wasn't new and had some signs of wear, but it made a notable impression. As it passed the tavern, Tommy Atwater and two other boys started to run along beside it.

"I had forgotten that the Ekland family comes from landed gentry. Why was Madelyn on the street selling tea?"

"Land holding gentry or not," he responded, "she believes in the nobility of work." He shared a buoyant expression with one eyebrow optimistically raised. "She'll make a precious bride for a good man some day."

I heard Louisa cough inside their home. He glanced in my direction and something struck the floor in the house.

Madelyn brought the horses to a halt and set the brake. We exchanged smiles, but aware of Reverend Ekland and the others, we addressed each other with less familiarity than the previous day. "Hello Madelyn. You drive superbly well," I said.

"Thank you. It is so nice to see you again."

Edwyn grinned at me.

"Thomas, it's fitting that you're here," said Reverend Ekland. "Come along with us to Warrington Hall."

"That's why I'm here, Pastor," he replied.

We climbed aboard the carriage. Madelyn leaned over the side, and promising to give Tommy and his friends a ride another day, asked them not to run alongside. She feared that the boys might be crushed by the wheels and told them they were upsetting the horses. The boys ran off, back towards the bridge. Edwyn and I sat in the back seat facing forward with Thomas Baumann and Reverend Ekland facing us in the opposing seat. Madelyn confidently sat in the elevated driver's seat.

Brynne stepped out onto the porch clutching a book she had borrowed from Edward Stewart. "Good morning, Madelyn. This is an impressive sight." Her mouth was agape and her eyes were opened wide.

"Hello Brynne. I'm managing as best as I'm able."

"Reverend Ekland, this is a wonderful carriage, but where's your one horse gig?" asked Thomas.

"This Landau was given to me as a gift from my father but it embarrasses me by its pretentiousness. I wouldn't want people to get the impression that I think highly of myself, nor that I use my salary for such worldly extravagance." He paused for a moment. "It's handy, however, when a number of people need to be transported, such as this morning."

Thomas repeated himself, "Where's your gig and Pilgrim, your old white mare?"

"I've sold Pilgrim to Mr. Kline's eldest son, George, and I still have the gig. Madelyn is training the horse on the left—"

"*Shadow,*" Madelyn interrupted. "Uncle, his name is Shadow."

"Yes of course, Madelyn."

Reverend Ekland continued. "She's training *Shadow* to be comfortable working on his own without his harness mate. There will be times when I only need the one horse gig. It's practical and comfortable for two or three people." He paused again and asked, "The lighter horse, the one on the right, what's his name, Madelyn?"

"Wonder," she responded.

"That's it. *Wonder* is being trained to carry a rider alone."

"These horses, being geldings, are quite manageable and a joy to drive," she said.

We turned up the country road away from the harbor, and Madelyn skillfully followed the winding road as it ascended through the majestic grove of oaks. Lord Warrington's men were harvesting some for the next shipment to Bristol but most of the woodland was left untouched.

I was awestruck. Great golden blessings of sunlight shone down between the lofty trees and through the openings in their leafy branches. Some of these oaks were of such a great girth and towering height, with shaded expanses beneath them, I felt that I was within a mighty cathedral.

The great windows of man's cathedrals are mere copies of these impressive portals. The green trees overhead with the bright blue sky beyond serve as a colorful cathedral ceiling.

Edwyn interrupted my reverie. He spoke to me of recent deer poaching on the estate and pointed out Lord Warrington's forest bailiff, a short man with a pack over one shoulder making notations in a book and standing amongst the trees. He was speaking to three well-armed soldiers as they examined the area around the carcass of a deer. *The poachers must've been interrupted to leave the deer.*

The road climbing from Oak Harbor to Warrington Hall was in excellent condition. It was bordered by occasional flowerbeds and decorative shrubbery, but within the sheep enclosure walls I noticed many tufts of wool caught in the briars and bramble.

At the hilltop, we crossed an ancient stone bridge above a pool and a picturesque waterfall boasting an expansive vista that overlooked the harbor far below. I remembered sitting on a high pedestal stone very near here years earlier, enjoying the view of the seaport, the lighthouse, and the distant teal blue sea. At the time, I wished that I was an artist with years of training and experience, that I might capture the inspiring sight. I'd never been farther up the road towards Warrington Hall than this point.

As we approached the hall, the stone walls bordering the road were intermittently clothed with ivy, and the groomed flower beds became more frequent. Beautiful hedges and curiously shaped ornamental trees were carefully placed amongst stone assemblages that were made to resemble ruins. Each of the structures sought to portray moments of ancient history.

I was amazed at the size of Lord Warrington's enclosed flocks and saw various breeds under the care of shepherds and well-trained dogs. I had heard that some of these sheep had been sold to Lord Warrington from Robert Bakewell, the breeder of Dishley.

Coming around the final curve on the lane, which was now cobbled, we were stopped by several heavily armed soldiers at the formidable but open gate of Lord Warrington's estate. It was of iron, protected by a stone gatehouse perhaps thirty feet in height, and manned by a dozen soldiers. Reverend Ekland seemed to know several of the men and after speaking to them, we were allowed to pass.

We entered and were presented with an imposing view of Warrington Hall. Massive doors were centered between the wide cobbled drive at the end of the building nearest us, and the massive stained glass windows of Blenheim Chapel at the far end.

Flanking the centrally located doors were magnificent flowerbeds along the front of the mansion. Delicate violets were nearest the lawn, interspersed and backed with low, dark green ferns and those were backed by tall dark red peonies.

Completed centuries earlier, this well maintained and attractive two-story hall boasted two towers: a wide three-story tower in the center, above the massive double doors, and a smaller one at the far corner of Blenheim Chapel. At our end was a stone wall with a high and impressively arched carriage gate. It served as the entrance to the rear courtyard with its auxiliary buildings.

Upon passing through this noble gate of oak and iron, with the apex of the arch well above Madelyn's head, we were surrounded by stables, a workshop, servant's quarters, soldier's barracks, and a rear wing of Warrington Hall. We were immediately met by the stable's head groomsman, Alistair Bletchley, who seemed to know Reverend Ekland and Edwyn well.

"Pastor, this is a fine surprise," greeted Alistair. He strode forward, smiling broadly, and shook Reverend Elkand's hand.

"Alistair, we missed you and Agnes in church last Sunday," observed the reverend with a little wink of his eye. He was always attentive to any missing from the congregation.

"Yes Pastor, I was home with my dear Agnes. She was smitten with a fever but she's in fine form now. I heard your sermon was well received."

We climbed down out of the carriage. Alistair led the horses to a trough in the shade of a great maple and removed their bits and bridles. Madelyn pulled a carrot from a small satchel at her side, broke it in two, and gave half to each of the horses. She stayed there affectionately stroking them.

Walking towards the rear entrance of the hall, an impeccably dressed butler met us wearing a scarlet velvet waistcoat. He politely blocked our way at the door. Respectfully, he asked the reason for our attendance at the estate of Lord Warrington. Reverend Ekland handed the butler his calling card and explained that there were criminal concerns in Lord Warrington's mountain district.

Standing in a nearby doorway, a middle-aged cook with a stained apron listened and watched closely. I later discovered that this was Agnes Bletchley, Alistair's wife. One hand held a large clever, glinting in the sun, and the other, a rack of pork ribs.

"Reverend Ekland sir, please wait for a moment as I inform Lord Warrington of your presence," said the butler.

"Certainly," he responded.

The butler invited us to enter and wait within the rear foyer, and a few minutes later, he returned accompanied by Lord Warrington's captain of the guard.

"Lord Warrington will see you now in his reception room," said the butler, gesturing an invitation to follow him down the hallway.

"Thank you. Is he in dandy spirits?" asked Thomas.

The button-polished butler, not wanting to express an opinion about Lord Warrington's mood, did not respond but merely proceeded along the hall. He paused before an stately set of tall double doors with a fearsome guard at each side. Grasping the brass handle of each of the shining oak doors firmly, he swung them open. We paused as he stepped inside and announced, "The Reverend Martin Ekland and his party are here at your pleasure, my lord."

We followed Reverend Ekland inside the reception room and were followed in turn by the captain of the guard. The butler, with head bowed, closed the great doors behind us.

"Gentlemen, please be seated," directed Lord Warrington. His spectacled and scholarly scribe was seated nearby with pen in hand and a sheaf of papers on the table before him.

"My lord, may I introduce those whom may not be of your acquaintance?" asked Reverend Ekland. "This, my lord, is Thomas Baumann of Cliffside, a man of integrity and wisdom derived from his reverence for our Lord and the abundance of his years, with which he's been blessed." Thomas rose to his feet, bowed, and seated himself as Lord Warrington nodded. Gesturing to me, I stood and he said, "This, my lord, is Michael Sterling of Cliffside, nephew of Edmund Sterling, humble gentry of Penrith, a servant of the crown. He is the grandson of Aaron Sterling that attended Fair Havens Church and passed away last year."

"Master Sterling, my deepest sympathy on the passing of your grandfather." He paused thoughtfully. "I heard you play at Penrith. Beautifully tender phraseology and a more exquisite oboe tone cannot be found. You must play for me again." Lord Warrington smiled as he bowed his head.

"Yes, my lord, if it pleases you, sir," I responded self-consciously, and took my seat.

Lord Warrington, with furrowed brow, asked Reverend Ekland, "Tell me now, what is the criminal concern that you would like to bring before me?" He turned to his scribe. "Record this carefully."

"Yes, my lord," the scribe responded.

Reverend Ekland presented the details of the death of Charles Hawthorne and the abduction of Myra Wood. I

We Both Shall Row, My Love And I

shared my story of the three brigands and placed in his hands the package containing the dirk and the letter, tied with the faded tartan ribbon. He examined them and asked a few questions. He was very interested. I gave him the amethyst pendant and the buttons found by myself and old Thomas, and his indignation grew. Next, I repeated the conversation that I had overheard about them brawling with a clay merchant. His anger and desire for justice was evident to us all.

"What are the names and the physical descriptions of these rogues?" demanded Lord Warrington angrily.

I shared the names of Gavin and Victor and their physical descriptions, and went on to tell him about the third man, the bowman, whose name I didn't know. The scribe's pen scratched dutifully, recording the details as I spoke.

Recalling what John the Rotund had said to me at Midway Bridge, I added that there might also be a suspicious family involved, traveling in a wagon, and I expressed that it would be wise to locate and question them. The captain of the guard nodded attentively.

When I had finished, Thomas shared his troubling account of the burning of Charles Hawthorne and added that the presence of the three men was known to the Stone Ridge villagers. Edwyn, who Lord Warrington truly respected as a man of integrity, stated that he and I had clearly observed that Victor wore a waistcoat with two remaining buttons, which matched the two that he had already been shown.

Thomas, not able to control himself further, spoke of the sorrow of the Wood family and his own distress at finding Charles Hawthorne's gruesomely burned body.

My heart pounded as I listened to him. We saw the anguish in the dear old man's face. We heard the pain in his trembling voice. We witnessed the suffering of his soul.

Having heard these details of dread once again, and remembering Lorena's sorrow, I stood and exclaimed, "Lord Warrington, we must do all that we can! Little Myra may have passed from the living, or worse, she may be experiencing great evil at the hands of these miscreants." I looked away towards the long gothic window and then, wincing, closed my eyes. I stood there for a moment, visibly shaken, as Edwyn stood and placed his hand on my shoulder. Regaining my composure, I apologized for my outburst and returned to my seat.

Lord Warrington's face manifested an angry redness, and grimacing, he declared, "Don't apologize. Where are these three loathsome brigands now? Justice shall find them and they shall reveal what has become of little Myra!"

I carefully described the location of their encampment and added, "They're under the surveillance of Mr. Kline and his son."

"Get the magistrate," he ordered the captain of the guard, "A warrant must be issued."

"Yes, my lord," the captain responded. He quickly rose to his feet and hurried out of the room.

A few minutes later, he returned with the magistrate. In a concise summary fashion, the evidence was read back to the magistrate, who listened intently. He asked us several more questions, and we responded clearly and honestly. Reaching into the leather case that he carried and extracting a formal-looking piece of paper, he looked at us and pursed his lips. "I am completely satisfied with what I've heard." He wrote out a warrant, which stated the pertinent details and his satisfaction with the veracity of the allegations. He dated it, signed it, and affixed a wax seal to the bottom corner. Lord Warrington also signed it, as did Reverend Ekland and Edwyn as witnesses.

Lord Warrington thanked us for bringing this matter of justice before him and said, "Those brigands will be apprehended, truth shall be extracted, the little girl recovered, and justice dealt out."

He then ordered the captain of the guard to apprehend the brigands and to keep them separate from one another during transport and incarceration. The captain once again hurried from the room.

We left the evidence of the wrapped dagger, the amethyst pendant, and the buttons with Lord Warrington.

By the time we were in the stable yard, the captain was leaving with his men. The thundering hooves of the massive horses was a foretaste of the justice the brigands would receive.

Madelyn, seeing us, climbed into the driver's seat of the carriage and expertly walked the horses towards us.

With eyebrows raised, Lord Warrington exclaimed, "I didn't know that Madelyn could drive a Landau. A little lady for such a big carriage."

"Yes, my lord, she is skillfully adept," responded Reverend Ekland.

Lord Warrington continued. "I find myself formulating an idea. Perhaps my son, and Madelyn, and you Michael would favor my wife and me with some music? Madelyn's an expressive flautist. Would that be possible, perhaps in a few days?"

Madelyn, overhearing Lord Warrington as she set the brake, grinned and nodded towards her uncle. He then glanced my way and I inclined my head affirmatively.

"Yes, my lord. Would Thursday be to your liking?" he asked.

"Marvelous. I'll tell Jonathan and he can select a few pieces of music. He's a splendid pianist."

Our party expressed appreciation to Lord Warrington, climbed aboard the Landau, and passed out through the great arched gate of the courtyard. Then, when we had exited the outer gate, we entered the lane and headed back towards Oak Harbor.

My mind, having been taken from the enforcement of the magistrate's warrant, was now mercilessly focused on my musical responsibilities—and my interest in Madelyn.

I had no idea that she played the flute, that Jonathan Warrington played the piano, and that I would be involved in something like this. Thursday's so soon. I need to practice. What music will Jonathan Warrington select? What if the music is not suited for flute, oboe, and piano? Perhaps Madelyn and I could play the sorrowful duet that I've written.

I was jolted back to reality. "Men, it is a great victory to have Lord Warrington so decidedly forthright in our quest for justice. Such a blessing," declared Reverend Ekland.

"Amen to that," responded Edwyn.

I sat quietly as Reverend Ekland, Edwyn, and Thomas discussed certain details of the matter.

Turning her shoulders slightly to the rear and slowing the carriage, Madelyn asked, "Uncle Martin, might I leave my driving and be dropped off at the waterfall? It provides such a grand view."

"My dear, with men being arrested and horsemen charging about, you might find yourself in harm's way."

"Oh Uncle, no harm will come to me. I'll be cautious."

Edwyn cast a glance in my direction, coughed, and gently elbowed me in my ribs.

"Excuse me Reverend Ekland," I interjected, "I would be honored to serve as Madelyn's escort and guide her home safely. It will also provide us with the opportunity to discuss what music might be suitable to meet Lord Warrington's request."

Edwyn grinned and looked away as he once again poked me with his elbow.

"Michael, a superb idea," said Reverend Ekland. "Not too late now. It's a long walk back. Be mindful of the heat of the day."

Edwyn, enjoying every minute of my unfolding plan and barely able to keep from laughing, repeated the reverend's instruction. "Yes Michael, be mindful of the heat..." He suppressed another chuckle. "Of the day." He burst out laughing.

Reverend Ekland and Thomas both looked at him, brows furrowed, as though he were mentally deficient or perhaps sun-struck.

Angry and scowling at Edwyn, I mumbled, "A few berries short of a full basket."

Thomas, having not heard me clearly asked, "I beg your pardon, Michael?"

I raised my voice and responded, "The ewe tarries short of a wool casket." I pointed at a thorn festered and muddy sheep in the adjacent field. It was lying down, struggling with its breathing, and a concerned shepherd was bending over it. He was trying to free it from the thorns and bramble caught in its fleece.

Thomas thought for a moment and said, "Nicely worded." He continued to nod appreciatively.

"Hmm, 'a wool casket'. Quite poetic, Michael," added Reverend Ekland.

Thomas repeated my poetic observation. "The ewe tarries short of a wool casket. Well said. Yes, very good indeed."

The Pedestal

We arrived at the bridge and Madelyn set the brake as Reverend Ekland and I climbed down from the carriage. He took his dear niece's hand and supported her arm with the other.

I passed old Thomas my wig. "Please put it on the high shelf above my cot when you get to the Brixtons."

I detest that sweaty thing. I'm glad to be rid of it. We seldom wear them in the mountains.

"Yes Michael," he responded. "Onto the shelf with it then."

I looked up at Reverend Ekland, now in the driver's seat. "I'll ensure that she gets back to the parsonage at a reasonable time, sir."

"I'm sure you will. Mind the heat of the day," he repeated.

Edwyn, looking off into the distance, pressing his fist over his mouth, suppressed an urge to laugh as the carriage pulled away. "Yes Michael, mind the heat," he chuckled. "Mind the heat of the day."

As they drove away, we stood on the bridge, resting our arms on the stone railings and looking down into the quiet and shaded pool below. I turned in the opposite direction, looking up at a distant stony peak, which would be a hike of several hours. "Would you ever consider hiking up there?" I pointed at the peak. "I've often wondered about it. There are people in the harbor who have. They say the view is breathtaking."

"I don't know if I would." She hesitated. "I might."

"Have you ever been close up to the waterfall?" I asked.

"No, but I crossed this bridge before today, when Uncle Martin took me to meet Lord Warrington's family several weeks ago. Jonathan Warrington is younger than you or I but he's a highly skilled musician." She wet her lips. "How long have you played the oboe?"

"When I was a child of five years, I played the penny whistle. A few years later, my grandfather purchased an oboe from an elderly friend. I've been playing it ever since."

"I started on the penny whistle as well," she responded. "Any ideas what we should play on Thursday night?"

"I've composed a melancholy duet for flute and oboe. We could play that for Lord Warrington."

"Is it demanding?"

"Not at all; slow tempo, interesting phrases, and quite somber. With a little bit of practice and effective intonation, it's deeply moving. I call it 'Evening Sorrow'."

"Sounds like a worthy choice to me. Lord Warrington said he heard you play at Penrith. Did you study music there?"

"That's right. I studied literature, mathematics, and the classics at the Hawkshead School in Penrith with Ann Birkett, and I studied music with Isabel Hetherington, originally of Devon. She had been a student of Frederick William Herschel."

She was quiet for a moment. "Did you ever hear one of the Parke brothers play?"

"John Parke, actually. One summer I studied with him at Penrith, but during the rest of the year, he was in London. He sold me a printed copy of the larghetto movement of one of his own concertos. It's a transcription for piano and oboe. Very lyrical and emotional."

"Do you have it here in Oak Harbor?"

"It's in my backpack at the Brixtons, but it's a bit crumpled."

"It sounds interesting." Madelyn quietly watched the pool beneath the bridge and tried to see down into the seaport. "There are too many trees blocking our view. It was much better from the height of the carriage."

"Come with me. I know a path through the trees to a tall pedestal stone at the waterfall's edge."

I led her down some step-like stones from the road to the side of the stream. We followed the path until it ended at some bushes.

"This can't be right," she said. "The path has come to an end."

Pushing aside some branches dramatically, I revealed that the little trail continued to the pedestal that I had described.

A moment later, we were there. I stepped across first in one casual stride, to show how easy it was. I suddenly felt very responsible for her, wanting to make sure that she was safe. The flat-top pedestal stone was the size of a large kitchen tabletop and a great height above the base of the cliff. I told her to wait for a moment as I firmly planted my feet.

"Here, take my hand," I said.

She grasped a fistful of her skirt, holding it against her thigh. "Are you sure, Michael?"

"Trust me."

Hesitantly, she looked at me, reached out, and firmly grasped my hand. Stepping across, we came face to face, unusually close, and her soft warm hand lingered in mine. Sitting, I noticed that there were dusty gravel patches on the stone, so I took off my jacket and spread it open for her. *She will think I'm so gallant.*

MARK G. TURNER

The Pedestal Stone

"Thank you." She seated herself beside me.

We sat, peering down into the seaport far below.

"Look, there's Uncle Martin's Landau turning onto the road alongside the harbor."

"Madelyn, you drove amazingly well. How did you learn to drive like that?"

"I've been caring for horses and riding my whole life up in the north."

I winked. "Some people call the north 'the secret kingdom'." I chuckled. "Why is it called that?

"I'm not permitted to say. It's a secret." We both laughed and she continued. "I'm from the little village of Flodden Field near Branxton, not far from Etal Castle."

"Etal Castle?"

"Yes, on the River Till, near our border with Scotland. The first couple of weeks in September, the village is quite somber. Some of the shops don't open and cautious mothers keep their children at home." She looked at me mysteriously. "In fact, there are a few people who leave days before to visit distant relatives and don't return for a week or more."

"Now I remember." I waved my index finger in the air. "I borrowed a copy of Daniel Defoe's touring book from Mr. Stewart. The Battle of Flodden Field is mentioned in it."

"That's right. My great uncle told me that he met Mr. Defoe and that he was asked countless questions about the area." She paused and swept some strands of her long auburn hair from her face. "Flodden Field often seems to be under a pensive grey weight every ninth of September. There's a shadowy, somber mood."

"Why?"

"That's the anniversary of the battle in 1513. The ninth of September was a day of death and affliction on that ancient battlefield. Right at that exact spot, my cousin found the rusted remains of an ancient sword in a field." She paused and looked away. "I don't want to speak about it further. It's unsettling."

The sun was high, there was no shade on the pedestal, and I was getting warm. I removed the cravat from my neck, my waistcoat, and undid a couple of shirt buttons.

We watched as an old, weather-worn three-masted barque left the harbor. The wind was not favorable, so it was tugged out by an eight-man longboat. When it had left the harbor and altered its course, it found a more favorable wind. Its sails were set, the longboat was retrieved, and it made its way between the protective island and the glistening white lighthouse as it headed north.

Madelyn sighed. "It would be grand if we had a telescope to watch the people in the town and the work of the men on the ships." She pointed far below. "Look, there's Tommy running along the street?"

"Edwyn's purchased a telescope." I leaned back enjoying the breeze. "There's your friend, still selling her pastries and buns."

"Michael, could I share with you a little poem I've written?"

"Of course."

"I've never read it to anyone," she said. "Promise you won't laugh."

"I won't laugh. I promise."

"It's about a person's point of view." She looked off into the distance. "A person's perspective of life. Who they are and what they think of their identity. I've captured my thoughts using a variety of animals."

"Your poem idea sounds interesting." I touched her arm. "I won't laugh. Share it with me."

She stated the title as a question, and then recited her poem.

We Both Shall Row, My Love And I

What Is Your Perspective?

I'd rather be an eagle, soaring 'bove a lane,
than a flea bitten beagle, tethered with a chain.
I'd rather be a beagle, with a master whom I love,
than a cruel and fearsome eagle, chewin' on a dove.

I'd rather be a robin, hoppin' on a lawn,
than a grumpy ruffled rooster, screamin' at the dawn.
I'd rather be a rooster, strollin' with my hens,
than a worm-pullin' robin, with my worm-breath friends.

I'd rather be a moth, with brightly colored wings,
than a scary buzzin' hornet, passin' out the stings.
I'd rather be a hornet, fearless an' on my way,
than a clumsy, dusty moth, who can hardly fly away.

I'd rather be a spider, with a finely woven house,
than a crawlin' shiny beetle, in the jaws of a mouse.
I'd rather be a beetle, amblin' with a friend,
than a furry, lonely spider, with a broken web to mend.

I'd rather be a turtle, sittin' on a log,
than a yappin' little puppy, or a mangy old dog.
I'd rather be a puppy, with a master who loves me,
than a hard-shell, lonesome turtle, sittin' 'neath a tree.

I'd rather be a kitten, warm and in a house,
than a cold and stinkin' street cat, the home of a louse.
I'd rather be a street cat, roamin' fancy free,
than a house-bound, little kitten, searchin' for a knee.

We were quiet for a moment. I reflected on the poem. It was marvelous. It was funny. "Madelyn, I like your poem. It's intriguing. I've often wondered about a person's point of view, who they think themselves to be. You've expressed that truth in an interesting and playful way."

"Really?" She smiled beautifully at me.

"Honestly, I love your poem. The part that compares the eagle and the beagle is my favorite."

"I'm glad you like it," she confessed. "I was a bit nervous about sharing it with you."

"Have you ever had a poem printed in a book or in a newspaper?" I asked.

"Yes, several in fact, in a Carlisle newspaper. I'll share them with you sometime." Something caught her eye down in the seaport. "Is that John Lyon walking towards the lighthouse?"

"It must be," I responded. "He couldn't be mistaken for another."

She looked disappointed that I'd said that. "It's unfortunate that people see him only for his size. He's a good man and a great friend to many people."

"You're right," I agreed. "He's friendly and has a great sense of humor."

"There's a clear view of Fair Havens Church and the parsonage from here." She shielded her eyes from the sun. "And we can see some of the larger stones in the cemetery as well."

I didn't want to talk about the cemetery, my grandfather's resting place, so to change the subject, I repeated her idea about the telescope. "Like you said, having a telescope up here would be interesting. My music teacher, Isabel Hetherington, said that William Herschel, who was also a man of science, had a large one that he carried in an old trombone case. We'll borrow Edwyn's next time."

"Next time?" Madelyn observed with a playful grin.

We were quiet for awhile and then, with a tender, almost wounded voice, she spoke. "Michael." She sounded concerned when she said my name. "You were looking at the tiny scar above my right eyebrow." She touched it with her fingertip.

"I'm sorry. I simply found it interesting. Scars speak of personal history and experiences."

"Maybe some time I'll tell you about it." She seemed angry or hurt. I couldn't tell which. "This detail of my personal history." She grimaced and looked away.

I smiled apprehensively and invited her to step back onto the path from the pedestal stone, that we might start heading down into the harbor.

She stood, brushed off my jacket, and passed it to me. Once again, I took her hand as she stepped across the gap, and once again, her hand lingered in mine.

I could do this all day. What a precious woman. So delicate, with her small soft hands.

We walked for a bit. I was uncomfortable, having made her feel self-conscious about her little scar. I wanted to move past it. "I know an interesting shortcut that will save us some hiking time."

She chuckled and shook her head. "Why do men always want to explore shortcuts?" She winced and laughed. "They always take longer, involve a lot of dirt, and usually people get lost, but the men never admit it."

Laughing, I responded, "Adventure. It's all about adventure." I paused dramatically and raised my eyebrows. "Adventure and discovery."

We followed the path but it turned deeper into a mysteriously shadowed oak grove. Our descent down through the forest began to follow a steeper slope. Colossal branches, high above, shaded us from the hot sun, and they served as perches for the woodland birds. A couple of wood pigeons were pecking the ground ahead of us in a little clearing and a magpie was having a conflict with a squirrel in some branches overhead. We hadn't been moving through the forest for more than a few minutes when we were startled by several young squirrel's chasing each other with much noisy complaint around tree trunks and leaping from branch to branch.

"That looks like so much fun." Madelyn clapped her hands together. "I wish I were a squirrel."

"That would be fine as long as some animal didn't prey upon you and eat you up." I hesitated and looked skyward. "I wish I were a hawk." Realizing that my prey might be a squirrel, I thought that I should present myself in a friendlier way. "Ahh, but I wouldn't eat you up, Madelyn." *What an odd thing for me to say.*

Laughing, she eyed me both cautiously and humorously.

We continued on our hike. The mossy stumps, rocky outcroppings, fallen branches, and huge ferns made the pathway seem more remote than it actually was. We were in the midst of a rustic menagerie.

In a clearing, we were surrounded by beautiful flowers: bluebells, snowdrops, and primrose. It was magical. I bent down and picked some flowers, forming a bouquet, and gave them to her. She beamed appreciatively with a tender sweetness.

The natural environment had often provided me with a sense of peaceful belonging and here I was in the midst of it, enjoying it with Madelyn.

"I've never been deep into a forest like this." She reached out and took my hand. "Thank you for sharing the waterfalls, the trees, the flowers, the ferns, and, and..." She paused. "Thank you for sharing *all* of this with me."

She didn't mention the stains on the hem of her skirt or her muddy and scratched shoes.

"I've always felt that my time in the woodlands, each animal, each moment, each shadow, was a gift. The forest has always calmed me, and helped me be, more..." I paused, looking for the right word. "More at peace."

"Do you lack peace, Michael?"

"Well, my father died when I was just a runt of a child, I barely knew him, and my mother lacked warmth. I suppose..." I paused, feeling exposed. "Maybe I needn't dwell on the past."

Why am I talking like this. Why am I so open, and yet holding back from her?

She stopped to look at several brightly colored butterflies. "Butterflies flutter by and tumbling streams stumble dreams."

"That's curious. What do you mean, 'tumbling streams stumble dreams'?" I asked.

"When I lived in the village of Flodden Field with my parents, our little home was beside a tumbling stream that led to the River Till. When the water tumbled by, dashing over rocks and splashing into pools, its sound gave me odd dreams. Do you know what I mean? Listening to it all night long. It had a big effect on me."

What she was saying made a lot of sense. "Listening to a splashing and gurgling stream all the time is bound to have a big effect on a person."

"Eventually, I learned to ignore it and got comfortable with it. I ended up enjoying its soothing sound."

We came upon the ruins of a small stone cottage lacking a roof. Flowers were all around us and throughout the ruins. On the walls, thick tangles of overgrown ivy had found a home.

My thoughts about how nature had reconquered the home and taken it back from the family that once lived there toyed with my mind. "The people left long ago and now the ivy is free of woe."

Madelyn frowned. "What does that mean, 'free of woe'?"

I responded, "With the people gone, the ivy will never be cut back. It can grow freely."

"Interesting." She crouched down and tried to break off some ivy vines but was having great difficulty. They were too bendable and wouldn't snap free.

"Let me help." I pulled my Sheffield knife from its sheath, cut some lengths, and passed them to her.

She wound them round and round, making a wreath-like crown, and placing it on her head, she took on a royal demeanor. With gestures and mannerisms suitable only for the nobility, she mimicked a queen commanding her loyal subjects.

"Just a minute, it needs something more suitable for a princess of the woodlands." I bent down and picked some flowers—bluebells, primrose, and marigolds—and wove them into her crown. Stepping back and giving her a low bow, I knelt on one knee before her, paying homage to her as my sovereign. "My lady, I am your humble servant."

With a lifted chin and a dramatically condescending nod, she said, "Thank you, my faithful squire." She then, quite humorously, picked up a crooked stick and knighted me, tapping one shoulder and then the other. "A simple squire you are no longer. Rise, Sir Knight."

Standing, slowly and theatrically, with my chest puffed, my head erect, and my chin lifted high, I drew my knife as if it were a long and mighty sword. Laughing, I raised it over my head. I resheathed my knife, she took my hand, and we were on our way again through the forest.

"We are very deep into the forest, but I feel safe with you." She grasped my hand more firmly.

We walked on beneath the beautiful canopy of the oak forest, and then entered a second clearing. Within it, atop a small hill, were nine standing stones. They looked foreboding. This was, I believe, a place of worship for the ancients. These monoliths, each greater in height than a man, were arranged in a great circle fifty feet across. In the center was a low, table-like stone with a number of beautiful Scotch thistles in full bloom growing beside it. The whole structure was almost entirely encircled by short blackthorn trees with their berries and fierce thorns.

We playfully began walking, weaving our way around and through the nine stones.

"This way we are walking, 'round and 'round the stones, is called a Druid's Weave," I said. "I've read about this in one of William Stukeley writings."

"What truly? Really?" She was shocked.

"Yes, the Druids were not only village leaders, lovers of the forest, and observers of the stars." I paused, wondering if I should continue. "Some say that they were also involved in unseemly worship."

"I don't like it here, let's go," she insisted.

Returning to the forest on a narrow path, we crossed a diminutive stream, bridged by a great slab of slate larger than a door. It may have had some connection with the standing stones.

She stopped walking, looked up at me, and asked, "Do squirrels actually enjoy chasing each other?" She grinned, her eyes sparkled green like the first leaves of spring after a sun shower. "Do birds like to fly?" She imitated a soaring bird with her hand. "Do you think that they enjoy singing as well?" She dropped her hand and looked at me intently with her eyes wide open, waiting for an answer.

"I believe they do. Why do you ask?"

"I've often wondered if there is more joy in nature than we see in the lives of some people."

"I love the forest, Madelyn, and I think you're right about some people lacking joy."

103

We followed the path farther and came out near the two lighthouses. One was short, old, weather-beaten, and made of stone. The other was tall, new, and white painted brick, glistening in the sun. We were both so overheated from the hike that the water of the harbor looked inviting. If I were alone, I would've stripped to the waist and gone in for a swim.

Walking along the road, we passed beneath the little hill, which I liked, and a few minutes later, we arrived at the Brixton's porch. Madelyn knelt down and affectionately petted Eutychus, which he thoroughly enjoyed. We then relaxed in a couple of the chairs and started removing burrs, sticks, and spots of mud from our clothing.

Brynne opened the door and stepped out. "Would you two like some hot tea or cold water?"

In unison and humorously, we responded, "Cold water."

She laughed and stepped back inside, returning moments later with large cups of cold water. "Here you go. I've got to work on supper."

"We've missed lunch," Madelyn exclaimed to me.

"Will your aunt and uncle be upset?"

"No, I don't think so, but I don't think it's a—"

Alarmed, Eutychus jumped to his feet as Lord Warrington's men passed by with their big Shire horses. They were being led by the captain of the guard, and upon seeing me, he slowed the procession. He acknowledged me with a slight raising of his hand and said, "Excellent information, Michael. We've apprehended Gavin and Victor, but the big bowman got away and one of my men took an arrow in the thigh." He grimaced and gestured towards the horseman behind him with a bandaged leg. He continued, "An amazing bowman, but then the rogue disappeared into the forest."

We Both Shall Row, My Love And I

Gavin, looking right at me, was close enough to hear the captain and would conclude that I had disclosed everything that led to their apprehension.

Careless captain. I can't believe he allowed me to be implicated. He put me, and Madelyn sitting here with me, at risk.

I said nothing and turned away as the captain of the guard and his men continued along the road.

Madelyn, looking puzzled, asked, "What was all that about?"

At length, I told her about our request for the help of James Warrington, Earl of Cumberland, and shared my details and opinions as well. She was shocked. The gruesome death of Charles, whom she'd met, and the abduction of Myra, impacted her forcefully.

Silent tears formed in her eyes and she struggled through them. "I'd better be getting back to the parsonage."

"I'll walk you the rest of the way. I don't want you to be alone right now." We stepped onto the street and headed off towards the bridge.

She was quiet for a while as we walked. "I imagine I'll see you at church tomorrow. Will I?"

"Yes, definitely."

Tommy and some other boys were jumping from the bridge into the river with great exhilaration.

Madelyn stopped to talk to them, especially Tommy, for whom she felt great concern. "Boys, a Reverend Raikes in Gloucester has started something new. It's called Sunday School. Have any of you boys ever heard about it?"

"No, I never be hearin' of it," said Tommy.

"Nor me either," said another.

"Not me, miss," added a third.

"Boys, it will be wonderful. We will read the most daring Bible stories." She was truly selling her idea now. "I'll help you with your reading, we'll draw pictures, and have a tasty snack. You boys will be my first pupils." She clapped her hands together. "Come to Fair Havens Church at ten o'clock in the morning."

"Can we bring our friends?" asked a thin lad.

"Yes, certainly."

The boys all looked at each other and cheered.

"I made up a dramatic song about David and Goliath we'll all sing, and I'll play my guitar."

They quickly got dressed from their bridge jumping and disappeared down the side streets of the community, presumably to tell their friends.

Surprised, I asked, "You play the guitar as well?"

"That's right. There's a special song that I'll sing at our concert on Thursday. I'll accompany myself on guitar."

"You're talented. I discover more of your mysteries moment by moment."

She chuckled. "I thrive on music. Music and singing are a gift from God." She looked thoughtfully at me. "Actually, more important than music, I would say that the Lord Himself is my song."

"That's an interesting thing to say." I grinned. "Tell me more."

"In the Bible, in Psalm 118, it says, 'The Lord is my strength and my song; He has become my salvation.' That's my attitude, not only about music but everything I do." With sparkling eyes, she looked at me intently.

Dramatically, I repeated the premise of what she had said. "The Lord is my song. It sounds like it could be a book title. I've never heard that before. It's curious. I'll give it some thought."

When we arrived back at the parsonage, Shadow and Wonder were behind a fence, head to tail, swatting flies from each other and enjoying the familiarity of their paddock after their long walk. A boy in the stable was busying himself with some chores, and the Landau was beside the parsonage.

Escorting her to the door, I was disappointed that our time had ended, but I was thrilled, looking forward to seeing her tomorrow. "The time I've spent with you today has been a great joy."

"And I with you, Michael." She smiled and ran her fingers through her shining auburn hair. "I'm looking forward to seeing you in church."

I was lost in thought. *She has interesting blonde highlights in her auburn hair. I wonder if it's soft to the touch.*

She repeated herself. "I'm looking forward to seeing you in church."

"Is the service still at two o'clock in the afternoon?" I asked. "Pastor Ekland used to preach out in a nearby town in the mornings."

"No, eleven. Uncle Martin comes home for lunch after our Oak Harbor service and then he often goes and preaches out at Harrington later in the afternoon, unless one of their elders preaches a sermon. He usually returns home for dinner at six or so in the evening."

"That's a long day for a Sunday," I observed.

"He's a seriously dedicated man."

"Yes, he is. He was of tremendous help to me when my grandfather passed away."

"Your grandfather?"

"Yes. I was grieved to my core." My voice trembled. "He's buried right there." I motioned towards the cemetery between the parsonage and the church.

We stood there for a moment and I turned to look out into the harbor, regaining my composure.

"I'll see you tomorrow, Madelyn."

She smiled radiantly. "Tomorrow then."

Stepping away from the door of the parsonage, I took a few paces, walked by the entrance to the graveyard, and stopped at the flagstone walkway in front of the church. Griping one of the iron handrails that flanked the steps leading to the door, I hesitated, tethered by my apprehension. Anyone passing by would've seen my distress. I was overwhelmed by memories of my grandfather, a loving man.

Grasping hold of my courage, yet fearing my own emotions, I turned around and took the few steps needed to reach the graveyard gate. Resting my hand on the low stone wall, I saw my grandfather's stone.

A single cluster of wilted flowers sat in front of the stone. I swung the wrought iron gate open with a long loud squeak. I closed it behind me, again with a squeak, and approached my grandfather's grave.

◊◊◊◊◊◊◊

Michael, lost in his memories and attentive only to his grandfather's grave, didn't see the movement of a parsonage curtain above him and off to the side. Madelyn's bedroom window, above the kitchen, overlooked the graveyard and she became, at a distance, a witness of his sorrow.

Her uncle stopped at her open bedroom door. "Time to join us at the table, dearie."

"Uncle Martin, Michael's in the cemetery. He looks upset."

He went to the window and stood beside his niece, sweeping the curtains open a bit wider. "He loved his grandfather dearly, and his grandfather cherished him. Such love is seldom seen." He put his hand on her shoulder. "Michael's father died when he was a small child." He hesitated thoughtfully, wondering if he should continue. "His mother is not a warm-hearted woman. Grandfather Sterling, a loving man, lived

We Both Shall Row, My Love And I

out his faith in God, every moment of every day. He loved the people around him." Uncle Martin hesitated once more. "Especially Michael."

"Did he and Michael do many things together?" she asked.

"They talked and made music. Grandfather Sterling played the penny whistle beautifully. They hiked into the mountains until his grandfather's health started failing. Then, about two years ago, Michael went off to the capital."

"Why did he go to London?"

Reverend Ekland stepped back from the window. "He was looking into old inheritance records and ownership papers about some property in the Bahamas. His grandfather had insisted that the matter be examined. Now with his grandfather's passing, I don't know if anything ever came of it."

"Look, Uncle Martin, he's writing something down on some paper."

Reverend Ekland let the curtain swing to a close. "Let's provide him some privacy, dear." He gently led her from the window.

Michael trudged along the cobbles, shoulders slumped, towards the new bridge. Stopping there for a time, he watched a father rowing with his son and fishing in a wide, slack water area of the river. They caught nothing but were enjoying each other's company, talking, and occasionally laughing.

Tommy passing by, approached Michael, and leaned on the stone sidewall of the bridge beside him.

◊◊◊◊◊◊

"Hello Mr. Sterlin'. Thinkin' of a swim?"

"No Tommy, not today," I responded.

"Did ya' have a nice walk with Madelyn? She's a charmer, you know."

"I think that I'm beginning to find that out. How did you know we went for a walk?"

"I be in the forest followin' a deer, near them tall stones. I saw the two o' you. I'm quiet in the forest, like a leaf fallin' to the ground or a tribesman, huntin' for 'is dinner." He chuckled.

"I suppose you are. We didn't know you were there."

"I be watchin' the doe that be watchin' you. She didn't be seein' me either." He changed the subject. "Madelyn's gonna' be takin' me for a carriage ride. She always 'as a kind word and always makes people 'appy."

"I've noticed that about her."

"I've got to be goin' now and 'elpin' me mom an' me sisters. She's 'avin' an' upset with Father. A real saber rattlin' row. She calls 'im a pub crawler and 'e calls her a..." He leaned over the stone sidewall of the bridge and spit into the river. "I guess I shouldn't be sayin' it. Bye, Mr. Sterling." He ran off and disappeared into the side streets beyond the end of the bridge, not waiting for a response.

"Goodbye Tommy," I said, long after he left.

Standing there on the bridge watching the father and son rowing, fishing, and laughing served as an invitation to reflect on the wonderful times I'd shared with my jovial and snowy-haired grandfather. His cheerful laugh embraced anyone nearby and his appreciation of people and patience with others was well known in the community.

My grandfather had first encouraged me towards music, books, and the wilderness. He also cultivated in me the desire to see the best in people and to be of a more optimistic disposition.

With a great cheer, the son fishing with his father realized that he had hooked a fish. I was snapped back to reality from my reverie.

The Harbor Master's Office

Walking along the harborside street, I saw Harbor Master Langley's office and thought that there would be wisdom in stopping to speak to him about the brigands and their crimes. I entered the office, sat in a sturdy chair, and found myself a witness to several conflicts.

Seamen and longshoremen exchanging blustery comments peppered with profanity were creating an intensely hostile environment. I wished I were back in the forest at Cliffside.

A harbor pilot, having struck a fishing boat with the ship for which he was responsible, and damaging it badly, was claiming innocence. "That little fishin' boat shouldn't've been anchored where it was. Only a fool seekin' clams in a privy would've put 'er there."

The first mate of a trading vessel, needing access to the largest loading crane for his big and impressive four-masted barque was demanding that Harbor Master Langley move two smaller boats so that his vessel could re-position itself on the wharf. "Blimey, those little bed pans aren't needin' the great crane, but I do."

Harbor Master Langley, after perhaps an hour, resolved these issues and others, and seeing me sitting on the bench asked, "What can I help you with, Mr. Sterling?"

"You can call me Michael. Have you heard about the tragedies at Cliffside, the death of Charles Hawthorne and the abduction of Myra Wood?" I asked, making sure to keep my voice loud enough to be heard.

"Yes, Lord Warrington's captain of the guard was here earlier," he responded. "The rogues, Gavin and Victor, have already been apprehended."

"Yes, that's right."

"Langley eased himself further back into his chair and shook his head. "Terrible tragedies. A little child abducted and Charles Hawthorne murdered."

"Did you know Charles?" I asked.

Langley reached across his desk, and taking his large cup in his hand, drank the remaining mouthful of tea and licked his lips. He then looked intently at the mug, inverted it, and held it out so that I might read the bottom. "CH" could be clearly seen. "Everyone new Charles and liked him."

"Did the captain of the guard tell you that others are being sought?" I asked.

"Like I said, Gavin and Victor have been apprehended. That's grand to be sure, but Robert Caine got away."

"Robert Caine? Who's that?"

"The tallest one of the three. The one who always carries the bow," he answered.

"How do you know his name?"

"That's what Tommy Atwater said."

"Tommy? How is he related to any of this?"

"When the captain of the guard came in, Tommy followed right in after him. He'd been walking along the road and decided to see why the captain entered my office. Not much goes on in our little seaport that Tommy doesn't know about."

"Did Tommy say anything else about the brigands?"

"I don't know," said Langley. "I didn't have an opportunity to find out."

"What do you mean?"

"Tommy interrupted the captain a few times and he didn't like being interrupted by a youth, so he ordered him out." William motioned towards the door.

"I need to talk to Tommy. Where does he live?"

"Go towards the bridge but don't cross it. Stay on this side," explained Langley. "Walk one street further upstream, past Kline's warehouse. Then turn left, away from the river. Go a short way up the hill with the river behind you." He gestured turning left and going up a hill. "You'll find a small yellow house. Truly well kept. White trim, neat appearance, and flowers in the garden. You know what I mean, a lady's house." He grinned.

"Is that Tommy's house?" I asked.

"No, not yet. Go up the small lane beside the yellow house. Past several beech trees, an old broken down stone wall, and a fallen down shack. Then you'll see where Tommy lives at the end of the path."

"How do you know the way so well?"

Langley chuckled. "The yellow house is my aunt's house. Tommy sometimes works in her yard to make some money."

"Thank you for your help, William. Did the captain of the guard tell you about a wagon being driven by a young man with a scar about here." With my index finger, I traced on my cheekbone the location of the scar below my right eye. "There was also an older woman and a whole family in the back of the wagon."

"He didn't say anything about a wagon. There are a lot of wagons in a town of this size, but I'll keep my eyes open for a man with the scar you've described."

I'll have to go and see Tommy. How in the world could he know the bowman's name? What else might he know?

"If any of these people come in looking for passage on a ship, let me know." I turned to walk away. "I'm staying with Edwyn and his family."

"Michael, what was the last thing you said?"

I faced him and repeated with a raised voice, "I'm staying with Edwyn." I thanked him for his help and headed out the door.

~~~~~~

Following Langley's directions, I soon arrived at the yellow house. As described, it was a well kept lady's cottage, boasting scrollwork at the eaves, louvered shutters at the windows, and a bird bath in the garden, surrounded by flowers.

I entered the pathway beside it and in a few minutes arrived at Tommy's derelict clapboard house. The carcass of a dead dog, writhing with maggots and buzzing with flies, was in the corner near a broken down fence. The stench was unbearable. A crow watched from a nearby stump and a lone magpie walked in the dirt, closer to the disgusting carcass.

"Good morning Mr Magpie. How is your lady wife today?" I asked jokingly as I passed by. It was a common superstitious greeting when you see a magpie here in the north.

From inside the house, I could hear a man and woman arguing and a young child crying. Bracing myself for the unknown, I knocked on the door. The arguing subsided and the woman that I had seen with the two small girls in front of the Royal Stag answered the door. A toddler with a tear stained face rode her hip and the bigger girl, with a fist full of her mother's skirt, stood beside her.

"What do you want?" the woman growled.

"Hello, my name is Michael Sterling. I'm a friend of Edwyn, the cabinet maker, and an acquaintance of Tommy's—."

"Who's at the door?" barked a surly male voice from within the home.

"If I might continue, madam." I cleared my throat. "I attend Fair Havens Church and know your Tommy. Might I speak to him, please?"

The surly voice from inside angrily barked again, "Belinda. Who is it? You stupid woman, who's at the door?"

The woman shouted over her shoulder, "A churchman, a friend of the Brixtons, looking for Tommy. Crawl back into your hellish pint and leave me be."

Smiling, I asked again, "May I speak to Tommy please?"

"Tommy's not 'ere."

Again, more surly barking, "What churchman? Ask him if 'es got alms for those that can't work."

I grinned, gave her my calling card, and asked her to tell Tommy that I came by. "Thank you, madam, for your time." I placed a few coins in her hand and she shared a crooked smile as I left.

~~~~~

When I arrived back at the Brixton home, having had nothing to eat since breakfast, Louisa gave me a large bowl of tasty oxtail soup. I took it out onto the porch and she followed me with her own bowl. She explained that her husband had taken old Thomas to see some beautiful maples, superb for fine cabinetry, in the forest above the seaport. Before going back inside, she told me that several years earlier he had purchased the timber rights for certain select trees in a modest woodlot from Lord Warrington. Soon he'd be harvesting the last of the carefully chosen trees.

Tommy passed by a few minutes later, coming from the direction of the lighthouse with several friends, each carrying an old piece of rusty iron.

Eutychus lifted his head, looked at the boys, and then went back to sleep.

"Tommy, step up onto the porch for a minute. I need to talk to you about a few things."

He gave his pieces of iron to his friends and told them that these treasures should be put on the pile behind his house. Waving them off, he joined me on the porch as Brynne brought me a large platter of cheese, fresh bread, and fruit to follow-up the soup. Hungrily, Tommy blinked several times when he saw it.

"Brynne, this is too much." I dramatically rubbed my belly. "Tommy will need to help me with this, and could we have an extra bowl of oxtail soup for him?"

"Right away, Michael." She quickly returned with a large bowl of soup and an extra plate. She put her hand on my shoulder and slid her thumb onto the side of my neck. "I'll bring the tea out shortly."

"Mr. Sterlin' sir, I'll be burstin' me belly if I be eatin' all this."

"Enjoy it. Louisa and Brynne are the best cooks in Oak Harbor," I said.

"No doubt 'bout that, Mr. Sterlin'."

"Tommy, I looked for you earlier at your home. I'm glad I can chat with you now."

"Are they still fightin', me mom an' dad?"

"Adults sometimes have things to discuss." I paused. "Can I ask you a couple questions?"

"I'm in trouble, right?"

"No, actually you could be a big help to me."

"Sure, Mr. Sterlin', anythin' to 'elp."

"The harbor master told me that you were in his office when Lord Warrington's captain of the guard was telling him about the evil men. The ones they're searching for."

"Yes sir. I be there."

"How did you know the name of the tall bowman, Robert, the friend of Gavin and Victor?"

"Not friends, Mr. Sterlin' sir. They be brothers. I know 'em all."

"You mean all three of them?" I asked.

"No, I know the 'ole family an' the others as well."

This is getting interesting. I don't want him to be hesitant if I ask too many questions.

I casually leaned back in my chair and calmly took a sip of tea.

"Tommy, what do you mean when you say that you know, 'all' of them? Tell me more."

"Well sir, if you go up the road that leads to the big cave, you know the cave, the one that's not far from the trout fishin' brook."

"No, I don't know the area as well as you. What street is it when it reaches town?"

He stopped and thought for a minute, counting with his fingers, imagining where the town's streets were, and then said, "That be the fourth street up from the bridge."

"Interesting. Tell me more."

"Well sir, start goin' up there, but not as far as you'd go to reach the cave. When you come to the path that leads to the old lady's place with all the chickens, keep goin' an' curve to the left."

"I think I know the place," I responded enthusiastically.

"Gavin, Victor, an' Robert lived in a camp at the ruins o' the old stone 'ouse, 'neath the giant tree. Walk the path a wee bit more, over a rise, an' through the forest a bit. There it be, their main camp."

"Who's in the camp?"

"Sabina. She's in charge o' the big wagon, an' there be a smaller wagon sometimes. She takes care 'er old dad, Alfred, but everybody be callin' 'm Gran' Freddie."

"How did they get their wagons in there? It's a narrow little path."

He laughed. "The path's not for 'orse an' wagon Mr. Sterlin'. It be only for people. Men an' 'orses can walk in. The captain, 'e be walkin' 'is men in. Then they grabbed Victor an' Gavin. There be no room for a wagon."

I repeated the question. "So, how did they get their wagons in to the area of the cave, beyond the ruins?"

"There be a lane windin' 'round through the forest. It be comin' out on the road, further 'long, near the cave."

"Tommy, how did you meet all those people?"

"Am I in trouble? I'm in trouble, right?"

"No, you're not in trouble. You're being tremendously helpful."

"A few days ago, I be fishin' for trout near the cave. Then they stopped for water an' asked me a bucket full o' questions 'bout Oak 'arbor, an' the ships that be comin' an' goin'. Then, they started settin' up camp. They be 'avin' two wagons an' some tents."

"Who else is in the camp?" I asked.

"There's Joseph Caine, 'e 'as a scar, 'e's Robert's youngest brother an' 'e's on the smallish side, not a giant like Robert." Tommy dropped his voice to a whisper. "But 'e be the most evil. I saw 'im chokin' the life out o' a li'l pup once jus' because it be barkin' at 'im."

"That's terrible. Who else is in the camp?"

There's Nicola, she be much younger than me. An' 'er sister, she be there, but I don't see 'er much an' I don't know 'er name. She's sickly, so they be sayin'. She's in the big wagon most o' the time. The little wagon, it comes an' goes."

"What does she look like, the sickly one?"

"Nothin' like 'em. They 'ave dark 'air an' be lookin' rough but she be 'avin' blonde 'air."

"Tommy, tell me more about the camp."

"Sometimes there be Victor's cousins, Chatwin an' 'oward. Chatwin knows how to throw a knife into a tree 'bout ten paces 'way, an' 'oward 'as a beautiful musket, not as nice lookin' as Gran' Freddie's but it shoots straighter. I saw 'im drop one o' Lord Warrington's deers at 'bout a 'undred paces. Mr. Sterlin' sir, there's a few others, but I don't be knowin' all their names."

"You've been a big help. Will you come with me to talk to James Warrington, Earl of Cumberland?"

Tommy lifted his chin and pressed out his chest. "Yes. It be my duty to speak to 'im." He looked shocked and then he hesitated. "I, I've never been speakin' to Lord Warrington. I might be fearin' to be sayin' the wrong things."

"You will be fine. He's a friendly man. Let's borrow a horse or a carriage and go up to Warrington Hall."

"George Kline, 'e be 'avin' a 'orse."

"Great idea. Let's go and talk to George, or maybe we can go to Reverend Ekland's parsonage and talk to him about using his carriage."

At the mention of a carriage ride and going to see Lord Warrington, Tommy bubbled with enthusiasm. "Yes sir, Mr. Sterlin'. Let's be goin'."

Without divulging the details, I told Louisa where we were going and we quickly left for Kline's warehouse. On the way, Reverend Ekland approached us with his gig, pulled by Shadow.

"Reverend Ekland, Tommy has more information about the brigands. We need to talk to Lord Warrington immediately. May I ask you to take us?"

"Michael, for anything as important as this, certainly."

Tommy and I climbed aboard the gig. As we traveled up through the oak forest, Tommy told Reverend Ekland all that he had told me.

When we arrived at the Warrington estate, Reverend Ekland spoke to the soldiers on duty at the gatehouse and we were readily waved through. We then entered the grounds on the cobbled lane and passed through the high arched gate that led to the courtyard and stables. Tommy, who had never been inside the outer wall, let alone inside the courtyard, was in awe of the compound. The powerful horses, well-kept stables, and armed soldiers, busy with their duties, instilled in him a sense of wide-eyed wonder.

Alistair Bletchley, the head groomsman, walked over to us and helped Reverend Ekland climb down. Tommy jumped down in one great leap.

"Tommy, you must be respectful when we meet Lord Warrington. We need to see the gentleman in you today. Do you understand?"

"Yes sir, Mr. Sterlin' sir."

Alistair's wife, Agnes, the head cook, leaned out the kitchen window across the courtyard and looked us over.

We went to the door and were met by the same button-polished butler I had met before.

He addressed Reverend Ekland, "Hello sir, may I be of service?"

"Yes certainly," said Reverend Ekland, passing him his calling card.

"One moment, please. I'll inform Lord Warrington of your presence."

The butler invited us to step inside the foyer and disappeared down the hallway.

"What'd the reverend give to that fancy-suited fella'?" Tommy asked me in a whisper.

"It's his calling card. It has his name on it."

"Why'd he give him the card? Will the butler be forgettin' the reverend's name by the time he be talkin' to Lord Warrington?"

Reverend Ekland shared a gentle yet stern expression. "No Tommy, it's simply the correct way to let the Earl of Cumberland know that there are visitors hoping to meet with him."

"Blimey, Mr. Sterlin', I can't see Lord Warrington. I be 'avin' no card for meself."

"That's fine, we only need one card. Reverend Ekland's calling card will suffice."

Tommy looked up at Reverend Ekland. "Sir?"

"Yes, Tommy."

"Your card, it be lookin' expensive. Will you be gettin' it back?"

"I don't know, Tommy. Don't concern yourself with it."

The butler returned and invited us to accompany him down the hall. He paused before the double doors, as he did in the morning. Tommy's eyes brightened as he stared fearfully at the two guards. The butler then grasped the doors' shiny brass handles, one firmly in each hand, and swung them open.

We paused as he stepped into the reception room and announced, "The Reverend Martin Ekland and his party are here at your pleasure, my lord." He gave a little bow of his head.

"Gentlemen, we meet again. It has been an eventful day," said Lord Warrington, with his scribe at his side.

As we entered Lord Warrington's reception room, Tommy grasped the butler's sleeve and mumbled, "Excuse me, Mr.

Butler sir, can we be 'avin' the fine reverend's card back?" The butler, ignoring him, didn't respond.

I whispered to Tommy, "Don't worry about the reverend's calling card. It's not a concern. Don't talk about it."

James Warrington, Earl of Cumberland, hearing Tommy's request, smiled. "Who might this young gentleman be?"

Reverend Ekland introduced him. "My Lord Warrington sir, this is Tommy Atwater, a lad from Oak Harbor. He has new information about the brigands."

"I'm pleased to meet you, Master Thomas Atwater."

Tommy, having never been called master, was very nervous. He responded, "My sir, Lord Warrington, your lordship my sir." He hesitated. "Glad to meet." He hesitated. "Glad to makin' your acquaintance." He was trembling with fear.

"Master Atwater, there is no need to be nervous." Lord Warrington smiled again and gestured towards the chairs in front of his desk.

We seated ourselves, and when I started to speak of the brigands on behalf of Tommy, Lord Warrington calmly but decidedly raised his hand, palm towards me. "I would much prefer to hear this directly from Master Thomas."

Tommy's eyes brightened, his chin lifted, and he sat up straighter.

Lord Warrington shifted in his chair and leaned in towards him. "Tommy, there are people in danger. Danger for their lives."

Tommy looked older and more serious than a moment earlier. "Yes sir, Lord Warrington, sir."

"Only you can help. Will you help me now?" asked Lord Warrington. "Will you help the people that are in danger?"

"Yes sir, Lord Warrington, sir. I be doin' that."

Tommy described the camp at length the two wagons and the comings and goings of the brigands. He described where the camp was, what it was like, and everyone who remained there, listing each of their names and their descriptions, as the scribe carefully recorded them. Alfred Caine, Sabina Caine, Robert Caine, Joseph Caine, Chatwin Smythe, Howard Smythe, young Nicola Smythe, and her seldom seen sister, who looked nothing like her. Tommy also shared that there were a few other men whose names he didn't know.

When Tommy had finished speaking, Lord Warrington was red faced with indignation. He abruptly leaned back in his chair, and striking his desk with his fist, rose to his feet. "Excuse me, gentlemen. I must see the captain of the guard." He stepped out of the room.

Tommy, staring at Lord Warrington's scribe, who remained with us, said to him, "I can write my name and a few other words and Madelyn Haversham is goin' to be 'elpin' me read an' write better."

"I have met her, Tommy. She is a pleasant lady," said the scribe.

"There be truth in that," responded Tommy. "Do you make good coin for writin' things down for Lord Warrington?"

"That's the gentleman's private business," said Reverend Ekland. "Questions like that shouldn't be asked."

Tommy stood and took a few steps towards the scribe. "Do you be writin' more neatly than Lord Warrington? Is that why you be doin' it?"

The scribed looked up from his papers and adjusted his spectacles. "The Earl of Cumberland has superb penmanship but it is my responsibility to record all matters of importance. I take my time and I do my best work."

"Sit down, Tommy," said Reverend Ekland. "Please show us your best behavior."

Tommy sat, but couldn't keep his eyes off the scribe.

Lord Warrington returned minutes later and grinned at Reverend Ekland and me, before turning his attention to Tommy. "Master Thomas, you are a fine young man and you have truly been a great help." He noticed that Tommy kept glancing at Reverend Ekland's calling card, laying on a nearby table. "Would you like that card?"

"Lord Warrington, sir, I think that we should be givin' it back to the reverend. They be expensive, so I 'magine."

"Yes, Thomas, I suppose they are." He gave the card to Tommy, who held it delicately and carefully studied the artistic lettering and amber edging. He then gave it to Reverend Ekland.

"Thank you, Tommy."

"Reverend Ekland?"

"Yes, Tommy."

"I think that my name, if you don't mind, Reverend, should be *Thomas* from now on."

Reverend Ekland and I nodded to one another, and Lord Warrington, smiling broadly, directed the scribe to alter the official record.

"Master Thomas, what is your middle name?" asked Lord Warrington.

"Cedric, sir."

Lord Warrington winked playfully at Reverend Ekland and me. "Do you mean Sir Cedric?"

"No," responded Tommy. "I'm not a sir." He hesitated. "Just Cedric."

Lord Warrington smiled. "Ahh, Cedric the Just. You must be a man focused on righteousness to have such a title."

"No sir," said Tommy. "My name, it be Thomas Cedric Atwater."

Lord Warrington turned to his scribe and in a formal voice stated, "Let the record show that Master Thomas Cedric Atwater of Oak Harbor, as a servant of the crown, was of significant help to His Majesty's subjects in the pursuit of justice on this day."

Tommy, brimming with pride, looked towards me, then at Reverend Ekland, and then at the scribe.

"Thank you, Lord Warrington sir." Tommy's voice seemed a little deeper, a little more confident.

"You're welcome, Master Thomas. I need to speak now to Reverend Ekland and Michael Sterling privately. Please accompany my scribe. He will take you to Mrs. Bletchley in the kitchen for a biscuit."

"Yes sir, Lord Warrington, sir."

Tommy left us and Lord Warrington described the details of Victor and Gavin's apprehension, the horseman's wounding, and his puzzlement that Robert, the bowman, had slipped through their grasp. He then shared that Gavin and Victor, up to this point, were saying nothing, and that he had sent out once again his men in overwhelming numbers to apprehend the remaining brigands.

We expressed appreciation to Lord Warrington for his pursuit of justice and like earlier in the day, we heard the thundering of hooves passing through the courtyard gate.

As the butler escorted us out, I made a request. "Lord Warrington, sir?"

"Yes, Michael."

"Sir, might I return tomorrow afternoon and meet with your son, Jonathan? I would like to practice the music with him for Thursday. I would truly like to do my best."

"Yes, a superb idea. I will let him know that he should be expecting you."

"Thank you, my lord."

We stepped into the courtyard and saw Tommy. With one hand, he was helping Alistair Bletchley feed Shadow and with his other, he held three large biscuits.

Alistair put the bridle back on Shadow and thanked Tommy for his help.

Climbing aboard the gig, Tommy's eyes were wide with the accoutrements of wealth around him and his heart was buoyant with the recognition that he had received from Lord Warrington.

Reverend Ekland let him take the reins for a short time on a straight stretch of road through the oak grove. With all of the new experiences of the day, you could see Tommy envisioning himself to be the young lord of the manor. He looked triumphant. With raised eyebrows and a slight inclination of his head, he acknowledged Lord Warrington's gardeners, grounds keepers, and shepherds as we passed. At one point, with well-mimed gestures, he pointed at some horse manure on the road ahead of us and seemed to be giving orders to some imaginary underlings to remove it.

Arriving back at Edwyn's porch, I climbed down from the gig and Reverend Ekland said he would drop off Tommy nearer his home.

The poor lad, with his derelict home, the dead dog in the yard, and his pub-crawling father. A striking contrast with the accoutrements of wealth he saw earlier and the respect he had received from Lord Warrington.

As they were about to leave, Tommy asked, "Reverend, could you please be droppin' me at the Royal Stag? Shannon always gives me the chicken bones from the plate scrapin's. I take 'm home and boil 'm up. I make a right tasty soup, and sometimes I be sellin' it to the sailors an' merchantmen that come in from the sea."

"You're a clever lad, Tommy," I said.

"Thank you, Mr. Sterlin' sir. Clever I be, when there's coin to be 'ad."

During dinner with the Brixtons, I explained all that had transpired with Tommy, Reverend Ekland, and Lord Warrington during the afternoon.

After dinner, Edwyn, Louisa, old Thomas, and I were on the porch enjoying our tea as Lord Warrington's men rode by on their way back up to the estate. By the light of the oil lamps on the rail and the full moon above, we witnessed more than a dozen troops escorting several of the brigands along the cobbled street.

With the canvas removed from the large wagon, we could see Grand Freddie, wrists shackled, sitting in the back beside a moaning soldier. Two other men were walking along behind the wagon with lead ropes to their necks and shackles around their wrists. The smaller wagon wasn't in the group, nor were many of the other brigands that Tommy had described.

"Such is the destiny of those who live by the sword and clothe themselves with violence," said Edwyn. "Michael, do you grasp how these wicked people have destroyed not only the lives of others but their own lives as well?"

"I believe I do."

He then said pensively, "The wicked shall fall by their own wickedness."

"That's from the Scriptures, is it not?" I asked.

"Yes, that's correct, from the Proverbs of wise old Solomon, the eleventh chapter."

The evening was wearing on. The sounds of the port floated through the harbor to meet us; officers of the watch, declaring all was well; a bell buoy towards the harbor entrance, sounding a dull clang, and some rope work, straining and sighing, as the breeze blew in from the sea. Boisterous laughter, crude exclamations, and the indistinct words of a drinking song reached us from the Royal Stag. Louisa, shaking her head and adjusting her shawl higher on her shoulders, made eye contact with her husband.

I shared that tomorrow I would go to Warrington Hall to meet Jonathan Warrington and practice the music that we would present to the Warrington household.

Edwyn leaned to his side and stroked Eutychus. "Quite a few townspeople will be in attendance at the concert as well."

"Yes, I've heard."

"I'm glad that you will be practicing, Michael. Thursday is merely days away. Practice makes perfect when mediocrity, quite simply, will not do."

"Well put, my love," said Louisa.

We sat on the porch saying little but enjoying each other's company and the cool of the evening. Brynne stepped out and joined us carrying a tray of scones, tea, milk, and sugar. She then sat quietly on the floor beside Eutychus, her faithful companion since childhood, and whispering a song, affectionately petted him. Murmuring in his sleep, he lifted his massive head from his crossed paws and laid it in her lap. Then Brynne, reaching into a cloth bag beside her, pulled out a brush and began grooming him. Eutychus, finding with her all that he sought in life, wagged his tail and murmured again in his sleep.

"I'm not feeling well and must seek my cot," said old Thomas. He rose from his chair and went inside. Edwyn, Louisa, and Brynne likewise went inside a short time later.

By the light of an oil lamp, I continued my reading of Captain Bridger's journal of 1764. He had faced many adversities and intrigues, yet relentlessly, he continued his travels. *Where will my life as a single man take me?*

Tired, I went to the room behind the kitchen. Thomas, whom I respected as a fine old gentleman, was already enjoying a deep sleep on his cot across the room. Snoring, he reminded me of my grandfather.

We Both Shall Row, My Love And I

I laid on my bed trying to sleep and wondered if I was kept awake by Thomas' snoring or by the events of the day. I couldn't escape the mosaic of my thoughts: my grandfather, the tragedies of Stone Ridge, the recent arrests, and sweet Madelyn.

Madelyn. I like how her name sounds. Her wide smile, luxuriant hair, her wit, and her beauty. Priceless. She is a treasure. Her life has purpose. Is my life as a single man as satisfying as I once thought it to be?

Fatigue embraced me, and finally, sleep found me.

~~~~~~

In the grey of early morning, I was awakened. Thomas, in the grip of a terrible nightmare, cried out, "No, don't make me look." He moaned in his sleep. "No Lord, that's not Charles. His face. Not human!" he shouted. He then became silent. By the early morning light, I could see that dear old Thomas was awake and laying on his side facing me, his eyes wide open.

"Are you alright now, Thomas?"

He said nothing but blinked a few times and wet his lips. I repeated my question. "You've had a dream. Are you alright?"

"It was no dream. It was a terrible nightmare." He closed his eyes, winced, and shook his head. "Charles Hawthorne was such a good man."

Fair Havens Church

After a breakfast of toast, eggs, and fruit, we strolled like a family, including Thomas and I, around the harbor towards Fair Havens Church. Eutychus stopping to smell every tree, followed along behind. Old Thomas, feeling much better, stopped to speak to an elderly woman that he had known years earlier. Nearing the church, a large number of boys, including Tommy, a special focus of Madelyn's love, boisterously approached us.

One of the boys, an effective reader, was dramatically reading aloud an introduction prepared by Madelyn of First Samuel, the seventeenth chapter. When he had finished, we witnessed a re-enactment of the story of David the shepherd boy, with King Saul of Israel, and Goliath, the Philistine warrior.

Tommy, as David the shepherd boy, boldly asked, "King Saul, who is this Philistine, that 'e should be defyin' the armies o' the livin' God?"

A boy, in the role of King Saul, with a crown of ivy wound around his head and a fence picket sword raised high above him, stood on a tree stump, flanked by other boys serving as his soldiers. Capturing the drama of it all, King Saul, with nobility but exaggerated condescension, stared at Tommy, as David the shepherd boy. He said, "David, thou art not able to go against this Philistine to fight with him. Thou art but a youth." King Saul then pointed at another taller boy, also wielding a fence picket sword, who stood on a nearby wall. "Goliath has been a man of war from his youth. He was slaying mighty warriors when you were in your nappies."

Then Tommy, still in the role of David, confidently tapped his chest and said, "I thy servant 'ave kept my father's sheep, and there came a lion." Tommy gestured towards Eutychus, who had stopped to lick himself indiscreetly. "That ol' lion, 'e took a lamb out o' the flock." He gestured towards a little boy, down on all fours, bleating like a sheep. "I went out after 'im and smote 'im, and delivered the sheep out o' 'is mouth." Tommy starred at King Saul confidently. "When 'e arose against me, I caught 'im by 'is beard, an' smote 'im, an' slew 'im."

The boys, serving as King Saul's soldiers, exclaimed in unison, "Oh!" Then one of them shouted, "Stop David. Aren't you afraid? You will be slain and be meetin' your maker."

Tommy, as David, spoke through gritted teeth. "Thy servant slew both the lion," he gestured again at Eutychus, "an' the bear." He gestured at a house cat that sat on a post licking its paws. He then declared dramatically, "This Philistine shall be as one o' them. This Goliath, 'e 'ath defied the armies o' the livin' God."

The boys serving as King Saul's soldiers began shouting, "No David, stop, stop! You will be destroyed by this giant of a man."

Tommy stepped closer to Goliath, who loomed over him on the wall, and shouted, "The Lord that delivered me out o' the paw o' the lion and out o' the paw o' the bear will deliver me out o' the 'and o' this 'ere Philistine."

The boy, standing on the tree stump as King Saul, wiped his hand across his forehead and mumbled, "Whew, better you than me." Thankful that he didn't have to fight Goliath. Trembling he added, "Go, and may the Lord be with thee."

Our dear Tommy, in dramatic mime, whirled his imaginary sling above his head, released it's stone, and pointed at Goliath, proudly standing on the wall. The giant, fatally smitten, screamed out in excruciating pain, and clutching his forehead, collapsed onto the grass, writhing in agony. Tommy rushed the last few steps towards him, picked up Goliath's fence picket sword, beheaded him, and lifted a red handkerchief into the air. Louisa's jaw fell open, Brynne dropped her Bible, and two old ladies passing by on their way to church gasped.

The violent realism on a quiet Sunday morning was obviously too shocking for the ladies, but the result was entirely the opposite for Edwyn, old Thomas, and me. We laughed and applauded their spirited drama.

"Boys, you inspire me," Edwyn declared. "If I had been there, I would've wanted to serve at David's side."

Old Thomas joined in the praise. "Well done, boys. Obviously you were all listening closely to Madelyn, and taking to heart what she was teaching."

"Where are you all going? Why aren't you staying for church?" I asked.

Tommy responded, "Some be 'eadin' home, some to work, and some be lookin' for adventure." He then ran up to me, stretched out his hand, and said, "Me card, sir."

I took from his hand a little scrap of tattered paper. "Thank you, Tommy." It was his calling card.

"Madelyn 'elped me with the spellin'." He then raced away to catch up with his friends.

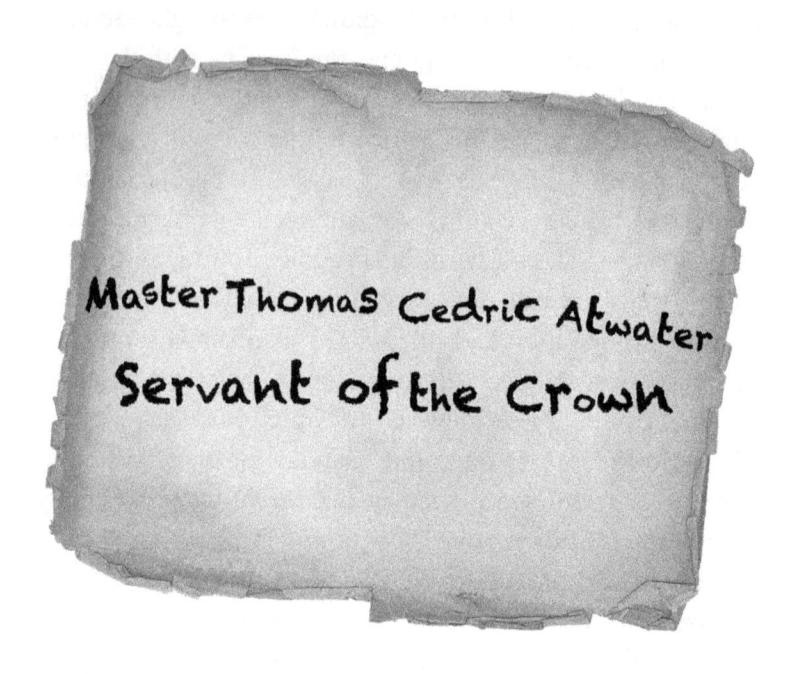

> **Master Thomas Cedric Atwater**
> **Servant of the Crown**

The boys disappeared up the street with their enthusiasm. *Tommy, such a character. Their drama was amazing. I wonder who else, quietly on their way to church, might meet them and be face to face with their graphic drama. A serene Sunday morning? I think not.*

As we neared Fair Havens Church, we passed other Sunday morning strollers. Some from other congregations, and some heading to Fair Havens. Our exchange of morning greetings was cheerful and genuine.

When we arrived in front of the church, Madelyn approached from the parsonage. She wore an attractive but unadorned dark green dress with a wide white belt. Her long hair, flaming red and glistening in the sun, was topped with a modest white hat, matching her belt. One of her white gloved hands clutched a well-worn Bible against her trim waist. She was the perfect picture of devotion.

"Madelyn, we saw your class on the street enthusiastically re-enacting the lesson you taught them. Why aren't they staying for church?"

"A few will, but others go to Saint Cecilia's or other churches, and some pursue their own interests, not being from church-going families."

In front of the church, James and Emily Scott stopped to greet us, and their three chatty daughters followed along behind. Next, Albert Kline, with his wife, Sarah Ruth, and their son, George, came to a stop in their wagon. Albert set the brake and his family climbed down. He then drove the wagon, pulled by Pilgrim, around to the back of the church.

Eutychus, having curled up beneath a beech tree, was enjoying the morning sun. Edwyn and his family, with Thomas, after entering the church and greeting several people, ambled up towards the front. They seated themselves there but I quietly sat in the back row and Madelyn slipped in beside me, holding the well-worn Bible that I had noticed earlier.

"This is for you." She gave me a handcrafted leather bookmark that she had been carrying, and leaning in to me, she rested her hand on mine. "A dear uncle made it for me when I was about ten years old. It means a great deal to me and I want you to have it." Upon it was inscribed, *Ye shall seek me, and find me, when ye shall search for me with all your heart. Jeremiah 29:13.*

"Thank you, Madelyn. It's beautifully made."

When she opened the Bible she was carrying to get the bookmark for me, I noticed its poor condition. Numerous pages were no longer attached, the binding was broken in several places, verses were messily underlined, and the margin notes were beyond number.

She must be using her uncle's old Bible. His devoted study has ruined it.

I gestured toward the Bible. "I see Uncle Martin has loaned you his Bible for the lesson with your boys."

"No Michael," she answered with a smile. "This is my Bible."

A young couple seated near us were discussing in hushed tones the tragic death of Charles Hawthorne, and the wicked abduction of little Myra.

Sarah Ruth, standing between the pews towards the center, was waiting for her husband Peter and praying with the veiled widow, Elizabeth Harcourt. Even through the veil, Elizabeth's grief was apparent. Muriel Ekland started to pump the reed organ and play, "Sheep May Safely Graze" by Johann Sebastian Bach. Upon hearing this hymn, Sarah Ruth said, "Amen."

Elizabeth quietly took her seat. Looking distraught, with shoulders bowed forward, she wept silently, none hearing but her Lord. I watched as her little daughter, seated beside her, reached up with a small handkerchief and dabbed at her mother's eyes. Few were singing although everyone knew the words. Their compassion for Mrs. Harcourt was profound. They grieved with her in her recent loss.

> Sheep may safely graze and pasture
> Where a Shepherd guards them well.
> By still waters 'ere he feeds them,
> To the fold he gently leads them,
> Where securely they may dwell.

Muriel stopped playing and the unsettled yet serene atmosphere in the church continued for a time. It was an unhurried tranquility, a moment of reflection for each present.

James Scott, a much-loved deacon of the congregation, rose from his bench and stepped over to the pulpit. He carefully opened the cover of the large pulpit Bible, and with a buoyant attitude, affectionately slid his hand across the page. He lifted his eyes from the Scriptures before him and allowed his gaze to drift from person to person. His brow became furrowed, and turning to the twenty-third Psalm, he authoritatively read:

> The Lord is my shepherd; I shall not want.
> He maketh me to lie down in green pastures:
> He leadeth me beside the still waters.
> He restoreth my soul:
> He leadeth me in the paths of righteousness for his name's sake.

Deacon Scott looked up from the Scriptures, wet his lips, and taking a deep breath, continued reading.

> Yea, though I walk through the valley of the shadow of death,
> I will fear no evil: for thou art with me;
> Thy rod and thy staff they comfort me.
> Thou preparest a table before me in the presence of mine enemies:
> Thou anointest my head with oil; my cup runneth over.
> Surely goodness and mercy shall follow me all the days of my life:
> And I will dwell in the house of the Lord for ever.

He quietly closed the Bible and returned to his seat, at which point Reverend Ekland rose and went to the pulpit. He led in prayer, seeking and expressing vital applications of the truths found within the twenty-third Psalm in the lives of these parishioners whom he loved. While he prayed, a few people, at various points, in hushed tones, said, "Amen," or, "Yes Lord," affirming what was being prayed. The unsettled and shadowed recesses of the valley, that some of the parishioners found themselves in, seemed to brighten.

Muriel began playing the organ once more as Reverend Ekland returned to his seat and deacon Scott, holding a hymn book, returned to the pulpit. "Let's join together in singing, 'My God, My Father, Blissful Name,' from Anne Steele's well-known hymn book." He then added, "This is one of Reverend Andrew Fuller's favorite hymns at his church in Kettering of Northamptonshire. Let us, each one of us, seek the consolation of God in this trying time."

To Muriel's accompaniment and Deacon Scott's leading, the congregation sang, 'My God, My Father, Blissful Name.'

> My God, my Father, blissful Name! O may I call Thee mine?
> May I, with sweet assurance claim,
> A portion so divine?
>
> This only can my fears control,
> And bid my sorrows fly:
> What harm can ever reach my soul, Beneath my Father's eye?
>
> Whate'er Thy providence denies,
> I calmly would resign;
> For Thou art just, and good, and wise; O bend my will to Thine.

Deacon Scott, holding his hymn book in his left hand and leading the congregation with his right, sang with even greater deliberation, dispelling any doubt or fear that might try and assail this little congregation.

Whate'er Thy sacred will ordains,
 O give me strength to bear;
And let me know my Father reigns,
And trust His tender care.

If pain and sickness rend this frame, And life almost depart,
Is not Thy mercy still the same,
To cheer my drooping heart?

My God, my Father! be Thy Name
My solace and my stay;
O wilt Thou seal my humble claim,
And drive my fears away?

The parishioners took their seats as Reverend Ekland began his sermon on the twenty-third Psalm. He described his experiences as a boy. He reminded the congregation that he was from a wealthy family but regularly went out and spent time with his family's shepherds. Often days at a time.

An old shepherd by the name of Esmond Fairchild had taught him to make sure that the flock had water and was situated on suitable grass. Old Esmond had also described certain ravines, rapids, and plants to stay away from, because they were dangerous to the sheep.

Reverend Ekland began telling the congregation, a true story, of which he was part. "One night, we were on a quiet hillside beneath countless twinkling stars. Patches, Esmond's faithful border collie, became violently ill, retching uncontrollably, and he kept the poor dog near him at the circle of shepherds by the fire. He nursed him as best as he was able. The flock was bedded down for the night, not too distant from the little fire, and the shepherds would take turns, two at a time, to watch over the sheep.

Several of the parishioners leaned forward, becoming quite interested in the story. Reverend Ekland paused long enough to dramatically lift a glass of water that he kept at the pulpit and take a sip of water, glancing at his notes as he did.

He continued. "Two of the shepherds, who knew the sheep well, returned to the little fire and said that one of the sheep was missing, having wandered, or having been taken, from the flock."

I rested my elbows on my knees and my chin on my knuckles, wondering what had happened to the sheep. I puzzled over what the shepherds might do next.

Reverend Ekland cleared his throat and rubbed his forehead. "It was decided that old Esmond and I would search along a pathway, which curved through a sloping meadow, and two other shepherds went out in the opposite direction towards a ravine, fearing that the little sheep may have fallen into it. Only two shepherds remained with the flock."

I hope the sheep is unhurt. I hope they find it.

Reverend Ekland took a sip of water. "Old Esmond and I came around a cluster of bushes and down a short slope looking for the sheep. What did we see?"

A little boy in the congregation shouted, "A pack of wolves."

An older lad rebuked him. "We don't have any wolves left in England."

A lady that had been sitting in her pew, knitting while listening, looked up and said in a questioning voice, "A pack of ravenous hounds?"

"No," responded Reverend Ekland. "None of these answers you've given are correct, but you all sense danger, don't you?"

The parishioners nodded and he returned to his story. "Old Esmond, a little farther ahead of me on the path, had surprised

We Both Shall Row, My Love And I

two poachers that were about to kill and butcher the missing sheep. I came hurrying along the trail behind him and burst into the clearing. They had dear old Esmond on the ground and a brutish looking fellow held his cudgel high." Reverend Ekland paused dramatically, having raised his fist as if it held a cudgel. "The poacher was ready to bring it down and crush old Esmond's skull."

Several women in the congregation gasped. Deacon Scott, with eyebrows raised, leaned forward, and someone said, "Lord have mercy."

Reverend Ekland winced and shook his head. "The poachers, cowardly ne'er do wells, ran away when they saw me, not wanting a witness of their crime. One of the poachers, carrying a large knife, scrambled up and over a low hill in the moonlight, and the other, spewing curses, disappeared into the shadows of the nearby glen." Reverend Ekland grinned. "They may have thought there were more shepherds right behind me. I knelt beside dear Esmond and saw that he was not seriously hurt, though he was bleeding from his nose and was quite shaken.

Reverend Ekland took another drink of water and gently set down his glass.

"The Lord is my shepherd," he declared boldly. He made eye contact with several parishioners and repeated himself more tenderly. "The Lord is my shepherd."

Is he looking at me?

"I will fear no evil." He glanced down at his notes. "We are told in the Gospel of John, twice in the tenth chapter, that our Lord Jesus declares Himself to be our Good Shepherd."

"Yes Pastor," said Deacon Scott with a subdued yet confident voice.

Pastor Ekland continued. "Precious old Esmond bravely sought and found his missing sheep at the risk of his life. Our

Savior, the Lord Jesus, sought us and found us and it cost Him." He paused and lightly struck the pulpit. "It cost Him His life!"

Reverend Ekland stepped back from the pulpit. His eyes scanned the congregation. Parishioners were visibly glad that old Esmond hadn't been badly hurt or even killed. Returning to the pulpit, he shared that people, like sheep, have wandered away from God. Using the poachers from his story as examples and even reminding us of our own failings, he spoke of the evil that is bound into the heart of man.

He boldly declared, "There is a stain on the heart of man!" He winced. "And a chain about his soul!"

He took a deep breath and more forcefully repeated himself, expanding slightly. "There is a stain of sin on the tarnished heart of man and a heavy chain around his weary soul."

Deacon Scott asserted, "Yes, Pastor. That is the truth."

Reverend Ekland took a sip of water. "Man is limited in his ability to do what is right but willfully and liberally engages in sin at almost every turn. Mankind's dreams are earth-bound, his understanding of truth significantly limited, and his vision of God tragically impaired."

I remembered my temptation to exaggerate the truth to Lord Warrington about what I had overheard the three scoundrels saying. *I'm so glad that Edwyn guided me and that I didn't lie.* Flashing across my mind were some of my other failings and shortcomings.

Reverend Ekland proceeded. "The Lord Jesus' death and resurrection purchased our freedom from this bondage. He took on the penalty for our sin. The Lord Jesus set us free." With a booming voice, he then read from the prophet Isaiah, the fifty-third chapter.

3 He is despised and rejected of men; A man of sorrows, and acquainted with grief:
And we hid as it were our faces from him; He was despised, and we esteemed him not.
4 Surely he hath borne our griefs, And carried our sorrows: Yet we did esteem him stricken, Smitten of God, and afflicted.
5 But he was wounded for our transgressions, He was bruised for our iniquities:
The chastisement of our peace was upon him; And with his stripes we are healed.
6 All we like sheep have gone astray; We have turned every one to his own way;
And the Lord hath laid on him the iniquity of us all.
7 He was oppressed, and he was afflicted, Yet he opened not his mouth: He is brought as a lamb to the slaughter, And as a sheep before her shearers is dumb, So he openeth not his mouth.

Madelyn's Uncle Martin, this humble man of God, then declared with a loud voice, "'Behold the Lamb of God, which taketh away the sin of the world.' That is what John the Baptist cried out when he saw our Lord, as recorded in the twenty-ninth verse of the first chapter of John's gospel."

Reverend Ekland wiped his forehead with his handkerchief. "John the Baptist saw the Lord Jesus as the fulfillment of Isaiah's prophecy from seven hundred years earlier. John the Baptist declared Jesus to be 'The Lamb of God'."

I looked down at the floor, then lifted my eyes, and scanned the congregation. *Everyone looks so attentive.*

He continued. "What say ye of Him?"

I swallowed hard. I could still hear his words echoing in my mind: *"There is a stain on the heart of man and a chain about his soul."*

My heart was pounding. I was breathing deeply. Feeling overheated, I loosened my cravat.

The good reverend seated himself and bowed his head in prayer. When we had sung our final hymn, prayed for little Myra, and received the benediction, we were dismissed.

As I hurried outside, Muriel Ekland stopped me a few steps from the door. "Have you ever heard Johann Christian Bach's Oboe Concerto No. 2, in F major?"

Distracted, my mind was relinquishing the weight of the sermon. I clenched my jaw but didn't speak.

"Michael, are you okay?"

I brought myself under control. "Oh, of course, yes, certainly." I collected my thoughts and grinned. "Yes, when I was in London about three years ago I heard it for the first time. I was deeply moved. I think he composed it in 1770. Because it moved me so, I chose to perform it with a small orchestra in Leeds about two years ago. Why do you ask?" The distraction from the weight of the sermon was a relief.

Muriel responded, "Lord Warrington's son has purchased a transcription for piano and oboe."

"I didn't know there was such a transcription available."

"Michael, I think that it would be wonderful if you and Madelyn and he would perform it at Lord Warrington's concert on Thursday."

"That doesn't leave much time for practice, but we'll discuss it."

"When will you be meeting with Jonathan Warrington?"

"Madelyn and I are going there this afternoon to practice with him."

Muriel was full of enthusiasm. "I am truly looking forward to the concert. It will be wonderful."

As we finished speaking, Elizabeth Harcourt passed by with her little daughter on her hip. She shared a pained grin as Muriel stepped away to speak to her husband.

I stepped out into the sunshine, walked over to the harbor's edge, and stood in the shade beneath a large spreading oak. Reverend Ekland's words echoed in my mind: *"There is a stain on the heart of man and a chain about his soul."*

Madelyn came and stood beside me, interrupting my reflection. "Michael, will you join us for lunch?"

"What? Pardon? Sorry Madelyn, I was lost in thought."

"Aunt Muriel and I would like to invite you for lunch."

"I'd be delighted to join you for lunch. I'll tell Edwyn and his family not to wait for me."

I walked across the lawn in front of the church and met up with Edwyn, who was gazing at the ships in the harbor. Brynne was sitting near his feet and petting Eutychus.

"I've been invited to stay for lunch with the Eklands. Sorry that I won't be walking back with you."

Edwyn winked and smiled. "That sounds like a special invitation. What did you think of Reverend Ekland's sermon?"

Pursing my lips, I nodded. "It was forceful."

"Yes Michael, it was. Enjoy your lunch and we'll see you later in the day."

Edwyn, Louisa, Brynne, and Old Thomas made their way along the cobbled street beside the water's edge as Eutychus stopped to smell the corner of the church. Then he hurried along to catch up to Brynne, who was calling him and holding out a treat.

Ah, the domestic life. A wife and family, a faithful dog, and a Sunday stroll.

"Michael, are you coming?" asked Madelyn from the front step of the parsonage.

I didn't answer but simply sauntered towards her with a wide grin.

I entered the Ekland's home and was met by the aroma of a delicious meal. Mrs. Ekland had a roast in the slow cooking Dutch oven while we were in the service. She was now in the kitchen completing other meal preparations.

"Michael, would you please get my serving platter from the high shelf?" she asked from the kitchen. I walked through the sitting room towards the kitchen, and as I passed by Reverend Ekland's study, I noticed the door ajar. Inadvertently glancing in, I saw him kneeling, clutching his Bible, and leaning with his elbows on a chair. *I imagine he's praying for his flock of parishioners and probably for little Myra.*

I quietly passed by and went into the kitchen as Mrs. Ekland pointed to a high shelf and slid a chair to a spot beneath it. I stepped onto the chair and retrieved the platter as I heard her say, "It's so nice to have a man, or in my case two, around the house."

After a wonderful lunch, I helped Madelyn harness Shadow to the Ekland's gig. She put her flute and music folder behind the seat in the gig luggage compartment. "Don't forget your duet, 'Evening Sorrow'."

"*Our* duet, Madelyn."

"Okay, *our* duet." She giggled.

On the way, we stopped at the Brixtons', where I picked up my oboe and music.

Blenheim Chapel

We overtook Tommy, who was trudging along carrying two huge but empty patchwork bags, as we began our climb up the road through the oak grove.

"Tommy, what are you going to do with those dirty, dusty bags?" I asked.

"I be an acquaintance o' Lord Warrington now an' thought that I'd be askin' the shepherds if I might collect the dirty and tangled tufts o' wool from the sheep enclosures."

"That's an interesting idea. I remember seeing hundreds of tufts of wool on the ground or tangled in the thorns and thistles."

"I've a question, Mr. Sterlin' sir."

"Yes, Tommy, what might it be?"

"Do you still 'ave me callin' card?"

Realizing I still had it in my pocket, I took it out and showed it to him.

"Could I 'ave it back now, Mr. Sterlin'? I'd like to be givin' it to the shepherds so they don't think I'm just a rough lad."

I hope the shepherds don't mock him and send him on his way when they see it.

Realizing I hadn't shown it to Madelyn, I did so, and when she saw it, she chuckled. Her eyes were sparkling with pride for this young man's optimistic diligence. "I helped him with the spelling a day or so ago," she said with a broad smile.

She loves Tommy and the other young people of Oak Harbor so very much. I returned it to Tommy.

Arriving at the first sheep enclosure, we were surprised to find Lord Warrington under the shade of a great oak and speaking to a wary shepherd. The captain of the guard, standing off to the side, held the bridle of Lord Warrington's carriage horse.

Skilfully, Madelyn slowed and stopped the gig. Tommy jumped down with his great bags and ran towards Lord Warrington as if he were a favored uncle.

The shepherd, startled by Tommy's running advance, was about to violently strike him with his staff, but Lord Warrington, raising his hand towards the shepherd, averted a violent defense.

Tommy came to a quick stop and gave his calling card to the old shepherd, who had blocked his path. The grey-headed man, with failing eyesight, raised the card towards his eyes, squinted, and shook his head. "Boy, are you daft? Did your mother drop you when you was born?"

Disappointed with the shepherd, Lord Warrington looked at him sternly. With his eyes on the ground, the old shepherd stepped aside and passed him the card.

Lord Warrington's serious demeanor was instantly replaced with a beaming smile. He winked at Tommy and read the card aloud. "Master Thomas Cedric Atwater, Servant of the Crown." He placed his hand on Tommy's shoulder. "How can I be of help, young Thomas? What are the big bags for?"

"Lord Warrington, sir, when I be 'ere last, I be noticin' great tufts of wool, more than can be counted, all through the enclosures." He pointed at tangled tufts in the brambles and trampled tufts on the ground. "When the wool gets long on the sheep an' they needs a shearin', tufts get caught on bushes or fall off."

"It sounds like you are going to share a grand idea."

"Sir." He paused. "Your enclosures are quite unseemly and need some tidyin' up. It's a shame to be seein' a fine lord, such as yourself, with enclosures such as this."

"To the point, Thomas. What would you like to do?"

"Me dear mom, she be a wonder with the spindle and knittin' needles and I'm 'opin' that you'd 'ave me clean up your enclosures for a modest fee." Tommy motioned towards the nearest enclosure with a swing of his arm. "A trifling fee, Lord Warrington sir." He hesitated and then gave a business-like nod as he spoke. "Just a few coins for each enclosure."

Lord Warrington, the captain of the guard, and even the sour old shepherd started to laugh and exchange cheerful glances.

Madelyn and I, some distance away but having overheard the whole exchange, started to chuckle quietly.

"He can be quite a brassy lad," she said.

"And with an eye for business," I added.

"Master Thomas, you are an enterprising fellow." Lord Warrington grinned appreciatively. "Yes, you may certainly collect all the tufts that you find in the enclosures."

Lord Warrington told the shepherd to make sure that the other farm workers knew that Tommy would be coming to the enclosures from time to time to collect the tufts. Lord Warrington directed the old shepherd to give Tommy a few coins whenever he came.

"Thank you, Lord Warrington sir. My mother will make some fine warm woolens for the cold weather. The chill rattles me bones when the winter blows in from the sea."

Tommy bounded away and scrambled over the nearest wall to begin his enterprise as the rest of us exchanged glances, wondering what might come of this.

"Excuse me, Lord Warrington. Madelyn and I were on our way to meet with Jonathan and practice for Thursday night. Is this still an appropriate time, sir?"

"Yes, by all means. Jonathan is expecting you."

"Might I enquire, Lord Warrington: has Grand Freddie or the others apprehended with him said anything about Myra?"

"No Michael, they have not. They are as silent and as sullen as ever I've seen anyone to be." He winced and looked at me gravely. "I'm sure that my men will have them willing to share what they know with the right amount of convincing. They will be seeking mercy soon enough."

Madelyn reached across to me, grabbed my arm, and looked away. No doubt she was imagining what was meant by the word "convincing."

We excused ourselves humbly and advanced up the lane. When we arrived at Warrington Hall, we were immediately invited in by the butler. "Master Jonathan is at the piano in the chapel. Please follow me."

As we neared the chapel, the mastery of Jonathan's piano playing became evident.

"He's a superb pianist," I exclaimed. "Listen to his smooth scale runs."

"I'm impressed by the booming octaves in his left hand. I've never heard the piece he's playing. Do you know it, Michael?"

"No, I don't think that I do."

When the butler opened the tall and beautifully carved doors of Blenheim Chapel, we entered the most attractive little hall that I had ever seen. The piano was at the front and as I walked up the aisle, I was awestruck by the beauty that surrounded me.

A series of honey-colored wooden arches, mounted upon a series of stone pillars, rose to the main ridge beam in the peak above us. Beneath our feet was the most lustrously waxed and polished slate flooring I'd ever walked on. Beautiful wooden panels were evenly spaced along the walls between the pillars, beneath richly grained oak crown molding. Near the front of the chapel, in each of eight wooden panels, four to a side, there were detailed and interesting paintings depicting events from the life of Paul the Apostle.

Each painting had the corresponding Bible passage beneath it in beautiful script on expensive parchment and framed in brass.

1. Paul (Saul) witnessing the stoning of Stephen. Acts 7:54-60
2. Paul (Saul) converted on the road to Damascus. Acts 9:1-9
3. Paul and Barnabas commissioned as missionaries. Acts 13:1-4
4. Paul and Silas singing in the prison at Philippi. Acts 16:23-26
5. Paul seated with Aquila and Priscilla, making tents. Acts 18:1-3
6. Paul arrested by the Roman Tribune. Acts 21:30-36
7. Paul speaking to the sailors during the storm at sea. Acts 27:21-26
8. Paul teaching about the Lord Jesus Christ while in Rome. Acts 28:30-31

Jonathan rose to his feet from his piano bench. "I'm so glad that you've arrived."

Madelyn and I set our instruments and music folders down on a side table and walked over towards him.

He was buoyant with optimism. "I'll be playing two pieces, and perhaps one we can do together as an oboe solo with piano accompaniment. Are you familiar with Johann Christian Bach's Oboe Concerto No. 2, in F major?"

I responded, "Yes, all three movements. I performed it a few years ago with an orchestra in Leeds. Mrs. Ekland said that you have it transcribed for piano and oboe."

"That's correct," he said. "Seeing that you and I are familiar with it, we might consider it for Thursday," he responded. "It's too bad that the flute can't be included. Take a look at the transcription of the concerto for oboe and piano." Jonathan pointed at several sections of the music spread out on the piano and added in a condescending way, "These passages, here and also here, might be the most difficult for you."

"A moment please." I examined it and discovered that it was almost identical to the original that I had performed in Leeds. "This will not be a problem," I said confidently.

Jonathan raised his eyebrows.

"Look here, Madelyn." I pointed at two lines in the music. "A soaring flute descant here would come through superbly well above the oboe melody and the staccato piano chords."

Johnathan looked puzzled.

"Madelyn, here's a spot for an oboe countermelody using chord tones and passing notes." I pointed with my index finger. "And over here." I tapped on a section of the music. "When the flute takes the melody an octave higher, I could provide some low oboe colorings using sustained notes."

Jonathan was quite perplexed. He shook his head, dropped his jaw, and mimed confusion with hands raised. "There's no flute descant and what low sustained oboe *colorings* are you referring to?"

"I'm a trained composer, Jonathan. I'll select some of the notes from the piano chords and add the passing tones I deem suitable to create the flute descant. Similarly, at a few points, I'll sustain certain low chord notes with my oboe to emphasize Bach's harmonies."

Madelyn concluded, "This is already a wonderful piece by Bach and your work on it will add some interesting features. It will be the highlight of the concert, no doubt."

Angrily, Jonathan resisted. "I'm not going to learn a new piano accompaniment when the concert is merely days away."

"Not to worry, Jonathan. Your piano accompaniment will not be changed, but we will need to listen to each other closely as we play to arrive at the required unity."

Jonathan, looking relieved, gave me an extra copy of the complete music so that I could do my composing and arranging. "Do you each have pieces that you'd like to play as well? If we can decide today, my father's scribe can pen an attractively scripted program for display at the concert. His calligraphy skills are superb."

"Michael and I have a duet, something he's composed," said Madelyn.

Jonathan looked intrigued. "Tell me about it. What's it called?"

"'Evening Sorrow'," I responded. "I've composed an intriguing set of variations which we will play. Here's an extra copy of the original flute melody with the oboe counter melody."

He looked at the music that I had handed him. "The minor key and slow tempo will truly invoke a somber atmosphere. It will come through with profound solemnity." He studied it for a few minutes more and handed it back to me.

153

Madelyn added, "I'd also like to sing 'The River is Wide', accompanying myself on the guitar, and Reverend Ashcroft from Saint Cecilia's would like to sing his favorite hymn from his seminary days, 'Let Us Plead For Faith Alone' by Charles Wesley."

"I hope it's not too stuffy," said Jonathan. "I'm not completely in tune with some religious sentiments and it is my view that a person's individual beliefs should be kept as a private matter." He paused and looked at Madelyn, waiting for a response that didn't materialize. For a moment, there was an uncomfortable silence.

He continued. "I can accompany Reverend Ashcroft as he sings his hymn and I've asked my father to read an excerpt of a poem that a recent Cambridge graduate, a friend of mine, has written. His name is Samuel Coleridge and he calls his poem *The Ancient Mariner*. It genuinely is quite poignant."

We Both Shall Row, My Love And I

We practiced successfully for more than two hours and committed ourselves to personal rehearsal during the days to come. Deciding to practice again as a group on Thursday evening before the concert, Jonathan said that he would send a carriage to the Brixtons' at 5:00 p.m.

He then wrote out the order of performance and said he would make sure to give it to the scribe who would design an exemplary and attractive concert program for display on an easel.

Following our practice, Madelyn and I drove down the lane through the trees on the gig. Near the base of the hill, we met Tommy. He was half carrying and half dragging his two large bags filled with cast off wool along the dusty road. His shirt was also stuffed with woolen tufts and he was sweating profusely. Rivulets of sweat were streaming down his grimy face and flies were buzzing about him. He was tired from his hard work, itchy from the wool shoved into his shirt, and smelly from the sweat of his labor.

"Tommy, you should rinse your tufts in the river near your home," I suggested.

"Yes sir, Mr. Sterlin' sir. That I shall surely do. I need to get the lanolin out o' it with a bit o' soap as well. Could I trouble you for some 'elp gettin' these great bags 'ome?"

"Of course you may—"

"Wait a minute, Tommy." Madelyn protested, with her hand raised. "You're not crowding up here smelling like that and covered in filth and sweat."

Before Madelyn could offer any further advice, Tommy had rammed the extra tufts of wool from inside his shirt into one of the great bags and had jumped into the harbor to get cleaned up. He disappeared beneath the surface and when we saw him again, he was quite a distance out from the harbor's edge.

"He's a dolphin!" I exclaimed.

"Well Michael, when the sun's shining, he's at the bridge almost every day, jumping in and splashing about. He's quite a water creature. Lately though, he's been looking for extra jobs to help his family."

Tommy returned to the gig, secured the two great bags behind the bench seat with a length of rope, and we continued along the road past Edwyn's porch.

"Now Tommy, rinse your wool and pick the sticks and sheep dung out of it before you take it to your mother."

"Yes sir, Mr. Sterlin' sir. I know how to wash it, sort it, tease it, an' dry it. Me auntie an' me dear mom knows how to be cardin' an' rovin' it."

"Who's going to spin it into yarn?" I asked.

"Stop your frettin', Mr. Sterlin'. Me auntie, me mom, and me, we knows all 'bout the wool trade."

We dropped him and his great bags near the bridge where the side street and the narrow lane lead to his home.

I accompanied Madelyn to her home, having expressed to her that I wanted to visit my grandfather's grave, and when we arrived at the parsonage, I helped her down.

A possibility came to my mind. "Do you think that we could go for a long hike to the south of the harbor in a few days, after the concert? I'd like to show you some ruins."

Madelyn thought for a moment and beamed with my invitation. "That would be wonderful."

I unhitched Shadow from the carriage and Madelyn led the beautiful horse into the stable.

She began brushing it. "Would you like me to help you?" I put my hand on hers as it came to rest for a moment on Shadow's hindquarter.

"That's not necessary. I enjoy the brushing and it strengthens our bond. Go and spend some time at your grandfather's stone."

WE BOTH SHALL ROW, MY LOVE AND I

I entered the graveyard quietly, the iron gate having been left ajar. Sitting atop the low encircling stone wall near his grave, I remembered his warmth and wisdom. I could hear his low, expressive voice, and was embraced by his laughter.

◊◊◊◊◊◊◊

Michael, having entered the cemetery, sought a few minutes of quiet reflection on his life with his loving grandfather. He would be warmed by his memories.

Madelyn, when she had finished brushing Shadow perhaps half an hour later, entered the parsonage, climbed the staircase, and went into her room. She tossed her jacket onto a chair, opened the curtain, and saw Michael, as before, deep in thought at the graveside.

Why is his grief so intense?

She watched as Michael took a few papers out of his pocket. He seemed to be reading them and then a few moments later he bowed his head. He looked so sullen. Tears formed in her eyes and she was gripped with a deeper fondness for him.

Why am I so drawn to him? I want to hold him and comfort him.

She brushed the tears from her cheeks as they gently flowed down her face.

Lord, comfort him in his sorrow. Cause him to deepen his trust in you. Only you can truly meet his need.

Remembering her uncle's point about providing Michael with some privacy at a time like this, she let the curtain swing to a close and left her room. She froze for a moment at the top of the stairs. *He needs comfort more than he needs privacy.*

Moments later, she stepped out of the door of the parsonage and hurried over to the cemetery entrance. Silently, she approached Michael and sat beside him upon the low wall.

◊◊◊◊◊◊

She tenderly took my hand as the fragrance of her perfume enveloped me.

Her hand is so warm, so comforting.

We sat there for quite some time, bathed in the sunshine of the afternoon. I turned, looked at her, and tried to look positive. *Her perfume, like rose petals, is all around me.*

"Madelyn, I wish you could have met him. You and he would've become the best of friends."

"I will meet him." She paused thoughtfully. "In heaven. He is with his Lord," she said sweetly. "Grandfather Sterling is in the midst of those who loved him and those who loved his Lord."

She drew me closer, held my arm, and leaned in against me. The wind blew a wisp of her long auburn hair up against my cheek. A curious tickle, never to be forgotten.

The Brigand's New Camp

I awoke to the sounds of a gathering on the Brixton porch, and skipping breakfast, I stepped outside a few minutes later.

Edwyn saw me and waved me over with his hand. "Join us; we need to take further action."

Edwyn, Old Thomas, James Scott, Albert Kline, David, and a couple other men I didn't recognize sat on a circle of chairs. There being no chairs left, I leaned against the front wall of the house at the side of the gathering.

"What's happening? Has Myra been located?" I asked.

James Scott replied, "We believe so. Tommy Atwater has seen them again in a new location."

"Where?"

Edwyn, holding a roughly sketched map in his hand, shared Tommy's story with me. "Yesterday, shortly before dark, Tommy was at his home spreading tufts of damp wool all over the stones of his walk, the bushes, and the broken down wall beside his mother's garden, when Robert Caine walked by. He was heading away from town, so Tommy followed him and discovered their new camp. He said that the remaining smaller wagon was in the middle of the camp, and several family members were cooking at the fire."

"Let's go. Let's apprehend them," I said.

"There's more." Edwyn held up his palm to slow my impetuosity. "Sabina, Gavin's mother, took a plate of food and a jug of water into the back of the wagon." He leaned back in his chair. "Tommy then heard her berating someone, and a short while later came back out empty handed."

"Why are we sitting here?" I asked. "We should be capturing them and freeing Myra."

"Oh, we'll be going soon enough." Edwyn confidently bobbed his head in agreement. "George has ridden Pilgrim up to Lord Warrington's hall to inform the captain of the guard."

Edwyn stepped inside the door and came back out with his two cudgels. He passed the blackthorn one to me.

James Scott was loading his musket and powerful David was holding the opposite ends of his own intimidating blackthorn cudgel while flexing and stretching his arms. Two other men, whose names escape me, were checking the sharpness of their swords, and one of them had a flintlock pistol tucked into his belt.

"Perhaps we should send for Reverend Ekland," suggested Albert Kline.

"No," Edwyn responded. "It's not the right thing to do. He's a man of God, our shepherd. He should be spared from violence of this sort as much as possible—"

"Even though it's righteous violence?" I interrupted.

"That's right. Besides, he has no experience in battle. He could be injured or gripped with guilt if he were to seriously injure or even kill someone. His conscience is quite strict."

"Edwyn," Albert Kline acquiesced. "You're perceptive on that point."

We all voiced agreement as Edwyn gripped my shoulder. "Men, we're about to face those that perpetuate the devil's work. They thrive on it. We dare not enter into this without spiritual preparation."

One of the two men that I didn't know grinned mockingly and rolled his eyes.

"You're right," said Albert. "Let's pray."

Edwyn clenched his hands around his cudgel, closed his eyes, and spoke with the conviction of an Old Testament warrior, Joshua perhaps. "Oh Lord, we need you now, and we seek your aid. May little Myra be located and released from her bondage."

Albert Kline and James Scott each said, "Amen."

Edwyn continued. "Lord, use us and bring justice to these brigands."

I looked up and saw Edwyn nodding as he prayed.

Again, several said, "Amen."

Justice, that's what this is about. Bringing justice. Doing justice. Justice shall free Myra. Justice shall fall upon the brigands like the fury of a storm on a foolish and unprepared captain in the harshest sea.

As the circle of prayer broke up, heads were lifted and hooves were heard coming towards us. The captain of the guard approached with more than a dozen soldiers. George, on Pilgrim, trailed behind, and still further back was a wagon pulled by two huge draft horses, being driven by one of Lord Warrington's soldiers.

The horses slowed and stopped in front and the captain of the guard. With his booming voice and looking quite serious, he asked, "Well then, who's with us?"

Edwyn passed him the map and pointed out several details on it. George motioned to me and I swung up onto Pilgrim's back behind him. The others climbed into the wagon as it came to a stop. Eutychus jumped on board and took his place beside Edwyn. Old Thomas wanted to join us but was dissuaded by Edwyn and Albert Kline. Reluctantly, he remained on the porch, assuring the group that he would pray.

When we arrived at the point that Tommy had described, we slowed our pace and came out into a small clearing below the crest of a hill.

The captain of the guard, with hand raised, whispered, "We'll stop here. Keep your horses quiet." He dismounted and took two of his men on foot up to the crest of the hill. Concealing themselves behind some bushes near the base of a great fallen maple, he could be seen pointing out features in the valley beyond them and in the brigand encampment below.

In the captain's absence, his sergeant, carrying a ball of stout twine, gave each man a generous length. "A captured man might speak, a dead one never will. Tie 'em up tight. These filthy rogues must be questioned."

The captain returned. "The brigand wagon is across a small stream, and there are eight people in the camp. Our position and their camp are separated by a small meadow. Men, a charge on horseback will be needed."

He then turned to George and me. "A path parallels the stream that runs through their camp." He gestured to a young soldier. "Owen, take Michael and George and conceal yourselves behind that sheep enclosure wall." He pointed out the stone wall. "Follow it until you meet up with the path downstream. Block any of the miscreants that try to escape in that direction."

We dismounted. The young soldier gave his horse to Edwyn and George gave his horse to his father. George and Albert, father and son, looked at each other, not knowing if either would survive the day.

The three of us left the main group and after a stealthy hike along the enclosure wall, we arrived at the path that the captain had described. It ran alongside a marshy area of the stream, bordered by thousands of marigolds. A little farther along, in the midst of a grove of massive chestnut trees, we located ourselves near the base of a hill at our position to stop any fleeing brigands.

Almost immediately, we heard the thundering of hooves and the sounds of battle: gun shots, clashing swords, cudgels striking shields, cursing, and shouting.

I'll never forget that sound. Sword striking sword. Such a loud and distinctive ringing.

After a time, the sound of the fighting began to die down, but we could still hear Eutychus barking and growling fearsomely. We found out afterwards that he had chased Sabina, the matriarch of the rogues, up a tree.

With the sounds of battle diminishing, our own aggressive tension lessened.

George, concealed near me, said, "Let's head up the path to the camp, nothing's happening here—"

"We'll hold this position as we were ordered," interrupted young Owen.

Suddenly, a short but powerfully built brigand came running towards us along the path from the camp. He carried a long and heavy sword.

I was concealed behind some bushes at the base of a sizable oak. He attempted to run by, but I thrust out a large branch in front of him, attempting to trip him. I moved too late. He simply jumped over it as he ran, and seeing me, turned, ready for battle.

A scar below his right eye. Is it Joseph?

Face to face for a moment, and breathing heavily, we studied each other as combatants.

"Drop your sword!" I shouted. "Another step and you're a dead man." His eyes scanned the path.

He burst upon me ferociously, raising his massive sword. He intended to split me in two. As it came down, I leapt to the side, swung my cudgel, and struck his shoulder with great force. I heard his clavicle break.

"Ahhgg! You cursed swine," he shrieked.

Off balance, he staggered but regained his footing. His arm was powerless.

"I'll stick you, you pig!" he shouted as he lunged towards me, seeking to pierce my belly.

I parried his thrust with my cudgel, and with the heavy bulbous end, I mashed his mouth. Teeth went flying. I found out later I'd broken his jaw.

"Nothing to say now?" I mocked him. "You conscience-crippled fiend."

In pain, he winced and moaned as blood filled his mouth. Then I smashed his sword hand with my cudgel. He dropped it, collapsed to his knees, fell onto his side, and lay there moaning helplessly before me.

My aggression burned within me. I lifted my foot to stomp his face but clenched my teeth and resisted such cruelty. Owen was farther away, so George rushed forward and grabbed the brigand's sword. I took the length of twine, tied his hands behind his back, and we cruelly dragged him to a tree and tied him to it.

"Stop your moaning," I ordered, "or I'll ram a stick in your mouth."

George and I returned to our well-concealed positions, but a few minutes later, I heard the sound of an arrow being released. I peeked out and scanned the forest above me as young Owen collapsed to the ground. I gripped my cudgel tighter.

"Where'd that arrow come from?" asked George.

"Up the hill, to our right."

George repositioned himself behind a larger tree and crouched down.

Scrambling over to the soldier, I lifted and cradled his head. Blood was spurting from his neck but there was no arrow to be seen. It had passed through his neck, slicing an artery, and was now sticking out of a tree a short distance behind him. Blood was everywhere. The top of his tunic uniform was soaked in it, and with futility, I tried to stop the bleeding. It was a hopeless task. His blood continued to pulse out between my fingers. *Lord, if you're going to take him, take him quickly.*

The young soldier looked up at me, eyes wide with panic, lips moving, but helplessly unable to speak. I couldn't save him. *Lord take him. Don't let him linger in this pain.*

He slumped motionless in my arms. I gently lowered him to the blood-soaked ground.

"Curse that bowman," said George. "He has us pinned down here."

I crouched a little lower. "Keep low," I whispered. "Listen."

Suddenly, an arrow pierced George's wrist and stuck him to the tree he was behind.

"Awww!" He dropped his sword. Reaching with his other hand, he broke the arrow and lifted his arm off the splintered shaft. "Aww!"

He hunched down and moved around the tree for better protection.

"George, it's useless to try to climb the hill. He'd slay us with those accursed arrows."

"He has us completely immobilized. We should have muskets and then we'd have a chance. Stay low and wait for any brigands that might flee down the path."

"Come down here without your bow!" I shouted. I hoped he would shout back, revealing his position. "Face me with some courage, like a man!"

"George," I whispered. "Do you think there's a path atop the hill or is he randomly finding his way through the forest?"

"I don't know. We should stay put. I've stopped the bleeding of my wrist."

"Take care of your arm. I'm going to work my way from tree to tree up the slope."

Abruptly, Robert Caine's voice echoed through the forest. "Let my brother go."

The scar, and now Robert's calling him his brother. We have Joseph Caine for sure, bound and tethered to a tree.

"Sterling!" his voice boomed. "You might live through the day, but you won't live through the week!"

How does he know my name?

"Come down here. Fight like a man!" I shouted back.

"Let my brother go. You've destroyed my family and I'll soon destroy you. You'll discover what real suffering means."

Three of Lord Warrington's men, two with muskets, came down the path towards us.

If Caine sees them, he'll kill them and escape.

I shouted to the soldiers, "There's a bowman with command of the path. Take cover!"

They did so. One of them seeing movement up the hill fired his musket and reloaded.

Moving slowly and carefully from tree to tree, I worked my way up the slope. When I arrived at the top of the ridge, I searched for the accursed Robert Caine. He was nowhere to be found. He had disappeared into the forest shadows.

I returned to the base of the slope, and rocking the arrow back and forth that had passed through Owen's neck, I freed it from the tree. I broke it, keeping only the arrowhead and a short piece of shaft. Next, I went to the tree that held the arrowhead and a few inches of shaft that had pierced George's wrist and forced it out.

"What are you doing?" asked George.

I put the arrowheads into the bag I carried at my belt. "He might come back to collect and reuse them. Taking them would limit him."

We heard more of Lord Warrington's soldiers heading towards us, and when we met, we carefully examined the hilltop once again. The bowman was gone.

Up the path to the brigand's camp we went. The soldiers carried Owen's body as I led the badly injured Joseph Caine with a tether around his neck. When we got there, we saw the rogues, bruised and bleeding—a testament to how hard they'd fought—tied up and sitting in a circle in the dirt.

Across the camp, I finally saw her, little Myra, sitting up behind the captain of the guard on his monstrously powerful shire horse. She was clinging tightly to him, safe and secure, with a wide grin and beaming eyes. The captain, with chin held high, displayed great satisfaction. Her freedom had been achieved. James Warrington, Earl of Cumberland, would be pleased.

George, supporting his pierced arm, climbed into Lord Warrington's wagon and sat beside the body of the young soldier who had been killed by Robert Caine. There were a number of other wounded men in the wagon; some bound as prisoners and several of Lord Warrington's soldiers. I followed along on Pilgrim.

We went back through Oak Harbor. Children ran alongside us, heralding our victory. Upon seeing us, people stopped and stared with their mouths open and eyes wide. A group of men in front of the Royal Stag, beaming with joy, cheered as we passed by. In front of the harbor master's office, several old men, shouting approval, raised their canes above their heads, as if they were in their memories or imaginations, weapons of war. A sense of justice, in celebratory joy, bathed the community.

As I dismounted from Pilgrim in front of the Brixton home, Madelyn apprehensively ran to meet me. She saw blood on my clothing and held me tight as tears streamed down her cheeks.

"Are you hurt, Michael?" She pushed me back at arm's length and looked at me with my bloodied clothing. She then embraced me tightly once again and whimpered, "Are you alright?"

There was so much love in her voice. "I'm fine. I'm okay, but it was terrible. Mind your dress." Now it was my turn to hold us apart at arm's length. "Look, you've soiled it."

She smiled, pulled me close, and started to cry. "If you had been hurt, I don't know what I would do." I could feel her heart beating against my body. "I can't lose you."

Over Madelyn's shoulder, I could see Edwyn with his arm around Louisa, smiling and nodding with approval at our obvious affection. We embraced and I felt her soft sunlit hair against my cheek. I tightened my hold of her, closed my eyes, and for a moment we were entwined in our love for each other.

"Madelyn, I feel as you do. I'll wash up and then let's go for a walk. I have something that I want to say." *It's so comforting to be held by her.* "I'll come to the parsonage later in the afternoon."

We looked deeply into each other's eyes as we parted.

I'll not be able to think about anything else until I see her. My love for her is an over-flowing, fountain.

Any lingering apprehension I had in expressing my feelings to her were fading.

George, his father, and I, along with a couple other men, went around behind Edwyn's home. I leaned through the back door into my room and tossed my cudgel, belt, sheath knife, and bag with the two arrowheads in it onto my bed.

Joining the other men encircling the rain barrel, we removed and rinsed our soiled clothing. We scrubbed our bodies clean of blood and grime. Albert Kline was concerned about George's pierced wrist and said that he'd take him over to the parsonage to let Muriel Ekland care for it. The other men at the rain barrel said that Robert Caine had been the only one to escape.

Elated that Myra had been freed from the brigands and that dear old Charles' death had been avenged, I was inwardly buoyant and yet apprehensive that Robert Caine had successfully eluded capture. Concerned that we hadn't heard the last from him, I would need to remain on my guard, not merely for myself but also for those whom I cared for in Oak Harbor.

When the others had finished their cleaning at the rain barrel and had wandered away, I alone remained. I noticed a curtain move in the back bedroom as I was hanging my rinsed clothing on a fence, and wondered if Brynne was in her room.

Moments later, she came out of the back door with an old, well-worn but clean piece of cotton cloth. "I knew there would be a purpose for my old cotton nighty."

"Hello, Brynne."

She started to dry my back and side as I held the rim of the barrel. "Michael, you've got a cut at your waist."

I felt the wound earlier but hadn't stop to look at it. Twisting to have a better look, I saw that it wasn't grievous. "You're right, but it's merely a shallow cut. I'm glad you noticed that, Brynne. I'll have Muriel put some of her healing salve on it."

Brynne, with gentleness, rinsed it once more and then, kneeling beside me, bandaged it. She looked up into my eyes at one point in an unusually mature way and brushed a long strand of her chestnut hair away from her face.

Taking my rinsed articles of clothing from the fence and washing them properly with soap, it was obvious that she liked helping me. She then rinsed them again, wrung them out, draped them over a twine cord, and stepped back into the house.

Going into my room, I pulled some clean clothing out of my pack, removed my damp trousers, and got dressed.

A moment later, Brynne came into my room carrying a tray. "Sit and rest, Michael. You've been through a terrible ordeal."

I sat on my bed and ran my fingers through my hair as she set the tray down on the little table beside me. A bowl of soup with a hint of spice. It smelled wonderful and beside it was a plate of inviting cheese, savory sausage, and a warm slice of buttered bread.

As she left my room to return to the kitchen, she stopped in the doorway and looked over her shoulder at me. "I'm relieved you weren't seriously hurt, Michael."

Book Two

The Parsonage

Later in the afternoon, I arrived at the other side of the harbor and sat upon the sea wall in front of Fair Havens Church. Small clouds sped across the bright blue sky, gulls and terns soared and wheeled above me, and the song of the sea breeze in the trees surrounded me.

Madelyn came and gently set herself down beside me and without a word, she took my hand and rested it with hers on her thigh. I enjoyed the feeling of her delicate hand within mine. It seemed as if time had stopped, and any remaining concerns I had were swept away in her attraction towards me. My heart belonged to her and a sense of contentedness welled up within me.

"Michael, do you love me?"

The sea birds continued soaring and wheeling overhead and the sea breeze maintained its song in the trees. Being struck by the directness of her question, I found myself speechless and lost in thought. I sat motionless and quiet.

She repeated her question, with greater tenderness. "Michael, do you love me?"

I turned, lovingly looked at her, and tenderly squeezed her sweet hand. "You sold me some tea when I arrived at Oak Harbor." I paused for a moment, enamored by the shape of her lips and their rosy color. "Madelyn, I was drawn to you when I first saw you. I became quite captivated by you when we hiked down to the harbor from the Warrington estate." I paused to collect my thoughts. "Earlier today, when we embraced and you expressed your affection for me, I realized that my own feelings had grown towards you." I looked deeply into her beautiful eyes. They were a deeper green than usual, jade perhaps, because of the shade we were in. "I love you more than I've ever loved anyone. From this day forward, I realize that our lives will be inseparably entwined."

We sat there silently, enjoying each other's company, watching the activity in the harbor with its ships and seamen. In the distance, some boys were jumping into the river from the bridge.

"I wonder what my parents or even Uncle Martin and Aunt Muriel might think of our love for each other," she mused.

"I have no idea what your family might think, but Edwyn and Louisa know of my affection for you. I think they approve."

Madelyn winced. "What? You told them?"

"Edwyn saw my interest in you on several occasions and I was the subject of his teasing, but now I think he understands and approves."

"What did they say?"

"At one point, after Edwyn had been teasing me, Louisa gave him quite a tongue lashing and said that I was a 'fine young man' and she also said that 'you had been through enough.' What did she mean by that?" I squeezed her hand a little tighter. "Madelyn, What have you been through?"

In barely a whisper, she began to speak. "I... um." She stopped and looked out across the harbor. "Several years ago, I was in the worst difficulty imaginable. It has troubled me ever since." She adjusted the neckline of her dress and then took my hand once again. "That's one of the reasons that I came here to live with Uncle Martin and Aunt Muriel. This is a time for new beginnings."

My hold on her hand, which rested on her thigh, tightened. "I love you, Madelyn. You can trust me."

With distress, she continued. "I was married once before." She hesitated. "It was a marriage that my parents pressured me into. He was eighteen years older than I, the younger son of Lord Haversham of Ridley, on the east coast. He was cruel and demanding." Her head bowed lower and she trembled.

"If you're uncomfortable or embarrassed, you needn't share this with me—"

"You mean a great deal to me," she whispered. "I would like to tell you about it. About him."

"Take your time, Madelyn."

She looked away for a moment. "Walter Haversham presented himself as kind and considerate at first. I was so young and inexperienced with life that I hoped for the best and followed my parents' wishes. He and his father, Lord William Haversham II of Ridley, approached my parents and then he became the center of every conversation we had. It was flattering that someone of his prestige took interest in me. I was hesitant, but he was charming and handsome with his curly blonde hair. He looked as though he had stepped off the canvas of an epic portrait.

She paused for a moment and shook her head. "I gave in and we were married. I didn't even know about his drinking and skirt chasing. He was cruel towards me, and the abusive way he treated me drove me to deepen my faith. There are some verses in Psalm 119 that express the truth of this for me. "Before I was afflicted I went astray: But now have I kept thy word. . . It is good for me that I have been afflicted; That I might learn thy statutes."

"I've noticed that about you: your faith and your knowledge of the Bible." I put my arm around her, comforting her further.

She paused for a moment, covered her face with her hands, and inhaled deeply. "I simply wanted a happy home. To love and to be loved. He was seldom kind." She leaned back and picked a petite wild flower. "He may have looked the picture of nobility, but noble, he was not. Fortunately, he began spending more time away from me and our estate." She gave a little laugh. "His absences were answers to prayer."

"Didn't your parents put a stop to his abuse?"

"They felt that I was simply exaggerating when I told them of it." She paused, raised her right hand to her forehead, and swept some strands of her cascading hair back over her shoulder. She lightly tapped the little scar above her eyebrow. "You asked me about this once. This interesting item of personal history."

"I'm sorry. I didn't know about your abuse."

"Michael, this little bit of history included his back hand and a signet ring with a sharp edge."

"I'm so sorry."

"He attended countless wild parties. One night he came home, staggering drunk, and I innocently asked him if he would like help removing his boots. His backhand knocked me off my feet."

"I don't know how you survived under his roof."

"Fortunately for me, he frequently went hunting in the Scottish highlands. His family had land north of Glasgow and they'd been going up there since he was young. The last time he was away, *hunting*, it was for more than two months. People said that he had women in the north." She crushed the little flower she had picked and threw it into the water in front of us. "Quite the *hunter*. I can imagine what his prey was." She guffawed. "The filthy skirt chaser."

Her demeanor and resolve strengthened as she unburdened herself of her pain.

"I don't understand how he could've been so cruel towards you."

She cleared her throat and bit her lip. "On his last trip, he had been away for more than two months and finally word came back to me that he had been killed in a hunting accident. Some hunting accident." She guffawed again. "There were staff at his hunting lodge in the highlands that said he had been shot and killed by a jealous husband."

I gently rubbed her back. "You were released from his cruel abuse."

The sun broke through the white and grey clouds. The sea birds were still wheeling and soaring overhead. "His funeral, an atrocious hypocrisy. His family and their minister presented him as a saint. They missed him, I understand that, but they must've known the truth about his character. They aren't stupid people. They spent most of their time with their eldest son, William III, who would one day inherit the title and the estate."

"Parents often overlook the sins and failings of their children," I said.

She looked up at the clouds. Great shafts of sunlight were breaking through. "Walter and I were married for only ten months and seven days. He passed several years ago. I don't want to talk about him anymore." She paused, took in a deep breath of fresh sea air, and closed her eyes. "So many bad memories, so many... so much pain."

Serene Breeze, the beautiful two-masted top sail schooner of perhaps fifty feet that I'd seen when I first arrived at Oak Harbor, sailed by. It sought the open water and freedom of the sea. A young man was on the forward deck unfurling a second headsail, and another, more smartly dressed, was at the helm holding course for the open sea.

"Where do you think the *Serene Breeze* is going?" I asked.

Madelyn had been looking down at the water near her feet and looked up when I spoke. "She usually does short runs to various ports in the Irish Sea and around to Bristol. Several months ago, she journeyed to northern France and the north coast of Spain but I heard that when she returns, in a number of weeks, she'll venture farther yet. She'll be sailing some regular runs to Gibraltar and then into the Mediterranean."

"It's a beautiful ship, and so well kept."

The Serene Breeze

"Two of Shannon's wealthy cousins own it."

"Truly? I had no idea."

"Yes. Apparently, they've owned it for many years and have started making this a regular port of call."

We sat there watching the activity in the harbor, quietly enjoying each other's company, and across the harbor we could see Edwyn's porch with a number of people on it.

They're probably talking about Myra's freedom and deciding what to do about Robert Caine's escape.

Farther along the road, in front of the Royal Stag, I could see Reverend Ekland driving his two-tone green Landau. "There's your uncle, almost at the bridge."

"He'll be here in a few minutes." She nestled her head into my shoulder. "Michael, please stay for supper."

"Do you think that your aunt will mind?"

"No, not at all. We enjoyed your company at lunch yesterday. I'll go ask her. Wait here for a few minutes."

I reflected on all that she had told me about her marriage to Walter Haversham. *I'd love to bring her some joy and peace. I want to do that. I need to do that.*

Madelyn was in the parsonage a long time, and when she returned, Reverend Ekland was passing our spot on the breakwater. He turned into the short lane beside their home. We walked over and offered to help with the horses.

"Uncle Martin, Michael is staying for supper."

"That's wonderful, Madelyn." Reverend Ekland took a few steps towards me, shook my hand, and put his other hand on my shoulder. "You are to be commended for your part in the freeing of Myra and the apprehension of those criminals."

"Thank you, sir. It was a community effort. We simply supported Lord Warrington's men. How's George's wrist?"

"It's been properly cleaned and bound up well. We're trusting that it'll be fine and that he'll not lose any use of it."

He gave me Wonder and I walked him into the stable. Madelyn followed with Shadow.

"These are fine-looking geldings. Which one are you training for the gig?"

"This one, Shadow." She affectionately brushed and then patted the horse's shoulder. "Perhaps later we should take the gig out for a ride. I want to show you a gorgeous country lane."

"The lane to the south of us? The one that leads up to the ruins?"

"Yes, that's the one, but I've never been as far as the ruins."

"I hiked up it two years ago," I said. "It's beautiful, being bordered by so many enormous trees and interesting rock formations, but let's wait until after the concert and make a full day of it."

"You're right. We'll have a wonderful outing." She smiled, confidently lifted her chin, and added, "Together."

I joined the family for a dinner of meaty soup, fresh baked bread, and some of Muriel's delicious pastries. The conversation was interesting and sitting across from her and seeing her in a domestic setting caused my mind to wander. A domestic life in Oak Harbor would be vastly different from my solitary life up in Cliffside. I enjoyed being in the midst of the forest there, with only a couple dozen homes. In Cliffside, the sound of the wind in the trees, the earthy smell of the forest, and the birdsong are beautifully peaceful, but here, in a seaport of this size, a certain bustling activity brings entertainment.

After dinner, Muriel Ekland, known by many locals as an excellent herbalist healer, removed my bandage and put some salve on the cut at my waist.

"Mrs. Ekland, thank you so much for having me for dinner and for the salve. I appreciate you and I enjoy the company of your family."

Madelyn giggled, Reverend Ekland smiled, and Mrs. Ekland said, "Michael, you're becoming as dear to us as your grandfather. A charming and warm-hearted man."

I took my leave and removed my jacket from the back of the chair, but being an exceptionally warm day, I simply draped it over my arm. Madelyn walked me to the door and stepped outside. I started down the steps in front of the parsonage until she grasped my hand in hers and stopped me. She looked up at me with a wide grin. Her eyes greeted me with joy.

What's going on in my heart? Even saying goodbye, knowing that I'll see her tomorrow, is difficult.

"Michael, my love, come back tomorrow, perhaps in the afternoon. We can practice together in the church."

"Splendid idea. Let's work on the concerto."

"And your piece, 'Evening Sorrow', as well." She adjusted her belt. "I'm glad we had that talk beside the harbor." She inhaled deeply. "Sharing with you about my life with Walter was difficult but I'm glad that I did. A weight has been lifted. I'm much less burdened about it now. I'm so happy that you shared your feelings towards me as well."

"So am I. My heart warms towards you with every moment we spend together."

She reached up, put her hand on my shoulder, and lifted her chin towards me. Pulling my head down towards her, she moved to kiss me on my cheek but actually made contact with the edge of my lips. My heart lifted. *Did she mean to kiss me like that? That was deliberate. Intimate.*

Her lips were satiny and warm. She had a fragrance of roses. A strand of her beautiful auburn hair, shining in the sun with its lighter highlights, blew across my face.

◊◊◊◊◊◊

Michael ambled up the road towards the bridge, enveloped in the intimacy of that brief kiss with such a lovely and tender-hearted woman.

Madelyn watched him as he walked away, with his jacket slung over his big shoulder. He removed his cravat and his waistcoat because of the heat, and undid most of the buttons on his shirt. She noticed that he slowed for a moment, as if to turn into the cemetery sidewalk to visit his grandfather's gravesite, but he didn't. Instead, he turned and looked back at her with a confident expression.

The wind tossing his wavy black hair and his shirt blowing open made an impression on her. She admired his masculinity and wanted to be held by him.

Her mind wandered. *He has comforted me in my painful memories. Have I eased his suffering and his grief? I hope so. He's so tall and powerful and yet so caring and sensitive. His broad shoulders are like a great stone warmed in the sun.*

Madelyn shifted in her thinking from her own simple thoughts to seeking the Lord's intervention for him. *Lord, please deepen his faith as you did mine. Whatever struggles he may pass through in the future, may those struggles lead him closer to you.*

◊◊◊◊◊◊◊

The Atwater Home

As I crossed over the bridge on my way back to the Brixton home, I stopped to watch some boys jumping into the river. I buttoned a few buttons of my shirt and put my waistcoat back on but left it open.

I noticed that Tommy wasn't among the boys. "Where's Tommy Atwater?"

"'e be workin' on 'is wool at 'is house," responded a little boy with swarthy features. "Who wants to be workin' when there be swimmin' an' bridge jumpin'?"

An older lanky boy mockingly added, "He says he mustn't lose any time from his business."

The boys laughed and then returned to their jumping and swimming.

I decided to stop at the Atwater home, which wasn't far from the bridge. As I approached, I could hear the singing of a rustic song:

> Pick and tease, to your heart's content.
> Card and rove all day.
> Spin and draw, 'tis time well spent,
> Winter's on its way.

The sight that greeted me was one of noteworthy cottage industry, but in the midst of poverty. Their dilapidated cottage with its faded paint, broken boards, and sagging porch served as a backdrop to their hard work. The dead dog was still in the far corner of the yard. Relieved that the wind wasn't blowing my way, I stopped and stood in the shade of a giant beech tree at the side of their yard to watch them work.

The oldest of Tommy's sisters sat picking debris out of large gatherings of wool and teasing open any matted clumps. Tommy's mother was using a set of carding paddles with great expertise and after carding each clump, she would shape it into a uniform roving. A woman, I later discovered to be Mrs. Atwater's sister, was spinning using a simple drop spindle with a large whorl. She carefully drafted beautiful lemon yellow rovings of wool into long groupings of fibers, spinning them into yarn. From time to time, she would hold the spindle between her knees, roll the yarn onto the bottom of it, and then expertly draw and spin some more, eventually adding the next roving.

Tommy, with sweat running down his face, was standing beside a huge cast iron pot full of boiling water. He was stirring it gently and adding handfuls of orange flower petals and small amounts of wood ash.

As I left my spot at the edge of the yard and approached the family, Mrs. Atwater stopped her carding and looked at me with a wide grin. "Oh now, you're the friend of the Brixtons that stopped by last week lookin' for me boy."

"Yes, that's right, Mrs. Atwater." I gave her a respectful bow of my head and touched the brim of my hat. "You have a busy family here."

"Idleness is the devil's playground." Her playful eyes twinkled. "An' 'e left an hour ago."

The others laughed and Tommy slapped his thigh. "I'm to thinkin' 'e won't be comin' back before nightfall."

Mrs. Atwater whimpered quietly. "And then 'e'll be 'eadin' off to the tavern with the pub crawler."

The others stopped their singing and laughter. There was an uncomfortable silence. I stepped closer to Tommy and his work.

"Tommy—"

"Thomas," he interrupted. "Please be callin' me Thomas."

"Thomas, are these marigold flowers that you're adding to the pot?"

Clutching a handful of the yellow and orange petals, he chuckled. "Indeed, these be marigolds, bright and beautiful like the summer sun." He tossed the handful of petals into the pot. "They'll fetch some good coin as winter woolens. Mittens and mufflers. Shawls and caps."

"I imagine they will. Why are you putting wood ash into the mix?"

"That'd be the fixin'. It 'elps 'old the color into the wool."

The uncomfortable silence had ended. The rest of the family had returned to their singing and their work.

> Pick and tease, to your heart's content.
> Card and rove all day.
> Spin and draw, 'tis time well spent,
> Winter's on its way.

Tommy continued his stirring and the rest of the family glanced over towards us from time-to-time. They gave our discussion little thought.

Tommy added another handful of the marigold petals to the boiling pot. "That'll just 'bout do it."

"What's next?"

"Next I be puttin' in an 'andful o' salt, stir it just a wee bit, an' then I be puttin' in me mother's raw wool rovins."

After he added the salt and stirred some more, he gave me his stirring stick and stepped towards his mother. She continued her carding on the dilapidated porch, and on the floor beside her was a large pile of raw woolen rovings. Tommy picked up an armful of these, returned to his iron pot, and gently dropped them in, one by one.

"Mr. Sterling, sir. Be passin' me the stick, if you please."

I passed him the yellow-stained stick and he then began to press the rovings down gently into the water, making sure that each was fully submerged.

Our discussion, or rather, my lesson, was interrupted as John the Rotund, who was passing by, stopped at the wall. "A fine 'ello, Mrs. Atwater. 'ow are you and your fine children this day?"

"We be fine and as you can see, we be 'ard at work. Winter will be 'ere soon enough," she said, raising her eyebrows.

"Yes Belinda," he said, with a wide grin and the stem of his pipe clenched between his teeth. "I'll be biddin' you a good day then."

She adjusted a clip in her hair and sweetly said, "John, 'ave a splendid afternoon."

Hmm, an interesting exchange between The Rotund and Mrs. Atwater. I don't think he noticed me.

Tommy cleared his throat to capture my attention. "Now, Mr. Sterlin', I let the fire die down a bit. It only needs to simmer for a short time."

Raising my eyebrows, I nodded.

This family is so diligent. I marvel at their unity and industry. "You and your family are expertly skilled."

"When coin's involved, skill puts weight in the pocket. Do you agree, Mr. Sterlin' sir?"

"Yes, I do." I caught his eye and smiled. *I am so proud of Tommy with his serious self-confidence and his eye for opportunity.*

"Mr. Sterlin', come an' take a look at these."

I followed him onto the porch beyond his mother. He led me to two more iron pots. One almost as large as the one he had used for boiling, and the other a bit smaller.

"Lift the lid on this one, Mr. Sterlin' sir."

I lifted the lid and looked inside. "Tommy, this is a rich deep amber. What flower petals did you use to make these rovings so much darker?"

Tommy grinned with attentive eyes. He kept himself from laughing. "These here be the same petals, but the rovin's been sittin' an' soakin' all through the night. Now lift the lid o' this 'ne." He tapped the smaller pot with his toe.

I lifted the lid and saw rich, dark brown rovings. "These rovings must've been soaking for a week."

Tommy shook his head, laughed, and covered his face with his palm. "These rovin's were put in 'ere a few 'ours ago. This 'ere brown be comin' from walnuts, not flower petals." He regained his composure. "This dark brown, it be far more manly. Mittens and stockin's and the like. Some men might not be keen for wearin' the soft yellow. We can be makin' reds and blues as well, but they be a might more costly."

He started to explain the use of beets for red and woad plants for blue. I nodded with a wrinkled forehead and pursed lips, trying to give the impression that I understood each detail.

Tommy, seeing me agreeing but out of my depth, said, "Mr. Sterlin' sir, for a man o' learnin', you do 'ave your limits."

The singing ended and there were a few giggles from Tommy's little sisters. His aunt looked stern.

"Tommy!" His mother stopped what she was doing and raised her voice. "Have some respect for the gentleman."

There was again, an uncomfortable silence.

"This work is interesting and practical, Thomas. I've learned so much from you and your hard working family."

"I'll be 'angin' 'em up to dry in a few minutes. Do you want to be 'elpin'?"

I looked at his yellow hands and decided that I would forgo the opportunity. "No, I think that I'll leave that to you. You're an expertly skilled worker."

"Mr. Sterlin', if you want to be writin' any o' this down, I'd not be faultin' you."

"I think that I can remember all that you've shown me," I said with a smile and a chuckle. "I need to be on my way now." I gestured towards the remains of the dead dog. "Thomas, before I leave, get your shovel and bury that dead dog over there in the corner."

"Mr. Sterlin', we don't 'ave a shovel." There was another uncomfortable silence, and the women and girls stopped their singing. Tommy continued. "I was tryin' to be puttin' it in the ground, scrapin' out an 'ole with 'n old piece o' steel, but me daddy, and right fine pickled 'e was, shouted to me, 'Leave that cursed beast alone, you gutter puppy.' Mr. Sterling sir, I be leavin' it right where it be layin'."

I stood there quietly for a moment, feeling quite uncomfortable at having perhaps offended the family. I was speechless, and then leaned down towards Tommy's ear. Whispering, I asked, "Does 'pickled' mean drunk?"

"Yes," he mumbled. "That it be."

I congratulated Tommy and his family on their hard work and decided to head back to the Brixton home. As I walked, I couldn't help but reflect on Tommy's creativity and energy. I wondered if some day his ingenuity and diligence might lift him, perhaps his whole family, from their poverty. Behind me, I could hear that the family's singing had resumed.

We Both Shall Row, My Love And I

Pick and tease, to your heart's content.
Card and rove all day.
Spin and draw, 'tis time well spent,
Winter's on its way.

Edwyn's Porch

As I neared Edwyn's porch, I heard The Rotund, who was seated in Edwyn's chair, call out. "Michael, blessings man. I was lookin' for you earlier."

When I reached the porch, he stood, and taking his hand, I shook it as his other arm warmly came around my back in a half embrace. Although there were empty chairs all around, I sat on the wide porch railing in front of him. He returned to Edwyn's rocker and wiggled himself into a comfortable position, with Eutychus at his side.

"You be lookin' right well," he said to me. "I was worried for you and the others when I 'eard that you were goin' to round up the rest o' the rogues. The dirty scoundrels."

"John, did you hear? Myra's free. I'm sure that arrangements will be made to return her, to her family.

"Yes, I did. Did you 'ear 'bout the young soldier that took an arrow through 'is neck? Those rogues."

"I was there." I shook my head and exhaled. "It was a gruesome sight. Let's not talk about it."

"George's wrist is all bandaged up and 'e be restin' at 'is parent's 'ouse. 'is father's fearin' that 'e might be losin' the use o' 'is 'and."

"Have you seen Myra?" I asked.

"I 'ave." John was beaming. "A dear child an' full o' life. She's been through an ordeal but she be seemin' none the worse for it." John leaned over and stroked Eutychus on the head. "I 'ear this wondrous ol' 'ound 'ere 'ad Sabina up a tree."

"You heard right. It was quite a sight. Where's Myra now?"

"She be up at Warrington 'all enjoyin' the fine life: a splendid bath, a fine dinner, and 'efore long, a cozy night o' rest."

"I'd like to take her back to her family in Stone Ridge," I said. "They were truly distraught at her disappearance. Lorena loves her and misses her so much."

"Michael, there be no need."

"What do you mean?"

"James Scott an' old Thomas left more 'n two 'ours ago and they'll be well up the road by now."

"There will be rejoicing in Stone Ridge when they arrive with the news. Why didn't they take Myra with them?" I asked.

"She needs to be restin' an' Lord Warrington wants the court to be 'earin' 'er testimony. The magistrate is up to Carlisle and 'e won't be returnin' 'til the day after tomorrow."

"They would usually hear the capital cases and have the hangings in Carlisle, wouldn't they?"

"That be true, but fear there be. There may be more rogues about and Lord Warrington doesn't want to be riskin' 'is soldiers in transportin' them. So, they be swingin' up at Warrington 'all. The magistrate will be bringin' the Crown's judge back 'ere the day after tomorrow. It be takin' the Crown's judge to swing a man. The court proceedings will be 'ere but the sentences, whether the 'angman's rope or time be'ind bars, will be in Carlisle."

"Justice will fall heavy on the brigands."

"O' that ye can be sure. Some'll be swingin' for the murder o' Charles 'awthorn as well as Myra's abduction."

"No doubt about that."

We Both Shall Row, My Love And I

"It be the truth. Swingin' like a clock's pendulum." He stopped and thought for a moment. "The pendulum o' judgement, swingin' for the timepiece 'o justice."

"Well said. Bye the way, why are you here, all alone on Edwyn's porch?"

"I'm not bein' alone. I have Eutychus with me and earlier I was a talkin' to Brynne. Then Louisa brought me out some bread an' cheese an' a cup o' tea."

"Brynne's a fine girl," I said.

"That she be. I was 'ere with the men, a chattin' away. James an' old Thomas left and Edwyn went in to rest. 'e got 'imself a nasty set o' bruises from the rogues. Then Brynne came out. She and I, well, we be talkin' all 'bout Eutychus."

"Eutychus?" I questioned.

"That's right. Me brother an' I 'ave a fine new Irish Wolfhound that I brought down from 'onister Pass. She be a fine young dog, tall, more 'an three feet at the shoulders." He gestured her height with his hand. Then forming his hands, width wise, he said, "Wide in the 'ips, good for breedin' pups." He leaned in towards me, grinned, and whispered, "Me brother an' me, we'd be likin' Eutychus to perform 'is duty with 'er."

I looked out over the water. Thoughtfully, I said, "An Irish Wolfhound."

Again, in a whisper, he leaned in towards me. "O for sure. An English Mastiff with 'n Irish Wolfhound would be a fine pairin'." He stroked his chin and continued whispering. "The pups, they'd be a spectacle to be'old."

I leaned in towards him. "John, why are we whispering?"

"I don't want Eutychus to 'ear, as 'e might be gettin' excited."

I started laughing and The Rotund joined in. "It be true, Michael, 'e needs to be savin' 'is energy for 'is missus. He needs be gettin' the deed done, good an' proper!" The Rotund raised his eyebrows, slapped his knee, and continued his robust laughing.

A tottering old man, clicking his way along with a metal tipped cane, stopped and stared for a moment. Then, after witnessing our foolish hilarity, he simply shook his head and continued down the road.

Eutychus sighed in his sleep and our laughing increased even further.

"Oh, did you 'ear that, Michael? The mastiff, 'e be thinkin' 'bout 'is missus, I 'magine."

A moment later, Brynne stepped out onto the porch holding a book. "Why are you two laughing? You'll wake Daddy."

John the Rotund and I were laughing uncontrollably and all I could do was point at Eutychus.

Brynne asked, "Did he have a funny doggie dream?"

John answered, barely able to remain in his chair for his laughing, "Oh Brynne, 'e'll be doin' more than dreamin' soon enough, missy."

I tried to speak but was having trouble catching my breath. "He's, he's, he's..."

Eutychus lifted his head and looked at me and then John, and laid his head back down.

Brynne, with anger starting to simmer, said, "You two should be quieter, more like Eutychus."

John, leaning towards the dog, whispered, "Well, Eutychus, you won't be a quiet doggie for much longer, will you boy?"

Almost on cue, Eutychus liked his lips, gave a doggie smile, and went back to sleep. With that, The Rotund, belly rolling with laughter, red faced, and tears streaming down his puffy cheeks, said, "Look, 'e be thinkin' o' 'is Irish bride."

Brynne, with anger at the boil, addressed us. "Is there no shame left among you?" She angrily stepped back inside, shaking her head.

We Both Shall Row, My Love And I

Eutychus

We tried to quiet down realizing that we may have gone too far. I bit my lip with tears coursing down my face. John, covering his mouth with his hand, was making laughing motions but with almost no sound coming out. Then, uncovering his mouth, a smile burst onto his face. Looking at Eutychus, he said, "Brynne, she be lookin' at you when she said that. Have you no shame, Eutychus? Have you no shame?"

With that, we were laughing uncontrollably again. Becoming over-heated, I removed my waistcoat.

Brynne stepped back outside with a big bone from a roast of beef. Eutychus, smelling the meat, quickly approached her, took the bone, and went down the steps and around to the back of the house.

"He left in a hurry," said Brynne.

John, still laughing uncontrollably, responded almost unintelligibly. "I think... I think 'e be savin' it for the missus."

Becoming further overheated, I opened several shirt buttons.

Not knowing who or what we were talking about, she asked, "Who? Who's saving what, for which missus? What are you talking about? You're both Bedlam bound for sure." She went back inside, rolling her eyes and shaking her head.

Our laughing eventually subsided as we sat on the porch wiping the tears from our cheeks and regaining our composure. We sat there for a few minutes looking out into the harbor.

Then finally John said, "Well Michael, I need to get back to the keeper, me dear brother, an' see if the light 'ouse'll be ready for tonight. The Argand lamp may need some care an' cleanin' and I need to be 'elpin' me brother with the oil reservoir."

Remembering that I wanted to ask him a question, I thought it would be a suitable time to do so. "Before you go, I've got a question. Who owns that little knoll of cleared land between the lane to Warrington Hall and your lighthouse? The knoll with the little strand of beach below it."

"Ahh, I know the little knobby 'ill you be referrin' to. It belongs to me an' the keeper. We were goin' to be buildin' an 'ouse there but decided to live in the ole' light'ouse because it be so much closer. We're lookin' to sell the 'ill as a buildin' lot."

"How much might you want for it?"

"I'll 'ave me a talk with me brother. For you, Michael, we'd be givin' you a fair price."

"Thank you so much. Have a peaceful night, John, and say hello to the keeper." I thought that I'd send him off with a little rhyme. I said:

> May the ships at sea,
> be safe with thee.
> May thy guiding light,
> lead them safe at night.

"Well said. Bless you, Michael."

He stepped off the porch and headed down the street.

I sat there, enjoying the sights of the harbor, and a few minutes later Edwyn came out with a couple of apples. I feared that our laughter may have awakened him.

He tossed me the second apple and sat in his chair. "That rest did me a world of good."

"I'm glad you're refreshed. John told me that you had quite a few bruises. Will you be alright?"

"Oh sure, I didn't see them until I removed my shirt and my trousers. When we actually stormed the camp, I got into hand-to-hand combat with two young brigands; one with a staff and the other with a cudgel similar to my own."

"Two against one. How'd you survive that?" I asked.

"We exchanged several hard blows, some blocked and some not, and then the combatant with the staff swung at my head. I dodged the blow, but his staff continued its arc. He struck his friend in the head and laid him out cold, motionless on the ground. A moment later, the brigand that had swung his staff, distracted by what he'd done to his friend, found himself an easy target. My cudgel glanced his shoulder and then on the backswing, I knocked him in the head. If he hadn't been wearing a heavy leather helmet, he wouldn't be shackled up in Warrington Hall, he'd be silent in the cool earth.

He took a bite of his apple. "Man to man combat is a dirty business. I abhor violence."

"It wasn't violence for violence's sake. It was to free Myra and to bring justice to bear for the murder of Charles Hawthorne."

"You're right, but I hate it nonetheless."

Edwyn took another bite of his apple. "The young soldier that took the arrow through the neck will be laid to rest tomorrow behind Warrington Hall."

"He died in my arms. It was terrible. Brynne got most of his blood out of my clothes. I'll need to remember to thank her again for that." I took a bite of the apple and looked out into the harbor. "I don't think that I'll go to the service. I didn't know him well and I'd like to forget the whole experience."

"I can understand that. It must've been horrendous for you," he said. "I want to go and check on George's wrist. We are all hoping that he won't lose the use of his hand."

"Sure, not a problem. I need to practice and prepare for the concert at Warrington Hall on Thursday."

Edwyn excused himself and we exchanged our good byes.

I went to my room and for a couple hours started working on writing out an exciting and interesting part for Madelyn on her flute. Then, I spent some time preparing my reeds and practiced the transcription of Johann Christian Bach's oboe concerto.

Eutychus, after some howling at my oboe playing, wandered to the back corner of the garden, and then went around to the porch at the front of the house.

I laughed to myself. *I suppose he's not a connoisseur of fine music. Why do dogs howl with woodwind instruments so much?*

For well over two hours, I labored on the piece, glad that it was almost identical to the original version I had performed the previous year.

My work on 'Evening Sorrow' also went well. Of course, with it being a slower and more somber piece the issues weren't fingering technique and dexterity, but rather, things such as phrasing, intonation, tone quality, and mood. It reminded me of a lonely mourning dove or a grieving nightbird.

The Sea Wall

The following morning I assisted Edwyn in his shop behind their home. He had me prepare some previously dried lumber for his cabinetry projects. I took to it with diligence, although I hadn't slept well the night before. I worked according to his careful instructions; cutting to measure, planing, sanding, and staining for several hours. Following his carefully made drawings and lists that he pulled out of his leather project folder, we worked with deliberation.

Across the shop from me he assembled previously prepared pieces and I stopped my work several times to watch him. His measurements for a maple cabinet were precise; his dove-tail joints in a walnut chest were tight; his finished pieces were artistic and sturdy in every way. It was easy to grasp how he maintained his reputation as a master craftsman.

We worked well into the afternoon, only stopping for short breaks when Brynne would bring tasty morsels out to the shop. Snacking on cold sausages, a variety of cheeses, and slices of fresh bread, we were content.

He appreciated my assistance and asked if I would be available to help him move a great maple log to a sawyer in a few days.

"Edwyn, I'd be glad to. I'm staying in your home and Louisa is feeding me marvelously well. You are my dearest friends."

After supper, I completed the arrangement of the Bach oboe concerto to include the flute, and then I practiced my oboe again. I was looking forward to playing through my arrangement with Madelyn. *She means so much to me. I want her to know me as a competent musician and composer.*

~~~~~~

When I arrived at the parsonage the following afternoon, I was greeted by Muriel Ekland. She had a great grin and an uplifted spirit. "Last night, Madelyn's joy and happiness was something to behold."

"I'm glad to hear it."

"She's been lacking in real contentment for the past three years, and to see her now…" Muriel paused and smiled broadly. "Well, she's like a new person or rather, her old exuberant self has returned. She was buoyant again this morning."

"She's a blessing to me and everyone around her," I said.

"Michael, I think the time she has been spending with you has been wonderful for her."

"Thank you, Mrs. Ekland. Is she still interested in practicing with me at the church?"

"I'm sure that she is, but she and Martin left in the carriage shortly after breakfast this morning. They went to visit Elizabeth Harcourt, wanting to be an encouragement to her, and will be back shortly. They took her some of my calming tea and a few other things."

"Oh yes, Elizabeth Harcourt. She lost her husband to a storm at sea while fishing."

WE BOTH SHALL ROW, MY LOVE AND I

She paused, brows furrowed. "Michael, that's only part of her sorrow. Don't you know what Elizabeth is going through now?"

"What do you mean?"

"The young soldier that was killed during Myra's rescue was Owen Harcourt, Elizabeth's younger brother. He was buried up at Warrington Hall early this morning."

My mouth dropped open and I was silent. "He was with me and George when he passed." I took a step back and looked at her in shock. "He died in my arms."

"Michael, that must've been terrible."

"It was. I'm sorry that I didn't know who he was. She and her little daughter have been through so much. Is the Harcourt home far from here?"

"Several miles up the south road, just this side of Sandwith."

Muriel Ekland was finding it difficult to continue talking about the tragedy. I let the conversation end. "Thank you, Muriel. Please tell Madelyn that I'll be practicing in the church."

"Certainly. She'll be along soon. I'm looking forward to the concert on Thursday."

I entered the church, which was usually left unlocked and set my music and Madelyn's up on the music stands at the front. After practicing for half an hour, I heard the sound of a carriage and a few minutes later, Madelyn came in.

"Aunt Muriel said you were in here. Sorry I'm late."

"Not a concern. I think it's a truly Christian thing to do that you and your uncle went to comfort Elizabeth Harcourt."

"We did what we could. She has suffered so much. Uncle Martin read some Scripture and prayed with her."

"How's the baby?"

"I sang to her and we played in the back bedroom so that Elizabeth wouldn't be distracted from what Uncle Martin was

203

reading. She loved Aunt Muriel's calming tea and her baking as well."

"What baking was that?"

"Aunt Muriel sent some bread and scones, along with her calming tea."

Madelyn and I practiced for about two hours and when we finished, we were confident that Lord Warrington would be pleased. She was thrilled by my arrangement of the Bach concerto and thought that it was clever how I had created the flute parts. We cleaned our instruments, put them in their cases, packed up our music, and stepped out into the sunshine.

"Michael, would you like to sit on the sea wall at the water's edge, like before?"

"Nothing would please me more."

We sat and I took her hand in mine. "I had difficulty sleeping last night. When I first went to bed, I was thinking of you and how much you mean to me."

Madelyn looked at me, grinned, squeezed my hand, and leaned into my shoulder.

"I finally fell asleep but was awakened by a terrible nightmare."

"Did you see an apparition?" she asked.

"No, not an apparition. It was a gripping memory."

"What do you mean? What memory?"

"When I returned from the expedition to apprehend the brigands and rescue Myra, you saw me covered in blood, right?"

"Yes, it was terrible. I was sure that you were wounded."

I breathed deeply a couple of times, and for a moment, without speaking, relived the death of the soldier. "It wasn't my blood. It was Owen Harcourt's. Robert had sent an arrow straight through his neck. Blood was pulsing out. I tried to stop the bleeding but couldn't. It kept gushing out between my fingers."

Madelyn was speechless. She parted her lips several times, as if she was about to say something, but nothing came out. This stirred my memory of Owen looking at me, his eyes wide with panic, and trying to speak but being unable to. I was quiet for a time. She squeezed my hand more firmly, turned her shoulders towards me, and searched my face, looking for eye contact. I simply looked out into the harbor.

"His blood, it kept pulsing out between my fingers. He was desperate and panic-stricken. He was trying to speak but couldn't." I hesitated, realizing that I had said too much. "I'm sorry for speaking in such a graphic way."

"I'll pray for you, my love." She bowed her head, right then and there. *"Lord, remove this terrible memory from Michael. Comfort him and may he—"*

"I wish I knew what he had been trying to say," I interrupted.

"No one will ever know." She hesitated. "Except God." She sat there silently, looking out into the harbor. "He probably found some comfort in being held by you."

She leaned in towards me again, and nestled into my shoulder. It was so comforting to have her close to me. I didn't tell her that I also had great pangs of guilt, having broken Joseph's collarbone, mashed his mouth, and that I had wanted to stomp his face. The things that I had done revealed in me an aspect of myself that I didn't like. The violence with which I had assaulted Joseph troubled me as much as Owen's death, but it felt right to stop him, bring him down, and rescue Myra. *Am I justifying myself, my actions, my violence?*

The breeze coming across the harbor was helpful in lessening my tension, as was the welcomed distraction of the men working on their ships and the sounds of the busy seaport.

"Thank you for listening, Madelyn."

"I want to bear your burdens with you. It's part of my love for you. I was comforted by you when I told you about

Walter and my life with him and now." Her voice trailed off, she paused and then continued in a whisper. "And now I trust that I've been a comfort to you."

"You have."

She looked at me with her sweet, comforting eyes. "Michael, you're easy to love."

Aunt Muriel came out onto the top step at the front of the parsonage. "Will you be staying for supper, Michael?"

Madelyn, not giving me a chance to answer, responded, "Yes Auntie, he'll be staying."

I chuckled at the way she decided for me.

"I thought he might," Mrs. Ekland responded. "A fine roast beef will be on the table in a few minutes." She returned inside.

Madelyn moistened her lips and smiled, her eyes sparkled in the sunlight. She didn't say a word but reached up, clutched my shirt collar in her hand, and pulled my face down towards hers. Her other hand rested firmly on my shoulder. She kissed me again, like before, on the side of my mouth. *Her lips are so soft and moist. She's the fragrance of flowers. She loves kissing me.* My heart beat faster. *It's warm sitting here, even in the shade.*

With my eyes opened wide, after she had kissed me, I said, "I like the fragrance of you, I mean of your," I paused and then stammered, "your, your flowers."

"You mean my rose perfume?"

"Yes, that's it. Your perfume." *Such a fool I am. I must look and sound like a little schoolboy.*

"I'm so glad that you like it, Michael. It's from London. I put it on when I arrived back from Elizabeth Harcourt's home." She looked up at me and licked her lips. "I put it on for you."

A few minutes later, I was sitting at the dining room table, Madelyn was in the kitchen helping with the meal's final

preparations, and Reverend Ekland was reading an old newspaper from Liverpool. I suppose it had arrived on one of the ships. He was engrossed in it although much of it was simply the retelling of old news from London.
"Michael, have you heard about William Wilberforce's speech?"
"Which speech was that?"
That's a delicious looking roast of beef on the table. Where's Madelyn and her aunt? I'm so tired. I blinked a few times and then yawned.
Reverend Ekland yawned too. "The news is a bit old, but in the House of Commons, on the twelfth of May, he made an impassioned speech to end the slave trade. He is a caring and godly Christian."
"I saw him once in a London shop."
"Did you? Did you speak to him?"
"Well yes actually, I did."
Reverend Ekland, eyebrows raised, looked up at me from his paper. "What did you say? What did he say?"
"He was buying a book and I was buying some printed music in the same shop. He's rather short in stature. Perhaps only five foot three or so."
Reverend Ekland looked at me with furrowed brows. "He might be diminutive in stature but a giant in spirit and determination." The reverend leaned across the table towards me with an even deeper interest and repeated the question. "Did the two of you have a conversation?"
Playfully, I wanted to toy with the reverend because of his interest in my chance meeting with such a great man. "I agree with Wilberforce on all of his social justice points. I cannot imagine one man being the property of another and I support him in his quest for societal reform. I understand that he was greatly moved by Doddridge's book, *The Rise and Progress of Religion in the Soul.*"

"I've also read it." He moved his spectacles up onto his forehead and repeated his questions. "Michael, what did you say to him? What did he say to you?"

"I asked him a question, actually." Not being able to help myself, I toyed further with the reverend. I took a slow sip of tea for dramatic effect. "I asked him if he thought that the rain might shortly come to an end."

Reverend Ekland froze there with great concern and his mouth dropped open. "You asked him if our sovereign George the III's reign would come to an end?"

"No, nothing as momentous as that. It had been a grey and wet morning and I simply asked him if he thought that the weather might improve."

"That's it? That's all that you asked him, a leader, a man of his stature?"

"Yes, that was all I asked him. He then said that he would prefer drier weather. He put his book down on the counter and proceeded to pay for it."

He looked pensive. "What book did he buy?"

"It was a beautifully bound version of *The Vicar of Wakefield* by Oliver Goldsmith."

"I've read that as well," he said. "It has some truly amusing sections."

Reverend Ekland returned to his reading and I believe that I heard a little chuckle from behind his newspaper.

Mrs. Ekland walked into the dining room carefully carrying a gravy boat, filled to the brim and steaming hot. Madelyn followed her carrying a platter of assorted vegetables, also steaming hot. Our eyes met as she set it down between an ample bowl of mashed potatoes and a basket of sliced bread.

"Aunt Muriel, you set a splendid table!" I said.

As soon as I'd spoken, I realized that I'd called her *Aunt Muriel*, with too much familiarity, and not Mrs. Ekland. Madelyn noticed it as well. She sat there smiling joyfully.

Reverend Ekland was still engrossed in his newspaper but Mrs. Ekland laughed and said, "Well now, Michael, you're becoming a regular member of the family. I can't say that I disapprove. Please call me Aunt Muriel."

Madelyn giggled. "We'll have to cancel his debt for all of the fine meals he's been having."

Reverend Ekland carefully folded, and then set down, his newspaper. "What debt? Who is having their debt canceled?"

The three of us laughed and Reverend Ekland simply looked at us curiously and then said grace over the meal.

After a wonderful feast, and stepping out into the cool breeze of early evening, I felt my tiredness abating. Madelyn lifted her chin and kissed me, as before, on the edge of my lips.

I wonder why she kisses me like that. Not on my cheek and not entirely on my mouth either. It's exciting and curious at the same time.

With my oboe in its case and my music folder under my arm, I made my way along the cobbles that followed the harbor's edge. I stopped a short distance up the street and turning, noticed that Madelyn was still watching me, she and I exchanged fond smiles and a wave.

On the walk along the south side of the harbor towards the bridge, I reminisced about the time that I had spent with Madelyn. The practice was superb and the meal with the Eklands was warmly family-like, but what I saw as a great personal relief was that I had unburdened my heart to her about Owen Harcourt. His death in my arms would be a terrible memory that I'd always have with me. By the time I reached the bridge however, her kiss and my affection for her firmly set aside all other concerns. *Why does she kiss me like that on the side of my mouth? What should I do? She's so sweet.*

As I crossed the bridge and approached the Royal Stag, I determined that I would stop in for a cup of tea and get some of the latest community news. I hoped that there might be some information about the brigands. Everyone would be talking about their capture, Robert Caine's escape, and Myra's freedom.

As soon as I walked in, one of the old men recognized me and pointed his cane at me. "There's one o' them 'eroes, right there. I saw 'im return with the captain's men."

"That's Michael, old Sterling's grandson," said another.

"Buy 'im a brew," said a longshoreman with a pint in his hand.

Another of the local men said, "Not 'im, 'e's a tea man like old Sterlin' and 'e'll not be tippin' no tankard with the likes o' us."

"Buy 'im a tea then," shouted the old man, still waving his cane.

"Your best tea," said the longshoreman, flipping a coin through the air to Shannon.

"Tea it is," she said.

Several men gathered around me as I seated myself and set my instrument case and music folder on the table.

"So Sterlin', tell us about the brigands. Empty the bag," said a surly, whisker-faced, man.

"Dancin' demons, did their blood run well Sterlin'?" asked another.

"There'll soon be a few more o' the rogues in eternity boxes, for sure. Some by swingin' on Warrington's rope," said a third.

I simply expressed appreciation for Lord Warrington's interest in justice and the community effort in freeing Myra. A few of the men were quiet and trying to listen, but most of them, having had a bit too much to drink, started to laugh. I recognized Tommy's father sitting alone sullenly in the corner with a tankard on the table in front of him.

A man shuffled over and sat beside me. Lifting his arm, missing a hand, he said, "Quiet down. I've got me a serious question for young Sterlin'."

Everyone quieted down and leaned in towards us. "Well Sterling," he whispered. When everyone was leaning in, he winced, passed gas, and laughed. "There you have it. That's me question."

Everyone started to laugh uproariously and a couple of the men slapped him on the back, congratulating him for his vulgarity, as drinking mates often do.

"Did you crack some skulls and knife out some bowels?" asked a young sailor with an ugly scar across his forehead.

I was speechless with this kind of bawdy talk.

Fortunately, as a relief from all of the crude attention being directed towards me, Shannon arrived with a pot of tea, some cups, and a few biscuits.

A moment later, at the far end of the long table, the Spaniard arrived with a huge tankard-filled tray, and close behind him, a serving girl with a large tin platter, heaping with chicken pieces: wings, legs, necks, and breasts piled high. The patron's eyes were wide with amazement.

"Ale and chicken for all!" exclaimed Shannon. "Three cheers to the grand men from Glasgow up the Clyde for their favor on the likes of us!" She pointed towards two well-dressed men, standing off to the side.

The patrons of the tavern shouted, "Hip hip hooray for the highlanders!" Levity filled the room.

"No bones on the floor men," shouted Shannon. "Leave 'em in the bowls."

The tavern was a menagerie of laughter, camaraderie, boisterous talk, and backslapping. Shannon and the serving girls were busy carrying trays of ale and platters of chicken. The kitchen was cooking more chicken, and the two grand men from Glasgow were receiving more praise than had ever been witnessed in the Royal Stag.

"Give us a song, Michael," shouted an old man who stood over my shoulder.

The one handed patron said, "Sterlin', play something for us."

I got out my oboe, wet my read, inserted it, and started to play. I went from one song to another. Short catchy tunes that seemed to repeat endlessly. It was hot and smoky in the tavern. Not the most enjoyable place to play.

While I was playing, a lad of perhaps only fourteen years started beating out the time with a hand drum, the Spaniard got his guitar into the mix, followed by two fiddlers, and then Shannon started singing. Twice while we were playing, Tommy passed through the tavern dumping the leftover piles of chicken bones and morsels of meat into an old sack. I shook my head when I saw him, and grinned when we made eye contact. I started to laugh and was almost unable to play, thinking of the soup he'd be selling down at the docks. A moment later, I saw him give a small slip of paper, probably his calling card, to one of the wealthy men from Glasgow as they sat with Harbor Master Langley.

After several songs, the Spaniard replaced a broken string, and someone with a commanding voice shouted out, "Play, *The Jig o' the Sun-Bleached Bones!*"

The sailors in the tavern raised their hands for quiet. Men set down their tankards and some patrons moved tables away from the center of the tavern. Several of the old salts, as well-weathered seamen are often called, rose to their feet and took their places in the center.

The Spaniard slowly played through four, one to a bar, down-strummed chords. He played them through again, accompanied by the lad with the hand drum. Then the fiddlers joined in with a slow deliberate melody. Finally, when it was repeated again, I joined in. I started slowly, much like a dirge for the dead, as is commonly done with this jig.

At each repeat, we would play a little louder and a little faster. Faster and faster, until we were flying through it at a furious pace and couldn't go any quicker. When we hit our top speed, Shannon joined in with her high descant melody of long held notes that carried the words of the song. A marvelous contrast to the faster moving jig being played beneath her. Young men were dancing, tables were being pounded, and old salts were swaying. It was boisterous, but it surely was great fun.

Then quite suddenly, the music stopped. Men looked down at the floor, Shannon left and went behind the bar, and the Spaniard, head down, sheepishly walked around behind a high shelf out of sight. I halted my playing, and puzzled, looked at several of the patrons that stood before me. My back was to the door and I caught sight of an old merchant staring at me. He motioned with his head towards the door and I turned. Elizabeth Harcourt stood in the open doorway with her darling little daughter on her hip. The tavern was dead silent.

"Michael, could I speak to you please? Perhaps outside?" she asked tenderly.

With a sense of shame for our lighthearted revelry and singing a song that minimized death, I quickly packed up my instrument, grabbed my music folder, and followed her outside.

Sitting beside me on the bench, with her little girl sprawled across her lap, she looked at me. "Is it true? Did Owen, my younger brother, die in your arms? I came from Fair Havens Church and Madelyn shared that with me."

I sat there for a moment collecting my thoughts, enjoying the cool breeze coming in from the sea.

"Yes. I cradled him in the crook of my arm as he left us. My deepest sympathy, Elizabeth."

I sat there quietly, still enjoying the cool breeze. Elizabeth Harcourt, looking down at her little daughter, adjusted a modest blanket to cover her against the cold.

"Did he die peacefully?"

There is no way that Madelyn would've shared with her the gruesome details of Owen's death. She's simply trying to find some peace. Some comfort.

"He never said a word." I looked out into the harbor and then back at her. "He died as a faithful soldier, obeying the captain of the guard's orders. He served James Warrington, the Earl of Cumberland, superbly well."

Looking down at her daughter, she sat there silently, further adjusting the blanket.

"Elizabeth, you must remember forever that he had a part in Myra's rescue."

She continued adjusting her daughter's blanket silently, avoiding eye contact with me. She wet her lips. "Thank you. It's comforting to know that he wasn't alone when he died and that he had been a dependable soldier."

"May I walk with you back to Fair Havens and carry the baby?"

"No, that's not necessary. I'd like to be alone with my thoughts. I'll return to the church. Pastor Ekland said he would drive me home."

"Good night, Elizabeth."

"Good night. Thank you for your kind words."

She started down the street, but stopped and turned back towards me. "I'm glad you were with him when he passed." She resumed her walk towards the bridge, away from the Royal Stag, and disappearing into the darkness, I was left alone.

Edwyn's Workshop

*S*unrise the next morning didn't truly arrive. There was no sun. The seaport went from the black ink of a moonless night to the grey, soul-gripping shroud of drizzle that no one would ever enjoy. The harbor wasn't as busy as it usually was, and my motivation was lower than what I would have liked it to be. When the drizzle ended, the harbor remained overcast with leaden clouds, and a short while later the rain returned.

Once again, I hadn't slept well. Owen Harcourt dying in my arms and my cruelty towards Joseph Caine weighed heavily on me. Robert Caine's threat, 'Sterling, you might live through the day but you won't live through the week,' grieved me as well. I wasn't worried for myself, but for Madelyn. *What if he wants to exact revenge at some point when Madelyn is with me?*

Edwyn had hoped to hire a team of horses and a skid to retrieve a huge maple log out of the forest, but it was far too wet for that. He had felled it a month earlier, set it up off the ground, and said that he would now like to have it cut into lumber for air drying.

Skidding it to the father and son's steam mill beside a nearby stream would have to wait. No one wants to work out in a dismal drizzle when you could work in a warm dry shop.

He suggested that we continue the kind of preparation and assembly work that we had done on previous wet days.

After breakfast, we went out to his workshop. We were followed by Eutychus, head hanging low but tail wagging, and reeking of that wet dog smell. He had been out for an early morning walk along the harborside, in spite of heaven's spittle.

We entered the shop and Edwyn bent down and scratched the top of Eytychus' head. "Come on, old fella, rise to the occasion. The Rotund is going to stop by in a little while and take you for a walk to meet someone special." The mastiff, licking his lips, walked in a tight circle and then laid down on a pile of old canvas tarpaulins.

Edwyn started a fire in the fireplace at the back, opened the damper, and pulled a variety of drawings and lists out of his leather project folder. He placed before me one of his drawings with its accompanying materials list, which showed the specific dimensions of the wood that must be cut. He opened his padlocked cabinet where he kept his best tools, and then a large padlocked chest, about the size of a one-person bed, where he kept his best pieces of hardwood.

My surprise that he would lock up pieces of wood was evident. With raised eyebrows and a little grin, he reached down into the chest, pulled out a couple of hardwood planks, and unwrapping them from an old sheet of cotton, passed one of them to me. It was about the length of my arm, half as wide as it was long, and perhaps one inch thick. Only preliminary finishing had been done to it, but even so, it clearly possessed many intriguing burls, and a highly contrasted grain passed through it on an angle. It would catch any artist's eye.

"It's obvious that this will be superbly attractive as a piece of furniture," I observed.

"Yes, it will," he said with vivid eyes. "Let me show you something that you'll truly enjoy." He paused dramatically. "You'll enjoy it, *artistically*."

Exposing his teeth, he shared a crooked grin and passed me the other plank of the same dimensions. "Take a look at this."

"This also would be attractive for fine furniture or cabinetry."

"Look closer, Michael. Compare them side by side. This one with the one I showed you a moment ago."

Again, I did as he asked. With the joy of discovery, I exclaimed, "Mirrored twins! They are identical to each other."

He leaned closer, pointing out several of the mirrored characteristics of the grain and the burls. "We call it book matching. Can you imagine what they would look like side by side, well finished and highly polished?"

"Exquisite. Without rival. They'd make a wonderful set of matching cabinet doors for some wealthy patron. I understand why you keep them locked up."

"Exactly." He rewrapped the pieces in the large cotton cloth.

He showed me several other interesting pieces of wood from his chest and I told him how impressed I was.

"They are interesting now," he said. "But wait until they are smoothed with pumice and oil, fitted, and polished to a high gloss. They will stand out as fine art pieces. Clock cabinets, jewelry boxes, and things of that nature require the Lord's finest artwork in the forest as well as my own best work here in the shop."

The woodworking that I do in the mountain district is nothing compared to this. His work inspires me. I would like to attempt some finer pieces like this. Who in Cliffside could afford craftsmanship of this quality? No one.

After working for several hours, the Lyon brothers arrived together.

Edwyn closed the door behind them. "Well now, if it isn't our future in-laws arriving from the lighthouse."

"John the Rotund bent over and let Eutychus smell an old cloth that their dog, Princess, the Irish wolfhound, had slept on the night before. Almost immediately, Eutychus rose to his feet and began sniffing the cloth more intently. He looked up at Edwyn and then over at The Rotund, smiled his doggie smile, and walked to the door.

We exchanged glances with each other and John said to his brother, "Well Stephen, it's not fittin' to keep a lady waitin'."

They left with Eutychus leading the way, and we returned to our work.

An hour later, Brynne brought a delicious lunch of bread, cheese, and flounder stuffed with crab out to the shop. Edwyn, noticing that the rain had stopped and that the cold breeze had ended, put out the fire in the fireplace.

"Brynne, would you please take our lunch out to the porch?"

"Yes, Daddy."

We carried a few of the smaller project pieces, which we were now ready to burnish and polish, out to the porch, and after we ate, we began our work.

"This mixture of beeswax and turpentine is almost all that I use up in Cliffside."

"It'll do a suitable basic job," said Edwyn.

"No one in Cliffside has any extra money for the beautiful varnishes and shellacs that you use on your fancier pieces."

Edwyn stopped what he was doing for a moment, looked at me, and said, "You might want to introduce a bit of coloring to your finishing, if you're not doing it already. Add a modest amount of artist's oil paint into your wax and turpentine solution. Modest amounts of yellow or red might add fire to ones imagination. A hint of blue or green introduces some cool intrigue."

"Really? I suppose that makes perfect sense. It sounds interesting and easy enough," I said. "I'll try that some time."

Edwyn asked, "How was your practice with Madelyn?"

"It went supremely well." I set down my finishing cloth. "She's precious to me, Edwyn. Yesterday, before our practice, she went along on a pastoral visit with Reverend Ekland to the home of Mrs. Harcourt."

Edwyn looked pensive. "Elizabeth Harcourt has gone through so much more than any young mother should have to face."

I resumed my polishing. "I saw Elizabeth late last night at the Royal Stag."

"That's odd. What was she doing in a place like that, and late at night?"

I looked up from my polishing work, out into the harbor, and winced. "Looking for me."

"You? What did she want with you?" he asked.

"She found out that I was with her brother when he died and wanted to know about his passing. I spoke of his dedication towards Lord Warrington, and she took comfort in knowing that he had a part in Myra's rescue."

"The loss of her husband was difficult, and now for her to have lost her younger brother as well," Edwyn shook his head and bit his lower lip. "It's such a double tragedy." Coughing, he cleared his throat. "How was she when she left you?"

"I think she was as contented as can be expected. She was satisfied with what I had told her about Owen and then she left to go to the Eklands."

We quietly continued with our burnishing and polishing. My mind wasn't on my work. I was still consumed by my thoughts about Owen's bloody death in my arms.

My somber mood was broken when Edwyn laughed. "Look, there's Tommy Atwater. He's selling soup to those prosperous looking men."

"They're from up the Clyde and were in the Royal Stag last night."

Edwyn laughed again. "Tommy, such a highly motivated lad. Too bad his father doesn't have even half of his ambition. You can be sure, if there's some possible way to make money, Tommy will find it."

I nodded. "Speaking a bit harshly, others have called Tommy's father a mere 'muck about'. He refuses to work and ruins everything he puts his hand to."

"You've got that right, but Tommy and his mother are hard-working souls. He and his family are washing and processing cast off wool from Lord Warrington's enclosures. Do you know what he started a couple of months ago?" asked Edwyn.

"No what?"

He smiled and stopped his polishing. "He's collecting any old metal that he can possibly find and selling it to the owner of the forge: iron, steel, brass, copper, tin." He coughed again. "Any metal he can salvage."

"Oh, that explains it. I've often seen him carrying broken metal bits about the harbor." I stopped and gestured up the street. "Look, here come the Glasgow gentlemen."

Tommy had continued on his way, but the well-healed men, one quite tall and heavy and the other rather short and thin, each carrying their large bowls of soup, approached us. When they were on the street in front of Edwyn's porch, they stopped to talk.

"Excuse me," the heavier man said. "We arrived yesterday afternoon on that grand ship." He pointed with his spoon at a ship anchored out in the harbor. "We need some local guidance—"

The shorter one interrupted, "Were you the musician that played the oboe in the tavern last night?"

"Yes, that was me."

"Superb playing. Well done."

"Thank you." I grinned. "I'm glad you liked it. How can we help?"

The heavier one said, "We're hoping to do some hunting—"

"Deer hunting actually," interrupted the shorter one.

Edwyn yawned and inclined his head down the street towards Tommy. "The lad from whom you purchased the soup would be interested in showing you where the deer are known to frequent. He'll also make sure that you don't wander onto Lord Warrington's land. He knows the area well and I'm sure that he'd like to make a little money."

"He's an enterprising lad," laughed the heavier one. The big Scotsman held out a little scrap of paper with Tommy's name scrawled on it. It was much like the one I had seen before. "He gave me his card and—"

The shorter one interrupted, "And his soup is delicious. It's quite satisfying."

Edwyn inclined his head to one side, and when our eyes met, he winked. "Make sure you tell him when he picks up the bowls and spoons."

The shorter one responded, "Oh he won't be picking them up from us. We purchased them."

The heavier man gave a friendly nod, we exchanged our good-byes, and they started up the cobblestone street towards the bridge.

"Edwyn, it's odd that two wealthy Scotsmen, from up the Clyde, arrive here to do their hunting."

He looked at me, brows furrowed. "I was wondering about that too. There are many majestic deer in the hills not far from Glasgow, and yet they travel here to hunt?"

"Right," I responded. "There's more that makes no sense. They're here to hunt, but have no hunting contacts and no guides waiting to show them some of the favored valleys and slopes where the deer are known to be."

"Astute observations, Michael. It sounds quite odd when you say it that way."

I paused thoughtfully. "There's something disingenuous about their whole story."

We returned to our finishing work, musing over the hunting plans of these two men.

Our work was interrupted once again as Alistair Bletchly, the head groomsman at Warrington Hall, came riding up on a beautiful chestnut mare. He had a large box wrapped up in a piece of canvas secured behind his well-worn saddle.

"Hello, Michael. Good day, Edwyn. How are Louisa and Brynne?"

"We're all fine. How's Agnes?" Edwyn asked, rising to his feet and stepping onto his flagstone walkway. "Is there any word on little Myra? How is she adjusting to life in Warrington Hall?"

"Oh, she's fine. Lord Warrington has discovered that she was not mistreated at all."

"That's a blessing." Edwyn looked skyward and clasped his hands together. "Thank you, Lord."

Alistair continued. "She and the little Smythe girl, Nicola, are spending a lot of time playing together."

"That's wonderful," Edwyn responded cheerfully. "I think that they're of similar age."

"That's right." Alistair straightened in the saddle, stretched his back, and removed his gloves as he dismounted.

"So Alistair, what's in the box?" asked Edwyn.

"Several small items that need repair and refinishing." Unwrapping and opening the box, he shared Lord Warrington's instructions as he lifted each item out.

"This picture frame has a split side, as you can see. Match the wood and finish it if you can, but if you can't, make a new frame of the exact same dimensions. This old mantel clock is quite solid, but needs some work. Remove the old finish and apply a new varnish. Finally, this maple jewelry box has a broken hinge. Replace it and repair the finish where this scratch is." He pointed out the scratch on the side of the box.

"I'm very pleased to do this work. Express to Lord Warrington my appreciation for his trust in me and in the quality of my repair and refinishing."

"Yes Edwyn, I certainly will. The Earl has always been pleased with what you've done in the past for him."

"How is the questioning of the brigands coming along?" Edwyn leaned forward and looked intently at Alistair. "What have you heard? Why would they kill Charles Hawthorne and then abduct Myra? Did she witness them rob and kill him?"

"No, it's the exact reverse," he responded. "Myra said that when she was taken from her home, Hawthorne saw it, tried to stop them, and then went running for help."

"Really? Why would the Caine family bother themselves with a little girl?"

"No one knows for sure, but it does seem that they knew of her having been found wandering in the forest many years ago."

"That's strange." I shook my head. "How did they know that? What's their connection to the little girl?"

Alistair continued. "I have no idea, but Lord Warrington's men are still looking for Robert Caine. They'll find him before long, no doubt."

"Let's all hope so," responded Edwyn.

"Little Myra truly loves Nicola and she talks about how Sabina protected her. The girls are actually staying with us, in our quarters, most of the time. They play well together and are great fun for us. Like the grandchildren we never had."

"That's a blessing," responded Edwyn. "Some of Myra's family will be here to pick her up in a week or so and the magistrate with the Crown's judge will be back soon as well. He'll run a court proceeding at Warrington Hall."

"Like I said, most of them aren't talking much, except for some of the members of the Smythe family. Chatwin is singing like a bird." Alistair laughed. "Some of the questioning of the younger men has been quite intense."

"The Smythe family?" I asked. "Why would they be so eager to talk?"

"The Smythes weren't involved until after the murder and abduction. They arrived from the north and joined up with the Caine family. A few of them came down the trail with Myra ahead of you, and then the others, Gavin, Robert, and Victor, came down when you did."

When did the Smythes come into the area?" I asked.

"Probably about the day after you arrived."

Alistair excused himself and said that he would need to pick up some items from the fabric shop and the butchers. He gave his horse a pat, mounted the beautiful chestnut, and rode towards the center of our little seaport.

As Alistair disappeared up the street, Edwyn said, "The Bletchlys always seem to know what's going on and who said what to whom, whenever there's a mystery unfolding."

"It's strange to hear that the Caines were aware of Myra's origin. Why would they bother to go all the way up to Stone Ridge to abduct a little girl? There must be more to the story, more to their crime that we don't yet grasp."

Edwyn returned to his polishing work. "There has to be."

"A question has been troubling me for much of the day." I leaned back in my chair. "Do you think that the bowman, Robert Caine, is still in the area?"

"I don't think that he'd leave them and run away. They seem as close as any family could be and Lord Warrington has them locked up." I ran my fingers through my hair. "Well, except for Robert."

"It's hard to imagine," I wondered aloud, "what family life would be like in a clan of criminals."

"It's a blessing that we'll never know what life is like for a family such as the Caines."

Having completed our work for the day, we set it aside on the porch and I leaned back in my chair. Edwyn moved over to his favorite rocker and winced as he gently seated himself. "These bruises and bumps from the fighting are such an annoyance."

We looked out into the harbor and saying little, simply enjoyed each other's company and the view of the busy harbor. We found ourselves in a quiet, reflective, calm.

Some time later, Edwyn broke the silence. "I wonder when The Rotund will be bringing Eutychus back."

I grinned. "The puppies will be amazing."

"They will be if they have the mastiff's strength and the wolfhound's height."

"How do you decide who gets the first pick of the litter?"

"The Lyon brothers will be getting the first and third picks." He paused buoyantly and shared a beaming grin. "I will get the second and fourth picks because there's no payment for Eutychus doing his duty with the wolfhound. Whatever other puppies there might be beyond the fourth one will also be theirs."

"Is that the usual arrangement here in Cumberland?"

"I don't know about the rest of Cumberland, but this is how we do it here if nothing is written down."

A few minutes later, as we were about to take the well-finished furniture pieces and Lord Warrington's repair work to Edwyn's workshop, The Rotund arrived back with Eutychus.

He took a seat in one of the empty chairs on the porch. "It was an amorous waltz for the mastiff and the wolfhound. At first, me wolfhound wasn't too enamored with the mastiff and perhaps not likin' the 'ole arrangement. Then, there was a wee bit more approachin' and sniffin' by Eutychus and backin' away by our sweet Princess and a lot more sniffin'. After a while, we were goin' to give up and try again on the 'morrow but then the Princess came an' stood beside Eutychus. They shared a few kind words, some affectionate nuzzlin', and a little face lickin'. A moment later, it be like springtime in Paris."

Eutychus looking tired, but wagging his tail, walked in a tight circle and laid down beside Edwyn's rocking chair. He quickly fell asleep.

Edwyn reached down and stroked his head. "In nine weeks we'll be seeing if you're a daddy, my faithful friend."

The three of us sat there talking about all of the happenings at Oak Harbor. A moment later, Mrs. Atwater, Tommy's mother, strolled by with her two little daughters. She had a dark bruise along her lower right jaw. "'ave any of you fine men seen my Tommy?" She addressed us all but was looking at The Rotund and smiling.

"No sorry, not recently we haven't," I responded. "We saw him a couple of hours ago though. He sold some of his soup to two wealthy men from north of the border."

"An' which way did 'e go when 'e be finished with 'em?"

"Back towards the center of town," Edwyn answered.

The Rotund, still receiving smiles from Belinda Atwater, offered to help search for the boy but she said that it wasn't necessary. She turned and walked back towards the shops at the center of the community.

The Rotund sat up straight with fire in his eyes and ran his fingers through his thinning hair. "Did you see the bruise on 'er jaw?" He shook his head vigorously. "That Belinda Atwater is a right stout beauty. I wish that Atwater, that drunken lout," referring to Tommy's father, "treated 'er and the children with more respect. No soul deserves what she be gettin' except maybe 'e 'imself."

Edwyn and I were quiet for a moment, exchanging uncomfortable glances and not knowing how to respond.

The awkward silence needed to be broken. "That's the truth." I then gestured towards the slumbering mastiff. "Eutychus is looking quite tired, Edwyn. Perhaps he needs to be inside and curled up in the kitchen."

"Well, I'll be on my way now," said The Rotund. He headed off down the street in the same direction as Belinda Atwater.

Lord Warrington's Study

Having not seen Madelyn the previous day, I was missing her greatly. I knew that we would be going up to Warrington Hall later in the afternoon and I was looking forward to it with great anticipation. It seemed to me that I was looking forward to being with her more than performing in the concert, and caring for her as much as I did, I wanted to give her a special gift. My grandfather had given me one of my grandmother's necklaces, a gorgeous silver one with an attractively mounted blue sapphire in the center. It was flanked by three pearls on each side. He had given it to me, along with several other pieces of jewelry, and I now wanted Madelyn to have it.

My morning was spent working with Edwyn in his shop and Louisa had provided, once again, a satisfying lunch.

By 4:30, I was on the front porch, resting, looking over my music, and waiting for Madelyn. She arrived a few minutes later with her flute, guitar, and music folder, and seated herself beside me. Without saying a word, she reached out and took my hand.

"Edwyn and I completed a lot of work yesterday and this morning," I shared.

"That's fine."

"Last night my practicing for the concert went well."

"I'm sure the concert will be a success," she said.

"Alistair Bletchley," I cleared my throat, "the head groomsman at Warrington Hall, was here yesterday and said that Myra was doing well."

Madelyn sat there with a sullen and detached look. "That's nice."

"He also said that the questioning of the Caine and Smythe families has shown that they knew all about Myra. They knew her history and that she had been found wandering in the forest as a toddler."

Madelyn sat quietly with no comment. She simply nodded.

"What's wrong? Are you alright?"

Still not speaking, she looked out into the harbor.

"Madelyn, something's troubling you. Please tell me what it is."

"On the way over, I stopped at the Kline's home to see how George's wrist was."

"How's his wrist?"

"People think that he'll not lose the use of his hand." She paused and looked deep within me. She seemed disappointed. "Do you not yet grasp how much I love you?" She looked at me sternly. "Why didn't you tell me about the threat?"

"What do you mean? What threat?"

She looked down at her flute case, which she was scratching with her thumbnail, and then looked out into the harbor again. "You know exactly what I mean." She looked directly at me. "George told me that Robert Caine threatened you when Owen was killed. Caine bragged that 'you won't live through the week'. Is that true, Michael? Is that what he said? Why didn't you tell me?"

"Madelyn, it meant absolutely nothing. Caine was simply trying to intimidate me. He's long gone by now, I'm sure of it."

"Is that what you think, that he would simply leave his family in Lord Warrington's jail, forget about them, wander away, and not want revenge on you?" She stared at me sternly. "Why didn't you tell me?"

For some reason I felt like a child once again, ready to be beaten by my mother.

I should've told her about the threat. She would've been filled with worry. Nothing will come of Caine and his boasting.

"I love you, Michael. You mean the world to me. Why didn't you tell me?"

"I'm sorry. I didn't want you to worry. It's not as if he could follow through with the threat. Lord Warrington's men are still out looking for him. He'll be hiding somewhere far from here, of that I'm sure. I'm sorry."

"You should've told me," she repeated.

"I won't keep things from you in the future. Forgive me. Let's not let this distract us from our love for each other or from tonight's concert."

We sat there quietly for a long time. I leaned towards her and tenderly stroked her arm, touched her shoulder, and took her hand. "I'm sorry."

We looked at each other deeply. "I forgive you." She squeezed my hand.

Was this my first scolding? From what I've seen with Edwyn and Louisa, it probably won't be my last. "Thank you, Madelyn. I will be open and honest with you in the future."

A few more minutes of uncomfortable silence went by and a small but attractive gig, similar to Reverend Ekland's but more finely painted, stopped in front of us.

The driver addressed us formally. "Mr. Sterling and Lady Haversham, Lord Jonathan Warrington requests that you attend to Warrington Hall. I have been sent to convey you at your earliest convenience."

"Thank you very much." We climbed up into the gig, leaned back into the luxurious leather seats, and off we went.

When we arrived at Warrington Hall, we were met by Lord Warrington's butler and escorted into Blenheim Chapel. Before us, in an attractive artistic script and mounted on a large hardwood easel, was the program for the performance. It was set up, off to the right, so that concert attendees could refer to it throughout the evening.

I took off my Inverness coat and put it in a nearby cloakroom with Madelyn's. Jonathan hadn't arrived yet, so we had some time to discuss things further, reconcile more fully, and get beyond our misunderstanding. It was helpful to be alone.

While Madelyn assembled and warmed up her flute, running through a few scales and difficult passages, I leaned back in my chair and simply adored her for a few minutes.

She wore a stylishly low-cut dress of dark blue with silver trim. It had puffy shoulders and around her waist was a wide sash belt of dazzling silver. Her auburn hair, in an upswept style, was decorated with tiny silver bows of silk. Each of these bows was mated with a dangling pearl in a silver setting which caught the light of the many candelabra around the room. She wore delicate black gloves of French lace, fingerless, so as not to interfere with her flute playing. She looked lovely, fashionable, enchanting.

"Whenever you wear this dress in the future, it will be the most special of occasions. You are the most beautiful woman I have ever seen."

She set her flute down and shared the sly smile, which she often did when she had a humorous thought. "Maybe you haven't seen many women." Her reddened lips were moist and full.

"Madelyn." I felt consumed by her beauty. "I love you. You mean the world to me and I would like to give you something. A symbol of my deep love for you." I reached into the pocket of my trousers and took out an embroidered, blue satin bag. I placed it in her hands as her jaw dropped in surprise.

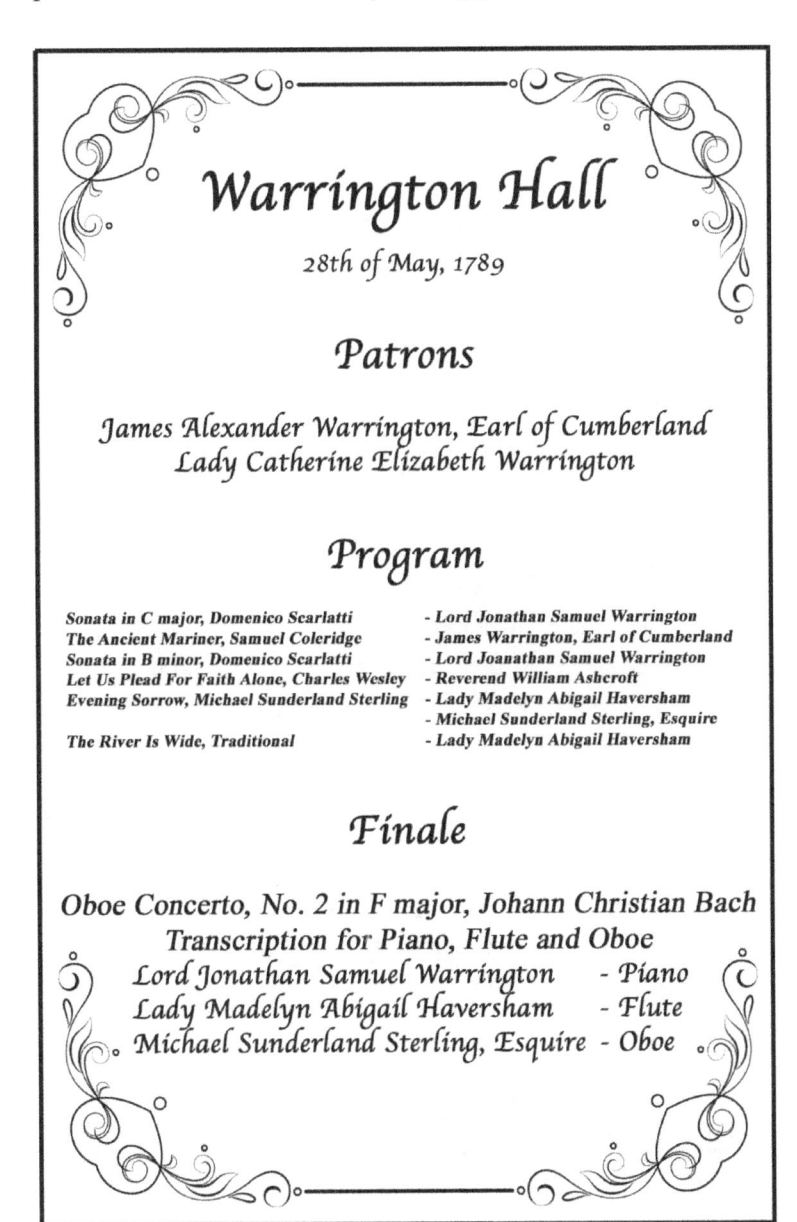

Warrington Hall

28th of May, 1789

Patrons

James Alexander Warrington, Earl of Cumberland
Lady Catherine Elizabeth Warrington

Program

Sonata in C major, Domenico Scarlatti — Lord Jonathan Samuel Warrington
The Ancient Mariner, Samuel Coleridge — James Warrington, Earl of Cumberland
Sonata in B minor, Domenico Scarlatti — Lord Joanathan Samuel Warrington
Let Us Plead For Faith Alone, Charles Wesley — Reverend William Ashcroft
Evening Sorrow, Michael Sunderland Sterling — Lady Madelyn Abigail Haversham
— Michael Sunderland Sterling, Esquire
The River Is Wide, Traditional — Lady Madelyn Abigail Haversham

Finale

Oboe Concerto, No. 2 in F major, Johann Christian Bach
Transcription for Piano, Flute and Oboe
Lord Jonathan Samuel Warrington — Piano
Lady Madelyn Abigail Haversham — Flute
Michael Sunderland Sterling, Esquire — Oboe

"What is it, Michael?" Her eyes flashed. "I love surprises." Her eyes were wide open, displaying the subtle emerald flecks that made them so captivating. Her smile was sensuous, revealing her perfect white teeth. Her hands were delicate, suggesting her femininity adorned in her stylish black lace gloves. She opened the bag and slid the necklace onto her lap. "I wasn't expecting—"

"My love, let me help you try it on. It will look so amazing with the dark blue and silver gown you're wearing tonight."

We stood, she lifted the dangling strands of her luxuriant hair, I put the necklace in place, and closed the clasp. Before I let go of the necklace, I leaned down and kissed the side of her sensuous neck.

"Michael, that tickles." She laughed and wiggled her shoulders. "That's the first time you've ever kissed me. I would've never dreamed that my first kiss from you would be a ticklish one." She paused. "There's no mirror in here. I wish I could see it on myself. She turned towards me, with one hand on her chest, as she slid her fingers along the silver chain and onto the pearls of the necklace. She then held me close and pulled my head down towards her face. She kissed me and whispered, her lips still against mine, "I love you Michael Sterling."

Briskly, Jonathan Warrington entered the chapel. "I am so pleased that you're both here. Was your carriage ride satisfactory?"

We both affirmed that the carriage ride was much appreciated.

The three of us, having warmed up, began our final rehearsal. Jonathan was genuinely pleased with my arrangement of the Bach concerto that included the flute.

The wind increased outside and the music on our stands was blowing about so we closed the windows. Unfortunately, that was the end of the cool and comfortable breeze.

After about thirty minutes, an exquisitely attractive servant girl, perhaps only fifteen or sixteen years of age, with long, light brown hair, entered the chapel. She was carrying two sizable vases of flowers. I glanced at her, then at Jonathan, and then back at her. Jonathan looked enamored, and with his eyebrows raised, he lost his performance focus entirely. His fingers stumbled over the keys like a beginner and his unity with us was totally lost. She was a distractingly beautiful young woman.

As our music tapered off and our instruments became silent, Madelyn looked up from her music stand, noticed the girl, and then looked at Jonathan. She shook her head and cleared her throat. "Jonathan, we still have some practicing to do." He wet his lips and inhaled deeply. The servant girl set the vases down on a side table and glided gracefully back out of the room.

She better not enter the room during the concert. Not only would Jonathan be distracted, but most of the men in the audience would be as well.

With her absence, he regained his composure, and we resumed our practice with diligence.

After rehearsing some intense passages at a tempo faster than they would normally be performed, Jonathan looked at his pocket watch. "It is 7:00 p.m. I made arrangements for a light tea, to be served in my father's study."

Madelyn and I cleaned our instruments, set them down, and followed Jonathan out into the corridor to his father's study. A few minutes later, he left us. While two servants were setting up the tea, biscuits, and pastries on a side table, Madelyn and I, like children in a toy store, roamed about the room. The best books were on the shelves, captivating paintings were on the walls, and intricate engineering models were upon the tables. What interested me most was on the wall behind Lord

Warrington's desk: an enormous, full color copy of the 1760 Bowen and Kitchin's map of Cumberland and Westmoreland. I would estimate that it was about four feet wide by six feet in height.

It served not only as an attractive piece of art, but also as a practical help to James Warrington, being after all, the Earl of Cumberland. The map was almost thirty years old and outdated, but it was beautifully done. It was flanked on the wall by smaller, yet more detailed, recently printed maps.

I couldn't take my eyes off them. Every detail was correct in respect to Cliffside, Stone Ridge, and all of the mountain villages that I knew. Every road, river, mountain, and bridge was accurately located on these newer maps.

Madelyn called me over to look at some paintings of the Battle of Flodden in 1513. She proudly declared, "This one is near our home, and this one, look at this one, that's where my uncle's farm is."

Jonathan re-entered the room and invited us to join him for some tea and pastries at the side table. We engaged in lighthearted conversation while we ate.

On one of the side walls, an attractively framed Scripture passage caught my eye. It was hand-lettered in a beautiful script and was carefully protected under glass. It spoke volumes to me about Lord Warrington as the leader I believed him to be.

> *Righteousness exalteth a nation:*
> *But sin is a reproach to any people.*
> *The king's favor is toward a wise servant:*
> *But his wrath is against him that causeth shame.*
>
> *Proverbs 14:34, 35*

Jonathan gave his final directions to the servants as they were sent to complete the concert preparations in the chapel. "I want it to be well-lit with fancy lamps and candelabra everywhere. It will be a concert of light and joyous radiance."

We returned to the chapel and almost immediately, invitees began to arrive. Each was impeccably dressed, strutting their appearance, complimenting one another, and sociably engaging in conversation.

Some quietly entered and seated themselves, but members of the nobility had their names announced as they strode into the room. It was an interesting mix of nobility, landed gentry, and well-respected commoners from our seaport.

A short time later, Alistair and Agnes Bletchley came in and were followed by the two little girls, Nicola and Myra. They were seated at the back of the chapel. A large number of the local leaders from Oak Harbor were there as well, including the Eklands, Reverend and Mrs. Ashcroft, the Klines, Edwyn, Louisa, and Brynne, and Edward Stewart. Harbor Master Langley was there with an ear trumpet. He seemed to be aiming it at various groups of people that were in conversation with one another.

"Look at Myra and Nicola." Madelyn gestured towards them. "Their fancy dresses and stylish shawls around their shoulders are striking." She adjusted her music on her music stand. "Such a contrasted pair: Nicola with her long, black hair and dark complexion; Myra with her curly blonde hair and fair complexion. The Bletchleys are treating them as the grand-daughters they never had."

"They look so happy together," I added. "Myra will be overjoyed when her family comes down from Stone Ridge to get her. Is this the first time that you've seen the girls?"

"Yes it is, but Myra reminds me of someone." Madelyn rested her flute across her knees and stared intently at Myra.

"Does she remind you of anyone? There's something very familiar about her."

Jonathan, interrupting, leaned over and said, "Sabina, Nicola's aunt, might be out of detention soon if Robert Caine is captured. It seems that she was actually caring for Myra and protecting her, although she didn't prevent the abduction."

Why would the Caine family go all the way up to Stone Ridge and abduct a little child? The question kept coming to my mind at the most inconvenient times.

It was getting quite warm in the room, with the many lamps and candelabra, and people had begun fanning themselves. Finally, at 8:05 p.m., James and Lady Warrington entered. Everyone respectfully rose to their feet.

Jonathan welcomed everyone to the concert, making special mention of the nobility, and introducing each of them one by one. Finally, he introduced his father and mother as the patrons of the concert.

James Warrington had a few fine words to say about music and the importance of the arts. He dedicated the concert to his wife, Lady Catherine Elizabeth Warrington, and he then introduced the first musical piece of the evening, Scarlatti's Sonata in C Major, also known as *The Hunt*.

Jonathan played the sonata superbly well, with its interesting rhythms and repeated figures. He was clearly a talented and well-rehearsed musician.

The rest of the concert continued, one piece after another, until Reverend Ashcroft, of Saint Cecilia's, introduced the hymn that he would sing. His introduction caught my attention. He began by reading a quote from Oliver Goldsmith's book, *The Vicar of Wakefield*.

> Almost all men have been taught to call life
> a passage, and themselves the travelers. The

similitude may still be improved when we observe that the good are joyful and serene, like travelers that are going towards home; the wicked but by intervals happy, like travelers that are going into exile.

Reverend Ashcroft clutched his Bible to his chest. "Life certainly is a journey. For me, a journey of faith. When I was a young seminarian, my personal experience of our Lord was non-existent, or at least quite limited. I sought the Lord, however, and found Him, or rather, He found me. My devotion now is to pray, read, and obey the Scriptures, and love those that the Lord brings my way. Our Savior, Our Lord, reached out and touched me with his love."

I heard Reverend Ekland say, "Amen."

Reverend Ashcroft continued. "I chose this hymn, 'Let Us Plead for Faith Alone', by Charles Wesley, as the hymn I would like to share this evening. It captures the depth of my feelings entirely."

He then quoted the second chapter of Paul's Epistle to the Ephesians, verses eight and nine.

"For by grace are ye saved through faith; and that not of yourselves: it is the gift of God: Not of works, lest any man should boast."

He closed his introduction by saying, "May we all, on our lifelong journey, humbly and repentantly seek the Lord, and grasp that we are saved by grace through faith."

He began to sing, and with a rich baritone, captured some of my recent thoughts about the Lord. I wondered if these related to the line that I could not forget from Pastor Ekland's sermon of last Sunday: *"There is a stain on the heart of man and a chain about his soul."* My memory of mashing Joseph Caine's face, and being tempted to stomp his head, came back upon me. I tried to put them out of my mind. *Reverend Ashcroft sings brilliantly. There's so much character in his voice in his lower range.*

The composition that I had recently composed, 'Evening Sorrow,' was solemn. Madelyn and I shaped the phrases with a voice-like quality, our intonation was perfect, and our unity complete. The harmonies that I had written were purposeful and a somber mood was established as I had intended.

Madelyn's rendition of the familiar yet always poignant song, 'The River Is Wide', moved me extremely. Perhaps it moved me to the extent that it did because it was my first time hearing it while being truly in love. When she began singing, she looked towards me and we made eye contact.

> The water is wide, I can't cross o'er.
> And neither have, I wings to fly.
> Give me a boat, that can carry two,
> We both shall row, my love and I.

I noticed that Edwyn, having grinned at me when Madelyn began to sing, was now broadly smiling at Louisa, his true love. Madelyn continued her deeply expressive singing and a moment later. we made eye contact once again. When she sang the stanza about the heavily laden ship, I knew that she was thinking of her love for me:

> There is a ship, she sails the seas.
> She's loaded deep, as deep can be;
> But not as deep, as the love I'm in.
> I know not how, I sink or swim.

She finished her heart-warming song with her delicate voice, and I saw both Edwyn and Louisa, with beaming grins, looking at Madelyn and me.

The climax of the evening was the finale piece, Johann Christian Bach's Oboe Concerto, No. 2, in F major, and I dare say that our performance of it was the best I'd ever heard. The hours of practice truly brought the best results. We were only distracted by the heat of the room. People were fanning themselves, removing their shawls, and opening their waistcoats. A few of the men briefly lifted or removed their wigs. I lifted mine several times when the music that was being performed didn't involve me.

After generous applause and Lord Warrington's personal expression of gratitude for our performance, the attendees began to exit. Many left for their homes, some stepped out onto the well-lit terrace for fresh air, and perhaps a dozen milled about the chapel looking at the artwork. The beautiful paintings depicting the life of the Apostle Paul, located at the front of the chapel, held the attention of many.

After most of the guests had left, Madelyn and I retrieved our coats from the cloakroom and carried them over our arms onto the terrace. We seated ourselves on a low wall that ran around the perimeter of the terrace, chatting about the evening and sipping some tea. It was cool outside and we enjoyed the breeze.

Our performance had been precise, unified, and well phrased, with slightly exaggerated dynamics, which I always preferred. Jonathan's prowess on the piano was evident in everything he played. I mentioned to Madelyn that I had seen Edwyn and Louisa looking at us, smiling and whispering several times during the evening. Hearing that, Madelyn laughed and took my hand with a sweet deliberation.

She looked over where the girls were playing. "Michael, are you sure that Myra doesn't remind you of someone?"

"No, I don't think so."

Mrs. Ekland stepped out onto the terrace, and with a tiny wave, indicated that we should join her.

"I think your uncle has the Landau ready," I said.

As we were about to stand from the low wall, the two girls went running by, chasing one another. Myra stumbled and fell at our feet and Madelyn immediately leaned forward to help her up but froze. Her jaw dropped, her face was ashen, and her eyes were wide with anxiety. She seemed to regain her senses, and lifting Myra to her feet, brushed the little girl's dress with her hand. Madelyn once again lost her self-control. She staggered backwards a couple of steps and sat down heavily on the low wall.

"Madelyn, what's wrong? Are you ill?"

"I feel faint. Please, let me rest." She clenched her eyes shut and shook her head. She then took a couple of deep breaths. "Let me rest for a minute. Just let me rest."

"Should I get Aunt Muriel? She went out to the carriage."

"No." She rubbed her hand across her face. "Just let me sit out here in the cool breeze." She set her flute case and music folder down on the wall and braced herself with both of her hands.

It was hard for me to see her, the woman I love, suffering like this. Sitting beside her I provided support with my arm around her shoulders. "Madelyn, my love, what's wrong?"

She started to stand but then flopped back down onto her bottom. She rested a little longer, looked up at me, lips quivering. "Take me to Lord Warrington."

The carriage had been left with one of Alistair Bletchly's stablemen. Reverend Ekland and I were at Madelyn's sides, supporting her as she walked. Visibly shaken, she was unsteady on her feet.

We Both Shall Row, My Love And I

The door to Lord Warrington's study was open and when we entered, he looked up from some papers that he was reading and signing.

"Oh hello." He pushed his paperwork aside. "Such a wonderful evening. You both played with such precision. I enjoyed your phrasing and your dynamics in particular." He paused and noticed that Madelyn was distressed. "What happened? Lady Haversham, are you ill?"

"Lord Warrington." Madelyn steadied herself with the arm of an over-sized chair as she sat down. "There's something that I must tell you. It's about Myra."

"Whatever could it be?"

"Did you ever have occasion to meet my late husband, Walter Haversham, the younger son of Lord William Haversham of Ridley?"

"No, I never met him." James Warrington looked concerned. "I've met Lord Haversham himself numerous times, and his eldest son once or twice." His brows furrowed. "I never met his younger son."

"As you know, we were married for less than a year when he was killed in a hunting accident up in the Scottish Highlands." She hesitated and looked embarrassed. "He was quite a bit older than I, eighteen years older in fact." She looked uncomfortable at having to describe her personal life. "It was his regular routine to go on hunting trips with a few friends, ever since he was about fifteen."

Lord Warrington was listening closely but he appeared bewildered as to where Madelyn's personal story might lead. "I don't understand. What's troubling you?"

"Throughout the evening, I was quite distracted by Myra's appearance. She reminded me of someone. I mentioned it to Michael."

I spoke up in agreement. "She did, Lord Warrington. She spoke to me at least twice about it."

Madelyn took a sip of the tea that had been brought in by the same strikingly beautiful servant girl that had made such a strong impression on Jonathan. "Myra has the same port wine stain, the same birthmark, as my late husband."

She reached up and traced the shape of it, a backwards 'c', on her own neck.

"Are you sure?" asked Lord Warrington. "Could you be mistaken? Many people have birthmarks."

"I am certain. It's the same shape and color, and it's at the same place on her neck." Madelyn then looked directly at Lord Warrington. "She looks and acts like him as well."

We were all speechless at this revelation. Lord Warrington reached for his teacup and the servant, noticing it was empty, refilled it. "Michael, little Myra is in the kitchen, I believe. Would you please get her and bring her to me?"

"Yes, my lord," I responded.

A moment later, I returned with Myra. She came skipping into the study with me, and having become quite familiar with Lord Warrington, she immediately approached him without hesitation. Her hair, no longer being held in place by her tartan ribbon, which she now held in her hand, was wildly askew. Lord Warrington, using the opportunity to see Myra's birthmark for himself, opened his desk drawer and pulled out a hairbrush. "Come here beside me, my dear. Your hair needs a brushing. Let me straighten it up for you."

As he brushed her hair, he paused for a moment and seeing the birthmark, nodded several times with assurance.

Not being able to help myself, I leaned forward and saw it exactly as Madelyn had described it.

"Is that your ribbon, Myra?" asked Lord Warrington tenderly.

"Yes, sir. It's the last one I have. My mother made me some from an old dress that I had long, long ago."

"May I see the ribbon please?" asked Lord Warrington, in his kindhearted way.

She giggled and passed it to him. He then opened the top drawer of his desk and pulled out the little highland dirk, wrapped as a package and bound with a faded tartan ribbon.

He laid the two ribbons side by side. The one that had been found on the floor of Myra's home the night she was abducted and the other that had been used to tie back her hair earlier in the evening. They were identical.

"You found my other ribbon!" Myra exclaimed. "It pulled out of my hair when the bad men took me away. I tried to scream but they covered my mouth."

"Yes Myra," said Lord Warrington. "I know. You told us all about that terrible night. Where did these nice little ribbons come from?"

"My mother made them for me from a dress that I had long ago. The dress that I was wearing when I was little and Lorena found me in the forest. I only wear these ribbons in my hair on special occasions, like tonight."

"Why only on special occasions?" asked Reverend Ekland.

"My parents say they are important." She chuckled and nodded cutely. "My mother says they are part of my heritage."

"*Heritage*, that's a big word," said Reverend Ekland, resting his hand gently for a moment on her shoulder. "You're so precious, Myra. Thank you for your help."

Lord Warrington walked over to one of the bookshelves at the side of the room and pulled a thick volume from his collection. He looked at the binding and then the cover. "No no, not this one."

He returned it to its position and pulled out another book. "Yes. Here it is. I have a picture volume of all of the tartans of the highland clans." He dropped the open book onto his desk with a thud and began flipping through the pages, forwards and backwards, searching for the tartan of the two ribbons.

"Hmm," he said to himself, "could this one be it? No. Not quite." He continued his searching and flipping of pages. Myra stood in front of Lord Warrington's desk, eyes wide, bewildered by the drama that was taking place in front of her, of which she was a part.

"Yes, this is it!" Lord Warrington stabbed his finger at the picture in the book.

Myra, leaning forward to have a look, shouted with joy, as if a game had been won. "My ribbon!" She pointed at the picture in the book. "This picture is the same as my ribbon."

Lord Warrington leaned back into his chair and looked at Madelyn. A moment later, Mrs. Bletchley, looking for Myra, stepped into the study, the door having been left ajar. "Lord Warrington, may I take Myra to our quarters to get her ready for bed? It is quite late."

"Yes, of course," he responded.

"Agnes!" exclaimed Myra. "Everyone likes my hair ribbon."

"We all love your ribbon," laughed Agnes. "Maybe you can wear it again tomorrow."

"Actually Myra," said Lord Warrington in a grandfatherly tone. "Could I please borrow one of your ribbons?"

Myra had been clutching the two ribbons in her hand. She passed one of them to Lord Warrington across his cluttered desk, and then skipped out of the room with Agnes. The young servant girl followed close behind.

He addressed us all. "The questioning of the Caine and Smythe families has indicated that they were aware of certain things about Myra's past." Lord Warrington sipped his tea. "They haven't been completely honest and open though." He set his teacup down on his desk. "I was going to release Sabina

Caine as soon as Robert is captured or turns himself in, but now, with this new information, I'll make her release conditional upon her full disclosure about the past. I will have these *heritage* details, relating to Myra, included in our questioning."

"Thank you, Lord Warrington," said Madelyn.

"I am aware of the valley of the Haversham estate in the highlands." He tapped the book on his desk with the flat of his hand. "The book states that it is one of the three valleys within which the clan is found that uses this tartan."

Lord Warrington now directed his attention in a quieter tone to Madelyn, "Thank you for bringing this to my attention."

"Yes, Lord Warrington," she responded.

He continued. "Lady Haversham, in the interest of arriving at a deeper understanding of the truth, may I ask you a few questions privately about your late husband's experiences in the highlands?"

"Yes, of course, my lord." She paused and then hurriedly started right into personal disclosure. "He was a heavy drinker and it was no secret that he was a skirt chaser from his early years and—"

Lord Warrington quickly raised his index finger towards her. "Lady Haversham, I believe it is best for us to speak privately of these matters." Lord Warrington glanced at the door, looked at the Eklands, and then at me. "Thank you for being of such assistance to Lady Haversham. She will join you in the hall in due time."

"Yes, my lord," said Reverend Ekland.

Muriel took Madelyn's coat for her and we stepped out into the hallway to provide her and Lord Warrington with some privacy for their conversation. She leaned over to me and whispered, "It is a time for discretion. One mustn't display one's dirty laundry to the neighbors."

Seeing three ornate chairs against a nearby wall, we sheepishly looked at one another, and wondering how long we would be waiting, decided to be seated. We heard the rain begin to fall and the wind begin to howl as we waited for our dear Madelyn.

"It's going to be a wet ride down to the seaport," said Reverend Ekland.

"I'm glad that I reminded you to put the carriage roof up, dear," added his wife.

Almost an hour later, Madelyn, with tears streaming down her cheeks, rushed out into the hall from the study, her beautiful gown rustling as she hurried by. Without stopping, she dashed towards the front door and the carriage, which waited out in the rain.

"Walter Haversham," she cried as she hurried by, "I wish I'd never met him. Even after his death, I'm still troubled by him."

The Eklands and I quickly stood and followed her out to the carriage.

The driver was focused only on the road on such a stormy night. Reverend and Mrs. Ekland were sitting together silently, facing us. Madelyn and I sat beside one another, but it seemed we were miles apart. The ride down the lane was painfully sullen. No one looked at anyone else. The gravity of the disclosure gripped each of our hearts. No one spoke. The sound of the storm established an aura of the fury within which we found ourselves. My darling Madelyn was suffering. I reached out for her delicate hand. She pulled it away.

The carriage slowed to a stop in front of the Brixton home. Madelyn, without looking at any of us, stared out into the harbor. "Walter Haversham," she growled loudly. "You carnal fiend!" Shaking, she bowed her head and angrily struck the inside of the carriage. She sat there trembling and slowly shaking her head, breathing deeply. She started to quiet down. "Lord Warrington is such an understanding and supportive man. He and Lady Warrington are so unlike the hypocritical Havershams. I don't want to talk anymore about any of this. I want to go to my room and get a proper night's sleep."

It was difficult to see her suffering like this. Still avoiding eye contact, she looked away as I leaned forward to rise out of my seat and leave. She covered her face with her delicate, lace-gloved hands. She mumbled, "What should've been a positively buoyant evening has turned into a tragedy from which it will be difficult to recover."

I climbed down out of the carriage, and turning, said to her, in the hearing of everyone, "Madelyn, know this. Whatever happens in the world around us, I love you. Whatever you face, I will face it with you. You will never stand alone." I clutched my oboe case and music folder more tightly to my chest. "I will always support you in life's challenges. I love you deeply." I rested my hand on her shoulder and gave it a light squeeze.

The strong wind grasped at my coat as I walked around the outside of the house and entered the back door. I stepped into my room, put my oboe case on a side table, pulled off my boots, threw my outer clothes on a chair, and flopped onto my bed.

That was the first time that anyone ever heard me say "I love you" to Madelyn. I dropped off to sleep.

Throughout the night, the increasing wind howled fiercely and great sheets of rain pounded on the walls of the Brixton home without abating. Thunder and lightning began part way through the night and it was obvious that a great gale had begun out at sea.

The Main Dock

The following day, a depressing, damp grey filled the seaport once more. Movement in the harbor and in the community surrounding it was at a standstill. Children weren't playing in the streets, birds weren't calling and soaring overhead, and the optimism that a new day often brings never presented itself.

I awoke to the sound of men talking in the kitchen and the distinctive clinking of spoons in teacups and on saucers. Pastor Ekland was telling Albert Kline and Edwyn about the meeting with James Warrington the previous night, after Madelyn's discovery of Myra's origin. He was relaying all that Madelyn had told Lord Warrington, describing Myra's birthmark and highland tartan ribbons. He also shared Lord Warrington's desire to find out more through the questioning of the members of the Caine and Smythe families.

Outside the home, the rain had stopped and the wind had lessened to a strong breeze. I laid there in bed with the blanket at my neck, trying to ignore what I was hearing from the kitchen.

My restless worries for Madelyn assailed me. I felt only minimally rested after the previous night's drama and the stormy weather that had violently struck the seaport. I wondered how she was feeling. She had been through so much anguish and now she was being faced with a new set of challenges.

Across the dim room, I could see my oboe case and music folder. On the floor beside my bed, where my arm was hanging, I could feel the vicious cudgel that I had fought with. Beside that, my belt, sheath knife, and the bag containing the two arrowheads.

I still laid there, motionless and detached from the discussion of the men in the kitchen, and the sound of the wind outside. At times like this, reflecting on all of the activity and stress of the past week, I missed the quietness of my mountain home.

Reverend Ekland spoke to Edwyn and Albert. "Well, I must be heading back to the parsonage and see how Madelyn and Muriel are doing."

A moment later, I heard him mount his carriage and speak to his horse at the front of the house. Next was the sound of the horse's hooves clicking and the carriage wheels rolling on the cobbles. The street sounds disappeared and my attention returned to the kitchen.

"I think I'll take a cup of tea to Michael," Edwyn said to Albert. "He's sleeping late and must've had a lot on his mind when he went to bed last night."

Not wanting to engage in conversation with anyone, I rolled over and faced the wall. Edwyn entered my room, stood silently for a moment, and then set the teacup down on the small table at the head of my bed. It was merely inches from my pillow. My mouth was dry. I imagined the taste of the inviting tea.

He returned to the kitchen. "The poor man's still sound asleep," he said to Kline.

"You're right to let him sleep," responded Albert. "George has been resting quite a bit lately because of his injured wrist."

I turned and took a sip of the tea and set the cup back down. *My bed and blanket are so cozy and warm. It's cold outside.* I pulled the blanket over my head. *It feels so good.*

I must've fallen asleep. I was now laying on my back and the smell of soup, fresh bread, and cut up apples drifted into my room from the kitchen. Leaning up on one elbow, I reached for the tea that Edwyn had brought me. It was ice cold but I was awakened by its distinctive flavor and the coolness in the room.

Laying back down and rolling over onto my stomach, my arm once again hung over the side of my bed.

What's that? I felt the fir on the back Eutychus' head. He sighed and licked my hand. I moved my hand and felt the cudgel. Sticky. Eutychus had been licking it.

Joseph's blood. Gruesome thought.

Beside it, my belt, sheath knife, and the bag with the two arrowheads lay on the floor. I reached inside the bag and felt the tips of the two dangerously sharp arrowheads.

Arrows! The thought struck me. *Caine will need arrows. He will need to buy or steal some.* My mind was flooded with questions. *How could he get some? He can't make any proper arrows while he's in hiding. He couldn't turn his own long straight shafts or perfectly affix the feathers. He can't forge his own arrowheads.*

My questions broadened. *Could he hunt for food without being seen? Where could he have been hiding from Lord Warrington's men? Where was he in last night's storm?*

Abruptly, I sat upright, found my trousers, and rushed into the kitchen still doing up my belt. Louisa and Brynne were there at the stove preparing a meal.

"Good morning, ladies. Have I almost missed breakfast? Where's Edwyn, I need to speak to him?"

Brynne laughed.

"Missed breakfast?" exclaimed Louisa. "We're preparing lunch and Edwyn's been in his workshop for three hours."

I pulled on my boots, hurried through the mud, and burst into his shop. "Arrows! Robert Caine needs arrows."

Edwyn, working at a foot operated lathe, immediately stopped. A quizzical look appeared on his face and then it dawned on him. "You're right. I'll send word to the captain of the guard."

"Let's also send for Albert Kline and a couple of his warehouse workers," I said. "It might be some time before the captain sends men to the arrowsmith's shop."

He set his chisel down and went around to the porch. I followed close behind.

One of the warehouse workers was passing by and Edwyn asked him to fetch Albert Kline. The worker took off running towards the warehouse.

The same attractive servant girl that had been at Warrington Hall the night before was riding past on a runty sway-back horse. She had a couple of bags of kitchen provisions tied onto a frame behind her. She was presumably returning to Warrington Hall with provisions needed for the kitchen. I called her over as Edwyn scrawled a note about Caine needing to obtain arrows. I gave it to her and made it clear that Lord Warrington's captain of the guard must be given the note.

"Yes, Mr. Sterling," she said. "I'll make sure that he gets it."

"Hurry now. It's vitally important. What's your name, by the way?" asked Edwyn as she turned away, about to trot up the street.

"Carolyn. I'll get it to him as fast as I can." She dug her heels into her horse's sides and its pace quickened to a gallop.

Edwyn looked at me, tipped his head on an angle, and blinked slowly. "That young girl is one of the Lord's finest works of art."

I smiled. "That, she surely is—"

"I know her," Brynne interjected as she stepped out onto the porch with a big tray of food and tea. "She's sixteen, and she lives with her aunt and older brother in a little home beyond the lighthouse. When she's not up at Warrington Hall, she's taking care of them."

"Does her brother have a job?" asked Edwyn.

"He's a fisherman, but she told me that he left for Carlisle a few days ago and won't be back for a month or more."

Edwyn was beginning to understand. "Ahh, I've never met her brother, but her aunt has lived down the road beyond the lighthouse for several years, right?"

"Yes, Daddy. Carolyn and her brother moved here from Briercrest Village a few months ago to stay with their old aunt when their mother died. Her father left the family when she was little. It's a family that has faced one misery after another."

Brynne returned inside as Albert arrived at Edwyn's porch. She came back out a minute later with my warm shirt and my coat. I still hadn't taken the time to get fully dressed.

"Thanks, Brynne. You're priceless." She gave me a sweet smile, put her warm hand on my bare shoulder as she passed behind me, and went back into the house.

"Well now, Michael, are you getting dressed on the porch these days?" quipped Albert.

I smirked and finished buttoning my shirt as Edwyn explained to him Caine's need of arrows.

"I'll set up several men to watch the arrowsmith's shop," he said as he left.

Louisa stepped out, gave Eutychus a huge bone, and returned inside. Edwyn, Eutychus, and I enjoyed our lunch together, slurping, chewing, and smacking.

"Tell Louisa that this is the best soup I've ever tasted. It's fortifying and the black pepper in it makes it come to life. This bread is the best I've had in months." I bit off a large piece of it.

Edwyn wiped his mouth with a cotton handkerchief. "The spicy pork ribs are my favorite. A man could live through anything if he could have a rack of these ribs each day."

The sound of our smacking and lip licking continued and anyone passing by would've thought that we hadn't eaten for a week.

"Is there any word on how Madelyn is?" I asked.

"Reverend Ekland was here several hours ago and said that she was upset but starting to come to terms with it."

"Part of me wants to go over and spend an hour or so with her."

"Sometimes, Michael, it's best to let people ask for help on their own."

"Maybe you're right. I should let her have some time to herself."

I started tearing the savory meat from a rib with my teeth but Joseph Caine, with his missing teeth, came to mind. I couldn't finish tearing it from the bone and tossed it to Eutychus.

Out in the harbor, the dismal grey was being swept away and shards of sunlight were cutting through the clouds. The sea gulls and terns had started their wheeling overhead and some shore birds were moving along the edge of the harbor.

"Michael, are you interested in skidding that maple log to the lumber mill with me?"

"Sure. I'll be glad to help."

We finished eating and as we stood to take our bowls into the kitchen, our eyes were filled with a shocking sight.

A badly weather-beaten, three-masted barque limped into the harbor, having suffered greatly in last night's gale. The mizzen mast, with its ripped sail, was busted part way up, and hung there like a bird's damaged wing. The foremast was

We Both Shall Row, My Love And I

intact and properly rigged but leaning awkwardly. The spars of the mainmast were in place but only carried the remnants of several ripped sails. Cargo, strewn on the deck, was being repositioned and secured by the crew, and the helmsman was having a control problem with the rudder.

"Look at that, Edwyn." My jaw dropped. "They've been through a vicious maelstrom."

"Let's forget about skidding that big maple log and hurry down to the waterfront. They need a lot of repairs. Maybe we can get a woodworking job."

"You've got that right." I wiped my mouth.

We left our dirty dishes where they were and hurried down to the main dock. Edwyn, with paper and pencil in hand, was ready to take any woodworking orders he could get, and I was at his side. The ship staggered towards the dock where Lord Warrington's Bristol-bound stacks of lumber awaited shipment. Without such a favorably directed breeze, they would've needed to tug it in with a long boat. The ship's name, *Eleutheran Quest*, in bright yellow lettering on a dark green background, puzzled me.

An odd name, Eleutheran Quest. I know of the name, Eleuthera, I've heard it, but I wonder what it means."

Two men and a woman arrived from the sail loft to see what new sails they could sell and what damaged sails they could repair. With them, we were amongst the first to arrive on the dock, but not before Tommy with one of his young soup vendors.

"Mr. Sterlin' sir," said Tommy. "'tis an excitin' time to be seein' people lined up, ready to make some good coin."

"You there, you men on the dock," a seamen shouted. "Grasp this line, draw the hawser, and secure it to bollard." He cast a weighted lanyard onto the dock. Men grasped it and pulled a heavier line towards themselves.

As the ship was drifting its last few feet in towards the dock, a cook leaned out of a large porthole with a cast iron pot. Having meant to dump out some dishwater, the pot slipped from his hands, hit the water on its side, filled, and instantly sank.

"Looks like salvage to me!" shouted Tommy. He dove into the water between the ship and the dock, with only inches to spare.

"Stop!" I shouted. Edwyn grabbed me as I lunged towards the edge.

"He'll be crushed!" yelled an old salt.

"He'll drown for sure," sighed another.

The ship bumped the dockside and then eased back a foot. The crowd was speechless.

"The poor boy's gone to meet his maker," cried an old woman.

Everyone held their breath. Some dockhands uncoiled and lifted the hawsers as several men pried at the ship with a timber, easing it further out.

"I dropped the cursed pot," shouted Tommy, out of sight from below the edge of the dock.

Leaning over the edge, I got sight of his feet, following his inverted body downwards once again.

Several in the crowd gasped.

"Ahh, no," moaned a young mother as she clutched more closely the toddler on her hip.

There was silence as we waited. Up came some large bubbles. Our waiting continued. Up came some smaller bubbles.

"Blimey, that was tight!" shouted Tommy as he surfaced with the pot in his hands.

Everyone applauded.

He looked around. "Why's everyone cheerin'?"

The crowd laughed, and many shook their heads and rolled their eyes. A couple of men pulled him out of the water as he clutched his prize.

As soon as his feet landed on the dock, an old salt, seeing the barnacle scratches on his back and shoulders, berated him for his reckless behavior. "You could've been crushed."

Tommy looked sheepish at being ridiculed but confidently clung, white knuckled, to the pot.

The cook looked back out of the porthole. "Pass the pot o'er here, that be ship's property."

The captain of the ship, leaning over from topside, bellowed, "No such thing, cookie! Any man whose fool enough to risk his life for an iron pot deserves to keep it."

The ship's cook slammed the porthole shut and everyone laughed and cheered again.

"Tommy, go and see Muriel Ekland and get some of her special aloe salve for those deep scratches," ordered Edwyn.

"Yes sir, Mr. Brixton sir," he replied.

The ship was secured to the dock. The gangplank was swung out and set in place, and Harbor Master Langley, followed closely by his assistant, ascended to meet the ship's captain on the deck.

A moment later, the ship's sailing master, Master Powell, followed by the master shipwright strode down the gangplank. Powell introduced the master shipwright and addressed the onlookers of Oak Harbor. "This here master shipwright has the confidence of the captain and myself and he is deserving of your respect. He speaks for the captain and will be seeking skilled workers of integrity." "Thank you, Master Powell," said the shipwright. "Carpenters, here on my right." He gestured with a swing of his arm. "Sailmakers, on my left. I need a glazier for some broken windows and a smithy for some iron straightenin'."

He gave a detailed list of the ship's sail needs to the sail makers and sternly said, "Look at this here list carefully, divide up the work yourselves, and give me an honest price or we'll do the repairs ourselves."

"We need a lot o' finished lumber and some quality woodworkin'," he declared. You'll all make good money but I've got a serious question first." He paused dramatically and looked at the eager laborers on the dock. "The top o' the mizzen mast, as you can see, broke, and its tip, coming down like Poseidon's trident, pierced the captain's skylight and speared its way right into his cabin." He swung his arm towards the damage up on the deck. "It smashed his navigational desk and split asunder a fine cabinet beneath that." Once again, he paused dramatically. "Be honest with me now. Who does your finest woodwork in this here seaport?"

The carpenters looked at Edwyn, one of them pointed, and another said, "He's the one. Edwyn does all of the fine work for the nobility in this part o' Cumberland."

Edwyn stepped forward. "I'd be glad to look at the captain's damaged cabinetry. Would you be able to show me to his cabin?"

The head shipwright addressed the captain's steward. "Mr. Tibbins take this here cabinet maker down to Captain Henderson's quarters. Let him take a look at the damage."

Edwyn followed Tibbins and I in turn followed them.

We spent at least an hour there. We moved things about and surveyed the damage as the men, working above us, hoisted the top of the mizzenmast, spear-like as it was, back upwards through the captain's skylight.

Edwyn had me make careful notes as he dictated his observations, measurements, and plans. With permission, we emptied the smashed cabinet of its contents onto the captain's dining table and set the larger busted pieces of the woodwork out on the floor to examine how it had been made. The cabinet was perhaps three feet long, left to right, two feet high, and two feet deep from front to back. The navigational desk, which had been positioned atop it, was likewise worthless. They had been a matching set of beautifully made French furniture pieces, but were now, nothing more than a depressing, mangled pile of splinters and unusable larger fragments.

Edwyn shook his head and winced. "Mr. Tibbins, you do understand that this isn't repair work. It's definitely a replacement job. There is no part of this cabinet that isn't ruined and that's true also for the navigational desk."

"Yes, I'm sure that is to be expected. I'll tell the captain."

Edwyn looked Tibbins in the eye and tapped his papers with his measuring rod. "I'll be expecting fair payment for work well done."

Tibbins nodded and pursed his lips. "Of course. The captain is a generous man for work expertly done. One expects to pay well for quality craftsmanship."

Later, as we approached the Brixton home, having carried some of the broken pieces of cabinetry along with us, we saw Reverend Ekland waiting out front on his gig.

"How's Madelyn?" I asked.

"She's improving. We've been talking and I think that she's grasping that her late husband's problems were his own, not hers. They mustn't be allowed to control her life here in the present."

"That's the truth," said Edwyn.

Pastor Ekland put his hand on my shoulder. "The long sleep did her a world of good and Muriel made her some calming tea. Of course, we've also been supporting her in prayer."

He looked at the broken pieces of cabinetry that we had set down on the porch floor and touched one with the toe of his shoe. "It looks like you've been down to the dock securing work for the *Eleutheran Quest*."

"That's right Reverend," responded Edwyn.

My brow furrowed. "What does the word 'Eleuthera' mean?"

Reverend Ekland, at great length, explained that it was a New Testament Greek word meaning *freedom*. He told us how some puritans in the seventeenth century, people of a sincere faith like ourselves, were suffering persecution in Bermuda. They hired a ship, fled the island, and headed south. They arrived at a beautiful island in the Bahamas and named it Eleuthera.

I reflected on what he had said and felt odd that he had included me in his statement about people *like ourselves* having a sincere faith. I didn't think that my faith was as strong as his or Edwyn's.

Reverend Ekland then returned to his purpose in coming and faced me directly. "When I was leaving the parsonage on my way to the lighthouse to play chess with Stephen Lyon, Muriel asked me to stop and see you."

"Yes, Reverend. Is there a message, sir?"

"We'd like you to stay for lunch after church on Sunday. Madelyn would like to have some time with you."

Edwyn, having grasped that the conversation was of a more personal nature, shifted a few steps away, sat down, and petted Eutychus.

"I'd truly appreciate that."

"That's wonderful. Madelyn will be so pleased."

A moment later, Albert Kline arrived at the porch riding Pilgrim. "I'm on my way up to Warrington Hall to find out why the captain's soldiers never arrived to watch the arrowsmith's shop."

"Why would men need to watch the arrowsmith's shop?" asked the reverend.

Edwyn and I explained Caine's need of arrows to him, and upon hearing that, he stroked his chin with his knuckle. "Hmm, yes. A definite possibility and an excellent idea."

"Albert, I could take a message up to the captain of the guard," he suggested. "I could always play chess with Stephen later."

"That's not necessary, Reverend," he responded. "I'll be delivering and installing a marble table top with my men in a few weeks and need to do some measuring."

Albert left, and Reverend Ekland pulled a piece of dried beef from his pocket and gave it to Eutychus. He climbed aboard his gig and headed up the street towards the lighthouse.

Edwyn and I went around the side of the house to his shop and began the work for the ship. We worked all day and into the evening, barely taking time for a quick dinner.

I slept well that night knowing that I would be seeing Madelyn in only two days. *She loves me and I love her. I will give her all the support that she needs.*

Saturday morning was glorious. The sun was shining. I was well rested and awoke to the sound of the Brixton family laughing uncontrollably in the kitchen. Between their bouts of laughter, I grasped that Brynne had accidentally spilled some black pepper onto Eutychus' head as the big mastiff pushed passed her while she worked at the stove. He was sneezing, rubbing his nose, and walking backwards all over the house.

When I reached the breakfast table, they were still laughing and with one look at his hilarious antics, I was gripped with it as well. Humorous contagion, pure and simple.

Brynne and I, pitying the poor animal, finally grabbed hold of him and took him out to the rain barrel at the back of the house. With a bucket in her hand, while I held the powerful mastiff, Brynne began pouring water on his head and rubbing his face. Eutychus, shaking his head and knocking the bucket out of her hands, drenched her thoroughly. We were consumed with laughter. Out of respect for her, I tried to look away and not notice how her wet clothing clung to her feminine form.

Still laughing, with her dress dripping wet, she threatened to throw a bucket of water on me, and when I let go of Eutychus to grab for the bucket, he dashed away. The huge mastiff ran back into the house and proceeded to shake himself; water, slobber, and fur were flung about the kitchen. Brynne then grabbed him by the neck and led him out the front door. He continued his shaking and then finally walked in a tight circle, curled up beside Edwyn's rocker, and promptly fell asleep.

With the old mastiff quietly relaxing on the porch and Brynne returning to the table after changing her dress, we settled down to a delicious breakfast. Everyone was in high spirits until Edwyn spoke of Tommy's pot salvaging adventure.

When Louisa heard of the danger that nearly cost Tommy his life, she was aghast and put the responsibility squarely on Edwyn. She scolded him for not having stopped him, not realizing how quickly Tommy had dove into the water.

There was a period of uncomfortable silence. Edwyn cleared his throat. "Well Michael, we made a fine start yesterday on the captain's cabinet. Let's take a break from that kind of fine work and skid the great maple I was telling you about to the sawmill. It needs to be cut and shedded for drying."

"Sounds good to me."

"Don't get hurt, Daddy." Brynne put her hand on her father's shoulder.

He reached across his chest and put his hand upon his daughter's, tapping it several times. "We'll be careful, sweetie."

I carried a couple of broad axes over my shoulder and off we went to the stables. Edwyn, promising a load of firewood for the use of a skid and a team of horses, struck a deal with the stable owner. A few minutes later, we were leading a matched pair of huge, sandy colored shire horses through town and up the hillside, to where he had chopped down the great maple.

We arrived at it and trimmed away the smaller branches, and proceeded to cut the thirty-foot tree trunk into three ten-foot logs. Moving them, even with a block and tackle, wasn't easy, but after some effort, we secured them in pyramidal fashion, one laying atop the lower two, on the skid. We began skidding the load with the powerful team of horses down the hill.

I offered Edwyn a drink from my canteen when we had a short rest partway down the slope. "Sometimes I have the impression that we are being watched," I said.

He leaned back against the huge logs on the skid and looked up and down the hillside. "Are you worried about Caine?" he asked.

"Somewhat. In a situation like this, with him being a formidable bowman and us out here busy with our work, he could drop us like deer." My mind went back to Owen Harcourt dying in my arms.

"Michael." He laughed uncomfortably. "You're giving me the shivers talking like this."

A branch snapped. We froze and listened, hearing only our heartbeats.

I pointed towards a cluster of bushes beside a little meadow, and whispered, "The sound is coming from there."

We slowly crouched down and continued to listen.

Edwyn picked up one of the axes. "There's someone moving towards us," he whispered.

Another branch snapped and a pheasant flew up from the little meadow. Eutychus came out from behind a tree. Looking at one another and taking a few deep breaths, we laughed in nervous fear.

We continued driving the horses and when we reached the first muddy lane at the edge of town, one of Kline's men stopped us. He was on his way home, having finally been relieved at the arrowsmith's shop by another one of Kline's workers. He said that the captain of the guard still hadn't sent any of his soldiers down to the shop. It was assumed that he hadn't gotten the note from Carolyn.

That was odd. She seemed so reliable and trustworthy when I saw her at Warrington Hall.

When the logs had been skidded to the lumber mill, Edwyn gave the sawyer his specifications about cutting, asking that all the sapwood edge cuts be kept for firewood. The drying details were clear as well: in a shed, dry against the weather, on a level platform with one-inch sticks between layers, and well-spaced for sufficient airflow.

We returned the horses and the skid to the stables and went back to Louisa's kitchen for lunch. As we ate, we told Louisa and Brynne how Eutychus had frightened us in the forest and they had a good laugh.

The ladies cleared the table and we resumed our cabinetry work for the *Eleutheran Quest*.

About twenty minutes into the work, Edwyn abruptly stopped, laid his coping saw down, and said, "It's so strange that Carolyn hadn't given the note to the captain of the guard."

"It is odd," I agreed. "She's not a simpleton. Maybe she was distracted by something or someone."

We resumed our work on the cabinet replacement and the subject never came up again.

~~~~~~

Later that night, I continued reading Captain Bridger's adventurous journal but just before midnight, I was disturbed by some noises behind the house. Something was knocked over near the rain barrel and that was immediately followed by the sound of a few quick footsteps. I jumped up and hurried to the window but saw nothing. The wind had increased and perhaps something was blown over. I was greatly fatigued and it started to drizzle. I opened the door and peaked out. *It's nothing. I'm not going out in the cold rain. I'll just bolt the door.*

What a beautiful day of work and domestic life in the Brixton home it had been. *Someday, a loving family life will be mine. Tomorrow will be a new day and I will spend much of it with my lovely Madelyn.*

The Harborside

Much like the previous Sunday, the Brixtons and I strolled along the harborside. Eutychus, like last week, stopped to smell every tree and every patch of grass, wondering if his Irish Princess had passed by. I stopped for a moment to watch a mother duck with her ducklings swimming in the backwater pool near the bridge, but the Brixtons continued on their way. Brynne, seeing that I was alone, slowed her pace that she might walk with me.

We did so, but in silence, until she shared a few curious observations. "Michael, do you know that my mother was only eighteen when she married my father?"

"I didn't know that."

"That's only one year older than me," she said. "And father was twenty."

"I didn't know that either."

"That's five years younger than you."

"You have wonderful parents."

"Eight years is all that separates us, Michael, in age I mean, and when—"

Our conversation was interrupted by Tommy and a number of the boys from Madelyn's Sunday School class rushing up the street towards us.

271

Tommy, playing the role of blinded Samson, stood between two small trees, wincing and moaning, with one hand on each tree, as if chained.

"O Lord God, remember me!" Tommy declared dramatically. "Strengthen me, I pray, that I may be avenged of these Philistines for my two eyes." Grimacing and flexing his muscles, he began to strain slowly. Shaking even more and seeming to push the trees outwards, all of the boys around him made crashing noises, collapsed in agony, and then abruptly became silent.

"Well, boys," I said. "It's apparent that Madelyn's lesson for you was about Samson and Delilah, and the armies that defied the Lord."

"That be it, Mr. Sterlin' sir. Madelyn says the book o' Judges, the sixteenth chapter, is full o' truth."

The boys jumped to their feet and were off, running up the street towards the bridge, peeling off their shirts as they ran. I caught a glimpse of the scratches on Tommy's back from his adventure in retrieving the iron pot.

Next, several young girls came walking up the street. "That Delilah," one of them said. "How could she treat her husband like that? Samson should've never married her."

"It's appropriate," I said to Brynne, "that there are girls in the class as well."

"Yes it is," she replied. "Next week, I'll ask Madelyn if she needs help with the class. We who are *older*, should be guiding those who are younger."

"You're right. Marvelous idea."

She stopped to pet Eutychus. He had curled up under his favorite tree near the water's edge in front of the church. We entered to the sound of Muriel playing the pump organ triumphantly. Edwyn and Louisa were already seated near the front and Brynne went and joined them, but I lagged behind and sat in the back row.

A moment later, Madelyn, with a vibrant smile, slid in beside me and took my hand. "I could hardly sleep last night thinking of seeing you today. How's your waist?" she asked.

"It was only a scratch. I'm fine."

"Let me have a little peek. Wounds need careful attention."

It was a warm day and I wore my waistcoat without my jacket. I gently pulled my shirt out of my trousers, near the wound, and lifted the bottom of my waistcoat. She peaked under the edge of the bandage. "You're right, it's healing well." She had a tiny jar of Muriel's salve and carefully dabbed some on the wound before putting the bandage back in place.

Deacon Scott, having arrived back the previous day accompanied by Mr. Wood and Lorena from Stone Ridge, stood at the front. "Let's stand together and sing Amazing Grace."

While singing, I glanced around the congregation and saw a visiting Chinese family that were smiling and worshipping with great enthusiasm. In London, at the churches, shops, and sporting events, it was not unusual to see people of other races from the far ends of the British Empire. Here, in these little northern towns, visitors of other races were seldom seen.

After the hymn, Deacon Scott welcomed the visitors and made special mention of the Chinese family. "A special welcome to you, Mr. and Mrs. Chen, and also to your lovely daughter, Meiling." The father and mother, with their beautiful daughter, stood and smiled broadly. Clutching their Bibles, they looked around the church, receiving the warm greetings of those present. Their sense of inclusion in God's family was evident.

I later discovered that they were from the *Eleutheran Quest*. Mr. Luke Chen, a trusted employee and longtime friend of the captain, was a superb navigator. Gloria, his wife, along with their twenty-year-old daughter, worked aboard the ship, usually helping the cook or the steward.

Deacon Scott, with his expressively masculine voice, said, "The Chen family are with us today and this reminds me so clearly of the ninth verse in the fifth chapter of the book of Revelation, as heaven rejoices and sings a new song to the Lord; "For thou wast slain, and hast redeemed us to God by thy blood out of every kindred, and tongue, and people, and nation."

"Amen," said Reverend Ekland. "God's family is made up of people from all around the world."

It was a vibrant service that was filled with thanksgiving. The hymn singing was uplifting, the preaching was challenging, and the pastoral prayer was encouraging.

Myra's freedom, and the Lord having provided justice for the murder of Charles Hawthorne, was on everyone's mind, but there remained an undercurrent of sorrow and a shadow of concern; Owen Harcourt had lost his life and Robert Caine was believed to be still in the area, looking for revenge.

The main point of Reverend Ekland's sermon was that people reap what they've sown, but it was hard for me to focus, thinking of the time that I would be spending later with Madelyn.

The sermon text was verses seven and eight from the sixth chapter of Galatians:

> Be not deceived; God is not mocked: for whatsoever a man soweth, that shall he also reap. For he that soweth to his flesh shall of the flesh reap corruption; but he that soweth to the Spirit shall of the Spirit reap life everlasting.

We Both Shall Row, My Love And I

Reverend Ekland mentioned the various court sentences that would be placed upon the members of the Caine family. He reminded us that they had taken the life of Charles Hawthorne and having been arrested, were now facing the consequences of their own actions. He made it clear they were reaping what they had sown.

He spoke of Jesus' declaration on the night he was arrested in the garden of Gethsemane, that whoever lives by the sword, shall also die by the sword. Then, with his confident voice, he read verses fifty-one and fifty-two of the twenty-sixth chapter of Matthew's Gospel:

> And, behold, one of them which were with Jesus stretched out his hand, and drew his sword, and struck a servant of the high priest's, and smote off his ear. Then said Jesus unto him, Put up again thy sword into its place: for all they that take the sword shall perish with the sword.

Reverend Ekland went on to say that in the eighteenth chapter of the Gospel of John we discover that it was Peter who had cut off the ear of Malchus, the high priest's henchman.

Peter certainly was impetuous at times.

The sermon was heightening my personal sense of guilt about having beaten Joseph Caine, even though he attacked me with a sword.

Was it wrong for me to cudgel him? I'm not usually a violent man. I was obeying Lord Warrington's orders to capture the brigands. They murdered Hawthorne and abducted Myra. I'm glad that I stopped his escape, but I'm also glad that I didn't stomp on his face as I was tempted. If I had, when he was already down and helpless, that would've been wrong. *Someday, I'd like to know exactly what the Lord meant about "taking up the sword."*

My mind wandered to Madelyn's difficult life with Walter Haversham. *It was a painful memory for her. Like a sensitive tooth, hurting when you bite down on it. Having discovered the truth about Myra, as a constant reminder, she would be biting down on it a lot.*

Hmm, Walter Haversham was dead, probably by a jealous husband's hand. He reaped what he had sown, I suppose.

I think I missed much of the sermon because of my wandering thoughts.

Lunch with the Ekland family was satisfying and following it, Madelyn suggested that we go stroll around the harbor.

As we were about to leave, Pastor Ekland invited me into his study. "Have a seat." He gestured towards an old oak chair. "Madelyn has agreed to go and visit Elizabeth Harcourt with me later in the afternoon. It wouldn't be wise for a ministerial man, such as myself, to engage in a pastoral visit alone with a young woman. Would you be able to have Madelyn back in time this afternoon, please?"

"Yes, of course."

"Michael, you've played a significant part in the apprehension of the criminals and in freeing Myra and I'd like to inform you of some of the recent Caine family developments."

"I'd appreciate that, Pastor."

"Lord Warrington's magistrate has returned with the Crown judge, their cases have been heard, and the sentences have been pronounced."

"I heard that he'd returned but not about the sentences."

"Victor and Gavin would probably be hung in a week or so and Grand Freddie, being quite elderly, might die while serving his ten year prison sentence. It appears that although he hadn't been physically involved in the crimes, leaving that to the younger men, he had been a prime instigator and planner for carrying out their devilish plot." Reverend Ekland rested his elbows on his desk and made deliberate eye contact with me. "The Caine family is a family of damaged consciences."

My eyes narrowed. "These judicial sentences fit your sermon exactly. Did Walter Haversham's parents have anything to do with this?"

"Lord and Lady Haversham of Ridley knew nothing of this. The Caine family was hired by Walter when Myra was born. She was to be killed to prevent any claims against his future inheritance, and to eliminate personal embarrassment."

"The desire to hurt an innocent child..." I was speechlessly appalled. "I can't fathom it."

"Nor can I," agreed Reverend Ekland.

"How does Sabina fit into all of this?" I asked. "I've heard some positive things about her."

"Sabina could not bring herself to be a part of the killing of Myra, but she believed that if her family refused, Walter would simply hire someone else. She conspired to take Myra, remove her from the area, have her found, and then raised by a caring family."

"Was Myra's mother part of the conspiracy?"

"No, absolutely not. She simply went along with it. She was terrified of Walter Haversham and wanted to protect herself and her child. She would have come to see or be near Myra but she died the following year."

Thinking of Walter's hunting trips, the tartan ribbon, and the thistle etching on the knife, I asked, "Did all of this originate up in the Scottish highlands?"

"Exactly right."

"And why was Myra abducted now?" I asked.

"The Caine family abducted Myra with a plan to blackmail Lord Haversham."

"Pastor, how is Joseph Caine's jaw? I'm disappointed in myself that I injured him." I hesitated to finish the sentence. "With such…" Again, ashamed of myself, I hesitated. "With such cruelty."

"His jaw isn't healing well. The bone isn't setting straight. His collar bone isn't setting perfectly straight either."

"Was he sentenced?"

"He was given three years."

"Three years! Why only three?"

"He convinced the Crown judge that his older brothers, Robert in particular, had forced him into it."

Madelyn knocked lightly on the door. "Uncle Martin, is Michael in there with you?"

"Yes dear, we are having a few minutes together. He'll be out in a minute."

When I'd finished speaking with Reverend Ekland, Madelyn and I stepped out into the glorious sunlight and started our walk around the harbor. When we were in front of the church, she took my arm.

She has taken my arm. What might this mean? She doesn't mind being seen like this with me. Everyone will know that we're fond of each other.

"You're very quiet," she observed.

"Hmm, I was merely thinking about lunch, or something."

"Aunt Muriel's an expert cook," she said.

"Let's walk all the way around the harbor to the lighthouse. We can look at the Lyon brother's Irish wolfhound. I've never seen her, have you?" I asked.

"Not yet. Her name is Princess, right?"

"That's right. We can compare her with Eutychus in size and disposition."

I shared with Madelyn what Edwyn had said about the pick of the litter and how the puppies would be shared. As soon as she heard that, she said she wanted to buy one. The pick of the litter in fact.

When we got to the main dock, we saw that it was a beehive of activity. Mr. Chen, up on the deck of the the *Eleutheran Quest,* was pointing at something on a large map and having an animated discussion with the captain, almost spilling his cup of tea. After a few minutes, they shook their heads, had a grand laugh, and returned their attention to the map.

Other men were busy on the dock stacking timber, moving crates, coiling ropes alongside the ship, and four women were folding enormous sails.

Tommy, with one of his younger helpers, was selling soup to a few of the men, and Shannon was carrying a large tray, stacked with empty teacups and a few ale tankards back towards the Royal Stag. She smiled and said hello as we passed her, and we exchanged greetings with two other couples we met.

When we arrived at the Brixton home, deciding to take a break on our way to the lighthouse, we stepped up onto the porch. The family wasn't home except for Eutychus, curled up and sleeping.

Madelyn stooped to pet him. "Hello Eutychus. Where's your family?"

She petted the great mastiff's head. *She's always so affectionate and caring.* She clutched and stroked the furry folds on his massive neck and slid her hand along his side. *What would it be like for us to spend our lives together and raise a family?*

We sat in two of the well-worn chairs on the porch. My mind began to wander. Our walk around the harbor and sitting here with her warmed me, moving me greatly.

Madelyn will be a supportive and loving wife. A wonderful mother. We would build our happy home here, in Oak Harbor. Like Edwyn, I would work in the community. Our children would be loved; Madelyn would read the Bible to them and I would take them hiking through the forest. They would learn to love the great spreading hardwoods and the awe-inspiring rocky cliffs.

"You're being quiet again," she observed. "What are you thinking about this time?"

"You, Madelyn. I was thinking about you." I hesitated. "Actually, about you and me."

Madelyn was speechless. Smiling but quiet, with eyebrows raised quizzically.

I decided to express myself more fully. "Earlier, as we strolled along the other side of the harbor, when you asked me what I was thinking, I said I was thinking about how tasty Muriel's lunch was. I wasn't thinking about her lunch at all." I reached towards her and took her hand in mine. She responded by lovingly squeezing my hand.

She leaned towards me, smiling, her green eyes alive with expectation.

"I was thinking about you. It meant a lot to me for you to take my arm affectionately. Some women have difficulty showing affection publicly. You don't. People saw our fondness for each other and understand now," I paused, "that we are a couple."

She leaned back in her chair, looked intently at me, and sweetly blinked at me with both eyes. "Michael, I don't simply care for you and I'm not merely fond of you. I love you deeply and—"

Noisily, coming around the side of the house, Myra, Nicola, and Brynne appeared. They were laughing and teasing one another and creating quite a disturbance. Following along behind them, in a more mature fashion, came Lorena of Stone Ridge.

Myra and Nicola went straight ahead, across the cobbled street, to look at the harbor, and throw stones into the water.

Brynne and Lorena came up onto the porch, slid a couple of chairs towards us, forming a circle, and seated themselves.

Lorena searched my eyes with intensity. "Michael, I'm so thrilled to see you again. I wanted to speak to you," she said enthusiastically. "With the help of Lord Warrington and his men, you've done it. My little sister is free and unharmed." She smiled, unable to hold back tears of joy.

"It was actually more the other way around. Lord Warrington and his men, with help from me and some others in Oak Harbor, set her free."

"You're too modest," she responded, wiping her tears away with her hand. "Thank you so much." She confidently rose out of her chair, approached me, and leaned down over me. Her long, soft, scented hair fell upon my face and shoulders. She passionately embraced me and kissed me on my cheek.

Brynne mumbled something and went into the house. Madelyn sat quietly, observing.

Lorena straightened up in front of me. "My family and I are forever in your debt." She provocatively combed her fingers of both hands through her long dark hair. "We will be staying at Warrington Hall for a few days, maybe a week." She continued combing her fingers through her hair. "Perhaps we could go for a stroll."

"I've been quite busy lately working with Edwyn." I took a deep breath. "Why would you remain here instead of returning to Stone Ridge?"

"Lord Warrington has sent a courier to Ridley and he'd like us to remain here. The Havershams might like to meet Myra. She is, after all, their grand-daughter."

"Myra has become quite accustomed to life at Warrington Hall," I said. "It will be interesting to see what the future holds for her."

Myra and Nicola returned to the porch and laughing, I don't know at what, went into the house through the front door.

Lorena looked over at Madelyn and then back at me. "I better go and see if Mrs. Brixton needs any help cleaning up. Myra and I joined the Brixtons for lunch and the Warrington Hall carriage will be returning for us shortly."

When Lorena left the porch, we were alone. Neither of us spoke for a few minutes. It was an uncomfortable silence.

"She was appreciative," observed Madelyn sarcastically.

"Anyone would be, having a cherished little sister returned to them." I was concerned about her sarcasm.

"Have you known her long?"

"No, dear." Her stare worried me. "I only met her once, the night that Thomas Baumann asked me to bring word that Charles Hawthorne had been killed and that Myra had been abducted."

"And you've been thinking about her ever since, right?"

"No dear, not me."

I wanted to get off the subject of Lorena. "Madelyn, let's continue our walk to the lighthouse."

"Yes, let's," she said sternly.

She rose to her feet in front of me and mimicked Lorena perfectly, combing the fingers of both hands provocatively through her long auburn hair. She then lifted one shoulder, blinked her eyes slowly, and mimicked Lorena's voice and mannerisms perfectly. "Perhaps we could go for a stroll."

We both chuckled but my laughter was mixed with apprehension. I feared that I'd hear more of this.

From her pocket, she passed me a velvety dark green ribbon. "Michael, help me tie back my hair."

"You'll need to guide me. I've never helped a woman with her hair." She looked at me over her shoulder suspiciously. I was gripped with more apprehension. "I hope I don't mess it up."

"There's nothing to it. Slide the ribbon under my hair, high at the back of my neck, tie it tight, and then make a bow. Make sure the two sides of the bow are even."

She looked at her reflection in the front window of the Brixton home. "Not too bad for your first time." She giggled. "It won't be your last."

We stepped off the porch into the sunlight and walked along for a while, neither of us talking. *I can't believe she trusted me with her hair.*

"Michael, I think your contact with her was innocent, but I'm not too certain of her contact with you."

"Yes dear. Don't be worried."

Madelyn once again took my arm. "I was telling you how much I love you before we were interrupted."

"And I had just mentioned how much it meant to me that you would allow others to see us as a couple."

She laughed and took an even tighter grip of my arm, this time with both of her hands, and rested her head against my shoulder as we walked. "We are, after all, a couple."

"I love you, Madelyn."

She stepped in front of me, looked up at me with her eyes beaming, and reaching up to my shoulder, pulled my face down towards her own. She kissed me on the side of my mouth and said, "I taste your passion."

Surprised, I raised my eyebrows.

She then kissed me high on my right cheekbone, beneath my eye, and said, "I see your love for me."

Stunned, I blinked.

Lastly, she kissed my ear and whispered something that I couldn't quite hear.

Speechless, I wondered what might happen next.

"Michael, what are your intentions towards me?"

"I have the best of intentions towards you. I intend to remain here in Oak Harbor. I intend to get to know you better." I leaned down towards her and gently lifted her chin with my fingers. "I intend to—"

A sudden crash startled us, and from the forest beside the road, out bounded Princess, the huge Irish wolfhound, that we had heard so much about. Panting, she ran towards us and abruptly stopped, only a few feet away. Inching forward and reaching out with her nose, she smelled Madelyn's hand. She detected Eutychus' scent, and licking Madelyn's fingers, she glanced up the road toward the Brixtons' and sat down.

"You must be Princess," Madelyn said to the wolfhound, taking a deep breath. "Are you looking for your prince?" She dropped her hands to her side. "Michael, look at the size of her! She's even taller than Eutychus but not quite as heavily built."

John the Rotund came stumbling out of the forest, his boots splattered with mud and his tattered wool jacket covered with burrs. He invited us for tea and as we walked along together towards the lighthouse, Princess and Madelyn hurried along up ahead.

"So Michael, the keeper an' I would be 'appy to sell you that—"

Interrupting, I whispered, "Shh, John, keep your voice down."

In a quieter voice he repeated, "We would be 'appy to sell you the cleared 'ill that you be interested in. We decided upon a price of ten guineas."

"Here's a downpayment of four guineas," I mumbled, covering my mouth with my hand and slipping him the coins unseen. "Let's not talk about this now." I motioned towards Madelyn.

He whispered in return, "Oh, I'm seein' your meanin'. Another time then we'll 'ave our talk."

We Both Shall Row, My Love And I

Walking along a little further, we passed beneath the little cleared hill that we had spoken about, he pointed at it, and in a normal speaking voice said, "It's a wonderful site for 'n 'ouse."

"John, don't mention it," I whispered. "Stop pointing."

"Right. 'nother time then."

I wondered if I should show it to Madelyn on our return walk.

Too soon. We may have a future together, but it's simply too soon.

We arrived at the old lighthouse where the Lyon brothers live, and John welcomed us in for tea. He placed before us some biscuits and pastries as he put the kettle on to boil.

"Do you fancy these tasty pastries? Are they to your likin'?" he asked. "Tommy brought 'em from 'is sweet mom."

Madelyn took a bite. "Yes, they're quite delicious."

The Rotund told us all about Princess, who had run up the slope into the forest behind their home, when we entered the kitchen.

"Princess is much more active than Eutychus," observed Madelyn.

"Well Eutychus, 'e be a quieter breed. 'es more like your reserved elderly statesman." The Rotund took a big bite of biscuit. Crumbs dropped down the front of his sweater. "The mastiff, 'e be much older than me wolfhound. I'm to thinkin' there be eight or maybe nine years 'tween 'em."

"I understand." Madelyn was nodding and smiling. She was eager to speak about getting a puppy.

"We purchased 'er up in 'onister area from a slate man needin' money. She be but three years old and a fine animal." He took another bite of his crumbling cookie. "'er pups, they'll be somethin' to be'old."

"Will you be selling some of the puppies?" asked Madelyn.

"That's a cer'ainty. Little pups become big animals and they'd be eatin' us out o' 'ouse an' 'ome," he said, laughing heartily. "Our salary for light 'ouse keepin' would be lost to the sea breeze."

The three of us sat at John's kitchen table. Madelyn, looking serious and tapping the table with her index finger, asked, "John, would you promise me the largest as your pick of the litter?" She grinned and her eyes twinkled.

"Yes me dear, I would."

"Name your price," she said, giving the table a singular firm tap.

He thought about it for a moment. "Ten and six. Yes, that be fair. These pup's 'ill be a marvel if they be tall like Princess an' 'ave the mastiff's weight an' width at the shoulders."

"Are you sure your brother Stephen will accept the deal?" she asked.

"No doubt," replied The Rotund. "We be agreed, the first pick be mine and the third pick be 'is."

"Okay then, ten shillings and sixpence," she said. "Here's a down payment." She reached into her jacket pocket and pulled out a petite embroidered change purse. She found five shillings and sixpence and slid the coins across the table.

"Only five shillin's remainin'. Thank you, missy."

"No." She playfully waved her index finger and nodded. "Thank you, John. I know I'll be happy with the puppy. Of that, I'm sure."

John scooped up the coins. "It's set then." He struck the table with his flat palm. "The pick o' the litter, it be yours."

"John, could I change the subject for a moment? May I ask you a question?"

"Ask away."

"You know that I'm motivated to learn all that I can in life. Tell us how the Argand lamp got its name and a bit about your lighthouse work."

He told us that the lamp was invented by a man named Argand in 1782.

"O' course, our light'ouse burnin' oil, with the tube for air, be much brighter than the old one 'ere or the one at Saint Bees 'eadland, they both bein' only coal on a tray."

Then, at length, he shared with us how he and his brother manage their lighthouse work.

He and his brother would usually divide the preparation work and the night monitoring so that one would be working while the other slept. His brother, the keeper, had a preference for being awake a larger portion of the night while John preferred more of the afternoon preparations and monitoring until about midnight. The keeper would then wake up and begin his monitoring shift until sunrise when he would shut down the light.

John decided that he better be heading over to the lighthouse to meet his responsibilities. He called Princess to go with him, and she boisterously bounded in through the kitchen door.

Madelyn petted the tall wolfhound. "Can I take her outside for a bathing and brushing?"

"Oh missy," he responded. "That'd be a blessing. It's a chore with most dogs, but Princess, she loves to be bathed and brushed. Still she stands, an' no fussin'."

John reached into a cupboard near the door and searched until he found a grooming brush. Searching a little deeper in the cupboard, he found a package of soap from James Keir's factory in Tipton near Dudley. "Madelyn dear, use a wee bit o' this. It'll be wondrously good for 'er coat."

Madelyn was pleased with the soap. "She'll be so clean that you may not recognize her. She'll look like the Princess that she truly is."

"When you be finished with 'er, 'efore you leave, would you be so kind to bring 'er to me at the light 'ouse? Me brother, 'e be shoppin' now an' returnin' shortly for 'is sleep. I'd 'ate to see 'is sleepin' disturbed."

"Of course, John," she replied.

I went outside with them, and sitting in the shade of a great hardwood, watching Madelyn groom her was a treat. The wolfhound enjoyed the pampering and Madelyn enjoyed the opportunity to transform a rugged looking animal into the impressive matriarch that she would soon become. Her dull grey coat took on a silvery sheen. She looked like canine nobility.

"Madelyn, I can't believe the way you've transformed her."

"I often helped the groomers and trainers with the Haversham dogs, but they had smaller breeds."

"You're a multi-faceted lady with many skills. That I can see."

"Thank you, my love." She looked at Princess and said, "Hmm, just one more finishing touch." She took the velvety dark green ribbon from her hair and tied it around Princess's neck. "Now she truly looks like royalty."

"Amazing. The Rotund's going to be quite impressed."

"Michael, can I mention something to you?"

"Sure, go ahead." Again, I felt some apprehension.

"Please don't take offence at this, but I think that we should encourage people to use his real name, John Lyon." Madelyn pulled some matted hair out of the brush. "Belinda Atwater told me a few days ago, privately, that it hurts him when people call him The Rotund. Michael, he's a good man and we should call him John."

I reflected on what she was sharing. "I've wondered about that myself from time to time. Thanks for mentioning it. I'll call him John."

We took Princess over to the lighthouse and when he saw her, his jaw dropped. "She be a blue blood aristocrat!" He scratched the top of her head and gave her a great hug. "A princess, that be the truth."

The wolfhound, with her tail wagging profusely, thriving on John's affection, licked his hands and his face.

When we returned to Edwyn's porch, we stopped to visit Eutychus. The mastiff lifted his head, walked over to Madelyn, sniffed a few times, and began licking her hands.

"I feel like a secret courier carrying love letters," she said, laughing.

Joining in her laughter, I shook my head. "Look at his madly wagging tail." Eutychus then went and stood on the top step to see if his true love might be coming for a visit.

Just as I was getting concerned that he might run off to his lover, Louisa stepped out with a large bone and gave it to him. He laid down with it between his paws for a serious chew.

"Hello," Louisa said. "I see you've been on a walk."

"We spent some time with John and his wolfhound at the lighthouse," I responded.

"Brynne's not feeling well. She's been in her room much of the afternoon."

"I hope it's nothing serious," said Madelyn. "Perhaps she only needs a good rest."

"I think you're right," agreed Louisa. "A sleep, both deep and long, will be a blessing."

"Louisa, I'm walking Madelyn to the parsonage and will be back in about an hour."

"I'll tell Edwyn," she responded. "He'll be home by then. He wanted to speak to you about some of the cabinetry on the damaged ship."

"I'll be back soon."

We exchanged our goodbyes with Louisa and continued our walk back around the harbor. Madelyn took my arm. It was wonderful. We arrived back at the parsonage but only had a few minutes to sit at the water's edge, knowing that Madelyn's uncle would soon leave for Elizabeth's home.

Sitting side by side, I put my arm around her and she leaned into my shoulder.

"I've had a blessed day," she confessed. "Such a contrast to the trauma of Thursday night and Friday when I was so downcast. It was like a grey veil had been thrown over a painting of a sunny summer day. Now, the veil's removed."

"I wanted to come and see you," I said. "But after talking to Edwyn, I decided to provide you with some privacy. I knew that if you wanted to see me, you'd have sent for me."

"Thank you, Michael. By mid-afternoon on Saturday, the sunlight started to break through in my heart, when I found the courage to pray about this whole situation."

"I guess the Lord helped you." I turned to face her, angled my head, and kissed her soft cheek.

We could hear Reverend Ekland in the stable preparing Shadow and the gig. She leaned into me again and we sat there for a few minutes more.

We stood as Reverend Ekland led Shadow out of the stable.

"Hello, Uncle Martin," said Madelyn.

"Good afternoon, dearie. Would you be able to accompany me now to Elizabeth's home?"

"Yes, Uncle."

Reverend Ekland was only steps away, but Madelyn must've been in the mood to declare her love for me by her actions. She went up on the tips of her toes and kissed me on my cheek as I leaned down towards her.

She'll be forever surprising me. This time her right hand secretly slipped inside my opened waistcoat and I was stirred by her warm hand against my side. Her fingertips moved along several of my ribs.

I was a bit startled. "I'll see what work..." I forgot what I was about to say, thinking only of her warm hand and her fingertips. "What... hmm, what work Edwyn has for me, but I know that the next few weeks there will be a lot to do. I want to start earning more than merely my keep at the Brixtons."

"That's understandable," she responded.

"I'm saving it up for something special for someone I love."

She looked up at me, brushed some hair away from her face, and had a playful grin. "Sounds mysterious."

The Cleared Lot

The next several weeks developed into a regular pattern: working with Edwyn most days, enjoying domestic life with the Brixton family, and spending time with Madelyn a few evenings each week. The regular highlight, though, was Sunday.

We would have a meaningful time at Fair Havens Church, have lunch with the Eklands, and then have a more personal time with one another. We'd stroll and end up at the lighthouse, where Madelyn would spend time with Princess, or we'd practice our instruments together in the church. Other times we'd simply sit, enjoy each other's company, and discuss things with one another.

I got to know her more deeply, discovering her interests and exploring her opinions. We both hated slavery, cherished justice, appreciated music, and enjoyed people. My love of nature was greater than hers, but her understanding of what it meant to have a relationship with God and apply His Word was much deeper than mine. Our love for one another grew stronger.

One Sunday afternoon, weeks later, we were sitting at the harbor's edge, Madelyn was holding my arm, and I realized that I had made a decision. It was time to show her the building lot and speak to her about our future.

"Madelyn, there's something that I would like to show you."

She chuckled. "I wonder what that might be. Some interesting woodworking project or maybe a scenic trail in the forest I suppose."

"Nothing quite like that. Let's go for a walk."

We strolled around the harbor, passing all the well-known places and all the familiar faces. I was determined to have nothing distract us from our walk. We saw some boys jumping into the river from the bridge, but we didn't stop to watch. We saw John Lyon about to enter the harbor master's office. He stopped on the top step as if to start a conversation, but we merely said hello and continued on our way. We saw Brynne, her father, and Eutychus in the distance returning from the forest and heading our way. We didn't wait for them but kept walking.

As we passed the bottom of the lane leading up to Warrington Hall, Madelyn stopped and pointed up the slope, high above the trees. "There's our pedestal, in the distance beside the waterfall."

"You're right," I responded. "It was a wonderful hike. It was the first time we were alone together."

Madelyn laughed and said, "Remember when you put the flowers in my crown of ivy and knelt before me?"

"You knighted me."

Madelyn looked at me with a twinkle in her eye. "Maybe sometime soon we can go up the country lane to the south, like we said we would."

"Let's do that."

"It's a tiring uphill climb much of the way," she responded, dramatically looking exhausted. "Let's ask Uncle Martin if we can use one of his carriages and we'll take a picnic basket."

"Two great ideas. It'll be a wonderful day."

We walked on a little farther and Madelyn asked, "So, where's this thing that you want to show me?"

"Right here." I pointed to the small hill, cleared of trees, about thirty feet above where we were standing. "Come with me."

Taking her hand, I led her up the little hill and when we reached the top, we sat side by side on a large flat rock, overlooking the harbor.

Madelyn looked confused. "You wanted to show me the harbor? I've seen it before." She chuckled. " I live straight across the harbor from here." She pointed at the parsonage across the water.

"I wanted to show you this clearing."

It wasn't enormous, perhaps only two hundred feet across, but it was wonderfully positioned at the end of a small ridge, protruding out from the oak forest.

"This is a pleasant little picnic spot." She stood and walked a few paces to look at some nearby wild flowers.

"Oh, it's more than a picnic spot," I said in a teasing tone.

"What do you mean?"

"I've had a conversation with John Lyon." A sly grin appeared on my face.

"What are you talking about? What does he have to do with anything?"

"I want to build a house here, overlooking the harbor, and the Lyon brothers own the lot."

Puzzled, she didn't say a word.

I stood. "Madelyn, from a porch, right about here, a woman could watch her children splashing and playing at that little strand of beach below us." I walked over to another spot about thirty feet away and said, "Right about here there might be a study, filled with interesting books. A man could practice his oboe, or beautiful harmony could be created between an oboe and a flute."

Madelyn's eyes were moist with tenderness. She was grasping what I was sharing and stepped towards me. We were face to face, merely inches apart. Her breath was sweet. "What are you saying?"

"I've been imagining what it would be like to begin planning our future. I want to—"

She quickly touched her index finger to my lips. "We've only known each other for a few months."

"How long do two adults, deeply in love, need to know each other before they realize that their lives, their hearts, will forever be entwined, and how long will—"

Again, with her index finger, she silenced me, and with her other hand around my shoulder, she pulled my face down to hers and kissed me fully on the lips. She was passionate. I embraced her and returned the kiss. Her lips, warm and moist. Her fragrance, rose petals. Our desire, intense.

"Will you marry me? I love you and cherish you beyond measure."

"Yes, Michael. I will marry you. I love you. I know that you will always love me and take care of me."

Once again, she pulled my face down to her own and kissed me. My arms held her close in a tight hug. I could feel her heartbeat against my chest. My heart throbbed faster for her love, and her warmth stirred my excitement. Our passion, bubbling up like a fountain, threatened to drown us in desire. Enveloped by the moist firmness of her mouth, my senses were consumed in my love for her. We sat together on the flat stone and kissed again, and then simply held each other for a long time. We rested peacefully in each other's love.

After a few minutes, I showed her the two boundary markers on the uphill side of our lot that John Lyon had pointed out to me. At the northwest corner, a great boulder the size of a wagon was well into the forest, and at the northeast corner there was a cedar post, taller than a man, that the Lyon brothers had set deep into the earth.

We sat on the flat rock overlooking the harbor and shared our dreams for more than an hour.

On our walk back to the parsonage, when we were passing by the Brixton home, we saw Louisa on the porch. With needle and thread in hand, she was repairing a pair of Edwyn's trousers. We went up and sat beside her.

"If you're looking for Edwyn, he and Brynne have gone to borrow some books from Edward Stewart."

Briskly, Carolyn hurried by, passing the porch. She was wearing a lace head covering, veil-like, and was watching her feet as she walked.

"Hello Carolyn," said Louisa.

She didn't stop or slow down. She merely raised her hand in a greeting and actually turning away from the porch said, "Good day." She then sped up her walk even more.

I had caught a glimpse of her face as she approached, before she turned away. For a moment her veil was caught by the breeze and trailed over her shoulder.

"Did you see her face?" I asked.

"No," Louisa responded, "but when she passed by earlier, I asked her about the veil. She said that she'd fallen and was embarrassed by a bruise."

I was alarmed. "It looked quite bad. How does someone fall on both sides of their face at the same time?"

I stepped out onto the street and followed her with my eyes, far into the distance. "She didn't turn towards Warrington Hall."

"She must be heading home to help her infirm old aunt," Louisa said.

Madelyn and Louisa stood, stepped out onto the street with me, and Eutychus, sensing alarm, came off the porch and joined us.

"Michael, something's wrong." Madelyn sounded worried. "I need to go and talk to her."

"Not alone," I said. "I'll come with you."

"I'm coming to," added Louisa.

We rushed along the cobbled road with Eutychus trailing behind.

"Come on, Eutychus." Madelyn slapped her hand on her thigh. "Keep up with us."

At the bottom of the lane towards Warrington Hall, we met the Kline's large wagon with a team of four, having come down through the oak grove. They had delivered and installed an enormous marble tabletop to the estate. George was driving, flanked by his father and Tommy. In the back was powerful David and a longshoreman that I'd seen on the docks, but whose name I didn't know.

We told them about Carolyn's facial injuries. Tommy, who had been in the arrowsmith's shop the day before trying to sell the shopkeeper some home-made arrowheads, said, "Carolyn's in no 'arm. She 'as 'er brother."

"How do you know that?" I asked.

"I didn't see 'im but she was buyin' a new bowstring and some arrows for 'im. Carolyn said 'e's goin' deer 'untin'."

Carolyn was fairly new to the community and Kline asked Tommy, "Are you sure it was her?"

"Of course it be 'er. She be a rare beauty. She's 'ard not to notice."

Surprised, I responded, "Her brother isn't here. Brynne said that he's gone to Carlisle." I hesitated. "Caine! The arrows and bowstring must be for Caine!"

We Both Shall Row, My Love And I

We all agreed that Louisa and Madelyn should return to the house for their safety. I jumped into the back of the wagon and Eutychus jumped up beside me. When we got to the lighthouse, we quickly explained to John Lyon, who was sitting on a stump brushing Princess, what we suspected.

"Dancin' demons," he said. "I saw dear Carolyn 'urry past a few minutes ago."

John rose to his feet. "Tommy, get down 'ere an' give me an 'and. We best be gettin' some weapons." John climbed the steps as Tommy dashed through the back door ahead of him.

David and the other man leapt out of the wagon. He grabbed an axe from the woodpile and the other man picked up a smaller hatchet.

Tommy burst out of the door with an old flintlock pistol and John followed with his Digbeth musket, the one used to provide the antlers for the Royal Stag. Tommy climbed into the back of the wagon, and with effort, John got up into the front seat beside George. Eutychus leapt down out of the wagon and followed along with Princess.

Carolyn's house was only a few minutes away and when we got there, everyone jumped out of the wagon and approached it.

Tommy, with the flintlock in hand and without thought for his own safety, charged through the kitchen door. George and I followed at his heels. We began searching the dilapidated house. The smell human grime hit us as soon as we entered. George rushed up a flight of rickety stairs to the upper floor. I hurried along a hallway towards a bedroom and Tommy passed through the kitchen towards a small storeroom. There was no sign of the bowman or anyone else.

"You're too late," whimpered a shaky voice from the ground floor bedroom ahead of me. "He's killed them both." It was Carolyn's aunt, bed-ridden and frail with age.

299

We continued exploring the shadowed recesses of the house. Carolyn and her brother's bodies couldn't be found. Our search continued.

"There's a fresh grave out here!" shouted Albert Kline. "Behind the house at the forest's edge."

"I found 'er," announced Tommy from inside the house. "Carolyn's alive!"

He had found Carolyn, crumpled like a rag doll, in a dirty corner of a windowless little storeroom. She was laying on her side, trembling. She had been badly beaten and blood ran down her face but at least she was alive. Tommy helped her walk, set her down outside on the back step, and sat with her.

Carolyn feebly pointed to the pile of fresh earth that had been found. "There lies my dear brother." She started to cry. "He escaped his bindings two nights ago and tried to save us, but Caine, the mindless beast, stabbed him."

I re-entered the house and told the feeble old woman that Carolyn was alive, but hurt. What I said didn't even seem to register with her. All she could do was lay there, moaning in her suffering.

Hurrying back outside, I scrambled up the slope, following the dogs as Tommy and the others had done. Farther uphill and to my left, I heard that wretched voice, echoing down through the trees from a cliff above us. "Sterling, you meddling fool. I'll be putting you in the ground when the time is right."

Boom! A loud musket shot resounded through the forest. Thwack! An arrow hit a large boulder beside me, splintering the shaft. Bang! The sound of the flintlock pistol echoed from the cliff above us.

Princess and Eutychus looked confused for a moment. They barked aggressively as they tried to reacquire Caine's trail. A moment later, it seemed that they had found his scent and were pursuing him again. George, David, and I continued our uphill scramble.

George caught up to me and paused to catch his breath. He was optimistic. "Caine won't get far with the dogs after him." He leaned forward, panting, and rested his hands on his knees. "Our guns will finish him off for sure. We've got him this time."

A moment later, my heart sank. The anguished whimpering and whining of a dog pierced my heart. We scrambled further up the slope and reached the base of the cliff.

Sweet Eutychus, motionless, his life having ebbed quietly away, lay on his side with an arrow through his body. Whimpering beside him was Princess, an arrow through her front left leg. Kneeling with them, I comforted her.

When John caught up, he gave his musket, powder horn, and shot bag to George, who was with David. The two of them kept going, running along the base of the rock face, searching for a way up.

Looking away, I hid my sorrow as Albert passed by coming from the other direction along the rock face. I stroked Eutychus' head and tenderly spoke his name.

I put my head on his chest and listened for his heartbeat, which I knew would never be found. "Eutychus."

Bang! Again, the sound of the flintlock pistol was heard from the cliff above us. John sat on the damp earth beside Princess, and reaching out his hand, placed it on my shoulder. She was biting at the arrow and licking her pierced leg. John was doing everything he could to comfort her as he broke the cruel arrow near the piercing and gently slid it out of her wound.

He put the short arrowhead end of the arrow into his pocket and wrapped his handkerchief around her leg. "I've got to get 'er to Muriel."

I, likewise, broke the arrow and pulled the bare shaft from Eutychus' lifeless body.

"Michael, put the arrow'ead from Eutychus in your pocket. Caine, if 'es desperate, might be comin' back an' lookin' for 'em."

"You're right John. I've done the same thing before." I slipped it into my pocket. "Why did Princess and Eutychus seem uncertain as to Caine's trail?"

"That Caine, 'es a clever demon. He probably spread some spices or tea leaves as he ran. When the dogs got a good smell o' it, they got confused and thrown off the trail when 'e casts it away."

Another arrow was stuck into a tree beside John. He worked it out of the tree, easing it back and forth and when it was out, he broke off the arrowhead and put it into his pocket with the other.

George and the rest of the men came stumbling back along the base of the cliff.

"You're giving up already?" I was incensed. "Give me the musket. I'll drop him like the rabid animal that he is."

George looked dejected and disappointed in himself. "I slipped in a stream and all the powder's wet. It's no use."

A moment later, quite near us, Tommy slid down a tall thin tree from the top of the cliff, gripping the flintlock. "I've no shot left." He returned the flintlock to John and continued down the slope. "I be needin' to check on Carolyn."

Albert shared what was difficult for each of us to hear. "You can't chase a bowman with such deadly accuracy, without having a gun or a bow yourself."

I knew he was right. We all knew he was right.

"This will hit the Brixtons hard," said George.

John shook his head. "Dear, dear Brynne. Devastated she'll be. A wee child she was when they got sweet Eutychus as a pup."

Looking at the dogs, powerful David offered to help. He picked up Eutychus and carried him across his massive shoulders and thick neck as a man would carry a slain deer.

John helped Princess up and she was able to hop along without using her pierced leg.

When we got to the bottom of the hill, Tommy and Carolyn were in the back of the wagon, and he was supporting her and gently dabbing her face. "Mr. Sterlin' sir, we've got to get Carolyn to Muriel. She'll be knowin' what to do."

David laid Eutychus down in the wagon with great respect, and John and I lifted Princess up and put her in the wagon beside him. She began sniffing his pierced, lifeless body and licking his face. John, with great effort, climbed up into the back of the wagon and held Princess.

Looking at Carolyn, Princess, and Eutychus, John sneered. "Caine killed Owen 'arcourt an' Carolyn's brother." He angrily slapped his leg. "See what 'e's done today to Carolyn an' these 'ere good dogs." He stroked whimpering Princess. "The demon." He spit. "'e mustn't be allowed to live."

David said that he would stay with Carolyn's frail aunt. It was obvious that a fast wagon ride would be far too difficult for her. He went into the house but came back out a moment later. He held up his hand, called to George at the reins, and then walked over to him and whispered something in his ear.

"Let's be goin'," shouted Tommy, still gently dabbing at Carolyn's face.

George flicked the horse's reins. "Walk on."

Madelyn and Louisa came down off the porch when we arrived, as Brynne and Edwyn got back from their walk.

When Brynne saw Eutychus, she ran over to the wagon. "Is Eutychus hurt?"

I hugged her. "Sweet Eutychus is gone, Brynne."

She achingly moaned aloud. She started hugging him and petting his lifeless body. Stopping several times to look into his sweet face, she tried to love the life back into him. Her tears and sobs were too much for Louisa and Madelyn to witness. They started to cry as well.

Edwyn and I lifted his body out of the back of the wagon and put him on the porch. Without thinking, we laid him down in his favorite spot beside Edwyn's chair, where he had always found peace and contentment. Brynne sat beside the lifeless mastiff, repeating his name. Cradling his head, swaying, and sobbing, she had lost her dearest friend to Caine, the reprobate. I climbed up onto the front seat of the wagon and joined Madelyn, who had already climbed aboard. Louisa, also distressed, stayed with Brynne, and Edwyn hurried down the street to be of help with Carolyn's aunt. I saw that he had his oak cudgel in his hand and revenge in his eye.

"George, let's be goin'!" shouted Tommy as he held Carolyn.

Again, George flicked the reins, alerting the horses. "Walk on."

In the wagon, Carolyn was looking faint and still being supported by Tommy. His care for someone to this level of intensely was something new for me. *I've never seen this kind of care and maturity in him.*

Albert Kline and the longshoreman were dropped off near their warehouse as we were about to cross the bridge.

"I'll ride up to Warrington Hall," said Albert. "All of this needs to be reported to the captain of the guard. If we can get enough men out looking for him, we might be able to apprehend him, now that we know roughly where he is."

For the third time, George vigorously flicked the reins and startled the horses. "Walk on!" he shouted, and the horses bolted, barely under control.

When we arrived at the parsonage, George expertly brought the team of four to a smooth stop. Tommy and I helped Carolyn down. Her facial bleeding had stopped but the dried blood, her bruised and swollen face, and her matted hair shocked Muriel. Madelyn and Tommy supported her as she haltingly walked, unstable and unsure of her balance.

"Mrs. Ekland, Carolyn, she be needin' your 'elp so very much."

Muriel could hardly believe her eyes. "Lord have mercy on this child." She looked at the big warehouse wagon with a team of four, and back at Carolyn. "Was there an accident? Was she hit by the wagon?"

I told her what had happened as Tommy and Madelyn, supporting Carolyn, escorted her through the front door and down the hall to the guest room.

When we entered the room, Muriel asked Tommy and I to remain in the hallway but Carolyn, through her swollen lips, insisted that Tommy stay with her. "Tommy," she mumbled. "I want Tommy. He helped me."

I stood in the hallway for a few minutes and then, going into the kitchen and sitting down, I waited for word on how she was doing. *The Eklands are such caring people. In their pastoral ministry, they've used their guest room to help others for many years. It was a place of comfort and care.*

I remembered that Edwyn had told me that when my grandfather was doing poorly, he left their home, and at Muriel's insistence, came to the parsonage. He had passed away in their guest room. Muriel's nursing skills and knowledge of pain relief and diet had made his last few months tolerable. I had heard how Muriel had fed, bathed, and comforted him. It spoke volumes to me about the real meaning of Christian love and mercy.

My mind was refocused onto Carolyn's desperate need when I heard her scream from the guest room.

Caine. He's no better than a rabid animal.

He reminded me of the fox that I'd seen shortly before arriving in Oak Harbor. It was unable to overcome and capture the large goose so it went after the little chicken. In much the same way, Caine had held Carolyn captive, and then had assaulted her. We later found out that Caine had smashed a bottle into her lovely face after beating her with his fists.

No decent man would ever treat a helpless young girl like that, beating her and smashing a bottle into her face. He must be brought to justice.

I stepped out into the sunshine as George was preparing to leave with the wagon.

He waved me over. "She's gone."

I was puzzled. "Who's gone? Gone where?"

"Carolyn's aunt." He paused. "By the time we'd returned to her from being up the slope looking for Caine, she had passed away. That's what David whispered to me when we left."

As George and the impressive team of four were leaving, he said that he would discuss with Reverend Ashcroft the burial arrangements for Carolyn's brother and aunt. We expressed appreciation and wished him well.

I was aghast. "That little girl has lost her whole family."

The Healer's House

Later in the day, Madelyn told me how Muriel had carefully cleaned Carolyn's wounds. She was relieved when she discovered that most of the blood on her face was from her nose and not from the cut on her face. She also shared with me that Muriel had observed that old bruises from abuse were in various stages of healing. *Carolyn's weeks of having Caine in her home must have been truly wretched and dangerous. I can't imagine what she must've experienced.*

Muriel was by far the best healer in Oak Harbor, and she had cared for many people. The local doctor was more of a businessman than a medical man and his investments up in Carlisle and over in Penrith often took him out of town for long periods. He was rarely in Oak Harbor, which left Muriel as the town's primary source of treatment and care. She held the confidence of the townspeople, who would often take their sick and injured to her, even when the doctor was in town. She was much more than merely an herbalist healer. She had a copy of Pringle's book on military medicine, Brockelsby's more recent book about contagious diseases, and numerous other books on the art and science of medicine.

I went outside and into the stable. Princess was whimpering and whining as she was being treated by John and Reverend Ekland. George and I quietly looked on.

They had lifted Princess out of the wagon, set her carefully on the ground, and looking quite forlorn, she had hopped into the stable on her three uninjured legs. John had then rinsed her leg in a solution of wine and boiled salt water, which had been left to cool. The initial rinsing was followed by some peeking and probing to ascertain that there was no dirt or foreign objects in the wound, and then followed by another rinsing. Finally, John had coated the wound with Muriel's best healing salve, mostly a mixture of aloe paste with a little olive oil, and it was covered with a clean cotton bandage to protect it from Princess's incessant licking.

At sunset, when Carolyn and Princess were both resting, Madelyn and I had time to sit and talk beside the harbor. I told her that Carolyn's aunt had passed away and that she no longer had any family.

She was shocked and gripped my hand firmly. "This is going to be so hard on Carolyn; so difficult when she hears it, and so difficult when she is faced with the truth of living alone."

I winced. "She has no one now."

"I'll talk to Aunt Muriel about it. We'll tell Carolyn in the morning after a good night's sleep. I imagine Reverend Ashcroft will perform the funeral service for her aunt. She used to go to Saint Cecilia's when she was younger and in better health."

We sat there calmly and Madelyn explained what had led to Carolyn's serious injury. She had refused to run into the forest with Caine when he saw the horses and wagon approaching. Frustrated, knowing that he couldn't outrun or elude his pursuers while dragging her along against her will, he had punched her and struck her in the face with a bottle.

We Both Shall Row, My Love And I

Madelyn, describing Carolyn's wounds, said that there were a number of scratches and shallow cuts but only one that was deep. It was a clean cut and followed the orbit of her left eye. It curved from the center of her eyebrow around to the cheekbone below.

Muriel had carefully rinsed the wound with a medicinal solution and gently examined it, looking for bits of glass. Finding none, she applied a mixture of aloe paste, wine, and olive oil, and matched up the two sides of the long curving gash.

"Michael, you would hardly believe how meticulously Aunt Muriel worked. She carefully joined the two sides of the cut with tiny stitches of the finest silk thread, while I held a large magnifying glass."

Muriel had told her that if she did it correctly, and if the Lord answered prayer, it might heal well and have minimal scarring. The wound was then covered with a clean, lightweight, cotton bandage. It would need to be changed each day and kept moist with a medicinal salve of aloe to encourage healing.

While Madelyn and I sat there by the harbor, a profound thing happened. Tommy, looking quite tired, walked over and seated himself on the other side of Madelyn.

Sounding more mature than his years, he said, "Carolyn be sleepin' now and so I 'ave a chance to be restin' and gettin' some fresh air."

Madelyn, with her heart so warmed towards Tommy, put her arm around him. "Thomas, you were caring and tender towards Carolyn. I'm so proud of you and the way you helped care for her. You never left her side."

"Mrs. Ekland, she be such a great 'ealer and a carin' person, I'm trustin' that dear Carolyn..." His voice caught in his throat with emotion. "That dear Carolyn will be fine."

"Aunt Muriel is a wonderful healer," Madelyn agreed. "She's a gift to the community."

"Carolyn 'as suffered so much, so very much." He looked out into the harbor and spoke through gritted teeth. "She's not deservin' the abuse levelled on 'er by that Caine fella."

"She has suffered greatly," I said.

Tommy continued. "Carolyn she be tellin' me and Mrs. Ekland that Caine been 'idin' there for some weeks. She was forced to stop workin' for Lord Warrington and made to get food and supplies for 'im."

"Carolyn is in loving hands now," I said.

"Carolyn's brother, 'e was all bound up." Tommy winced. "Carolyn's dear aunt, she was bed-ridden. Caine made threats to Carolyn to kill 'em both if she didn't do what he was demandin'."

"She has all of us now to care for her," said Madelyn.

Tommy looked out into the harbor and then back at Madelyn. "Carolyn's a fine dear girl to be takin' care o' 'er loved ones like that." Tommy clenched his jaw. "She's not deservin' the abuse brought on 'er by Caine." His voice tapered off. "She will be needin' our 'elp in carin' for 'er aunt."

"You are a great encouragement to her." Madelyn looked at Tommy and took his hand. "There's something else that I need to tell you. You'll need to be strong for Carolyn's sake."

"What would you be likin' to be tellin' me?"

Madelyn, wanting to be comforting, started to rub his back gently. "Carolyn's aunt has passed away. She was so old and frail. All the stress of having that abusive Caine in the home was too much for her. Muriel and I will tell her in the morning."

Tommy firmed his lower lip and held back his tears. "That's it then." He slapped his thigh. "She be without family an' alone in the world now."

Madelyn looked at him with great tenderness. "She's without family but she isn't alone. We're her friends and we will all be helping her. We will be her family."

"Oh, Lady Madelyn, you be right on that. Friends is all she be 'avin' now." Tears sat in the corners of his eyes, but wanting to be strong, to be a man, he didn't let them roll down his cheeks.

I grasped that Madelyn and Tommy needed a bit more privacy. "I'll leave you two alone, I need to go and check on Princess."

Upon entering the stable, which was actually quite large, being both stable for Wonder and Shadow and drive shed for the two carriages, it took my eyes a moment to adjust to the dim light.

With a wedge of sunlight penetrating the darkness between two wallboards and reflected light from an open window high above, I saw John Lyon huddled in a corner, sitting beside Princess. He was gently singing a comforting song, but having heard me enter, stopped his singing and asked me to sit with them.

"Loss Michael. This be a day of loss. Come and sit with Princess an' me."

"That's the truth, John. It's a day of loss."

"Wee Carolyn 'as lost 'er brother an' 'er auntie." John was speaking with such great sorrow. "Brynne 'as lost 'er best friend, an' Princess 'as lost 'er true love. The daddy o' 'er pups."

I sat with them in the stable for some time without speaking, reflecting on what the events of the day would mean to each concerned, and then I rejoined Madelyn and Tommy at the edge of the harbor.

A while later, Reverend Ekland came out of the parsonage. "It has been a challenging day for everyone. Muriel anticipates that Carolyn will sleep through until morning. Princess seems to be resting well. Muriel and Madelyn will take turns monitoring Carolyn through the night and I will go to the stable and check on Princess from time to time."

"Thank you, Reverend," I said. "It has been a long day."

Madelyn, who was now standing beside me, squeezed my hand and kissed my cheek. "Michael, I need to go in and speak to Aunt Muriel." On her tiptoes, she kissed me on the cheek.

Reverend Ekland gently but firmly insisted that each of us get a good night's rest. "I'd like to give the three of you rides home."

"I'll come by tomorrow," I said, "to see how everyone is doing."

Tommy was concerned. "Reverend, may I go and see Mrs. Ekland, just for a minute?" He didn't wait for an answer, but quickly rose to his feet and took a few cautious steps towards the front door of the parsonage. Reverend Ekland shared an agreeable expression and gestured for him to go inside.

John and I climbed aboard the one-horse gig with Reverend Ekland. It was a tight fit. Tommy bounded out of the parsonage door, leapt down the several steps, and climbed up onto the gig's small luggage rack behind the seat.

Tommy, bubbling with joy, was relieved. "Mrs. Ekland said that I could be comin' back tomorrow afternoon."

His eager desire to be of help stood out. "Thomas, I truly am pleased with the maturity and helpfulness that I see in you."

"Thank you, Mr. Sterlin' sir."

"Thomas," added Reverend Ekland, "I've noticed a change in you as well. You are becoming a caring and helpful young man."

When Reverend Ekland arrived at the north end of the bridge, a short walk from the Atwater home, Tommy jumped off the gig but remained standing beside it, near John Lyon.

John, feeling quite positive, having been re-assured that Princess would be fine, tousled Tommy's curly black hair and said, "Tell your dear mother all that's 'appened today. Give 'er a special 'ello for me."

"Yes sir, Mr. Lyon sir."

Arriving at the Brixton porch, I climbed down, thanked Reverend Ekland for the ride, and went around the side of the house to the back. I was met with something that I didn't expect see, although it made perfect sense.

In a low corner of the backyard, beside a beautiful bed of globe flowers between the house and the shop, stood the Brixton family. Edwyn, flanked by Louisa and Brynne, each with their heads bowed and clutching handfuls of flowers, were facing a mound of fresh earth. A muddy shovel was leaning against the corner of the shop.

Louisa saw me and gestured for me to join them. As I stepped towards their family circle, Brynne looked up at me with her eyes red and swollen from crying. She firmly took my arm and leaned in towards me.

Edwyn led in prayer. "Oh God, we thank you that Eutychus was a faithful friend. We thank you God for the way that Eutychus pulled Brynne out of the harbor when she was a little whisper of a girl. I thank you..." He paused for a moment to let his deep emotions pass. "I thank you God that Eutychus was such a faithful friend and companion on so many hikes into the forest to search out the best trees for cabinet making. Amen."

Brynne began sobbing once again, and releasing my arm, dropped to her knees beside her sweet doggie's grave. She placed the flowers she had in her hand on the cool mound of earth, and Louisa bent down and did likewise.

I knelt down beside Brynne and put my arm around her back. I felt her heavy breathing and rubbed her back with each of her sobs.

Eventually her weeping ended. She took a couple of deep breaths and began praying. "Thank you, Lord Jesus, for my Eutychus." She paused and started to cry again. "My loving friend. I, I pray…" there was a long pause, "I pray that Princess will have her leg mended to full strength and that her puppies…" She paused again. "*Their* puppies, will all be big and healthy like Princess and Eutychus. I pray that each of the puppies will have kind homes. Amen."

The four of us went inside and although we spoke little, we enjoyed our evening meal together followed by a cup of tea. We were quiet but after a while, we began sharing our favorite stories about Eutychus. I hadn't been aware that he had pulled Brynne out of the harbor when she was a toddler until I had heard Edwyn's prayer, and I hadn't heard that several years ago Brynne had a young hedgehog as a pet that Eutychus cared for like a puppy. He would sometimes lift a puny piece of meat out of his dish and drop it in front of the hedgehog and it would sometimes snuggle down for the night in the fur of Eutychus' forelegs.

After Brynne and Louisa went to bed, Edwyn and I sat on the porch for a long time. We discussed all of the tragedy that Caine had brought to the community. At one point, while he shared with me that Reverend Ashcroft would conduct the funeral for Carolyn's brother and aunt, it appeared to me that he reached down to pet Eutychus or scratch his head, but regrettably, the sweet dog wasn't there.

There was so much on my mind after such an eventful day that I found sleep difficult to find. I felt like a man split in two. My heart was full of the joy of showing the cleared lot to Madelyn and our deep expressions of love for each other. My mind was crowded with the stresses of scrambling up the slope after Caine, Carolyn's injury, the loss of her loved ones, and the sorrow of the Brixton family. Eventually I drifted off. *The trees behind our future home. The smell of the forest mingled with Madelyn's rose scented perfume. her warm hand.*

~~~~~~

Awakened by the sound of the back door closing near the foot of my bed, I blinked a few times, rubbed my face, and sat up. Someone had passed through my room, which led out to the back garden and Edwyn's shop. I crawled out of bed and staggered out to the rain barrel. Taking a bucket, filling it, and pouring it upon my head in one great deluge, I felt quite refreshed. I was fully awakened and shockingly invigorated.

After dressing, I went directly out to the shop, choosing not to eat breakfast. I discovered Edwyn hard at work.

"Good morning, Michael," he said in a somber tone, leaning over the edge of his grim woodworking project.

"Good morning. Yesterday was a day that the people of Oak Harbor will never forget."

Edwyn stepped back from his work and examined the coffin for Carolyn's aunt. "I dislike earning a living like this. When someone passes away from Fair Havens Church, I insist that I work without pay. When I do work for people of other churches, I'm payed, but am uncomfortable receiving the money."

"One of these caskets is for Carolyn's aunt. Who is the other one for?" I asked.

"Her brother. His body will be retrieved from the shallow grave behind Carolyn's home. Carolyn and Reverend Ashcroft wanted them to have proper burials in St. Cecilia's cemetery."

I approached the coffin nearest myself and examined the joinery work. "Edwyn, let me give you some help."

"Thank you. Earlier, when I was drinking tea on the porch after breakfast, several men and several women passed by from Saint Cecilia's heading towards Carolyn's home."

I picked up some powdered pumice in oil and started sanding one of the caskets.

"The women would've been going to prepare her aunt's body for burial. The men would've been going to dig up her brother's body, wrap it in old canvas, and then put it in a bag of tightly woven fabric."

I shook my head and winced. "The body preparation for Carolyn's auntie would be challenging, but digging up her brother would be gruesomely terrible." I paused. "I'd never want to be involved in digging up a body."

"No one ever wants to be digging up a body." He stopped what he was doing and looked at me in a fatherly way. "Some things in life need to be done, quite simply, because they need to be done, whether one likes them or not."

"You're right."

He returned to his work. "She attended Saint Cecilia's for many years before losing her strength and becoming bedridden. Reverend Ashcroft told me yesterday that he hadn't been to her home for quite a while. He was going to visit her after their Sunday service—"

"If he had visited her when Caine was there," I interrupted. "He'd be buried in the back garden as well."

"Probably right, Michael."

"When is the funeral service?"

"Later this afternoon. Carolyn's aunt and her brother will be laid to rest in St. Cecilia's cemetery." Edwyn walked across the shop and got a set of files out of his large tool cabinet. "Muriel, so I've heard, won't be going to the funeral, as she has a fever. Madelyn will be staying to take care of her."

"I'm sorry to hear that she's sick. She was a big help to Carolyn."

In the afternoon, long after the two coffins had been picked up by a wagon from St. Cecilia's, I chose to remain with Brynne. She was still grieving the loss of Eutychus and I didn't want her to be alone. Edwyn and Louisa said they would attend the funeral to be supportive of Carolyn, although they didn't know her aunt well.

Half an hour later, after Edwyn and Louisa had left, Brynne and I watched from behind the lace curtains in the living room as the simple procession from Carolyn's house to Saint Cecilia's passed by. First came Reverend Ekland with Carolyn and Tommy in the landau, followed by a black wagon, which carried the two coffins in the back. These were followed by Reverend and Mrs. Ashcroft in their carriage, and following them, several other community members, including Edwyn and Louisa, walked along behind.

The Ekland's Landau Carriage

"Carolyn looks so grown up and dignified with that black dress on. I wonder who she borrowed it from," asked Brynne.

"I imagine from Madelyn."

"There are some bandages beneath her veil. Look how she reached across to hold Tommy's hand. They look like a respectable older couple."

After the procession passed by, we sat upon a comfortably padded sofa. "Tragedies like yesterday cause everyone to grow up quickly and leave their childhood." *I shouldn't have said that. Brynne is still grieving the loss of Eutychus. Why did I say that?*

She took my arm and looked up into my eyes for an awkwardly long time. "Thank you for comforting me yesterday. You're such a caring man and I love..." She paused. " I love..." Her voice trembled with emotion. "I love and miss my Eutychus so very much." She hesitated. "Hold me, Michael."

Holding her, she leaned in towards me. She didn't cry but I felt her heavy breathing and her warmth through her thin dress. "Yesterday was a difficult day for everyone," I whispered.

Brynne went to her room a short time later and I went out to Edwyn's shop to continue some of the work that I had started earlier.

An hour later, she came out to the shop. "Michael, I've made some tea. Please come and sit with me on the porch."

I followed her to the front of the house. While we were having our tea, we saw Brynne's parents and several others returning from Saint Cecilia's. Out of respect, and not wanting to appear as simple gawkers, we hurried back into the house.

Edwyn and Louisa stepped inside. "That was quite trying." Edwyn shook his head. "Carolyn's only seventeen—"

"Sixteen, Daddy," corrected Brynne.

"Sixteen? I thought she looked older. Okay sixteen then," Edwyn continued. "So young and she's lost what remained of her family."

I shook my head. "I can't imagine her living alone. I think that—"

"Oh she won't be living alone," Louisa interrupted. "The Eklands have said that she can have their guest room for as long as she likes."

My eyes opened wide and I nodded. "The Eklands are a ministry-minded couple. Can you imagine what Oak Harbor would be like if everyone was as caring as them?"

Louisa smiled. "Like heaven on earth. What has surprised me though is the change I see in Tommy. He's growing up. I don't merely mean getting older. He's becoming much more thoughtful and understanding of people's needs."

"Beyond a doubt, and he's the main support for his family," Edwyn said. "Madelyn has been having a big influence on him and some of the other children in the community with her Sunday school class. Are you aware that she's giving him, and a few of the other young people, reading and writing lessons each week?"

"I didn't know that," said Brynne. She smiled at me. "I've helped her a few times with Sunday School." Brynne, looking thoughtful, paused. "I think that I'll help her with the reading and writing classes as well."

Brynne glanced at me as Edwyn gave her a hug. "We have some of the finest young people in Cumberland in our own little seaport."

"Thank you, Daddy."

Edwyn and Louisa went to change out of their funeral clothes, leaving Brynne and I sitting in the living room. She picked up a book that she had borrowed from Edward Stewart and when I was about to stand and leave the room to go out to the shop, boisterous laughing and giggling came from her parents' bedroom.

I grinned. "Your parents truly love each other."

Brynne giggled. "They're passionate about each other and the shapely black dress that mother wears on such occasions has a powerful effect on daddy. Your room is in the back. You don't hear what I hear." Brynne's controlled giggling became laughter, which started me to chuckling. It was a source of relief to all of the stress that had gripped us.

"I think that I better get back to the shop. Your father will join me there in a while, I'm sure."

"And I better get started on the supper preparations," she added.

I glanced back at Brynne as I was about to leave the room. She remained sitting there, holding the book, acting as if she was reading it.

The laughter and giggling of her parents began to taper off, becoming punctuated with a few sighs and moans. Brynne's hand went to her mouth as she unsuccessfully tried to hold back her laughter.

I froze in the doorway, between the front room and the kitchen, with my hand on the frame of the door. Brynne was unable to cease her laughing, which started me laughing as well. I tried to keep myself under control and had my palm pressed over my mouth.

With our hands over our mouths and tears of laughter in our eyes, we rushed through the kitchen, through my room, and out through the back door. When we got there, we looked at each other and had a wonderful laugh together.

Brynne, still bathed in mirth, was almost unable to speak. "I hear that..." She laughed. "I hear that a couple of times a week."

I was embarrassed that Brynne and I were relating to each other about such an intimate subject. I got myself under control but my giddiness was still brewing deep within me. "I think we've gone a bit too far. I need to get to my work in the shop."

"And I should be in the kitchen." She giggled again, and as she passed behind me slowly, she placed her warm hand on one shoulder and slid it across my back to the other as she headed inside.

By Tuesday, Edwyn, with my help, had completed the cabinetry repair work for Lord Warrington; the new picture frame, the refinishing of the old mantel clock, and the jewelry box repair were all expertly done.

We were nearing completion of the cabinetry work for Captain Henderson as well, and by the end of the week, we were almost ready to install the navigational desk and cabinet in the captain's quarters. The *Eleutheran Quest* had contracted with Lord Warrington to deliver the large supply of oak lumber that had been accumulating on the dock because the previously contracted ship did not arrive at port. There were rumors that it had been lost at sea. The *Eleutheran Quest*, having sailed for Bristol, was scheduled to return in a few days.

The entire week following consisted of me working alongside Edwyn, Tommy visiting Carolyn each afternoon, and Muriel nursing Carolyn and changing her bandage, with Madelyn's assistance. I was able to visit my love only twice during the week.

On Sunday morning, it was encouraging to see Carolyn at Fair Havens Church, veiled for both her grief and her bandaging. She was flanked by Tommy and Madelyn, and they sat a little closer to the front than I would normally have liked, but I joined them in the fifth row. Madelyn took my hand as soon as I sat beside her and held it tight to the side of her thigh.

It was a powerful service. Pastor Ekland preached on the story of the Pharisee and the tax collector from the eighteenth chapter of Luke. I determined to be more like the tax collector and not like the Pharisee. I wanted to pray, "God be merciful to me a sinner," as the tax collector had prayed but I felt unworthy to pray like that. I wasn't sure if I was a sinner or a saint and I was struggling with my deep emotions.

Both Tommy and Carolyn were moved by the message and Madelyn asked me to wait for her outside, which I did. Sitting on the sea wall, I enjoyed the wheeling seabirds overhead and the sunshine breaking through the clouds. A pair of dolphins entered the harbor and seemed to be chasing a school of fish. They were thrilling to watch.

Madelyn came out of the church half an hour later, walked over to me with a broad beaming smile, and said, "Both Carolyn and Tommy have trusted the Lord. They've begun a relationship with Him, just like the repentant tax collector in Uncle Martin's sermon. They repented of their old lives, asked forgiveness, and now they are God's children like it says in the first chapter of John's Gospel."

"Oh that's good." *What does she mean by that? Is that how someone becomes a real Christian? What will she think of me if she finds out that I'm not close to God like that? I'm not so dedicated. I'll think about doing that someday.*

"Michael, I asked Carolyn if you could be present when her bandages are taken off in a few minutes. Aunt Muriel removed the tiny parts of the scab that didn't come off on their own last night and she carefully removed the stitches. She then recovered the wound with a clean bandage, which she had soaked in her healing salve."

"I don't want to be superficial, but I hope that she won't lose her beauty," I said.

Muriel Ekland appeared at the door of the parsonage. "Carolyn would like you both to come in now. She's nervous but would treasure your encouragement, I'm sure."

"We're on our way in, Auntie," said Madelyn. We walked hand-in-hand towards the parsonage. I assumed that Carolyn wanted Madelyn to be present and that I was invited simply to accompany her.

In a few steps, we were in the kitchen. Carolyn and Muriel were seated facing each other across the corner of the table. Tommy was sitting beside Carolyn, holding her little hand in both of his and biting his lip. Reverend Ekland and I stood farther back.

Madelyn gently lifted and set aside Carolyn's black hat and veil she had worn to church. Muriel, with tender expertise and assuring words, began removing the bandaging from Carolyn's face as Madelyn held a mirror. When the bandage was removed, Pastor Ekland and I leaned forward. Tommy turned his shoulders to face his dear Carolyn, and Madelyn tried to angle the mirror so that Carolyn could see herself.

Madelyn's eyes were alive with wonder. "Aunt Muriel, how did you do it? Is this an answer to prayer or strictly effective medicine?"

Reverend Ekland clasped his hands together and bowed his head in prayer. "Thank you, Lord, for your love and kindness to Carolyn. Amen, Lord, amen." He opened his eyes and looked at each of us. "Marvelous, just marvelous. Sometimes the Lord uses efficacious medical treatment as part of an answer to prayer."

Madelyn, being unable to get the mirror angle correct, passed it to Carolyn. Tommy's lips were parted, and he inhaled with a sigh. "Amazin', I don't know 'ow you did it. There be only a fine pink line where 'er wound used to be."

Carolyn was holding the mirror, trying to get the best possible view of her injury. It curved from the center of her left eyebrow, followed the bone around the side of her eye, and ended on her cheekbone.

Carolyn, with mouth agape, said, "Thank you so much, Aunt Muriel, I mean Mrs. Ekland." Tears formed in her eyes. "Thank you so much."

Muriel began giving Carolyn some clear directions. "I have made a creamy salve from a potted aloe plant that came from the Bahamas. It's hard to find in the shops of London and quite expensive."

The mention of expense made Tommy, who was always attentive to financial opportunities, lean forward. "Well 'ow much does it cost? Is it possible to start new plants from cuttin's o' a single plant? Can aloe be grown in a glassed green'ouse 'ere in England?"

Muriel lifted one hand to hold back Tommy's questions. "Tommy, let me finish my directions for Carolyn."

"Yes, Mrs. Ekland," he responded.

"Carolyn, each morning, please follow this plan for one week. Start tomorrow morning and finish the plan next Sunday morning. Then we'll make a new plan."

Muriel gently lifted Carolyn's chin with her fingertips. She described the steps. "First, wash your hands thoroughly. Second, gently rinse your face with cool, clean water. Third, pat it dry carefully with a soft, clean cloth. Fourth, take a bit of the salve on one of your fingertips from this jar and spread it on your scar, and the area around it." Muriel leaned back in her chair, closed the jar, and set it on the table. "Fifth, leave it on your face for an hour. Perhaps you could read a book or a passage from the Bible that Madelyn gave you." She leaned in even more closely towards Carolyn's face. "Finally, gently rinse your face with cool, clean water, spread a tiny amount of the salve on the wound, and leave it alone."

Carolyn looked shy or perhaps embarrassed for a moment. "I've a problem with the reading part."

Muriel put her hand on Carolyn's shoulder. "What do you mean?"

"I don't know how." Embarrassed, she looked away. "I can't read."

Madelyn immediately reacted to what had been said. "You can join my class. I'm teaching several boys and one of the girls how to read."

Carolyn brightened with hope. "I'd like to learn to read. Please, can I join? Can Tommy come too?"

"I'm already one o' 'er readin' students," Tommy said enthusiastically. "You should join us, Carolyn."

Tommy and I enjoyed a delicious lunch at the parsonage, having been invited to stay, and we all engaged in wonderful conversation with one another. Without being noticed, I examined Carolyn's scar. *Remarkable healing. The thin pinkish line seems merely interesting and not disfiguring. Muriel's medical skills are amazing.*

Following the meal, Madelyn and I excused ourselves and stepped out to enjoy a walk along the harborside. We ambled along, Madelyn taking my arm, as far as the bridge. There we stopped to watch a mother mallard duck being followed by seven little ducklings, wobbling along on a grassy area beside the backwater pool of the river.

"Oh look, Michael. They're so cute."

"They truly are."

As we watched, to our horror, a big magpie landed at the end of the little parade. It grabbed the last duckling, poking and tearing, devouring it with delight.

"Michael, save the ducklings. Stop the magpie!"

I ran out onto the grassy field and the monstrous magpie launched into the air with the duckling's remains dangling from its beak. Mother mallard, frantically calling the surviving ducklings towards the water, stood guard at the edge of the backwater pool. When the last one flopped into the water and the family swam away, we were spared any further horror. Madelyn, tender-hearted woman that she is, needed my tender consolation.

Caine, like the murderous magpie that had devoured the little duckling and escaped, was still free in the area. I trusted that Lord Warrington's men might locate and capture him, but until then I would be wary of him and the possibilities of terror he might bring.

Book Three

Captain Henderson's Quarters

The following Tuesday afternoon was remarkably bright and cloud-free, although it was quite cool. Above us, a brilliant blue sky served as a spirit-lifting canopy, and our little seaport was set free from its previous dismal shroud.

Sunday evening and all through Monday, it had alternated between a heavy rain and a light drizzle. Most people had stayed in their homes. Those that did venture out used umbrellas or covered themselves with whatever they could find, as they dashed from awning to tree. Today, however, was the kind of day that a cheerful person would write about optimistically in their diary.

My sunshiny optimism was challenged by a miserable grey cloud of pessimism when I overheard several old women outside. Clutching their shawls about their hunched shoulders and standing in a circle beside the shop next door, there seemed no limit to their criticisms. They were having a scathing chinwag about people in the community for nearly an hour. When I heard Carolyn and her aunt being discussed in unpleasant terms, I was compelled to intervene.

I opened wide the side window and leaned out near them to interrupt their gossip. "Good morning, ladies. Are you enjoying the sunny weather?"

"Good day, sir," said one.

"We be 'avin' a wet spell," said another. "'til today."

I continued to lean out of the window and as they grasped that they'd not be able to return to their gossip, the gaggle of rumpled old grey geese dispersed, waddling down the cobblestone street.

This morning, with the sun shining through the last of the clouds, the muddy puddles drying up, and the activity of the harbor resuming, the seaport was once again bustling. The *Eleutheran Quest* had returned from delivering Lord Warrington's lumber to Bristol and it was now tied up at the main dock, as it had been before.

Edwyn and I delivered the new cabinet and navigational desk and looked forward to seeing Captain Henderson's reaction. It was covered with soft canvas and was in the back of a borrowed wagon. He and a few of his men approached the wagon on the dock and stopping at its back gate, waited for the unveiling.

Above us, Mr. Chen and his alluring daughter watched from the ship's rail. Meiling's hair was wound up into a topknot but long strands of it, having fallen from the knot, framed her attractively exotic features.

We loosened and removed the tie down ropes, dramatically lifted the soft canvas cover, and backed away from the cabinet and desk. Jaws dropped, eyebrows raised, and one of the older salts actually gasped. Captain Henderson was silent, and leaning into the back of the wagon began examining these objects of our labor. He pursed his lips and scratched his chin. He then opened a few of the drawers, examined the dovetailed joinery, and rubbed his hand on the lustrously polished wooden surfaces, glistening in the noon-day sun.

"This is not only displaying a beautiful grain and artistic finishing, it's rock solid," said the captain.

The older salt that had gasped removed his hat and held it over his heart as an act of respect.

As I stood back, reexamined our work, and listened to everyone's positive comments, I was proud to have had a part in the design and construction of such fine pieces of furniture.

The cabinet was one of the most attractive and awe-inspiring examples of quality workmanship that I'd ever seen. The navigational desk, with its instrument drawers and sundry other compartments, was not only practical and sturdy but beautiful as well.

The captain, taking a step back and removing his hat, looked at Edwyn with wide-eyed appreciation. "Brixton, I've been to many fine cabinetry and chandlery shops in all of our great coastal cities, and I've seldom seen anything approaching this level of quality, even John Beltier's shop produces nothing finer than these."

"Thank you for your kind words, sir. My man here," he gestured towards me, "Mr. Sterling, is to be recognized as well as myself."

"Well, if either of you two is ever looking for a position aboard this ship," he clapped his hands together, "don't hesitate to contact me."

"Thank you again, captain."

He reached into an interior pocket within his coat and took out a change purse. He looked into it, and with his index finger rattled and slid some of the coins. "This is not enough," he mumbled to himself. "Not for work like this."

"Come down to my quarters and supervise the positioning of the desk and cabinet. I would like to supplement our agreed on fee."

Edwyn grinned and gave a little bow of his head. "Certainly, sir." He covertly winked at me.

"You men there." The captain pointed to four of his men gawking, from the deck above. "Come down here and lend a hand."

A moment later, the four men arrived. Two for each of the pieces.

Edwyn, seeking to block the men politely, stepped in between them and the two beautifully crafted articles of fine furniture. "Captain, we mustn't allow only two men per item." He held up a hand. "They are powerful looking men but four might be the better number for each piece to avoid scratches and abrasions on the stairs and through the passageways."

"Yes, quite right you are." The captain grinned and nodded his head in agreement profusely.

He called over several more men to join us. We went with the captain aboard and below deck. The men, four to a piece, cautiously followed us. Edwyn and the captain positioned the pieces where the earlier mangled and splintered ones had been. Captain Henderson then pulled over his padded high back stool, with its comfortable arms, and positioned it in front of his new navigational desk. He sat in the stool and rested his arms on the inclined desktop. "The angle that you've made the desktop is perfect. This is superb."

"Captain would it be possible for you to ask your men to leave us for a few minutes?"

"Yes, of course." He eyed Edwyn and me curiously. "Men, back to your other tasks! Tibbins, wait in the passageway."

Edwyn leaned towards the captain and whispered, "Captain, my man Sterling suggested I include a secret compartment for your private papers, a weapon, and perhaps some emergency funds."

Henderson, with eyebrows raised, held his chin with forefinger and thumb. "I've heard of such things but have never had one."

Edwyn stepped back and rested his hands on his hips.

I smiled with a sly look and whispered, "It's in the cabinet, not the navigational desk. See if you can find it."

Captain Henderson searched in each drawer, reached his hand in, and pressed suspiciously at several points, but to no avail.

"I give up. Where is this secret compartment? How can I open it if I can't even find it?"

I stepped closer to the cabinet and knelt down before it on one knee. Describing to him the three-step process, I carefully went through the motions. "First, pull this small drawer on the left most of the way out. Second, pull the middle drawer only halfway out and then, finally, reach around the right side to the third dovetail point from the top, and press it."

Just as I pressed on that specific dovetail joint, an outer panel on the left sprung open and the top tipped out by about eight inches.

"That's finer than any magic trick I've ever seen," said Captain Henderson, as he clapped his hands together.

He stepped around to the open panel on the left side, and seeing that it was quite substantial, asked, "How did I not notice such a large space?"

I was pleased that he hadn't found it. "The opening edges are all concealed by decorative work. The cavity is fourteen inches tall, eight inches from front to back, and two inches deep from left to right."

"It's huge," he said.

I moved over to the left side and pointed out to him a few of the features of the compartment. "I've lined it with two layers of felt so coins or anything metallic might not rattle and be heard. Here and here, I've positioned two pegs." I touched each of them with my fingertip. "They'll hold and support the weight of a flint-lock pistol and, as you can see, there are several leather laces that can hold other items in place." I leaned back on my haunches. "Even with the pistol within the compartment, you would still have room for extra shot, powder, a dagger, and an envelope for bank notes and personal correspondence."

"Brixton, this is amazing!" exclaimed the captain.

"Don't congratulate me." Edwyn put his hand on my shoulder. "This secret compartment is entirely of Michael's design."

Captain Henderson shook my hand, pumping it enthusiastically, and gripped my shoulder with his other hand. "Well done. Splendid. Well done, Sterling." He chuckled. "There will be no more hiding of my valuables in shoes and books, nor under my mattress." Humorously, he laughed at himself.

Winking, I raised my index finger and corrected him. "I would actually suggest that you do leave a few less important items in places such as you've mentioned. Decoys might cause a thief to stop looking when he finds them."

"Yes, I suppose you're right."

Captain Henderson closed up his glorious new cabinet. He reached into a broken drawer beneath his bed and pulled out a shoe with a great laugh. He then poured from his shoe onto his bed a handful of coins, a tied up roll of bank notes, a silver toothpick, and a dead cockroach. Picking out five guineas and a dozen shillings, he gave them to Edwyn, congratulating us again on our work.

"Thank you, Captain, for the opportunity to design and build these for you." Edwyn bobbed his head in agreement and shook the captain's hand.

The captain then shook my hand again as well. "Thank you men for such quality craftsmanship." He smiled. "Tibbins, escort these master cabinet makers through the ship to the dock."

We Both Shall Row, My Love And I

We dropped off the wagon and the canvas tarps at the warehouse and Edwyn flipped a shilling coin through the air to George. "Thanks for the use of your wagon."

"You're welcome. Is Captain Henderson a generous man?" asked George. "He transported the Earl's lumber down to Bristol and we'll be completing our repair work below deck with him later this week."

"I found him to be both generous and appreciative," responded Edwyn.

"How's your wrist?" I asked.

George opened and closed his fist several times. "I'm lucky I caught the shilling," he laughed. "It's almost back to normal, but it stiffens up from time to time."

We said our goodbyes and headed home. When we arrived at the porch, Edwyn sat in his rocking chair and I sat beside him. He pulled the rest of the money from his pocket. "The remaining shillings are for the materials, the sawyer, and the drying."

I leaned forward. "Are you sure that's enough?"

"For sure, and these," he passed me two guineas, "are for you."

"Thank you so much, Edwyn. Every time I work with you, I learn so much more about
woodworking, especially the finishing work." I rose to my feet, a bit suddenly. "I need to go and speak with John Lyon right away."

"It sounds urgent."

"Oh, it is." I grinned as I stood. "I'll be able to tell you all about it in a few days."

"Will you join us for supper in an hour or so?" he asked.

"Of course. It will be my pleasure."

I headed off down the cobblestone road toward the lighthouse with my two gold guineas, and was welcomed into the

Lyon's kitchen. Princess met me at the door, limping a bit but wagging her tail.

"John, Princess is doing so well. Muriel's healing salves are truly amazing."

"That they be, Michael."

He seated himself at the table, and gesturing towards the opposing chair, I seated myself.

With a broad grin, I pulled the two guineas from my pocket and slid them across the table to him. "Four plus two makes six. Add these to the down payment John."

"That's grand. Saints be praised. There be only four remainin'."

"Edwyn and I completed and delivered the work for the *Eleutheran Quest* earlier, and the captain was more generous than expected."

John pet Princess and then pulled three little pieces of dried beef from his pocket. "Watch this."

"Watch what?"

"Princess, sit." Princess sat and he gave her a dried beef treat. "Princess, over now." He gestured with his hand. Princess rolled over, and he gave her another dried beef treat. "Now Michael, you'll be appreciating this next command. I don't 'magine you 'ave ever been seein' one like it before."

"I'm looking forward to it," I said.

John, with mock anger and a loud voice, pointed at me with his closed fist and shouted, "Princess, don't let 'im move!" He repeated himself with more emphasis. "*Do not* let 'im move!" Princess immediately directed herself towards me. She lowered her head, narrowed her eyes, and started a deep, back of the throat growl, with bared teeth.

My head snapped back and I pulled my hands in towards my chest, expecting the wolfhound to start ripping into them. I sucked in a lung full of air and my heart rate exploded.

"Michael, would you like to try standing up?"

"Is, is it safe?" I leaned forward slightly, brought one of my feet under my body at the front of the chair, and started to raise myself up out of the chair. Princess reacted instantly. She lunged, barked, and snapped at me, merely inches from my knees and arms. I shuddered and imagined myself being viciously attacked. "John, call her off. Call her off!"

"Okay me Princess, stop now. My sweet doggie." He gave her the third dried beef reward and petted her head.

John started laughing but I didn't. My heart rate and breathing hadn't returned to normal.

"Princess, show 'im that you be friendly still." He grinned and gestured towards me with a confident expression.

Princess took a calm step towards me and gently licked my shaking hand. After a moment, I found my confidence and pet her head as she licked my hand a few more times.

"That is quite a command." I rubbed my chin. "If you were ever in danger or felt threatened, that command would stop an attack, or even save your life."

"We've worked on it for two weeks. Lay down now, Princess." Immediately she went over to an old mat in the corner of the kitchen, walked in a tight circle, and laid down. He tossed her a treat.

"Oh, did you 'ear?" John leaned back in his chair and tapped the table a few times. "Sabina 'as been released and she an' Nicola 'eaded south to be with some o' their family."

"I didn't know that." I raised my eyebrows and wondered what her future would be like. "Nicola is a fine little girl."

"There be bigger news than that."

"Go ahead, tell me more."

"Lord Warrington's men searched 'igh an' low for Caine but found nothin'. There be not a sign of 'im 'til a squad of Lord Warrington's men were transportin' all the rogues to Carlisle."

John Lyon slapped the tabletop with the flat of his hand. "Victor and Gavin shall be 'ung right proper." He dramatically mimed a hanging by pulling an imaginary rope up the side of his head and wincing. "Their last sunrise, it shall be in Carlisle, and that'll be the sunset o' their days."

My eyes opened wide and I sucked in some air through my parted lips.

John continued, "Grand Freddie, Joseph Caine, and Chatwin Smythe, under 'eavily armed escort, were taken to Carlisle as well to serve their prison sentences. The Crown 'as fine lodgin' for 'em, I 'ear." He laughed heartily. "But the tea is nothin' to be cherishin' and they might be 'avin' a difficult time findin' servants to their likin'." John chuckled and slapped his leg.

"John, what about Robert Caine? Has anyone seen him in Carlisle? We've all heard many rumors and even some detailed reports that he's up in the Carlisle area."

"Let me tell you. That rogue Caine, 'e attacked the armed escort an' tried to free the pris'ners only a few miles short o' Carlisle. Caine's first arrow missed the wagon driver's 'ead by an inch." He gestured with finger and thumb. "Then, 'is second arrow went 'alf the way through the squad leader's arm." He gestured with his right thumb point, striking his left upper arm. "Finally, 'is third 'it a soldier in 'is knee." John then smacked his knee firmly and Princess lifted her head, looked at him, and laid her head back down.

"What happened next?" My eyes opened wide. "Did the rogues get away?"

"No. The escort was a dozen armed men. They saw 'im on a nearby cliff an' shot a few musket rounds at 'im but 'e got away."

"Too bad he escaped," I said.

We Both Shall Row, My Love And I

"Four o' the escort men went up on the cliff, where Caine be shootin' 'is arrows from, to take a look. Guess what 'e saw?" John paused. "Spots o' blood."

"He must've gotten hit with a shot. Did they find him? Did they find Caine?"

"No, 'e wasn't about. They followed a wee blood trail an' then it started to be rainin'. It seemed that the trail o' blood led to a place where there'd been three 'orses tethered."

"Does anyone think that he'll be coming back here?" I asked.

"No one be knowin' for sure. We don't be knowin' if 'e be shot or if a mate be shot. We be all needin' to keep an eye open. 'e might be lookin' to 'is family in Carlisle or 'e might be returnin' 'ere."

John got up from his chair and went over to the wood stove where a pot of tea had been steeping. He brought it over to the table and set it down on a scorched cloth beside a sugar bowl and a little milk pitcher.

"Thank you, John."

He then got a plate of biscuits and baked goods and set them down in front of me, put his big hand on my shoulder, and gave it a squeeze. "Michael, you 'aven't told me about your plans for the lot but you did seem to be keepin' it quiet from dear Madelyn. Are you 'avin' plans in that direction?" He had a sly grin.

"Yes, I think that I am."

He produced a genteel laugh and gave me a wink. "Madelyn, she be a right fine lady. Let me write you out a receipt for the building lot. It be the correct way to be doin' business." Without getting up out of his chair, he squinted and peered around the kitchen. "Where's me spectacles? Me eyes aren't so good as they once be. Hmph, perhaps someone with poorer eyesight than meself 'as walked off with 'em."

Spotting his velvet spectacle bag across the room on a little side table, I retrieved it and passed it to him. "Here's your spectacles."

Carefully opening the drawstring at the top of the bag, he withdrew his wire-rimmed spectacles with the cracked lens.

He took a scrap of paper and a Borrowdale pencil from a drawer beneath the tabletop and wrote out the receipt showing the two payments, the first of four guineas, today's of two guineas, and the remaining balance of four guineas. He wrote the date on the top and signed the bottom. All in a truly business-like fashion.

"There now, 'ere you go, Michael, an' if you know anyone be needin' to rent 'n 'ouse, please be sendin' 'em my way."

"What do you mean? Are you leaving your home? Who'll run the lighthouse?"

"No, no, me brother an' me, we be ownin' the 'ouse that Carolyn's aunt 'as been livin' in, rest 'er soul, an' now we be lookin' for a new tenant. It was a terrible job cleanin' up the blood and filth."

"You and your brother are quite the active businessmen, with the lighthouse, the slate transport, house rental, and selling me that building lot."

"Well, one must be stayin' active. I 'ave two more lots, a wee bit smaller though, that I'd be willin' to sell an interested party, but I don't want to be gettin' to braggin' and bein' puffed up."

"By the way, there's only a few more weeks until Princess delivers her pups."

He gave a great smile. "That be right, maybe three weeks, but keep your voice at a whisper. We don't want to worry 'er."

"That will be a great day. Brynne has been praying for a safe delivery and for healthy pups."

"That Brynne is a precious missy, an' I be thinkin' that the young man who be findin' 'er will be blessed indeed."

"I'm sure of it." I stood and pushed in the chair. "I should be heading back now. I'd like to do a little more work with Edwyn before supper."

"By all means, and a fine thank you for the payment." John turned in his chair as I rose and walked towards the door.

We exchanged our goodbyes and I stepped outside into the dazzling afternoon sun. On my way back to the Brixton home, I noticed movement in the forest shadows up the hill behind the cleared lot. Quietly I moved off the road and stood still amongst some bushes. Watching and listening. My hand slowly went to my side, and opening the release clip of my knife, I drew it from its sheath. Carefully placing each step as I moved, I made my way up the hill, from one point of cover to the next. When I arrived at the top, I concealed myself behind a tree, took a few deep breaths, and waited for a moment. Breathing deeply and evenly, I waited for action. Peering around the side of a big old maple and scanning the area, I saw an outline of someone moving through the shadows.

The Field Of Retribution

Behind the building lot there appeared to be a woman dressed like a man. Her hair was tucked up under a working man's well-worn three-cornered hat to keep it clean and out of the way. She wore a man's tattered bush coat and light brown pants. Carrying an armful of small branches and piling them in the forest beyond the back corner of the clearing, she worked with diligence. A few minutes later, being a hot day, she removed her coat and draped it over a low branch. She then removed her hat and hung it on a broken, peg-like branch. Her luxurious auburn hair fell out and cascaded down around her shoulders. She pulled a length of yellow ribbon from her pocket and tied back her hair.

Madelyn? Why would she be here? What's she doing? Hmm, time for a little amusement.

I returned my knife to its sheath, refastening the clasp. Keeping low in the underbrush, not wanting to be seen, but still able to see her, I snapped a dry stick, *crack*. She stopped, lifted her head, and looked around. A moment later, she returned to her task. I quickly snapped another dry stick twice, *crack, crack*. Again, her head shot up. She stood still and listened intently as she scanned the forest before resuming her work. I had difficulty keeping myself from laughing.

"Is anyone there?" she shouted.

I let her return to her work for a few minutes. She dropped the armful of debris and then went into the clearing and picked up another armful. With her movement around the clearing, I was now only forty feet from her.

I'm so bad but this is such great fun. She won't think it's Caine. Everyone is aware that he's long gone up to Carlisle. I quietly picked up a couple olive-sized stones. Pitching one high and beyond her, she quickly spun around to look, at which point I tossed the other stone off to one side. She twisted around towards the direction of the second stone and froze. I started laughing but had my hands tight over my mouth, not wanting to be heard. Beastly sounds came through my fingers. Scanning the forest, bending down low, then lifting her head and moving it from side to side, she tried to see into the potentially dangerous shadows of the forest around her.

"Who's there?" she shouted.

I shouldn't be scaring her like this. She's cheerfully clearing our lot. This is such great fun.

She quietly set her armful of debris onto the pile, as if she didn't want to bring attention to herself from any potential danger. Picking up a heavy branch about two feet long, she scanned the forest. At the opportune moment when she was looking away, I made a vicious growling sound and came crashing out of the shadows like an animal, with my head down so that she couldn't immediately recognize me.

Thwack! With blood gushing from my mouth and nose, I bent over in great pain, moaning, barely able to recall who I was and what I had been doing.

"Ahhgg." *What happened?*

She had thrown her club-like branch at just the right moment, and when I looked up, it had struck me in the face.

Smitten, I was in excruciating pain. With my split lip and bitten tongue, I dropped to my knees. Falling onto my side, I lay there moaning. My ears were ringing. Stars were circling. *What happened? Am I going to die?*

"Michael, is that you?" Madelyn took a step towards me. "What are you doing?" I couldn't respond and continued moaning. When she was certain that it was me, she ran to where I lay suffering and knelt down beside me. "Were you chasing something? I heard a vicious animal moving about and I didn't know what it was. I thought that I needed to defend myself. I'm so sorry. Are you alright?"

"I' wath me. I wath thwyin' to fwighthen you." I couldn't form the words properly with my swollen lip, bitten tongue, sore teeth, and dazed condition. "I wath havin' tho muth fwun."

"What are you saying? Why are you talking like that?"

"I' wath tho muth fwun," I repeated.

She was quiet for a moment and shook her head. "Why do men always think that boyish behavior and trying to scare someone would be fun?" She grimaced and laughed. Mocking me, she said, "Ith no' tho muth fwun now ith i'?"

Moaning, I answered, "I tho thorry, Mathelyn."

I took a handkerchief from my pocket and started to dab my bloody lip, swollen face, and the abrasion I had on my forehead.

"You helpless man. You're smearing the blood all around your face. Give me your handkerchief."

She spent the next few minutes stopping the bleeding from my swollen mouth and scratched forehead by direct pressure. I pinched my nose, trying to stop its bleeding. She then tried to wipe up the blood on my clothing, but seeing that the stains would probably never come out, her hands dropped to her side in frustration. I was in such terrible pain.

Disappointed, she mocked me, saying, "Michael, I'm tho thorry tha' I hith you in the fath."

"I learn my lethon. I tho thorry," I mumbled and laughed through my injured mouth.

We laughed together, knowing that this would be a humorous drama that we would never forget. I would never underestimate her again. *This woman is fearless.*

"Michael, let's go and sit on the rock so we can see the harbor. I'll get some water to clean you up." She retrieved her hat and coat from the branches, and returned to help me.

I stumbled along like a disciplined and forlorn schoolboy as she led the way into the sunshine of the clearing and towards our sitting rock.

Madelyn dropped her hat and coat on a small fallen tree beside us and then helped me to sit. I was still a bit unsteady on my feet.

"Give me your shirt. I'll rinse it in the harbor."

The pain was subsiding. My mind was shrouded in stupidity, but even so, I was embraced by the beauty of the location. *This is a beautiful building sight we have. This is our clearing. Ours.*

I removed my coat with her help and tossed it on the fallen tree beside hers. It was still clean because it had been open but the shirt was another matter. It was spotted with drops of blood. Helping me unbutton it, because I was still pressing the handkerchief to my face, I didn't notice how she was looking at me. I tried to ignore the throbbing pain.

◊◊◊◊◊◊◊

Michael, with Madelyn's help, removed his shirt, held the handkerchief to his face.

We Both Shall Row, My Love And I

Her imaginative mind wandered. *He's a powerful man. His chest and arms are even bigger and firmer than I thought. I should've had his shirt off long before this. Madelyn, get yourself under control. This isn't proper.*

◊◊◊◊◊◊◊

Madelyn walked down the hill towards the water's edge with my shirt in one hand and the bloody handkerchief in the other. The wind blew her beautiful long red hair and in the sunlight, some blonde highlights caught my attention. She removed her boots, rolled up her pant legs, and stepped, knee deep, out into the water at our little beach.

My mind couldn't escape her beauty. *What a gorgeous woman. This wonderful woman that I love so deeply. My Madelyn. My love. She's as alluring as any woman could ever be.*

I was smitten, more by her beauty and her love for me than by her accuracy with her club. I started to laugh. *Ouch. It hurts too much to laugh.*

Madelyn dropped my shirt into the water to soak. She then rinsed and wrung out my bloody handkerchief repeatedly until it was almost clean. Finally, she rinsed and wrung it out one last time, and then after shaking it in the breeze, trying to dry it, she folded it and tucked it into her belt. She then started to work on my shirt. Rinsing it and wringing it out repeatedly, she made her best attempts to remove the spots of blood. When it was almost clean, she did the knuckle swishing motion, both in the water and above it, that one does when rubbing and agitating a difficult stain. Eventually, she stopped and held it up and looked at it.

It looks clean to me.

She looked at it, shook her head, and repeated the process twice more.

I shouted down to her. "Mathelyn, ith fine."

She looked up at me with a wide grin. Mocking me, she said, "Ith not fine. Ith thoiled, peeble will lath at you."

I'm going to be hearing about this for the rest of my life. What a sweetheart. Our home will be filled with joy and laughter. I started to laugh again. *Ouch, that hurts.*

Madelyn made her way back to the shore, crossed the road, and as she was about to climb the slope of our property, along came John.

"Well now, we 'ave a truly domestic scene 'ere. 'ave you been doin' your man's laundry, Madelyn?"

They climbed the hill towards me as she responded to his questions.

"What 'appened?"

"Michael's had a little accident."

"I can be seein' that, missy." He was becoming quite concerned. "What 'appened?"

"Something bumped his mouth."

"What 'it 'im in the mouth? Was you attacked, Michael?"

I envisioned John sending word to the captain of the guard and gathering a group of townspeople to search for some rogues. "I wathen't athacked."

"Why 'e be talkin' in such a way?"

Madelyn gave John the handkerchief, who began cleaning up my face and forehead as she walked into the forest beyond our lot. She picked up the club-like branch that had been my undoing and brought it to John.

"Was 'e 'it with this?" asked John.

"Yeth, I wath hith with i'."

"Who be 'ittin my friend with this 'ere club?" He gripped the heavy branch, looked at it, and swung it, testing its weight and use as a weapon.

Madelyn was looking quite embarrassed and glanced down at the ground before looking back at John, who was now holding the club in his right hand and smacking his left palm with it.

"This be a right formidable weapon," he said.

She winced and said, "He tried to frighten me when I was clearing our lot." She sheepishly looked down at the ground again. "I generally don't scare too easily. I reacted before I saw that it was my Michael. I threw it at him." She bit her lip and looked at the ground. "And down he went."

John drew his chin back into his neck and opened his eyes wide. He looked at me, then at Madelyn, and then back at me. After a moment, it dawned on him what was being said. "Oh Michael." He started to laugh. "You be tryin' to scare our dear missy but she not be the easy scarin' kind o' woman you 'magine." He let out a great chuckle. "She put you down like David dropped Goliath on the field o' retribution."

Madelyn came to my defense, perhaps feeling guilty that John might be embarrassing me. "It wasn't like that. He didn't go down easy like you say."

"Go on, missy, be tellin' me more."

"He fell to his knees—"

John mockingly interrupted, "Oh I see, 'e didn't go all the way down then. Big man that 'e be."

"No, not right away," she said.

John shook his head and laughed. "This be getting better all the time." John stopped laughing to catch his breath. "What do you be meanin', 'e didn't go down, not right away, what be 'appening next?"

"Well, after he dropped to his knees, then he fell onto his side."

I could hardly believe how the story was unfolding. *She's enjoying this. It's embarrassing to be dropped by a woman like a bag of dirt. I guess I deserved it. Hope she's having fun.* I started to join in the laughter. "Outh, tha' hurths."

Madelyn saw that I was in fine spirits and she was starting to enjoy John's comical reaction to everything that she said.

Everyone enjoys a good audience, including my Madelyn.

John saw that I was smiling in spite of my crooked mouth and swollen lip. "Oh, 'e suffered in silence then."

"No John, not *too* silent," she corrected him. "Not exactly. He was moaning something awful."

He saw that I had dribbled a spot of blood onto my chest and pointing at it he said, "You better wipe up your wee laddie, Madelyn, 'e be seein' more o' 'is friends in a minute." He gestured at Tommy, Carolyn, and Brynne as they approached us on the cobbled road.

Madelyn wiped the little spot of blood from my chest with the handkerchief.

"This be quite a story," said John. "A story worth rememberin' or writin' down."

I was painfully trying to grin and said, "Ith not ober ye'." I opened my mouth and stuck out my tongue. I then gently pulled open my lip and revealed that there was a cut on the inside of my mouth as well as the outside. "Lowk a' thith," I said, and realizing that I had a loose tooth, added, "My thooth ith looth." I gave it a little wiggle.

John started laughing again and wiped the tears from his eyes. "Bless you two. You be quite a pair. Meant for each other, I s'ppose." John ran his fingers through his thinning hair. "Madelyn, you better be practicin' your medical skills with Muriel if this be what the future be 'oldin' for you."

Madelyn put her hat on her head, rolled down her pant legs, carried my shirt under her arm, and carried her club. I picked up both of our coats and flung them over my shoulder

We Both Shall Row, My Love And I

as we walked down the hill hand in hand. Tommy, Carolyn, and Brynne, climbing up the hill, saw my injury.

Brynne touched my bare shoulder and looked up into my eyes. "Are you okay? That looks painful. What happened?"

Carolyn inhaled and exclaimed, "Did you have a terrible fall, Mr. Sterling?"

"Can we be 'elpin' you, Mr. Sterlin' sir? What 'appened? Did you be fallin' from a 'uge tree?" asked Tommy

I shared a crooked grin with them and Madelyn simply said, "He'll be fine but I think he needs to lie down and rest. John Lyon will tell you what happened."

When we got down to the road, I glanced back at the three youths crowding around John, who was now sitting on the flat rock in the midst of his story telling. He was gesturing and miming, and Tommy and Carolyn were starting to giggle, but not Brynne. She looked down the hill at me, and sharing an understanding smile, gave me a worried look and a wave.

When we arrived at the Brixton home, no one was there, so Madelyn led me directly through to my room at the back. She pulled back the blanket on my bed. "You need to get some rest."

She put my handkerchief on the small table at the head of my bed and hung my shirt on the twine rope in the yard after rinsing it out again in fresh water.

"Wait a minute, Michael." She spread an old towel on my pillow so that I wouldn't bloody the pillowcase. "You'll be fine. Get some rest and don't wiggle that tooth. No one wants a sweetheart with a gaping hole in his face."

She kissed me on the side of my mouth, opposite the cut on my lip, bringing back memories of how she used to kiss me.

"Michael, forgive me. I'm so sorry that I hit you in the mouth with that nasty old branch."

"I mo' thorry than you, thweet 'eart."

She gently seated herself beside me, and her gaze, having fallen on my chest, slowly rose to my eyes. With tenderness she said, "I think that you're beginning to grasp how much you mean to me and how deeply I cherish you."

She placed her nearest hand on my shoulder and placed her other hand on my chest. She leaned in towards me from the chair, softly kissing the side of my mouth, my cheek, and then my ear. She whispered something into my ear again.

What did she say?

She giggled and then sat back down.

Even her little kisses are warm and passionate. She can be such a tease. What did she say?

"Mmmm," I moaned.

"Was that a good moan?" she asked.

"Mmmm," again I moaned. I nodded slowly. "Yeth. It wath a gooth moan."

She smiled, baring her perfect white teeth. "Get some rest. I need to help Muriel with Elizabeth Harcourt and her child tomorrow. Come and visit me on Thursday evening." And with that she stepped out through the door.

I took off my trousers, got into bed, and pulled the blanket up to my neck.

Maybe tomorrow will be a better day. She takes good care of me. I love her so much.

Thinking of my sweet Madelyn and her love for me, sleep wasn't easy. Eventually, to the subdued cooing of a forlorn mourning dove, perhaps near Eutychus' grave, I fell asleep.

The Traveler's Studio
July 1789

At various points the following day, I discovered that while I had been sleeping, recuperating from the suffering I had received by the hand of my true love, life had carried on without me.

Life, entwined within time, had moved along. Three events relating to me, none of them earth-shattering nor epoch-making, would continue to unfold. Each would enkindle within me, a simple sense of thanksgiving.

First, as soon as Madelyn had put me to bed with my injuries, she had hurried to the parsonage. There she obtained from Muriel a little jar of healing salve, a large alum crystal, and a tiny bottle of laudanum. Returning quickly to the Brixtons, she had given them the medications and instructed them as to how the items should be used for my care. I would find myself thankful the following day that prayerful benevolence would be walking hand-in-hand with effective medication.

Second, a little later in the evening, John Lyon, who I dare not call The Rotund, had gone to the Royal Stag. He told his many friends the humorous anecdote of my dear Madelyn having smitten me. I would find myself thankful that I wouldn't need to repeat the story endlessly to those who might ask about my injuries.

Finally, late at night, long after the saintly doves of our seaport had snuggled into their cozy little nests, leaving the midnight ravens at the Royal Stag to their own misadventures, Captain Henderson's steward arrived at the Brixton home. Upon his arrival, Tibbins shared with Edwyn the detailed plans for a large roll-out chest that was to be positioned beneath the captain's bed. I would find myself thankful that I would have another project from which I might further develop my craftsmanship skills.

I was awakened the next day by the heartwarming chatter of cheerful women in the kitchen. There's no other sound in the world as consoling as that.

The light-hearted, expressive style of a third woman, in addition to Louisa and Brynne, was attracting my attention. The voice was familiar, to a certain point, but possessing the traces of an interesting accent. *Meiling? I wonder why she's here. In church, her father does most of the speaking for the family. His English is fair but Meiling's is superb.*

Brynne tapped on the door and entered my room, carrying a cup of tea. "Michael, you're awake. Here's some tea to start your day." She set it on the small table at the head of my bed. "Breakfast will be ready in a few minutes."

She walked over to the window beside the door and flung open the curtains. "It's a glorious morning." Sunlight, reflecting from the windows of the shop, flooded the room. She then stepped over to the door and fully opening it, stood there in the sunlight. The intense beams reflecting from the shop windows radiantly poured in, along with a great gust of wind. Her pale green gingham dress, cinched tight at her waist, was not only lightweight, and being blown by the inrush of wind, it was also quite sheer. Out of respect for her, I looked away.

She came over to my bed and sat down on the edge. "Last night, Madelyn brought over some of Muriel's healing salve, a large alum crystal, and some laudanum for the throbbing pain." She wet her lips. "We've got to get you feeling better. I wish she hadn't hit you with that stick." Taking the little jar of Muriel's salve from her pocket and removing the lid, she leaned towards me. "Michael, let me see your injuries."

I leaned up on one elbow and the sheet fell from my shoulders, exposing my chest. With a dab of the salve on her fingertip, she reached towards me and applied it to the abrasion on my forehead.

"Thank you, Brynne."

With a sly smile, she lifted my chin with her other hand. "Pucker your lips out like this." She formed her lips into an exaggerated pucker.

I did so and as she leaned in even more closely, her sweet breath caressed my face. She smiled tenderly while applying the salve to the outside of my lip.

"Here's an alum crystal. Place it gently on the wound inside your lip, even though it stings." She enjoyed demonstrating, revealing both her knowledge and her maturity. "It will deaden the sting, and if you have a lot of pain, talk to mother about the laudanum."

"Thank you so much. You're a precious friend."

Brynne arose and passed me a fresh shirt. "Would you like me to help you with your shirt?"

"No, thank you. I'm able to manage it myself."

"Breakfast will be on the table in a few minutes. Have a sip of your tea."

"Thank you, Brynne, you're very helpful."

After getting dressed, visiting the privy, and washing my hands and face at the rain barrel, I stood for a few minutes to look at Eutychus' grave. I remembered the loyal companionship he had provided for the family. Edwyn had carved the dear mastiff's name onto a wide hardwood plank, and had set one end of it, deep into the ground to mark his resting place. Brynne had planted some delicate wild flowers, entirely blanketing his grave, beside the globe flowers that were already in the yard. *A beautiful dog. A faithful friend.*

A pair of mourning doves was on a branch above his resting place and as they cooed, they leaned in towards one another and rubbed their heads against each other's shoulders. I couldn't help myself, I thought of Madelyn and me. These two mourning doves were so very content.

Louisa and Edwyn, having eaten breakfast earlier, left for the shops, while Brynne and Meiling were resetting the table as I entered the kitchen.

"Thanks for the tea, Brynne. It was a pleasant start to the day." I set my empty cup on the table.

Brynne paused for a moment, put her hands on her hips, and grinned. "You're welcome, Michael."

"Meiling, how are you this morning?" I asked.

She yawned and smiled, accentuating her white teeth, high cheekbones, and two tiny beauty marks beside her right eye. They were alluring and captured my attention.

"Sorry." She blinked and yawned again. "I'm doing well but I'm a bit tired." She stretched and then giggled.

"Why are you so tired?" asked Brynne, as she herself yawned while pouring my tea.

"My family stayed up late last night. Father was showing me things on a map and then we went up on deck with a star chart to look at the constellations. It was a beautiful night. Not

We Both Shall Row, My Love And I

a breath of wind. We were up there for a long time, and when we finished looking at the stars, he began playing his dizi."

"A dizi? What's that?" I asked.

"A Chinese wooden flute. His music floated out across the harbor and some of the men aboard the ship came and sat with us. No one spoke. It was a special time. When we finally returned to our cabins, mother recited some Chinese poetry, and then she and I took turns singing for my father. I accompanied our singing with my pipa."

I set my cup of tea down and leaned forward, listening more attentively. "A pipa? Tell me more. What is a pipa?" *I'm having a whole new area of music opened up to me this morning. So wonderful.*

"It is something like a four string tenor guitar or a lute. Have you never seen or heard one?"

"No, I haven't." I yawned. "Sorry." I rubbed my face. "Would you play it for me sometime? Perhaps Madelyn could play her flute and I'll join in with my oboe. We could—"

"I'll play my hand drum," added Brynne, not wanting to be left out.

"When could we get together? Where can we play?" I asked.

Brynne passed me a plate of biscuits. "This evening. Here, in the front room or on our porch."

Breakfast was satisfying and the conversation was stimulating, but Brynne and I did much more listening than talking. Meiling told us of her life at sea with her parents. She had an endless number of interesting stories, humorous anecdotes, and curious observations. She had been almost everywhere but East Africa, Australia, and South America.

She showed us some of her interesting sketches of the places that they had been and the things that they had done. It was wonderful artwork and we were impressed by her talent.

She spoke of the Bay of Fundy on the North American coast with its forty foot tides; the mysterious sixty-foot-tall Khao Phing Kan Rock on the coast of Siam with its enchanting beach, and the majesty of the rock of Gibraltar with its labyrinth of caves beneath it. The Brixton's kitchen had become a traveler's studio, as Meiling captivated us with her stories of distant lands.

Most of Meiling's life, since the age of eight, had been with her parents aboard a variety of blue water merchant ships. Their past five years aboard the *Eleutheran Quest* had been their longest length of service on any one ship. In her twelve years at sea, she had seen an almost limitless number of exotic places and had experienced many life-challenging situations. They had faced storms, pirates, loss of food supplies, fire, and on one occasion, an attempted mutiny by members of a dissatisfied crew.

Brynne was so excited to hear of Meiling's adventures that she slapped the table with the palm of her hand. "That's the life for me. Excitement and adventure."

"It can be dangerous," added Meiling, sipping her tea, examining Brynne and me with her beautiful almond-shaped eyes. Her gaze was alluring.

Nodding, Brynne ran her fingers through her chestnut hair. "Reading about exotic ports and adventure is all I get to do." She was so disappointed. "You actually go to those places."

Meiling and I smiled at one another, inwardly applauding Brynne's youthful desire. "That's what I'd love to do," she continued. "Maybe someday my father will return to the sea and take my mother and me along." With both arms raised, a bit provocatively, she adjusted a sterling silver pin in her hair.

Her dress and her actions are difficult to disregard. I looked away and stirred my tea.

"Your father was a sea-faring man?" asked Meiling.

"That's right. Before I was born, my parents had a modest home in Bristol. My mother worked as a cook in a rich person's home, not far from the Baptist Bible college, but my father was often at sea. He worked as a ship's carpenter and—"

"Madelyn told me about that Baptist College," interrupted Meiling. "Her cousin, Colin Graham, was there. He has just completed his studies and is assisting an elderly preacher in a nearby town."

"Graham?" I asked. "Madelyn's family name is Ekland."

"Her mother's maiden name was Graham. There's more interesting details yet. Colin is engaged to an amazing Spanish woman, Penelope Mendoza."

"Penelope Mendoza," repeated Brynne. "That's an interesting name." She chuckled. "Penelope is a very English name and Mendoza is very Spanish."

Meiling passed Brynne the plate of buttered toast. "Her father was a wealthy Spaniard and her mother was a highly educated mulatto."

"Was?" I questioned.

"Her parents have both passed away. Now it's Colin and Penny against the world!" She giggled, dramatically raising both her hands. "Very romantic."

Meiling took a sip of her tea. "Sorry to interrupt your story, Brynne." She took a bite of toast. "I didn't know that about your father, that he had worked at sea."

"That's okay," responded Brynne. "My father loves woodworking. His love of wood is the story."

They both chuckled. With furrowed brow and my chin pulled into my neck, I didn't see what was so humorous.

Meiling picked up the last piece of toast, took a bite, and turning, faced me more directly. "Captain Henderson let my father and I take a close look at the cabinet and chart table that you and Edwyn built." Smiling, she pointed at me with her toast, licking her lips. "You both did marvelous work. It's both beautiful and sturdy."

"He's a master cabinet maker, and every time I've worked with him, I've learned something new."

Brynne passed Meiling a pewter serving dish with pieces of fried pork piled onto it, followed by a selection of cheeses on a small wooden plater.

I continued. "I've seen my own craftsmanship improve greatly during these past few months here with Edwyn—"

"My father would be gone on the ships," Brynne interrupted, "as a carpenter for months at a time, but when my mother became pregnant with me, that put an end to that." She nodded decisively. "He decided to stay ashore and do his woodworking on land. There was no one who did finishing carpentry or quality cabinetry work here in Oak Harbor, so we came up from Bristol when I was still a baby."

"Bristol's a busy seaport," said Meiling. "There were more than a thousand ships that passed through the harbor last year. About equal numbers of coastal traders and foreign vessels."

"How do you know that?" I asked.

"The Bristol harbor master took me out for tea when we were there last week with Lord Warrington's lumber." She leaned towards Brynne and whispered, "He couldn't take his eyes off my dress."

Brynne chuckled. "He wasn't looking at your dress Meiling, he was looking at you."

Meiling continued. "He told me all about the seaport." She laughed and leaned towards me. "It might not be pretty in all respects but it always captures a sea farer's heart. It's becoming one of my favorite cities in the world."

"Bristol? The whole world?" I asked.

"That's right. It's a busy city and there are ships from everywhere. The harbor master told me that there are more than fifty thousand people living there now."

I finished my cup of tea and set the empty cup down on its saucer with a clink. "Did you ladies hear that John Wesley preached there last year?"

"No, tell us about it," said Meiling.

I leaned back in my chair. "John Wesley gave a thundering speech against slavery, and some of its notable citizens have become anti-slavery advocates." I rapped the table with my knuckles. "Should one man own another? Of course not." I paused, meeting each of their eyes. "There is no justice in it."

Meiling winked and poured me another cup of tea. "I absolutely agree with you."

My mind wandered. *Why does she always have her hair up in a topknot? The fallen strands of her hair frame her face so well.*

Brynne clinked the spoon loudly in the sugar bowl and then added some to my tea. "I agree. Slavery is wrong!"

When we'd completed breakfast and the ladies finished the kitchen clean up, Brynne went with Meiling to have a tour of the *Eleutheran Quest,* and shared that she'd be staying out with her until after supper. They assured me that they'd invite Madelyn to join us in playing some music on the porch later in the evening.

Minutes after they left, Louisa and Edwyn returned from the shops carrying a few packages while I was on the porch looking out over the harbor with my third cup of tea.

Edwyn and I worked all morning on the low roll-out chest for Captain Henderson, and then after a light lunch of soup, cheese, and bread, we returned to our work.

At one point in the mid-afternoon, and quite unexpectedly, Edwyn put his arm around my back and gripped my shoulder.

"That's a well-positioned building lot atop the little hill on the way to the lighthouse, isn't it?"

"You've got that right." I sensed that he was wanting me to divulge my intentions about Madelyn, but I playfully decided to toy with him.

"You've always enjoyed keeping an eye on the harbor from our porch." He walked across the shop, and fetching a dovetail saw, returned to the joinery he was working on. "A house with a porch, up on that hill..." He gestured the height of the hill. "Would be splendid."

"It would be. There's no doubt about that."

"The little strand of beach below the lot would be perfect for children." He inclined his head and pursed his lips. "They could be seen from the porch. It would be a safe place to play."

"You're right. It's a nice beach of clean sand."

"There's a woodlot for sale directly behind the building lot. Did you know that, Michael? Have you ever seen the impressive trees there?"

"No, I haven't. Who's selling it?"

"George Kline. It's about ten acres." Edwyn went across the shop again, picked up a hand drill, and returned to his project. "The cleared lot, and the ten acres, would make a wonderful estate."

"I'm sure they would."

He plumped himself down on an old chair across from me. "Well Michael, are you going to make me ask you outright what your plans for the future might be? I feel like a dentist digging and picking in your mouth."

I winced. *Such a gross thought.*

He continued. "The whole seaport's talking. I know about the four guinea deposit."

Having started my polishing work on the top of the chest with a mixture of pumice, linseed oil, and alcohol, I didn't want to stop. With a little guffaw and shaking my head, I decided that I would tell him about my intentions towards Madelyn. "It's actually a total of six guineas that I've deposited and only four remain."

Edwyn laughed and bobbed his head in support. "You're not one for wasting time, are you?"

"He who hesitates is lost," I declared. "She's marvelous. A caring and beautiful woman. I refuse to imagine my life without her." I picked up more of the abrasive pumice with my cloth. "I intend to marry her."

This feels so affirming to confess my love for her to Edwyn. "I desire to spend the rest of my life protecting her and caring for her." Setting my polisher down and placing both hands on the table before me, I confessed the depths of my devotion for Madelyn. "I intend to love her for all of the days of our lives."

Edwyn's jaw dropped. "That's wonderful. Congratulations! She's an honest, God-honoring woman, and she lives a purposeful life."

"Yes, she does."

"Do you remember, I told you long ago," he chuckled, "'She'll make a precious bride for a good man some day'."

"I remember." I rolled my eyes. "She's been an encouraging and faithful friend in all the challenges I've faced and—"

"You'll be going through a little more yet, my friend," he interrupted.

I was shocked at his abruptness. "What do you mean?" I looked up from my work. "What are you talking about?"

Edwyn, still sitting, put his hands on his knees and looked up at me with concern. "You and Madelyn are mature adults. In fact, Madelyn, as you well know, was married once before, but there would be wisdom in corresponding with her parents in Flodden Field." He paused dramatically, enjoying how he had caught my interest. "The sooner, the better."

"You sound a bit worried."

"I imagine that Madelyn has been corresponding with her mother about you. They're quite close."

"I only decided I'd marry her about a week ago."

"I met her parents last fall." Edwyn looked at me with gravity. "Her mother is a lot like Madelyn; amiable and encouraging. Her father, on the other hand." Another dramatic pause. *Is he toying with me?* "Well, he isn't as warm and friendly as you might like. In fact, he can be quite severe and demanding. Difficult to please. You know what I mean. If he's not in support of the marriage, he could make things..." he licked his lips, "difficult. Significantly difficult."

I stopped polishing for a moment. "This is discouraging." I slumped down onto a bench. "I'm a gutted fish."

"If he doesn't support the marriage, you'd be well beyond that."

"Beyond that? So, I'm not merely gutted?" Michael winced. "I'm a gutted fish that's slid out of the sizzling frying pan, and I'm about to find myself in the blazing fire?"

Edwyn raised an index finger towards me. "That's only if you don't get him approving of you, and supporting the marriage."

He stepped nearer to me and in a fatherly manner, put his hand on my shoulder. "Like I said, Madelyn has probably been corresponding with her mother. Any good daughter would be."

I raised my palm towards him. "Tell me more about her father," I pleaded.

"Her mother is a sweet lady."

"Her father!" Impatiently, my eyes burrowed into his. "Tell me more about him."

"He's driven by appearances, wealth, and influence. He'll want to know that you will not only love his daughter but also take care of her and provide for her. You wouldn't want him to think that his daughter's marrying a poor jam eater that can't afford meat with his bread."

"Don't make a joke. This kind of talk makes me nervous." I shuddered.

Edwyn chuckled. "You sound more fearful about her father than the day we went to apprehend the brigands."

"You've got that right."

"Michael, you're a man of learning, a great musician, and I think the world of you. If it were me as the bride's father, I'd support the marriage."

That's a strange thing to say. Is he thinking about Brynne? He can't be. She's only a child.

He continued. "I would be honored to be your father. Madelyn's father might not consider you to be..." He hesitated.

I completed his sentence. "To be a man of wealth and influence, worthy of his daughter."

Edwyn nodded. "You've got that about right."

"Madelyn's father sounds entangled and caught up in the world."

"I trust that I'm not being too negative, but yes, I think that's the case. He doesn't have the same heart of loving Christian devotion that Madelyn does."

I slumped down onto a bench beside my table.

"May I represent your intentions towards Madelyn to her father? I would like to write a very supportive letter on your behalf. I've met both of her parents."

"Thank you, Edwyn. That would be truly helpful."

"Thinking about how I might present you in the best positive light, tell me a bit about the inheritance that grandfather Sterling left you. I mean, if I'm not being too forward."

"You're not being too direct and I appreciate your help." I stood and returned to my polishing as I talked. "He left me a twenty per cent interest in a substantial farm in the Bahamas.

The farm manager and the workers are newly arrived from South Carolina, not wanting to break their ties with England after the rebellion. I don't know much about the farm, mostly pineapples, bananas, and some cattle. I think it's near a fishing village called Alice Town. It has paid workers. Grandfather and I had discussions about slavery and we agreed entirely that it's wrong and that no man should own another."

"I also have an investment account of £1,900."

"£1,900! That's a substantial amount of money. I don't understand why you live so humbly up in Cliffside. Why are you slowly scraping enough money together for a down payment on a small, though superbly positioned building lot?"

"Most of the money is invested, tied up so to speak, in trade, and I don't have ready access to large amounts for personal use. That might require a trip to London and a few weeks to liquidate it and turn it into actual bank notes.

Edwyn inclined his head in understanding and raised his index finger again. "I have an idea. The timber rights agreement on the small woodlot that I lease from Lord Warrington is almost done. It was merely a three-year agreement. If you were to buy the ten acres of forest behind your cleared lot, I would purchase the timber rights from you."

"Some of my assets would need to be liquidated."

"That's right, but probably not too much."

I shook my head. "I wouldn't want all of the trees to be cut down. I'd be interested in allowing the forest to regenerate."

"Of course." Edwyn scratched his chin. "My agreement with you would be for a specific number of the big hardwoods. I'd leave many of them to be coppiced near the ground and a few I would pollard, a little taller than my height, because of the deer here about. Then, in ten to twenty years, for smaller purposes, you'd have opportunity for them to be harvested again. Small projects, firewood, and things like that."

We Both Shall Row, My Love And I

I got a piece of scrap paper from Edwyn's planning table and began jotting down some points and doing some calculations. "This plan interests me a great deal."

Edwyn grimaced a little bit and scratched his chin again. "It might be a bit complicated, I'm afraid."

"Let me spell out the steps." I numbered them off on my fingers as I stated them. "First, I would redeem a small amount of my investment assets to pay off the cleared lot and come up with a down payment for the ten acres. Second, I would seek to obtain an open mortgage with Albert Kline for the balance. Third, I would write up an agreement regarding your purchase of the timber rights and you'd pay me in advance. Fourth, I would then pay off, or greatly reduce, the mortgage with Albert Kline. And finally, I would contract with someone to build an attractive home for my sweet Madelyn."

"Good gracious man. I had no idea that you had such a mind for business."

I smirked. "I'm not just a simple jam eater." I laughed and looked again at my calculations. "Even from a simple investment point of view, I like the structure of this.

"It's a pity that your investment in London is not easily retrieved," added Edwyn.

"I do have a smaller investment of about £210 at the Arthur Heywood Bank in Liverpool. I can readily redeem that personally or by courier."

"Well Michael, I'm catching you're excitement."

"When I find someone to build it by post and beam, would you do the finishing work and the cabinets?"

"I'd be delighted to." Edwyn laughed. "Where do I sign?"

"That's great." I held up my index finger towards him. "One last question."

"What's that?"

"Have you started writing the letter for me to Madelyn's father yet?"

We shared a good laugh together. The time I spent with him was always a great joy. "I'll get right to it." He chuckled.

"I'll need to ask George or David to travel down to Liverpool with me. I wouldn't want to return alone with that much money."

"That would be a wise decision. Both of them traveling with you would be a fitting security against robbery."

"Thank you, Edwyn." We returned to our work in silence. There was much to think about and so little time.

The Brixton Home

Later in the evening, the Ekland's Landau came to a stop out front. Not only did Madelyn and Meiling arrive with their instruments, but Reverend and Mrs. Ekland, along with Carolyn, did as well. When the Ekland household had heard that the Brixtons were having a musical evening, they didn't want to miss it.

Muriel went into the kitchen to help Louisa finish baking some biscuits, and within minutes, Edwyn and Martin, smelling the baking, found themselves in there also. Carolyn remained in the sitting room, watching us prepare our instruments and music.

While Madelyn put her flute together and ran over a few scales to warm up, Meiling carefully took her pipa out of a simple cloth bag and began tuning its strings. After trimming my reed and adjusting its position, I also warmed up but needed to play from the side of my mouth because of my cut lip.

"Meiling, is a simple cloth bag enough protection for your pipa?" I asked.

"No, not really, but I don't have a case."

Madelyn made eye contact with me, and then slyly nodded. We later discussed having Edwyn build her a more protective wooden case.

Brynne went to her room and came back with her Celtic hand drum.

"Should we start off with a little improvisation?" I asked the group.

Madelyn was enthusiastic and Brynne, merely playing a hand drum, said, "Sure. Not a problem."

Meiling looked a bit apprehensive. "I'm not sure what you would like me to do. I'm not familiar with how to improvise with others. I usually play alone unless I'm accompanying mother when she's singing or father when he's playing his dizi."

"Not a concern, Meiling. Can you read a figured bass or chord progressions?"

She winced jokingly. "I can't read a figured bass, I'm not even sure what that is. I can follow European chord progressions, as long as they aren't too complicated. They are notated differently for Chinese music."

"I've written out a few interesting progressions and jotted down the notes within each chord as well." I passed her the piece of paper. "Do you think you would be able to play them through in a simple four beats to the bar pattern at a moderate tempo?"

"Yes, I can do that." She started strumming, much like one would a guitar, and within minutes, she confidently included some attractive and interesting finger-picking patterns at appropriate places.

Meiling was flanked by Madelyn and myself. "Madelyn, if you'd focus on creating scale-like phrases and melodies in the upper register, I'll join you when you repeat it in eight bars. I'll play longer chord notes beneath you."

"Sure, I'll do that," she responded.

"What would you like me to do, Michael?" asked Brynne.

"Keep a clear four beats to the bar pattern and emphasize beats one and three."

After a few false starts and ugly mistakes, our improvisation started to sound quite proficient. We played like that for about twenty minutes and were becoming truly unified as an ensemble. Madelyn then suggested that we pass our melodic phrases back and forth. I would repeat her four bar melody with a few variations of my own and she would play longer sustained notes. It was starting to sound interesting, even enchanting.

The sound of the pipa was mysterious and everything we did took on an exotic quality. Meiling then suggested that she would start repeating fragments of the melody that we were passing back and forth. The music we were presenting was the most unique material that I'd ever heard. Even Brynne was adding quite a number of interesting rhythmic patterns. I previously had no idea that she could play so well.

Louisa wearing her apron, Edwyn with a cup of tea in his hand, Reverend Ekland, carrying a plate of biscuits, and Muriel pushing a tea trolley came into the sitting room. They were joyously surprised at our musicality.

Edwyn, with a pleasant look on his face, stepped towards us with his mouth open and eyebrows raised. "It's been many years since I've heard a pipa. When I hear it, I imagine myself back in Shanghai or Hong Kong. I knew a pipa musician on the island of Formosa very well. He was an amazing elderly man."

"You all play with such deep feeling," said Louisa. She winked at her daughter. "Well done, Brynne."

Reverend Ekland was beaming. "That was quite evocative of the mystery of the Orient. Perhaps you should play for Lord Warrington."

"Not me anytime soon." My eyes met Edwyn's. "It's off to Liverpool for me."

Madelyn stopped playing and snapped around to face me. "Liverpool! Why would you be going to Liverpool?"

"Merely a quick trip. We'll talk later," I whispered.

Meiling, sitting between us, set her pipa across her knees. "Liverpool, Michael?"

I made eye contact with Edwyn and Louisa, and then I winked at Edwyn, knowing that he knew the reason for my trip.

"I'd like to go to Liverpool again," said Brynne. "I've only been there once and that was more than three years ago."

I didn't respond to her expression of interest.

One of the highlights of the evening was when Meiling sang a Christian worship song in Chinese, accompanying herself on pipa. Not understanding her language, I didn't grasp its meaning, but she sang with a loving and worshipful intensity. *I must ask her to translate it for me some time.*

We finished off the evening with tea, biscuits, and buoyant spirits. Shortly before Reverend Ekland and the others were to head home and drop off Meiling at the dock, I took Madelyn by the hand out onto the porch. Holding both of her hands, giving her a little wink, and hoping for the best, I tilted my head, leaning down towards her.

Madelyn gently put her index finger up to my lips. "No kiss, not yet. Tell me about this trip to Liverpool. It's a few days travel to go there and return."

"My bank, well one of them, is the Heywood Bank in Liverpool. I need to make a withdrawal."

"Whatever for?"

"It's time for me, for us, to prepare for the future. I'm going to not only purchase our lot, but I also want to purchase about ten acres of woodland up behind it."

"Michael, ten acres plus our building lot! That's a substantial piece of land here in our little seaport."

"It's manageable, sweetheart."

"Don't be building a house for me quite yet. We should talk to my parents."

"Oh I shall. That's part of the plan. Edwyn suggested—"

"Edwyn suggested?" She stepped back and, having balled her fists, she firmly planted them on her hips. "I'm not marrying him. What does he have to do with this?"

"Edwyn and I had a talk—"

"Edwyn again. He's a good man but what does he have to do with us? With our plans?"

I reached out for her, we smiled at each other, and she took my hand. "Let's hear it," she demanded.

Is this my second scolding? No, I think it's my third.

"I want to present myself in the best possible light to your father. I know that at our age and with our life experience, we don't require your father's permission, but his blessing, the blessing of both of your parents, would mean a great deal to me..." I paused. "To us."

Madelyn was quiet for a few minutes. "That's true."

"If I own a substantial piece of land in a busy seaport and have a house under construction, he'll know that I'm not some penniless woodcutter down from the mountains. When he knows about the building lot and the ten acres behind it, and finds out about my other investments—"

"Other investments? You mean your cabin up in Cliffside?"

"No, my farm enterprise in the Bahamas."

"The Bahamas? What are you talking about?" Madelyn laughed playfully. "I didn't know that I was marrying the governor of the Bahamas—"

"Mr. Sterlin' sir. I didn't know you were the gov'na' o' the Bahamas!" exclaimed Tommy, who had stopped at the bottom of the porch steps as he was walking by. "We all knew you'd be gettin' married but none o' us knew that you be the gov'na' o' the Bahamas."

We hadn't seen Tommy come walking along carrying an old steel barrel hoop. His amusing reaction and his way of speaking made Madelyn and me to start laughing. "I'm not the governor of the Bahamas. I have a small interest in a farm enterprise there. Tommy, I mean Thomas, set down your barrel hoop where no one will trip over it and go into the house for some tea and biscuits. Madelyn and I are having a serious conversation."

Madelyn waited for Tommy to step inside. "What do your investments in the Bahamas have to do with the Heywood Bank in Liverpool? Are they managing it?"

"No, my bank in London manages my larger investments."

"Bank in London. Investments. You mean there are more?"

"I do have some other business interests."

Madelyn shook her head. "Who am I marrying here? Why were you living up in Cliffside in a humble cabin?"

"Edwyn asked me the same question." I nodded slowly. "Like my grandfather, I'm drawn to a simple life, enjoying the forest and desiring to live quietly."

Madelyn was calming down, grinning, and staring up at me with her radiant eyes. She went up onto her tiptoes and reaching upwards, took hold of my shoulder and passionately drew my face down towards her own. She planted a memorably sweet kiss on my lips and started to laugh while we were still kissing.

What a woman. There's never a dull moment with her.

"Why are you laughing?" I asked.

"A moment ago, I overheard Tommy telling everyone inside that we're getting married and that you own half of the Bahamas."

"I was once told something about him, wasn't I, Madelyn? 'Prankish Tommy means no harm but mischief does find him from time to time'."

Madelyn rolled her eyes. "It must have been a wise person that told you that."

"You two are getting married?" exclaimed Brynne, having stepped out onto the porch.

"Hello Brynne. Yes, it's true. We just haven't formally announced it yet."

"Michael wants to write my parents first," added Madelyn.

Brynne, without smiling, and in a dull tone said, "Congratulations." She then stepped back inside and the door closed firmly behind her.

A moment later, Louisa rushed out onto the porch, followed by Meiling, Tommy, Carolyn, Reverend Ekland, Muriel, and Edwyn. Each of them shook our hands and congratulated us. The women went back inside to discuss flowers, dresses, and more feminine things. The men, with Tommy, slapped me on the back, drifted along the porch, away from the door, and seated themselves with me, forming a circle.

Reverend Ekland leaned in towards me and whispered in my ear. "You will want to correspond with Madelyn's father. I know that you are both a little older but you will want to make sure that he sees your marriage in the most advantageous way possible."

"We be 'avin' a blessin' right soon now!" exclaimed John Lyon. He had been ambling along the cobbled road and having overheard the congratulations, felt the need to stop. "My brother's mindin' the light'ouse that I might be meetin' some mates at the Royal Stag." He stepped towards the porch, tapped the contents of his pipe out onto the ground, and without coming up the steps, rested his elbows on top of the railing near us.

"Mr. Lyon, would you be fancyin' a biscuit?" asked Tommy, holding a basket of them out towards him.

He nodded, took three, and bit one in half. "Such a blessin' it is, but I've been knowin' it for some time now. Michael, I know that you 'ave the finest of intentions towards dear Madelyn." Crumbs fell down the front of his coat.

Standing tall with Madelyn at my side, having taken my arm, we formally thanked everyone for congratulating us and wishing us well. "Thank you, one and all, for your congratulations and blessings."

Madelyn cleared her throat. "We wanted to make our formal announcement in Fair Havens Church, this Sunday, but somehow here we are tonight with the people we love and we are so glad that you could share this time with us."

Madelyn hugged me in front of those gathered and then took my arm in both of her hands. "We intend to make our home with you, here in Oak Harbor. We appreciate each one of you so very much." "Madelyn and I, starting our lives together, couldn't hope to find better friends than we've found here," I added.

There was a round of applause and a few "Amens" from those gathered.

Reverend Ekland held up a hand and said, "Let's pray for this young couple." We all bowed our heads and when he had finished praying, several people once again said their "Amens."

When I raised my head, I saw a curious thing. Tommy looked as though he was silently holding back tears and Carolyn, having taken his hand, was looking at him with tenderness.

"Thank you all," I said, "for sharing this evening with us, but I need to slip away and make plans to do a bit of traveling."

"Where are you going tonight?" asked Madelyn in a whisper.

"I need to go and see if Harbor Master Langley is in the Royal Stag and ask him if there are ships bound for Liverpool tomorrow or the next day that I might secure passage."

She touched my arm. "I'll miss you so much when you're gone, even if it is only for a few days. I'm so happy and content when I'm with you."

We Both Shall Row, My Love And I

They congratulated us again and off I went. As I stepped from the porch, I overheard Reverend Ekland ask Edwyn why I would need to be going to Liverpool.

When I entered the Royal Stag, John Lyon followed close behind, right on my heels. We had no sooner stepped inside than he called everyone to attention and shouted like a herald with the king's most important news. "If I may 'ave the attention o' one an' all 'ere, please." He stepped towards the center of the room and raising both hands, loudly cleared his throat and repeated his request. "Please, if I may 'ave your undivided attention."

Conversations tapered off. Shannon who had been singing as she carried a tray of ale mugs, stood still and looked at John, and then at me. A couple old salts, arguing about sail trim in heavy weather, stopped talking and looked at John.

One of them shouted out, "The Rotund 'as a voice as big as 'is belly."

The other old salt asked, "Who's minding the lighthouse? You don't want to be leading any ships onto the rocks because you need a brew and a platter of chicken." Everyone laughed.

John scowled and waved one hand. "My brother's mindin' the light'ouse an' that be the truth. I 'ave big news." He gestured towards me and placed his heavy hand upon my shoulder. "Michael Sterlin' 'ere, 'e be weddin' dear Madelyn 'aversham."

The patrons of the Royal Stag were silent for a moment. Jaws dropped, men looked with eyebrows raised from me to their mates, and Shannon flopped her tray down onto the nearest table. Big David, who I hadn't seen earlier across the room, set down a huge piece of chicken and wiped his shining mouth with his hand.

"Hurrah for young Michael," shouted the patrons. This was followed by a smattering of congratulations, table banging, and a few unseemly comments.

377

Shannon rushed over to me and hugged me, a bit too motherly, as if her wayward son had returned from a distant land. She released me from her crushing embrace, smiled tenderly, and held me at arms length. "I wish grandfather Sterling was here to congratulate you and offer some words of advice."

"I do as well, Shannon, and I would wish that—"

"Advice, that's it! It's time for some advice!" shouted a tall thin fisherman.

Several older men clustered about me and one of them, with a huge arm around my shoulder, set me down on a nearby chair.

The large number of men crowding around me began their chorus of advice.

One said, "When you be gettin' scolded," he shook his index finger at me, "simply say, 'yes dear. You're absolutely right sweetheart'." He slapped his palm to his forehead, emphasizing a husband's contrition. "'What was I thinkin'?"

"If ever you be distracted," said another, "and not mindin' what the missus be sayin', you need to answer 'er with this: 'I be so sorry my precious, I be thinkin' 'ow beautiful you be today'."

A third man, grey headed and much older than the rest said, "If ever you be strollin' with the misses and pass by some comely flowers, she might ask thee, 'my dear husband aren't these the most beautiful flowers that you've ever seen?'" He held up his index finger and gave it a little shake. "Respond by sayin, 'these flowers, fair as they might be, are not so beautiful as thee my love'."

And finally, a fourth added, "Michael, listen closely. Dear Madelyn, having dressed for church," he feigned the sweeping back of long hair over his shoulder, "might ask you a question." He paused dramatically, and put a stained dishrag atop his head as if it were a lace hat. Then, with a feminine voice and mannerisms, he said, "Michael my love, am I dressed tastefully for church? Do I look both attractive and yet respectable?" He then switched to a masculine voice, and said, "My love, you look respectfully angelic, and I dare say, you've come as close to the divine as any woman might without distracting from the stained glass windows or the heavenly singing."

Everyone burst out laughing as they returned to their tables, their friends, and their tankards.

Someone shouted, "Sterling needs a right proper send off to marital bliss. Time for the 'Jig o' the Sun-Bleached Bones'."

Men set down their tankards, conversations ended, and some of the patrons moved tables aside. The Spaniard grabbed his guitar from a shelf behind the counter and a scrawny lad with a dirty face and a hand drum began beating out a simple four to a bar pattern. An old man started to play the melody sorrowfully with a penny whistle.

They started playing slowly and quietly as three young sailors took to the floor and started dirge-like marching movements in unison. At the next repeat, as is common with this song, it got louder and a bit faster as the three young men began dancing a slow jig. At the next repeat, everything began to accelerate and the three young men, with perfect coordination, added some stiff, corpse-like motions as they danced the jig. Finally, Shannon joined in with her high descant of long held notes that carried the words of the song. Many of the patrons started to dance in little groups, tables were being pounded, a couple of chairs tipped over, and old men swayed to the beat.

Smirking, I gave my head a shake, stepped outside, and sitting on one of the benches, I enjoyed the cool breeze.

A moment later, along came Brynne. Without saying a word, she pensively sat beside me, reached into a small handbag, and pulled out a pale blue envelope. From within it, she took a folded piece of pale blue paper.

"It's late. Do your parents know you're here?"

She didn't respond, but quietly sat beside me, looking out over the harbor. The boisterous sounds of the men inside began to die down as they ended their jig and took to their tankards. The rigging of the ships creaked in the breeze, and a clanging bell buoy could be heard from further along the shoreline.

"Brynne, are you okay?" I tenderly put my hand on her shoulder and she leaned, ever so slightly, in towards me. "You look upset. Can I help?"

Still avoiding eye contact, her lips parted, and she took several deep breaths, as if she were about to speak. She didn't. She silently sat there beside me and put the piece of paper back into the envelope and back into her hand bag. She rose to her feet, still saying nothing, and walked off towards her home.

That was odd. She must be missing Eutychus. Maybe she has a letter for someone in Liverpool. I suppose she changed her mind about sending it with me.

Reentering the Royal Stag, I saw Harbor Master Langley at a corner table examining his record book so I sauntered over, sat beside him, and picked up a biscuit from the plate on the table. "Hello, Master Langley."

He looked up from his papers. "Hello, Michael." He grinned.

"Are there any ships sailing off to Liverpool tomorrow?"

He furrowed his brows. "What did you say?"

I repeated myself with a raised voice and leaned closer towards him. "Are there any ships sailing off to Liverpool tomorrow? I'm looking for passage."

His head bobbed profusely. "Just one, the *Merry Weather*. She's a sturdy little two-masted brig. She'll sail through the night and enter Liverpool harbor the following morning, weather permitting. The captain is Percy Nicholson." He pointed him out to me, sitting near one of the windows.

"Thank you, Master Langley."

I went over to him and leaned over the crowded table. "Hello, Captain Nicholson?"

"Yes, that's me. Congratulations on your upcoming marriage. How can I help you?"

"I'm looking for passage for myself and a couple friends to Liverpool, and then we'd return here. I'm wondering—"

"Sure," he interrupted. "I could use some coin. I've room for you and your friends but no berth. If you're tired you could sit on some crates or lay down on some canvas."

"What's your fare?" I asked.

"Two shillings a man, but I'll not be returning. After Liverpool, we're headed down to Bristol, around to Portsmouth, and then off to Antwerp. You'll need to find your own return passage."

"That's agreeable to me, Captain Nicholson."

"Call me Percy. Only my crew calls me captain. Be at the *Merry Weather* mid-afternoon tomorrow. We're heading out with the tide so don't be late."

"Yes sir. Are you alongside one of the docks or anchored out in the harbor?"

"At the small dock nearest the bridge."

"Tomorrow then. Thank you, Percy."

"Don't mention it, but come with your shillings in hand and don't be late. The tide waits for no man."

George came into the pub, and seeing David across the room, went and sat with him. It was obvious that they were discussing our engagement. They kept looking over at me, nodding and talking. A moment later, they were at my side congratulating me and wishing Madelyn and me a happy and prosperous future. They were good men and trustworthy friends.

Sharing with them that I needed to go to Liverpool to do some banking the following day, I asked them if they would be willing to sail with me. I offered to pay their fare and expressed my confidence in them.

"Michael, that suits me right well. I have a shipment of dinnerware and some other items for the warehouse and I would've had to go even if you hadn't asked me."

"Wonderful. How about you, David? Are you interested and available?"

David leaned forward and put his elbows on the table. "Me? Sure, but I'm a little light in the pocket right now."

"I'll be glad to pay your fare and give you an extra shilling for coming along. What do you say?"

He feigned a whisper. "Hmm, I'll need to check with my boss. He's been a might grumpy lately." He laughed and turning, jokingly addressed George. "Well boss, how about it? Am I off to Liverpool?"

All three of us laughed, David and I shook hands, and George smacked his hand down on top of ours.

"Tomorrow afternoon it is," chuckled David.

"With the tide in mid-afternoon." I winked and clicked my tongue. "It'll be an interesting little trip. Thanks for coming." I stood to leave.

George stopped me. "There's one more thing, Michael."

"What's that?"

"Please do extend our deepest condolences to Madelyn on her upcoming marriage."

After a round of laughter, I exited the tavern and headed off towards the Brixton home. Entering the back door and feeling quite fatigued, I sat upon my bed. My hands felt a cozy warmth on the bed.

Odd. My bed feels warm. Someone must've been resting here.

Liverpool

Edwyn and I limited ourselves to work within the shop the following morning because of the heavily overcast weather. We were doing the finishing touches on the brass work of Captain Henderson's roll-out chest, and polishing the wood to a lustrous sheen.

Once again, Edwyn had designed and built, with my help, an attractive and sturdy project. The chest was about four and a half feet long, thirty-six inches from front to back, and about ten inches deep. Like a huge drawer from beneath the captain's bed, it would roll out on wheels that could be locked. It was divided into four sections, each with its own hinged lid; two larger sections and two smaller ones. One of the larger sections was only one foot from front to back but fully four and a half feet long. It was lined with heavy felt and made to store a sword and a short barrel musket side by side. The whole project was an impressive piece of well-finished woodwork.

Captain Henderson, aware that his roll-out chest had been completed, sent two of his men with a four wheeled hand cart to Edwyn's home. We carefully wrapped the chest in old canvas and secured it onto the cart.

"Brynne wasn't at breakfast this morning. Is she not well?" I asked.

Edwyn responded with a grimace. "Louisa thinks that she might have a cold or some other ailment."

"The poor girl," I said.

"She's spending the day in bed." Edwyn steadied the cart. "Last night, after the music, she didn't seem her normal self."

I put my hand on the cart, stopped it, and tightened one of the ropes. "She's usually so full of energy and she has a wonderful sense of humor."

"Michael," he mumbled. "It might be one of those womanly things. Louisa put some herbs in a cup of tea and took it to her earlier."

I touched his elbow, wanting to fall behind the men pushing the cart. I whispered, "Don't even mention Aunt Flo coming for a visit. Talking about those womanly things can be a bit disconcerting."

Edwyn gestured for us to lag even further behind the men. In a hushed voice he said, "When we were first married, Louisa told me that 'the painters were coming into work but that they'd be gone in a few days.' I thought she meant real painters, so wanting to be helpful, I started moving the furniture away from the walls." Edwyn chuckled. "She thought I was daft."

Feeling faint, I leaned against a low fence. "Edwyn, talking about, or even thinking about, those womanly things makes me queasy. Let's just drop it."

When we arrived at the dock, Tibbins met us and then sent for the captain. We positioned the exquisite project after Captain Henderson inspected it. With great praise, we were once again offered jobs aboard his ship. The captain paid Edwyn three guineas and eleven shillings.

We thanked him for trusting us with the work and as we left the ship, Edwyn stopped me on the dock. "Michael, I'd like to pay you for your hard work." In his palm he counted out one guinea and five shillings and put them into my hand. "If I had a son, I would like him to be the kind of man that you've become. Your grandfather would be so proud of your diligence and your integrity."

"Thank you so much. It's been a joy to work at your side, and you've taught me well."

I walked along with him as far as the warehouse and then I stopped to speak with Albert Kline.

"Mr. Kline, how are you this morning?"

"Oh, I can't complain. I imagine that you're here to speak to me about the ten acre woodlot."

"Yes sir, that's right." *News travels fast in these little seaports.* "I think that I've arrived at a price."

"Yes sir, and what might it be?" I asked.

"It is a prime woodlot of sturdy trees."

Nodding, I agreed. "Yes it is."

"Michael, let me tell you, it's marvelous that you and Madelyn intend to marry. You are a fine couple."

"Thank you, Mr. Kline."

"There's more that I would like to express." He put his hand on my arm.

I was puzzled. "Yes, go ahead."

"When my son was wounded, you stood by his side. That means a great deal to me, and had you not been with him, Caine may have come down from the ridge above and taken my precious son's life."

"George is a dear friend."

He looked like he wanted to restrain his emotions. "Back to the business side of things," he said abruptly.

"Yes, Mr. Kline."

"There are many great oaks, beeches, and maples on the property, but much of the land is impractically steep and would never do for building or planting because of that."

"I'm aware of that. I've walked the property, and steep it truly is."

Mr. Kline smiled and continued "The woodlot runs up the slope, includes a cliff about thirty feet high, and then slopes higher still, another seventy feet above that. It is also to my understanding that you intend to build a substantial home on the lot in front of it." Pausing, he licked his lips and made serious eye contact with me. "How big will your home be and will you be buying your building materials from me?"

"Indeed. I do imagine that I'll be buying most of them from you, but Edwyn will do much of the interior finishing work.

"Certainly," he responded. "He's a master craftsman. What size of a home do you intend to have built?"

"The home I have in mind would have six bedrooms, a study, a dining room, an ample kitchen, and a number of other substantial rooms on two levels. About four thousand square feet." I gave him a list of our home's required details and shared with him that we would show him some rough plans in a week or so.

I need to convince him that our agreement would be a wise business decision on his part. "You will be supplying me with brick and mortar, and almost countless linear board feet of lumber, and lots of other materials will be needed. I'll be requiring quoined corners of red sandstone block as well. It's my understanding that you have men in your employ that do quality post and beam construction."

"That is true, I do. I have some of the best post and beam men in Cumberland working for me."

"So then, selling me the woodlot would be the beginning of a beneficial business relationship. Are you grasping my point, Mr. Kline?"

"Certainly." He grinned and lifted his chin. "Please, call me Albert." He thought for a few minutes and started jotting down some figures. "I can let you have the woodlot for £70. But that is with the understanding that my men will build the house and my company will supply you with most of the building materials."

I ran through a few figures in my mind. "Let's bring the materials and labor costs together. How much might you charge to build our home, including materials and labor? Excluding most of the finishing work."

He made more calculations, wrote some things in his notebook, and asked me a number of additional detail questions to which I responded as accurately as possible. He halted what he was doing several times, looked at the list I had given him, and glanced up at me. "Michael, a fair price would be in the vicinity of £140." He coughed a couple times. "Of course, that depends on the rough plans that you submit to me and the quality of the materials that you might expect. I will be able to give you an exact cost when we have agreed on a final plan."

"In principle, I agree with that amount and I'm sure we can make any specific modifications and adjustments that might be needed."

We shook hands. He was beaming, knowing that there would be a stream of payments and materials flowing through his company in the months to come.

"I do have one more request."

"Yes?"

"As you've probably heard, I'm heading off to my bank in Liverpool to secure some funds. I'll need to establish a mortgage with you. It's a large project. I will pay for the ten acre woodlot at the agreed on amount of £70 as soon as I return from Liverpool."

Albert's brow furrowed. "It depends on how big of a mortgage you need but I do require some working capital. Of course, you must understand that."

"Yes, I grasp that. Here's what I would like to suggest." I numbered off the points on my fingers. "First, up front I will give you £70 for the woodlot. Second, I will make a £20 first payment for the labor and materials, to total £140. Third, if you would be willing to hold a four-year mortgage at three percent for the £120 remaining balance on labor and materials, that would be within my financial capabilities."

He once again spent some time on critical calculations. "Your plan is close to my acceptance but we're not quite there yet. Seventy pounds for the woodlot is agreed but for me to hold such a large mortgage isn't to my liking. Instead of £20 as a first payment, I would need £50 and I would be willing to hold a mortgage of £90." His brows wrinkled once again as he looked at me. "Would you be able to handle that?"

I made a few notations on my scrap of paper. "Yes, I can manage that. It makes good business sense."

"Michael, it's a suitable agreement."

We shook hands and he wished me well.

Albert grinned and jotted down a few things in his notebook. "I'll have our agreement written up and we can record the specific details when next we meet. I truly do need to see your rough plans before we can move towards finalization."

"Splendid. I'm hoping to get started as soon as possible. I'll see you in a few days then."

He touched the rim of his tricorn hat. "Yes, in a few days."

He congratulated me on my decision to marry Madelyn and I departed towards the parsonage.

When I arrived and knocked on the door, Muriel answered.

"Hello, Mrs. Ekland."

"Call me Muriel or Aunt Muriel, please. We'll be family soon enough."

"Alright then. *Aunt Muriel*, is Madelyn home?"

"No, I'm sorry. She and Martin went to visit the widow

Harcourt earlier and they were going to make a couple other ministry stops. I don't imagine that they'll be back for a couple hours."

"Okay, that's fine. Thank you. I'll be leaving for Liverpool shortly."

"Michael, before you leave, would you please come in for a minute? I'm quite baffled by something."

Curious, I stepped inside the hallway. "How might I help?"

She pointed to a high shelf near where we were standing in the hall. "What is that? Is it important?"

Following the direction of her index finger, I saw what perplexed her. High on the shelf above us, as if on display, was the stout branch that I had been struck with.

"It looks frightful. Several days ago Madelyn came in carrying it, and barely able to suppress her giggling, stood upon a chair and placed it up there."

"It's nothing of concern." I grinned broadly. "Our dear Madelyn, when we were amusing ourselves in the forest, won a game." I thought for a moment. "She cast it an impressive distance and struck an intended target square on."

"Oh, I understand now. Something of an accomplishment."

"Yes, that's it." I grinned. "An accomplishment."

She tenderly touched my shoulder and then shook my hand. "Congratulations on your engagement, Michael. I know that you and Madelyn will be as happy as mice in a pantry when the cat has been caught by the dog. I'll let her know that you stopped by."

"Thank you, Aunt Muriel. You and the reverend—"

"*Uncle* Martin," she corrected me.

"You and Uncle Martin mean a great deal to both Madelyn and me."

"Blessings upon you."

"Have a wonderful day."

Someday, Madelyn and I shall tell our sweet children the story of me being smitten by their dear mother. I justly deserved what I received. Smitten by a branch, like Goliath having been smitten by David. We'll have a great laugh. It will be a humorous anecdote in our family history.

Leaving the parsonage and sensing inclusion in the family, I walked along beside the harbor. It was odd thinking of Reverend Ekland as *Uncle* Martin.

The overcast clouds had started to break up and great patches of sunlight were flooding the harbor. By the time I reached the Brixton home, most of the clouds were blown away and an intensely blue sky domed the seaport. A steady wind from the northeast promised to make the passage to Liverpool a good one.

From my room at the back of the house, I got my bank papers, extra clothing, and a few other items and stuffed them into my travel bag. I pulled on my Inverness coat, hung my Sheffield knife on my belt, and headed out the door.

Meeting George and David on the dock and stepping aboard the seventy-foot *Merry Weather,* we were ready for the journey to begin.

"Hello, Captain Nicholson, I mean Percy."

"Good day to you. Please pay your passage to Master Robson." Captain Nicholson climbed the stairs leading to the quarterdeck, from where he would captain his ship.

"Thank you, Master Robson, for providing us with this passage." I dropped the required shillings into his palm.

"You're quite welcome. Now, if you three gentlemen would kindly go to the forward deck and have a seat on those crates, you'll be out of the way and we'll ease out on the breeze and the ebbing tide."

We followed his directions and seated ourselves.

Being on the downstream and downwind side of the dock, and with the bow of the *Merry Weather* facing out into the harbor, our leaving would be made easy.

A moment later, we became witnesses of the captain's commands, the first mate's support of those commands, and the expert seamanship of the men.

"Make ready to leave port, Master Robson," commanded Captain Nicholson.

Master Robson immediately, in a much broader voice, shouted out the subset of orders required to complete what the captain had commanded and at each point, as soon as he spoke, men obeyed and moved quickly.

"Haul in and secure the gangplank."

Men moved expertly and smoothly as they carried out the command.

"Mount the handrail."

A big fellow mounted the handrail into place across the opening where the gangplank had been.

"Stand by at the bollards. Free and stow the spring lines."

Three men stood ready at the big bollards while other men freed and hauled in several of the smaller lines known as spring lines.

"Helm, sway the wheel ropes and steerage."

This order was followed by a short pause as the helmsman turned the wheel one way and then the other and finally set it straight.

"Free and haul the bow line."

The two men at the bollard, nearest the bow, lifted the hawser from the bollard while others hauled it aboard.

"Free and haul the stern line."

Two men on the dock lifted the stern hawser from the bollard while others hauled it in.

"Stow the fenders."

Three younger lads pulled up the protective fenders that had been hanging between the dock and the ship.

"At your places, men. Prepare to set sail."

"Set sail, Master Robson," commanded Captain Nicholson.

Master Robson once again shouted out his subset of commands to carry out the captain's wishes.

"Haul the jib and set it broadly." Robson paused and then observing that the men could have put more effort into it, he shouted out, "Smartly now, you bunch o' landlubbers." Men hauled up the largest of the headsails at the bow and then others trimmed it in a bit as it filled with the breeze.

"Release the main topsail gaskets and set it fore and aft." Men at the top of the mainmast removed the bindings that held the square topsail in a furled position. The sail fell and filled as other men on deck adjusted it to capture the breeze perfectly.

"Helm, steady, straight and true."

The *Merry Weather* left the dock as smoothly as I've ever seen it done. With the jib and topsail full, it drifted from the dock and eased forward as it was caught by the wind.

"Take her to sea, Master Robson," directed the captain, with the full authority of his position.

Master Robson then shouted out numerous additional orders, leading to all of the sails being set as they filled with the breeze from the northeast. It was fascinating to see the way that the men, knowing exactly where they should be and doing exactly what they should do, resulted in the precise movement of the ship.

It was only a seventy footer but Captain Nicholson's dignified bearing, Master Robson's expert follow through with the subset commands, and the men's practiced obedience made it seem like it was a leading warship in His Majesty's Navy.

Captain Nicholson looked at us squarely and with authority. "Michael, you and your friends may move about the ship.

Don't get in the way of my men and do not come up upon the quarterdeck."

Nodding and touching the brow of my hat, I gestured compliance. "Yes sir."

Master Robson raised an eyebrow and whispered, "Ascending the quarterdeck," he gestured to the elevated deck at the stern, upon which Captain Nicholson stood, "is by invitation only."

As we sailed past the end of the main dock, where the *Eleutheran Quest* was moored, I saw Meiling swimming. *Again, the topknot. Her hair is always up in a topknot.* She was near the stern of her ship and a big, brutish, pockmarked deckhand stared at her from the ship's rail above. His stare concerned me for her safety. She smiled and waved as our eyes met, and the *Merry Weather* increased speed and moved away from the dock.

George and David stood at the rail on the south side of the ship and pointed out features near Fair Havens Church to one another. I was at the opposite rail and glancing through the rigging to the shore near the church and parsonage, I sought my love, my dear Madelyn. She was nowhere to be found. I was disappointed. I stayed at the starboard rail on the north side of the ship, searching the street for her.

A moment later the ship passed by the Brixton home. Louisa, who saw me first, was in conversation on the street with John Lyon and Belinda Atwater. She pointed me out to them and they waved profusely. I returned the wave, and David, having crossed to my side from the other, joined in the waving.

Sailing through the harbor and approaching the cleared lot atop the little hill, I saw a woman wearing a hat that completely covered her hair. She sat upon the large flat rock, where Madelyn and I often sat, and looked out towards the harbor entrance and the sea beyond.

Is that my sweet Madelyn? David and I waved persistently, but for quite a while, we were unnoticed. Finally, as we passed the spot, she turned towards us, stood, and removed her hat. It was Brynne. Her long chestnut hair and her full skirt, of a cheerful canary yellow, were being swept out from her by the breeze and her tight belt accentuated her feminine form. Upon seeing us, she waved her hat vigorously.

She must be feeling better. She looks so much more mature now than when I first met her several years ago, when she was only a child.

"How old is Brynne?" asked David. "Is she the age to be courted? She looks it."

Being lost in thought, I didn't respond.

"Excuse me, Michael." He cleared his throat to get my attention. "Would Edwyn and Louisa think that Brynne might be courted?"

"Hmm, they might agree with her being courted. You'd need to talk to them first."

"Of course I'd speak to Edwyn," he said.

"That would be the right thing to do, David."

Our ship, having sailed past Brynne's location, was now passing by the lighthouse and changing course to pass through the southerly opening at the bottom of the barrier island.

"I've chatted with her several times," said David. "She strikes me as being a woman of good character."

"It is true, I suppose. She's a fine girl."

The ship sailed on. David seemed quite taken with her. "Michael, a mere girl she is not. She's an attractive woman with a womanly figure. She's quite beautiful in fact. A woman such as she is a treasure."

Looking back, I saw that she had returned to sitting on the rock. "She is attractive and a kind-hearted person. A bit young, perhaps."

"How old is she?" asked David.

"She's seventeen," I responded. "She'll be eighteen in late November."

It finally dawned on me. Having known the Brixton family for so many years, Brynne's maturation had snuck up on me. *She's no longer a child, a youngster, a frivolous missy. She's a truly attractive young woman.*

David looked back into the distance to where Brynne had been standing, and raising his flattened hand above his eyes, he searched for her. "Hardwicke's Act of 1753 says that someone can be married without permission at age twenty and with permission it could be much younger than that."

My lips parted. It was shocking to hear David speak of her like this.

He continued, "Of course, without permission, a young couple might secretly run up to Gretna Green. It's only a couple of miles into Scotland and they could legally get married as teenagers without permission. Two witnesses are all that are needed and you don't need the bother of clergy—"

"A minister is not a bother, David. The Brixton family deserves more respect than the things you are saying about Gretna Green." I was fearing for Brynne and her future. "How old are you?"

"I'm twenty-five."

I looked at him sternly. "Brynne, being seventeen, should be protected and cared for. She shouldn't be coerced into a course of action that might bring her to harm or unhappiness. Edwyn and Louisa, along with Brynne, deserve more respect than would be provided at Gretna Green."

David, having been rebuked, wandered away towards the bow of the ship, and I joined George, who was watching the shoreline.

An hour or so later, high above us, and not too distant, were the startling three-hundred-foot-tall red sandstone cliffs of the Saint Bees headland. They glowed in the late afternoon sunlight. Their weather-beaten lofty heights and smoothed boulders, having been sculpted by thousands of years of abusive storms, were the most westerly point of Cumberland. Atop the cliffs stood the little coal-fired lighthouse built more than sixty years earlier by Thomas Lutwige.

When we go to the ruins of Saint Begas, we should stop and have a picnic there. It will be forever a precious memory for Madelyn and me.

Some time passed and Master Robson informed us that we were invited to dine with the captain in his stateroom and he led us below. Captain Nicholson aptly entertained us with stories of some of the places he had visited. He said, with some regret, that he had never been to the Americas, nor further south than Gibraltar, nor deeper into the Mediterranean than Italy. We assured him it was much farther than any of us had ever been.

After a substantial meal and exchanging our good nights and best wishes, Robson returned and led us to a storage area where we might stretch out upon some sails and get a reasonable night's sleep. I straightened some folded sails and found a more diminutive one to use as a blanket. Laying down, I pulled it up to my jaw and hooded the back of my head. *The smell of canvas. Stiff shoulder. Warmth.*

~~~~~~

The sounds of the busy harbor jolted us awake the following morning and when we went up on deck we were met with all the activity and clamor that a prodigious modern city provided. Oak Harbor was busy compared to Cliffside but Liverpool was much busier still.

Liverpool, at the mouth of the River Mersey, was a bustling seaport city of almost seventy thousand people. We disembarked at the canning dock and were immediately witnesses to the outfitting of several stinking slaving vessels. Some would leave for the shores of West Africa in a few days, and from there, after having been laden with their cargo of chained human souls, they would sail to the West Indies. The thought was repugnant to me. Slavery was, beyond all doubt, the most immoral and evil institution of mankind.

We went to the Harbor Master's office and secured passage on a ship that would be leaving the same afternoon back to Oak Harbor. Grasping that we needed to move quickly, George arranged for his warehouse order to be delivered to the ship immediately, and David accompanied me to the Heywood Bank, where I made a withdrawal of £190. While there, I also made arrangements for some business to be done with my London bank using an agent. I sought to redeem a £700 investment and have the proceeds transferred to the Heywood Bank here in Liverpool. I also had a security box at this bank. Among its contents were the partial interest ownership papers of the farm in the Bahamas and my dear grandmother's jewelry, which included a ring that would serve well for our engagement.

Near the harbor, David and I stopped at a bookstore and while he examined some maps, I saw a book that immediately spoke to me of Brynne's interest in adventure.

The Coastal Cities of China was a marvelous book, and I enthusiastically flipped through the pages. The writing was descriptive, the maps and diagrams were detailed, and the pictures were colorful and numerous. Knowing that she would cherish the book, I purchased it without hesitation and slipped it into my satchel. I also bought several newspapers that Edwyn would enjoy, which had stories about the revolution in France. One of the articles was entitled, *The Storming of the Bastille*.

Having arranged to meet at a specific tearoom near the harbor for a light lunch, we were amazed how efficient we had been in completing our tasks. We returned to canning dock, located the ship that we had booked passage on, and found ourselves alongside it as George's warehouse order arrived. We were on board an hour before the set time for sailing.

The passage back was horrendous. We left Liverpool beneath a grey sky with intermittent drizzle. By the time we were at sea and heading north, the drizzle had turned to heavy rain, coming down in great sheets, and the breeze of eight knots had become a wind of twenty knots with six foot waves.

For us landlubbers it was a fearsome experience but the seamen around us laughed and said that it would simply get us to Oak Harbor ahead of the expected time. They said it was a good wind and they described it as "broad on the port quarter," but I wasn't sure what that meant. Later it was explained to me that the wind, being both behind us and coming in from the sea to the west, would push us nicely northward to our seaport entrance and then in and through Oak Harbor. It would get me to my darling Madelyn that much sooner.

We spent most of the passage below deck. The hatches above us leaked and water was sloshing on the floor beneath our hammocks. I was thankful for my Inverness coat, my dry clothing, and my fatigue, which enabled me to sleep intermittently. George found the passage particularly difficult and heaved up what little food he had been able to swallow earlier. David slept deeply, having the good fortune of having the best hammock.

When we arrived, I paid David two shillings for accompanying me on the journey, for which he was pleased, having expected only one.

Finding my way to the Brixtons', I stuffed my travel bag under my bed, removed my wet coat, and nestled my way into the cozy blankets. Louisa told me not to get up from resting, and the Brixtons, a few minutes later, clutching their umbrellas and Bibles, headed off to church.

~~~~~~

In the early afternoon, I was awakened by the cheerful domestic sounds of Louisa, Brynne, and Madelyn chatting and working in the kitchen. The smell of fresh baked bread and spicy soup filled the house. Madelyn tapped on the door as she entered my room, and sitting beside me on my bed, brushed some strands of my wavy black hair from my sleepy eyes.

"I missed you so much." She kissed my forehead as if I was her little child, and she rested her hand on my side. "David came to church this morning. It was the first time that I ever saw him there. He sat with the Brixtons, next to Brynne. *He's wasting no time. Should I speak to Edwyn about my concerns?*

"Next to Brynne?" I asked.

"Yes, and when he arrived in the entrance and he said that the sea had been quite rough."

Madelyn leaned down towards me again and kissed my cheekbone, tenderly, below my eye. *Her lips are so soft and her rose perfume is captivating.* "Would you like to come to the table for some soup or should I bring it to you here?"

I was lost in thought, still thinking of the kiss and her fragrance.

My love repeated herself. "Would you like your soup at the table or would you like it here?"

"Sorry, I was daydreaming. I'll come to the table," I responded with a yawn and a smile.

She busied herself about my room putting my boots by the door and hanging my coat up on a hook above them.

Madelyn's wonderful. I love it when she takes care of me.

She returned, and sat again on the edge of my bed with some clean clothes. "Here's a fresh shirt. Give me your soiled one so that I can wash it." I removed my shirt, ducked under the covers, pulled off my trousers, and passed them to Madelyn.

"Your squirming around under the blanket looks like a hedgehog," she said, laughing.

I put on the dry shirt, she passed me a clean pair of trousers and I repeated my hedgehog squirming under the blanket. "Thank you, Madelyn. I'm looking forward to the day when we'll be wed and have our own home."

"Me too."

As she stood and turned to leave the room, she tripped over my travel bag, which was protruding from beneath the bed.

"Sorry, I should've moved that farther under the bed. Are you alright?"

"I'm fine."

"Wait a moment. May I pull a few articles of soiled clothing from inside my bag?" I asked.

As I pulled some of the clothing from the bag, out fell my leather pouch, and bursting from it, coins and bank notes totaling £190.

"What have we here?" She laughed. Dramatically, she stood with her hands on her hips, and with an exaggerated, feigned accent said, "Well now, 'ave ye brought your sweet'art a fist full o' treasure from the gran' ol' seaport o' Li'erpool?"

We giggled and laughed as I scooped up and returned the money to the pouch. Louisa and Edwyn entered the room, and not noticing them, I followed Madelyn's humorous lead, responding in kind. "Ah now me darlin' this be but a wee trifle o' me love o' thee."

Madelyn continued. "What be ye doin' with 'em 'andfulls o' the kings coin? If ye be thinkin' 'bout buildin' me a li'l 'ome 'ere in Oak 'arbor for the wee ones, that the sweet Lord be providin' the idea be a fine one for sure."

Edwyn, laughing, shook his head. "It'll be entertaining to have such a fun loving couple as neighbors."

"It surely will," said Louisa. "But for now, the bread's on the table and the soup's getting cold."

Madelyn piled my soiled clothing beside the back door and the two of us joined the Brixtons for a much-appreciated lunch.

Afterwards, we all took our tea onto the porch and I told them about the beautiful sailing weather heading south, our time in Liverpool, and the rough weather returning north. Brynne was thrilled with her book, *The Coastal Cities of China*, and said that someday she would like to visit distant ports and move forward with her plans of adventure. I then gave Edwyn his newspapers with stories about the revolution in France. Several dramatic sketches of the fortress were included in the article, *The Storming of the Bastille*. The fourteenth of July and the weeks following were a time of terror. It was a turning point for the French people and the history of their nation.

In due time, the Brixtons left us and Madelyn put a folder on my lap. "Open it up and take a look. I've been working on house plans ever since you asked me to marry you when you showed me our lot." She grimaced. "Sorry if they're a bit messy."

We spread the plans on the table and examined them and I made some observations about their similarities. "All the homes are u-shaped structures, with an enclosure wall at the back, forming a courtyard. They're not too immense but do have about ten rooms each, lots of windows, and each of the designs feature an expansive porch across the front."

"That's right, Michael. You're correct on every point."

I shared with her the financial details between Albert and me: the agreed on price for the woodlot, the cost of materials and labor, and the consideration of a mortgage. "He was enthusiastic to sell us the lot and the building materials."

"Oh Michael, this is so thrilling."

"He's looking forward to building and I told him that we'd like to start as soon as possible."

Madelyn clapped her hands together like a young schoolgirl. "I'm so excited about our life together. We'll have a home filled with sunshine and happiness."

I love watching her when she's so happy.

"Tomorrow I need to speak with John Lyon and pay off the building lot and also Albert Kline to pay for the woodlot, make a substantial first payment, and sign our agreement."

Madelyn clapped her hands together again. "I'm so excited."

"I'll show him your wonderful plans, Madelyn."

"My plans?"

"That's right. I want you to be as happy as possible and I'll make sure that he designs a house that includes all of the common elements from your three plans."

"It's actually happening. Our home is being built," she said.

"Then, I'll write up an agreement with Edwyn about some limited timber rights on the property."

She leaned towards me with eyebrows raised. "It's going to be a busy few days but I have full confidence in what you organize about contracts and money. You don't need my approval."

"Thank you for your confidence." I hesitated and grinned. "There's just one more thing." I knelt down upon one knee. "Madelyn, I should've had this for you when I proposed. Will you marry me? I refuse to imagine living my life without you."

"Michael, of course I'll marry you, my darling." She had a beaming smile. "Where did you find such a gorgeous antique ring here in Oak Harbor? It must be from Liverpool."

I kissed her hand and slipped the ring onto her finger. "It was my grandmother's. She was very dear to me and I kept it for the day that I would give it to the love of my life."

~~~~~~

In the days following, the financial arrangements were made, we approved the final design that Albert Kline showed us, and we discussed a few finishing points with Edwyn. Albert Kline's men eagerly started to clear the land, measure out, our future home overlooking the harbor, and dig the footings.

I had written a letter to Madelyn's father expressing my intentions towards his daughter, and Edwyn and Uncle Martin had sent letters endorsing my character and supporting our marriage. We waited and hoped for the best. Several weeks later, a favorable response came back, and Madelyn and I were relieved that there would be no impediment to our marriage.

Our Home

October 1789

The days turned into weeks and the weeks into months. Now our home, the symbol of our intention to spend our lives together in love and in joy, was becoming a reality.

The foundation, the brick walls of the ground floor, and the quoined corner blocks of red sandstone were complete. The posts, beams, and joists for the upper floor were impressively stout and the Tudor stucco that was being applied between them was of the finest quality. Great rafters, steeply pitched, rose skyward, and formidable tie beams spanning the base of the roof structure provided us with two large additional attic rooms.

Our four fireplaces were complete and it was evident that Kline's men had taken great care to construct a large, practical, and attractive kitchen.

During August, in the grip of summer, work had slowed considerably. Progress had continued each morning but on many of the hot afternoons, older men would stop and rest in the shade, and younger men would swim at the beach below. During September, the pace of the work had picked up again, and now in October, Madelyn and I were rejoicing that the cooler temperatures had reinvigorated the men. The work was proceeding at an amazing pace.

A new feature of our relationship was caring for and training Jester. This comical and good-natured puppy, the pick of the litter, which Madelyn had purchased from the Lyon brothers, was well on his way to becoming everything that his name suggested. He was developing into a lively and mischievous companion. The other puppies had been sold and we were surprised that Brynne hadn't asked for one. She said that nothing could take the place that Eutychus had in her heart. There were times when she would carry a chair from the porch around to the back and sit beside the resting place of her much loved companion.

Each Saturday, Madelyn and I would walk through our home and dream together of the day we would be wed and the children we might have. Often, sitting on piles of construction materials, we would look out over the harbor and reflect on the memories of our time together.

Early one evening, Madelyn, sitting beside me on a workman's bench and snuggling against me in the cool breeze, suggested that she and I, with Meiling, work on a trio and present a concert. She mentioned several piano trios and suggested that I transcribe the piano chords for pipa.

"Let's not leave out Brynne." Madelyn adjusted her shawl. "She could provide the beat on her hand drum and play some interesting rhythms to keep things moving."

"A concert is a wonderful idea if we picked the right date." Madelyn took my hand in hers and rested it on her thigh. "The *Eleutheran Quest* is doing quite a few lumber runs to Bristol for Lord Warrington and we'd need to make sure that Meiling would be in port."

I put my arm around her shoulders, trying to warm her. "It's in port now but I've heard that the ship will be heading back to the West Indies in a few weeks before our northern winter sets in. We also need to make sure that Brynne and David aren't busy."

"What do you mean, Brynne and David?" asked Madelyn.

"They're a couple and take quite a bit of each other's time, right?"

"Not anymore." Madelyn turned to look at me more directly. "Didn't you hear? Their relationship has come to an end."

"When did that happen?" I had debated with myself whether I should share the things that David had said to me about Brynne and Gretna Green. I decided against it, and was now relieved that they were no longer together. The things that David had told me were worrisome and Brynne deserved better. "I'm always the last to find out about these domestic details."

"Michael, I would've thought that you might have heard something at the Brixtons'. Their relationship ended last Sunday after church."

"Why? What brought it to an end?"

"Brynne told me that David was suggesting some sort of pre-engagement commitment but she admitted to him that her heart belongs to another."

"Really? Another?" My brows furrowed. "Who could it be?"

Madelyn shook her head. "I don't know. She wouldn't say."

We sat there enjoying the cool evening breeze while Jester entertained us. Even in the darkening evening, he explored the lot, our home, which was nearing completion, and the strand of beach below. He was a rousing joy to watch, and had more of the robust Irish wolfhound than the relaxed English mastiff flowing in his veins. He'd be an active playmate for our children, if the Lord gave us such a wonderful blessing. They would grow up with Jester as Brynne had grown up with sweet

Eutychus. He would also be a wonderful protector and guard for our home.

Madelyn, with a twinkle in her eye, looked at me as if she had a great idea. "Do you remember that we were always talking about going up to the ruins of the Priory of Saint Bega, on the south road?" She looked quite happy with the thought. "Let's do it. You've worked so hard with Edwyn every day. Take a break from your woodworking."

"Great idea. Edwyn won't mind. I've been working six days a week for more than two months."

"Let's go Saturday." She gave me a great tight hug. "It's only a couple of days from now." She was thrilled with the possibility. "Michael, let's do it."

I nodded thoughtfully. "If we take Jester, we'll have to keep a close eye on him near the precipice."

"There's a cliff up there?"

"That's right, spectacular cliffs overlooking the sea. The red sandstone cliffs are over three hundred feet. I saw them clearly from the sea when we passed them by on our way to Liverpool."

"Tell me about the ruins."

"They're truly mysterious, being from ancient times. There's an interesting lintel above a doorway." I gestured with my hand depicting a doorway lintel. "It's a relief carving of Saint Michael fighting a dragon."

"Saint Michael!" Madelyn gestured towards me with both hands in mock admiration. "I have one of those."

"One of what? A dragon?"

"A Saint Michael." She chuckled with trusting eyes. "You're my Saint Michael!"

I rolled my eyes and laughed at her lighthearted comment. "I suppose you do, sweetheart. I will always protect you."

"If you are my St. Michael, what or who might the dragon be?"

"Hmm, I'm not sure," I answered. *Carolyn faced an evil and malicious dragon. I wish I had been there to protect her from Caine.*

"You're day dreaming again. What are you thinking of?" she asked. "Tell me more about the ruins."

"There's an amazing sandstone doorway called the West Gate. It's beautifully carved from red sandstone. You're going to be so impressed."

"What makes the ruins so special? What's their origin?"

"It's hard for me to believe that you've never heard about this before." I shook my head. "Saint Bega was a young and beautiful Irish princess that was being forced into an arranged marriage with a Viking prince."

"It's a long way across the Irish Sea. Why is she venerated here and not in Ireland?"

"Saint Bees, that's what the locals call Saint Bega's. It's the most westerly point of Cumberland and that is where she fled in a boat. For the rest of her days she lived a life of devotion and piety."

"She never married?"

"That's right," I responded. "She lived a quiet but lonely life."

"I imagine that she got a lot of personal strength from the Lord."

"I'm sure she did, but it would've been a lonely life nonetheless."

"That's a sad story. Not the devotion part but the part about her parents pressuring her into an arranged marriage and then having a lonely life."

MARK G. TURNER

St. Begas, West Entrance

I hadn't made the connection, the similarity between Madelyn and Saint Bega, until now. I wanted to say something but not knowing what, I remained silent.

"I'm free of my pressured marriage and I thank God for that," she sighed. "But I'm glad that I have you and not a monastic life." She gave a little laugh. "Now that you've told me her story, I want to see the ruins even more."

"Edward Stewart lent Brynne a copy of an engraving by Samuel Buck showing the ruins of the priory about fifty years ago."

"I'd like to examine that," she said.

"He also lent her a book about St. Bega's priory, which includes a number of outstanding sketches. There's a sketch of the red sandstone west entrance, built in old Norman times. It's truly impressive."

We walked through our soon to be completed home on our perfectly positioned hill, overlooking the harbor.

A beautiful location. Such a roomy, well-planned home.

We had been waiting for the flooring to be completed on the upper level and now that it was, nothing could hold us back. It was the first time we wandered about up there. Our bedroom was nearing completion, as were the bedrooms for our children.

"Michael, how many children do you want to have?"

"Maybe two or three, I suppose. What do you think? What would be a good number?"

"Hmm, three or four." We were holding hands as we walked. She planted her feet, tugged me around to face her, and said, "Three or four... or more!" She smiled, rose on her tiptoes, and with her eyes sparkling, pulled my face down to meet hers. We shared a long sweet kiss. My hands were at her waist. *She's so shapely.*

Seeking sleep that night in my little back room wasn't easy but it was cozy and comfortable. The door to the kitchen was open and there was a slow burning small fire in the stove. I added some firewood from time to time.

My cozy bed invited me and my warm memories of Madelyn enveloped me. I rested as an infant, being cradled in a loving mother's arms. My mind was infused with my love for her. *Her lips so soft, so warm, so moist. My breathing slowed. Love... tender love, peaceful love.*

~~~~~

Breakfast with the Brixtons was an embracing domestic experience and afterwards, Edwyn sent me to record some specific measurements in our home. We agreed that he would complete all of the cabinetry and finishing work for £70. The kitchen, dining room, and study were the largest cabinetry features, and some of the pieces, being built in the shop, were almost finished. Today he would be starting to close in our home against the weather. His goal was to complete the window framing and hang the doors in place next week.

When I arrived at the building site, Albert Kline, standing atop a high scaffold at the eaves, was examining our completed roof, which was a lustrous green slate from the Honister mine. The work was impressive.

"Hello down there! Your home is coming along beautifully." He had his hands cupped around his mouth. "The men have done an expert job."

Looking up, I craned my neck to see him. "They truly have," I shouted back. "It's a home that will stand for centuries."

"Have you and Madelyn chosen a date?"

"Not yet, but we want to be married before Christmas." *The weeks are passing by quickly. Here we are in mid-October. We'd better set a date.*

George, who was inside at the back, was doing an inventory of building materials, and when he heard my voice, he leaned out a window and gestured for me to join him. I climbed the stairs and met him in what would become the study. There were still five or six workers at various points around the structure but none were with him there.

"I was up in Carlisle a few days ago picking up building supplies for our warehouse." He looked serious and firmed his lower lip. "I found out that there have been some developments with the Caine family."

"What developments?" I asked.

"When the three prisoners—Frederick Caine, the one they call Grand Freddie, Joseph Caine, and Chatwin Smythe—were being walked from a court administrator's office back to the jail, an attempt was made at freeing them."

Alarmed, I stepped backwards. "What happened?" My fists clenched. "Did any escape?"

"Three men attacked and one of them, Robert Caine by the description, put an arrow into a guard's shoulder."

"Curse him." I hammered a pile of shelving boards with my fist. "Are we ever going to hear the end of this miscreant? He keeps coming back like a rat in a warehouse."

George grimaced. "Our warehouse has no rats. We have one of the best ratting terriers in Cumberland."

"Sorry George. It was merely a figure of speech." I paused. "You were saying?"

"When they got the three prisoners into the jail, the guards and the prison governor, were viciously abusive. The injured guard was a nephew of the governor, and a respected friend of the other guards."

413

"What do you mean, 'viciously abusive'?"

George set down the building material record sheets that he had been working on. "Grand Freddie is dead and Joseph was beaten badly."

My chin dropped and my eyes opened wide. "Grand Freddie's dead?"

"There's more. Robert Caine, one night a few days later, went to the home of the prison governor and attempted to murder him."

"Caine, such a demoniac. He never lets up."

"I don't know all of the details, but the governor survived. Joseph's incarceration was increased from three years to five because it was discovered that he knew about Robert's intentions. The authorities called it a conspiracy."

Hearing more about Caine angered me, and again, I hammered the pile of boards. "Caine's a demented fiend. He's barking mad."

George put his hand on my shoulder. "He's consumed with revenge for his father's death and Joseph's increased prison term." George, it was obvious, wanted to reassure me. "The Carlisle constables are looking for him. I'm sure they'll find him. Sorry that I brought it up. Don't let the thought of him take away the joy you have with Madelyn."

Remembering the tragedy that struck Carolyn's family, I clenched my jaw. "It's a relief to know he's up in Carlisle."

George agreed. "You've got that right. It's a long way from here. He'll probably try again to free Joseph."

Saint Bega's Priory

On Saturday morning, I awoke early. The same pair of mourning doves was once again cooing sorrowfully, on the branch above Eutychus' grave. Their sunrise lament was such a common occurrence that I knew memories of Eutychus would come to mind whenever I heard mourning doves for the rest of my life. He had been such a good-natured, precious friend.

I was looking forward to our exploration of the ruins of St. Begas, but I was thrilled even more with the idea that I would be spending the day alone with my Madelyn.

The special day that I had looked forward to, with my lovely bride to be, didn't turn out the way I had hoped. When I arrived at the parsonage, Tommy was harnessing Shadow and Wonder to the Landau, Carolyn was dusting off the leather seats with an old cloth, and Madelyn was walking Jester on his leash, near the water's edge.

"Good morning, Mr. Sterlin' sir. 'ow are you this fine day?"

Why are they here? I hope they don't see my disappointment. This was to be a special time for Madelyn and me to be alone.

"I'm fine, Thomas, how about you?" I was angrily frustrated on the inside but pleasant on the outside.

It struck me that Tommy was well dressed. He was wearing the clothes that I'd seen him wear to church lately. He wore a clean cotton shirt, a simple but presentable waistcoat, and clean trousers. Today, he had added to his church clothes, a tricorne hat, edged with silver brocade, not new but presentable and a clean cravat about his neck.

"No complainin' from me. Not a word. The sun, it be shinin'. My Carolyn, she be 'appy, and my friends, they be smilin'. Even me mom had a quiet night with me father gone off on the south road to Sandwith."

Madelyn sent Tommy and Carolyn into the kitchen to get the picnic lunch. She approached me, gave me a great hug, and scratched my whiskers, as she often liked to do. Then, rising up on her tiptoes, she gave me an affectionate kiss.

"I was hoping that we'd have the day alone so that we could talk," I whispered into her ear.

"Oh, sorry Michael. Yesterday, when I mentioned to Carolyn that you and I would be going to the ruins today, she seemed interested, and then when I told her the story about Saint Bega, she was so highly motivated she asked if they could come."

This was to be a special time for Madelyn and me. "You did the right thing I suppose, Madelyn. You, your family, and Tommy are all she has now."

"And you too, Michael. She thinks highly of you."

I reflected on Carolyn's new life situation. "You're right. We're her family now."

"Thanks for being so understanding. Besides, this will give me more cuddle time with you."

"What do you mean?"

"I've been teaching Carolyn how to handle the horses. She's been out with Uncle Martin and me many times in the gig and a half dozen times in the Landau as well."

"I didn't know that. I suppose being stuck in Edwyn's shop six days a week keeps me from seeing what's going on in town." I shook my head and shared a forlorn crooked grin. "Sometimes I imagine myself to be one of his tools."

Madelyn laughed. "You poor lad." She reached up and tousled my wavy black hair, and again scratched humorously at my short whiskers.

Maybe I should've shaved. She has a thing about my whiskers.

I grimaced at her teasing. "On Monday things will be a lot better. Exciting in fact."

"Why would that be?"

"Next week, the window framing, door jambs, windows, and doors will all be finished and installed. Our home will be closed in and protected from the weather."

Her mouth opened. Her hands dropped to her side. Her eyes sparkled. "It's happening. It's really happening. Our home is almost done." She held me at arm's length and gave me a wide smile, accentuated by her glistening emerald eyes.

"Then for two weeks following that, Edwyn and I will finish installing the cabinetry, shelves, and woodwork in the stairwells."

"Glorious! She exclaimed, clapping her hands together. "Can I come and watch?"

"It's best if you don't. Wait a few days or better yet, a week or two. Then you'll actually get a clear idea how things will look."

"I'm so excited." She clapped her hands again. "We should pick a date soon."

"You're right, sweetheart." I embraced her firmly. My hands held the small of her back. "The sooner the better."

"By 'sooner' do you mean weeks or months? I think weeks. What would you like?" she asked.

"Weeks."

"Hmm, my new name. What will it sound like?" She cleared her throat.

417

She dramatically responded to her own question. First, in a lighthearted feminine voice, I think she was mimicking one of the church ladies. "Excuse me, *Mrs. Sterling*, would you and your husband care to lead the congregation in the hymns next Sunday?" She clapped her hands together. Next, in a masculine voice, mimicking a low-voiced storekeeper in the seaport, she asked, "*Mrs. Sterling*, may I please discuss with you your grocery bill? It seems that I might've made a mistake in the figures."

"This is too much," I said with a wink and a grin.

Finally, in a formal voice, such as a master of ceremonies might use at a concert, she said, "Ladies and gentlemen, Michael and Madelyn *Sterling* of Oak Harbor in Cumberland will now bring us a selection of their favorite duets from their recent concert series in Manchester, Huddersfield, and Leeds." Once again, she excitedly clapped her hands and giggled like a schoolgirl.

I couldn't resist and wanting to get in on the humor. I emphasized the word *wife* with every sentence. I asked, as Uncle Martin might, "Michael, would you and your *wife* like to join us for lunch after church next Sunday?" I then turned the other direction, as if answering him, and said, "I'm not sure, Uncle Martin, let me check with my *wife*. My *wife* may have made other plans. I need to discuss it with my *wife*."

We shared a great laugh together and she grasped my hands as she swayed side to side. She was beaming. "We are going to be so happy. So gloriously happy." Tears of joy formed in her eyes. She looked up at me. A few tears rolled down her beautiful face. I kissed her several times on her cheeks. *So salty. Sweet with my bubbling love for her but salty from her tears. An exciting combination.*

"Michael, don't let anything keep us from this happiness—"

We Both Shall Row, My Love And I

Jester barked a few times, wagged his tail wildly, and was climbing all over Madelyn's shoes. She picked him up and held him between us. He thrived on the close attention.

"Madelyn, my love, we will be so happy, so content. Each night as we drop off to sleep, we will fall asleep in each other's arms, in each other's love."

Madelyn looked up at me. Her big, glistening, beautiful eyes communicated her intense love for me and her hope for our future. "I love you, Michael. I love you so much that somehow..." She paused. "I didn't know that life could ever be this joyful."

"My love." I brushed a long strand of hair from her eyes. "Each morning as the sun peeks through the window, we will hold one another and know that we will never face the day alone."

Tears ran down her cheeks, and Jester in the midst of our embrace, pushed his nose up and licked her salty, tear-stained face. We held each other and stood there resting in each other's love.

My heart was pounding. "I love you." My voice trembled with emotion.

Madelyn, still crying, was sniffling, and Jester was still licking her face. "I feel so silly."

"What 'appened out 'ere?" interrupted Tommy, as he and Carolyn came down the steps carrying a large blanket and a picnic basket.

"Are you two alright?" asked Carolyn.

"We're fine," responded Madelyn through her sobs and embarrassed silly laughter.

Taking the picnic basket and blanket from Tommy, I added. "We were thinking how wonderful it will be when we're married."

Madelyn rubbed her eyes with the back of her hand. "We should be on our way."

"Can I drive the team?" asked Carolyn. "Thomas has never seen me drive the Landau, only the little gig." She climbed aboard and tapped the seat beside her with the flat of her hand, looking at Tommy. "Jump up here and sit with me."

Tommy jumped to the driver's seat.

"Wait a minute," Madelyn said. "I'll put Jester in the house." She gave him a hug and petted his head as she walked towards the steps. "I wouldn't want him to be falling over any cliffs."

We climbed aboard and sat facing forward, and set the picnic basket on the empty seat in front of us.

Tommy turned for a moment to face us. "Carolyn's amazing. She's a wonder, that's for sure."

We started up the road and almost immediately turned towards the south and started the long climb up from the harbor valley. I was braced in the corner, facing forward, with Madelyn nestled in my arms.

Carolyn managed the team with competence. After a little less than an hour, near Elizabeth Harcourt's home, Madelyn decided to relieve Carolyn and I joined her on the driver's bench. "Maybe on the way back we can stop in and visit Elizabeth for a few minutes."

"That sounds like a splendid idea. You're always so concerned for others."

As we approached the little village of Sandwith, she waved at a gentleman who was keeping a close eye on some workers building a large structure close to the road. The man waved and his little terrier barked at us.

"Madelyn, we've been trotting along for more than an hour. How do you know someone this far from Oak Harbor?"

"That's Mr. Partridge and his dog, Shilling."

"An amusing name for a dog," I said. "How do you know Mr. Partridge?"

"Uncle Martin and I have met him a couple times when we've visited Elizabeth Harcourt. She's been receiving the occasional visit from him during the past month or so."

"What's he building?" I asked.

"It's an inn with a pub."

"If it was any closer to Oak Harbor, it might compete with the Royal Stag."

While passing through Sandwith, Tommy shouted to us, "If you be seein' me father, tell me. 'e came up this way yesterday. 'e was seein' a friend 'ere abouts. I told 'im we would be passin' by and could be given' 'im a ride but 'e didn't want to be waitin' 'til today."

There is no way that we would've given a drunken fool mouthed man like him a ride. I can't even imagine my sweet Madelyn in his presence.

"Okay, Tommy. If we see him we'll let you know."

I had no idea that Mr. Atwater would have the motivation or the energy to walk this far to be 'seeing a friend.' This is quite a distance, mostly uphill, from Oak Harbor.

We travelled on a little farther through the tiny hamlet and I pointed at the lane that led out to the headland. "There's the small carriage trail that leads to the lighthouse and the precipice."

"That would be a great spot for our picnic," said Madelyn. "We can look out over the Irish Sea."

"That's a superb idea."

A few minutes later, we crossed a picturesque stone bridge, beneath which a stream called Thorny Brook babbled along. All along this part of the road, we enjoyed the big shady trees that overhung us, swaying in the refreshing breeze.

Finally, after a journey of about two hours or a little more, we arrived at the ruins of Saint Bega. It was an interesting cluster of ancient red sandstone and limestone ruins, some of which were a thousand years old. The main hall was still being used as the church for the townspeople.

We tethered the team and Madelyn gave them a basin of water and a few minutes of care before starting our exploration. Deciding to look inside the church before the ruins, we approached the massive doors of the West Entrance. The impressive carved gateway of red sandstone struck me as powerfully today as when I first saw it several years earlier.

"It's a sight to behold," said Carolyn.

"This 'ere be a solid gate for sure," said Tommy. "I'm to thinkin' that Emperor 'adrian 'imself would've built it."

"Actually, Thomas." Seeking to correct him without embarrassment. "Not a bad guess, but it was built by the Normans over six hundred years ago."

"Blimey! That be older than Lord Warrington's fine 'all."

"Absolutely right, but not as long ago as the Romans."

"Michael, I like the three leaded windows above us here. Will we have any leaded windows such as these in our home?"

"Yes sweetheart, quite a few. The most attractive ones are on the upper floor and look out over the harbor. Leaded windows of twin panes in each of our three dormers. A little wider than these."

"They sound wonderful. You're building me a beautiful home."

"It's not finished yet, dear, though it's nearly so, now that the roof is complete and Edwyn will be hanging the doors and setting in the windows next week. Nothing can stop us now."

"Nothing can stop us now," she repeated joyously. Madelyn did her schoolgirl hand clapping again and giggled with glee.

Sometime I should mention to her that her hand clapping habit can be a bit distracting if it's overdone.

We opened the massive doors and stepped inside, but it was difficult to see. On any given Sunday, there would be abundant light provided by numerous lamps and candles, in addition to the windows, but not being a Sunday, the light provided by the windows high above was barely enough. It took several minutes for our eyes to adjust. Even with the poor lighting, we were awestruck with the artistically rich stonework pillars, arches, and polished woodwork. As our eyes began to adjust to the poor light, we walked towards the front of the church and located a doorway to the room at the base of the tower. We entered, found the steep steps that led up into the tower, and started our climb.

In the top of this square brick tower, avoiding the bells hanging in the middle, we went back and forth between the louvered openings on each of its four sides. Peeking through the louvres, many of which were missing, we were able to enjoy the four views that presented themselves to us.

Towards the north was the slope up towards the hamlet of Sandwith and to the west was the glistening Irish Sea. To the south, across the Pow Beck valley, we could see the most southerly part of the town with its sturdy buildings and peaked roofs, and in the distance to the east rose the mountains not too far from my home at Cliffside.

Tommy, realizing what we were looking at in the distance facing east, came and stood with us. He rested his hand on Madelyn's shoulder. "Look, there be the 'ome o' your betrothed. That be the mountain man's 'ome, for sure."

Madelyn winked and grinned. "He is my mountain man, no doubt about that."

She moved to the window facing south and looking puzzled, pointed out through the gaping hole left by several missing louvers. "What are those buildings right across the street?"

"That's Saint Bees School." I brushed some cobwebs from between the louvers. "The Archbishop of Canterbury founded the school two hundred years ago and it's been a grand place of learning ever since."

"It may have had some difficult times but it has weathered them all. It will never close."

When we descended the tower, we saw a gentleman wearing an academic robe kneeling beside the altar table. He noticed us and with some effort, rose to his feet. He introduced himself as Reverend James Hutchinson, a graduate of Oxford and the headmaster of Saint Bees School.

"Greetings to you, sir," said Madelyn.

"Happy to meet you, sir." I smiled and shook his hand, as did Carolyn and Madelyn. Tommy for a moment was quite distracted, digging in each of his pockets, searching for something. A moment later, he found and pulled out a piece of paper. *Oh no, not the scrawled, homemade calling card. The headmaster will think we're daft.*

Tommy, with a raised eyebrow, stepped towards the headmaster. "Hello, Headmaster Hutchinson. We are so glad to make your acquaintance on this fine day." Tommy, bowing in a gentlemanly fashion, removed his tricorne hat, swept it towards his waist, straightened, and held it under his left arm. Then, with their right hands, they shared a cordial handshake. Tommy inclined his head slightly and passed the headmaster his card. They looked like men of significance: a polished London businessman meeting a notable scholar for the first time. I caught a glimpse of his card as Headmaster Hutchinson read it. I was shocked. It was a professionally printed calling card with silver edging and embossed silver corners. Tommy continued, "Should you need any assistance with your business interests, it would be my pleasure to be of service."

Master Thomas Cedric Atwater
Servant of the Crown

Entrepreneur & Agent
For The Finest Craftsmen
Oak Harbor, Cumberland

"I will be sure to contact you when I am next in Oak Harbor," he glanced at the card, "Master Atwater."

Tommy affirmed Headmaster Hutchinson's intention with another respectful bow. "Thank you, Headmaster Hutchinson. I would truly be pleased to be of service to you and your fine school."

Taking a step towards him, my eyes met his. "We apologize for disturbing your time of prayer."

"Not to worry. I was just finishing up. Have a good day."

He took a few steps, stopped, and turned. Addressing Tommy, he said, "Actually one of our larger buildings needs new windows and a new roof. I need to find the best price for quite a large number of lamps as well."

Tommy, looking every bit the consummate professional, took out a pocket-sized notebook and recorded a few points of what had been requested. He then responded maturely, "I will return early next week with several samples of lamps and I will have my most expert associates provide estimates on the windows and roof."

"Fine then. Would eleven in the morning on Tuesday be a suitable time?"

"Yes, that would serve our purposes quite well," responded Tommy.

"Well, Master Thomas, I'm so glad that I have had the opportunity to make your acquaintance."

"And I yours, sir." Tommy dropped his notebook and was distracted. "Be 'avin' a good day then, 'eadmaster 'utchinson."

The headmaster was startled at the alteration of Tommy's speech, "I beg your pardon, young man?"

"Headmaster Hutchinson sir, I do wish you well on this fine day. I will be looking forward to our appointment on Tuesday at eleven."

"Master Thomas." The headmaster had regained his understanding of who he believed Tommy to be. "I will be looking forward to meeting with you in my office at Saint Bees School."

Tommy gave a respectable nod of departure.

Having completed his conversation with Tommy, Headmaster Hutchinson likewise inclined his head respectfully. He walked up the aisle with his academic robes flowing behind him, and stepped out through the great doors.

Madelyn, believing that she had witnessed a miracle, seated herself heavily on a nearby chair. Carolyn, with a beaming grin, staggered and rested her hand on the back of a bench for support. The two young women were speechless.

"Tommy, I mean Thomas." I was dumbfounded beyond words. "You're so mature. Where did you... Where did your accent go? What...? How did you...?"

"I've been practicin'." He gave me a respectful bow and returned his hat to his head. Then, with Reverend Ashcroft's

We Both Shall Row, My Love And I

mannerisms and a near perfect imitation of his rich baritone voice, he said, "My motivation has garnered certain opportunities. Of that, Mr. Sterling, I am quite certain. Contact me when you need my assistance in the future and please be advised that some of my associates might know me by the name of Cedric Atwater."

He looked me in the eye and laughed. Instantly, his normal stance, demeanor, and speech style returned. "I've been practicin' with Rev'rend Ashcroft, Rev'rend Ekland, and Edward Stewart. They've been 'elpin' me to be improvin'."

"You sounded and looked like a London businessman, with these new skills and top-notch clothing. Are you still actually you?"

Tommy laughed thoughtfully and returned to his more refined speech style. "I can assure you, each of you in fact, I am my maturing self. I seek to present myself to others in a more respectable fashion." He paused with one eyebrow raised and slipped his little notebook into his pocket. He looked in every way the ambitious businessman, the confident college student, the worldly traveler.

Carolyn grinned and winked, Madelyn froze and gasped, and I simply held my breath and stared.

Tommy balled his fists and placed them on his hips. "Even a mockin' magpie can be singin' like an 'armonious nightin'gale when 'e be settin' 'is mind to it."

With his switch back to his normal way of speaking, we were once again beyond words. A moment later, we were giggling and laughing, not at him, but with him in celebration of the new direction his life had taken by his own stalwart determination.

"You could be a great actor," said Madelyn.

"A person that can change from one character to another," I added. "Like a lizard that can change his appearance."

"A chameleon," clarified Madelyn. "That can change his color when he needs to." She was buoyant at the positive change in her reading student.

Carolyn started to giggle again, and I marveled at how Tommy had matured far beyond my expectations.

I slapped him on the back. "Well done."

"Your speech and manner were superb," said Madelyn.

"Until you dropped your notebook," giggled Carolyn.

Tommy adopted a cheerful expression with a great beaming grin. "I'll be 'avin' to 'old it more firmly in the future."

We walked down the church aisle laughing and chatting.

"There's never a dull moment when Tommy..." I cleared my throat in a genteel manner. "I mean, when Master Thomas Cedric Atwater is near."

The ladies giggled as we stepped out into the sunshine of the churchyard and began examining the various ruins. They were astonishing. The statuary, engravings, gravestones, and monuments drew our imaginations back to ancient times. The tumbled down, ivy-covered walls created for us an atmosphere of being visitors in another era.

What held Madelyn's attention the longest was some weather-beaten stonework near the red sandstone gate, through which we had entered. It was a stone lintel above a doorway, and carved upon it in relief from years long past was the scene depicting Saint Michael slaying a dragon that I had told her about.

Madelyn was walking arm in arm with Carolyn at the time. "I have one of those," she said to her.

Carolyn looked at the carved lintel and back at Madelyn quizzically. "A dragon?"

"No, my Michael. He'll slay any dragon that comes my way. He'll always protect me."

We Both Shall Row, My Love And I

Hearing my name, I joined them in their scrutiny of the lintel, and a moment later Tommy joined us.

Realizing that Tommy and Carolyn were listening, and that she was influencing their understanding, she decided to be careful of what she said. "Let's find out what the Bible teaches about Saint Michael, who is actually Michael the archangel." She went over to the Landau, reached into the picnic basket, and pulled out her Bible. "Michael the archangel is mentioned in a few places but the passage that I would like to read is in the book of Revelation" I leaned against a nearby wall, warmed in the noonday sun. Carolyn and Tommy sat upon a wooden bench.

"Let me share a powerful passage with you." She flipped through a few pages in her Bible. "Here it is, the Revelation of Saint John the Apostle, the twelfth chapter, verses seven through eleven."

> And there was war in heaven: Michael and his angels fought against the dragon; and the dragon fought and his angels, and prevailed not; neither was their place found any more in heaven. And the great dragon was cast out, that old serpent, called the Devil, and Satan, which deceiveth the whole world: he was cast out into the earth, and his angels were cast out with him. And I heard a loud voice saying in heaven, Now is come salvation, and strength, and the kingdom of our God, and the power of his Christ: for the accuser of our brethren is cast down, which accused them before our God day and night. And they overcame him by the blood of the Lamb, and by the word of

their testimony; and they loved not their lives unto the death.

Madelyn put her thumb into her Bible and held it with one hand. She looked over at me for a moment but then focused her attention on Tommy and Carolyn. "Do you understand what this is about? The Devil or Satan, also known as the dragon, was cast out of heaven and now he has been defeated by the sacrifice and resurrection of our Lord Jesus Christ."

"Madelyn, that's a powerful passage you have there," said Tommy.

She continued. "In our youth class last Sunday morning, we talked about temptation. What is the first action word used here to describe the Devil's activity that relates to the whole world?"

"Might I be lookin' at your Bible?" asked Tommy.

She passed it over to him. "You sure do 'ave a lot of underlinin's in it." His index finger slid down the page. "Here it be. The devil '*deceiveth* the whole world'."

"That's right," affirmed Madelyn.

Carolyn ran her fingers through her fine, light brown hair. "He's a trickster. Sometimes we're tempted to do wrong. We get an idea to do something improper and we say to ourselves, 'that's not so bad' but the Bible says it is."

"Yes, Carolyn, that's right." And with that she closed her Bible. "I wasn't expecting to get into a long study in the scriptures but I do like to refer to them sometimes."

"Sometimes?" Carolyn winked and grinned.

"Okay, okay," laughed Madelyn. "Often."

Tommy gave a cheerful laugh but looked pensive. "Miss Madelyn was I bein' deceivin' when I was talkin' to 'eadmaster 'utchinson?"

Madelyn was lost in thought for a moment. Her head tilted and she looked up. "Thomas, I'm under the impression that you weren't trying to deceive but that you were trying to rise to your new place in life." She paused to look at a butterfly that had landed on a wall beside a caterpillar. "The person whom you believed you might become. The way that a caterpillar becomes a butterfly."

"I be supposin' that you be right," responded Tommy.

My Madelyn is so perceptive. I imagine she could add a line to her poem, 'What Is Your Perspective,' about Tommy.

I'd rather be a street lad, struttin' burden free,
than a duty-driven banker, lookin' for his fee.
I'd rather be a banker, with a partnership to join,
than a foul smellin' street lad, lookin' for some coin.

Tommy, often more of a leader than he intended to be, brought us back to our purposes for the day. "Let's be goin' to 'ave a look from the cliff out over the Irish Sea."

We climbed aboard the Landau and headed north towards Sandwith. Madelyn was driving the team with me at her side. Tommy and Carolyn were behind us in the seat facing forward.

The Precipice

We turned from the road onto the lane and as we approached the lighthouse, we were dazzled by the great expanse of blue sky above the Irish Sea.

"We'll tether the team at the lighthouse." I pointed towards it, about a quarter mile up ahead, as I shielded my squinting eyes from the afternoon sun. "After that there's nothing to tie them to. Grasses, flowers, and a windswept terrace is all there is atop the cliff. We'll need to walk and carry the picnic basket and blanket the rest of the way."

"You've been here before?" asked Carolyn.

"Yes, with my grandfather." Looking out over the sea, bathed by the breeze rising up from the great body of water, I was warmed by my memories. "We came here several times."

Madelyn flicked the reins. "Walk on," she coaxed the slowing horses.

Traveling a little further along the lane, we reached the lighthouse and Madelyn secured the horses to an iron ring atop a solid hitching post.

Thankfully, there was water deep enough in the trough that we didn't need to remove the horses' bridles and bits for them to drink easily. Madelyn told us that it is difficult for a horse, with a bit in its mouth, to drink when the water in a basin is shallow.

We knocked on the door of the lighthouse for a few minutes, without response, and assumed that the lighthouse keeper was away.

Perhaps he's at the shops getting some groceries. I'm sure he'll be back before dark to prepare for the evening.

Walking towards the nearest cliff carrying the basket and the blanket, we soon arrived at a grassy crest. We stood there, awestruck with the view before walking down the short slope, about a man's height, onto the large flat sandstone terrace.

"Look." Carolyn pointed to the west, out upon the horizon across the sea. "That island can be hardly seen. It looks mysterious. What's its name?"

"The Isle of Man. It's just over thirty miles away and you can only see it on clear days like today."

"It seems so close," exclaimed Carolyn. "I've heard people talk about it in Oak Harbor but I imagined it to be much farther away."

On the sandstone terrace, beaten clean by the rain, the sea breeze, and the sun, the women spread the blanket and opened the basket. Tommy and I walked first to a narrow crevice, about two feet wide and as deep as a man is tall, and then over to the edge of the precipice.

"Tommy, look how far down it is. Be careful. This is dangerous." I was feeling fatherly.

"Blimey, that be a long way down." Tommy picked up a stone the size of his fist and tossed it over. It fell about a hundred feet before it smacked against a protrusion of the cliff face, bounced, and then fell the remaining two hundred feet, before impacting the sea-swept boulders at the bottom.

"Mr. Sterlin', if someone be fallin' o'er the edge, 'e be 'avin' time to write a letter to 'is mates before 'e 'it the bottom."

With a chuckle, I blinked. "You have a way with words, Tommy, but you're right. People say that it's about three hundred feet to the bottom. There are a few edges and points sticking out, here and there, but it's quite a height."

"Thomas! Michael!" shouted Carolyn. "We're starving. Come back from the edge. Let's eat."

We turned to go along the edge towards the women but I grasped Tommy's elbow. "Wait a minute. Look how beautiful our ladies are."

Carolyn, standing beside the picnic basket, beckoned us. The strong wind from the south was tugging at her long, light brown hair. Her pale lavender cotton dress billowed out from her slender body.

"Mr. Sterlin', a blessin' it is, that Carolyn's long scar is 'ard to see. It be but a small line, even up close. It is a miracle at Muriel's 'and."

"Yes, it is, Thomas."

Madelyn, always so beautiful, living art, stood beside Carolyn. With her chin held high, she was watching us, shielding her eyes from the bright sun with her flattened palm.

"Thomas, those are two of the Lord's most exquisite creations. What's most beautiful about them is their goodness; their desire to always do what is right, their care for others, and their care for you and me." I turned towards him and rested my hand on his shoulder.

"That be true and with care our ladies made us lunch. Let's be goin', Mr. Sterlin'. I be starvin'."

"Wait a moment, Thomas. Please call me Michael. You're older now and I've grown to respect you so very much." I grinned and tipped my head to one side. "You're a good man. You're such a blessing to Carolyn and all of us in Oak Harbor." I paused. "I'm proud to call you my friend."

Tommy lifted his chin and looked at me. "Michael, you've just now said far more than me own father 'as ever said to me. Thank you for 'elpin' me to be a better man."

We walked back over to the women and sat beside them. Madelyn and Carolyn had laid out the blanket, opened the picnic basket, and spread out the food on a tablecloth.

Before us was a feast that Tommy and I weren't expecting. Madelyn and Carolyn had put special effort into the generous meal. Slices of smoked ham, disks of spicy sausage, and blue Stilton cheese wedges were on a sizable platter. Beside it were sun dried apple slices, a fresh loaf of mixed grain bread, a small stoneware jar of strawberry jam, and a protective, quilted, pale blue bag. It was a tantalizing feast and we were the invitees.

"What do we have in the bag?" I asked.

Madelyn opened the drawstring, lifted out a bottle of wine, and passing it to me, I examined it. "Well now, 1770, the year that Ludwig van Beethoven was born," I said. "I've heard of Painshill Winery, but not being a wine connoisseur, I'm not expertly familiar with it. Tell me more."

"Pop the cork, Michael."

As I did so, she told us about the winery. "It was the best in England but it was sold in 1773 for £25,000."

Tommy dramatically bugged out his eyes. "That's a 'eapin' pile o' coin."

"The 1770 vintage year was considered the best and I brought this bottle from the Haversham estate for a special occasion. I believe that this picnic, with our dear friends Carolyn and Thomas, is that special occasion."

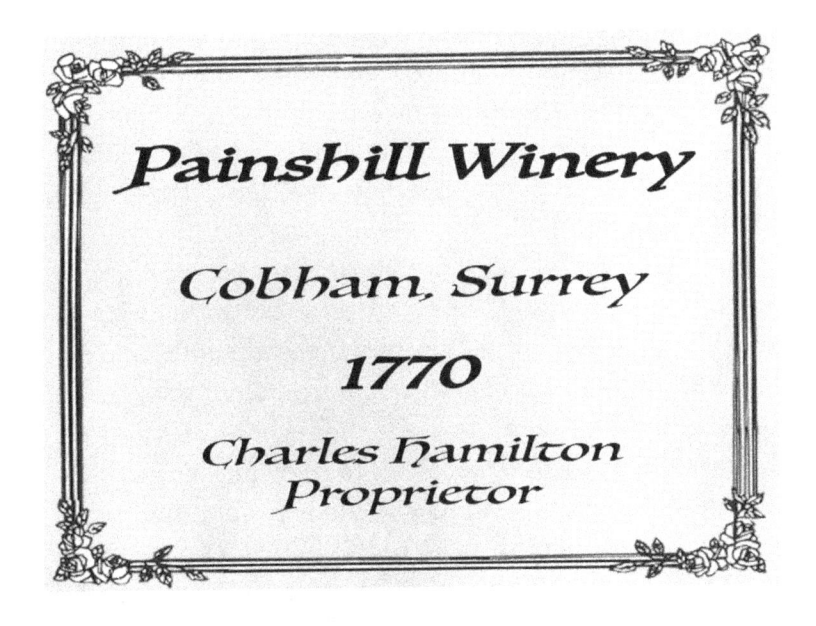

> **Painshill Winery**
>
> **Cobham, Surrey**
>
> **1770**
>
> **Charles Hamilton
> Proprietor**

Carolyn cleared her throat and smiled broadly. "Madelyn, you truly know how to make people feel special. Thank you so much." With a tender grin, she reached out and took Madelyn's hand.

"I'll be makin' a suggestion, if you don't be mindin'?" Tommy looked seriously at each of us in turn. "Thank you so much for bringin' this 'ere bottle of your finest wine dear, Madelyn. You all be knowin' my family and the life that I be comin' from." He paused, holding back some emotion. "The Bible, it be teachin' moderation and I be supportin' that. Me father and me family 'ave been ruined by drink. Moderation, that be all I'm sayin'. Moderation."

"Thomas, I agree with you completely," said Carolyn.

Madelyn pursed her lips. "Well said."

"Thank you for sharing that, Thomas," I said. "We all agree." *I truly admire him for the maturation and the changes that are taking place in his heart.*

Carolyn's face bore an expression of pride. Without her saying a word, you could see how she thought so highly of Tommy.

Madelyn politely cleared her throat as we sat in a circle on the blanket. "Let's pray." She paused for a moment. "Thank you, Lord, for our picnic lunch and the beautiful scenery. Thank you also for our dear friends and the fellowship that we can have. In Jesus' name, Amen."

When she finished, we set about to enjoy the fine meal and we were all buoyantly savoring one another's company.

Madelyn, realizing that she had forgotten a knife, passed me the stoneware jar of strawberry jam. "Can you cut this twine from the canvas covering, please?"

When my hand went to my belt, I realized that I'd forgotten my sheath knife. "This is going to be difficult. You're not the only one who has forgotten a knife. Mine is back at the Brixtons' and the cover's sealed with a heavily waxed and knotted twine."

"Not a problem." Tommy went up onto his knees from his sitting position, and fishing around in his trousers' pockets, came up with a little folding pocketknife. "My knife's quite small but it be truly sharp. Pass me the jar."

With a quick slice, the waxed twine was cut and the heavy fabric cover was removed.

"It's so nice to have a man around the house," said Carolyn with a wink and a nod. "I learned that line from Aunt Muriel. We should always praise our men."

Tommy set down the jar, picked up the loaf of bread, and cut several slices as best as he was able with his tiny two-inch blade. He generously spread some of the jam on a slice and passed it over to me. "'ere, 'ave some bread and jam."

"Thank you, Thomas."

"You'll be fancyin' this as well, Carolyn. Of that I'm sure." Grinning, he added, "I guess we truly be 'jam eaters' up 'ere in the north."

We were gripped with hilarity and Carolyn was laughing so hard she started choking until she coughed up a piece of bread. She coughed a few more times, cleared her throat, and Tommy, looking very worried, began to rub her back.

"Thank you, Thomas, you're always at my side when I need you."

Madelyn and I exchanged a glance and a wink, having heard what Carolyn said about Tommy.

I was pleasantly surprised by the bread and jam. "This is supremely delicious." I remembered having had some similar to this at Aunt Muriel's table, but this seemed more tangy.

"Madelyn, you have to try some of this." I licked my lips. "It's splendid."

Tommy passed her a piece of the jam-coated bread.

She took a bite. "It is good. Aunt Muriel made this and I know why it's so tasty."

"Is there a secret ingredient?" asked Carolyn.

Tommy wiped his knife on a napkin, closed it up, and slipped it back into his pocket. He took a monstrously big bite of the jam-coated bread. "This 'ere jam could be sold for an 'andsome profit in any o' the big cities."

Madelyn had a confident expression. "I know the secret. There's a hint of orange marmalade in it."

"Amazing," responded Carolyn. "Aunt Muriel is a clever lady."

Our picnic lunch atop the cliff was wonderful and our conversation with Tommy and Carolyn was playfully friendly.

When we had finished our meal, we looked out over the Irish sea. For a time we discussed our hopes and dreams for the future until a group of five dolphins passed by the base of the cliff, capturing our attention. Enthusiastically, we enjoyed watching them swim, jump, and tail slap.

After the dolphins moved off, Tommy and Carolyn, perhaps bored with us older people sitting and discussing things at great length, decided to go for a walk.

"Carolyn and me, we be goin' strollin' to the south."

I wanted to tell them to be careful near the edge of the precipice but resisted, not wanting to sound too fatherly. We watched them as they strolled along, side by side at first, and then hand in hand. A few steps further and they disappeared, out of sight, over the grassy knoll atop the headland.

I laid back on our terrace rock and looked heavenward. The intensely blue sky and the few fluffy white clouds that were skidding past created a dreamy winsome mood within me.

Madelyn sat beside me leaning on one arm, and with one knee raised.

"Michael, am I going to be a good mother?"

Looking at her tenderly, flooded with confidence in her, I conferred upon her my absolute certainty. "You're going to be a wonderful mother." Thinking of my own cold mother, I feared sounding harsh but there was something that I needed to say. "Madelyn, I wish that someone like you had been my mother and had raised me." I hesitated. "I would be a man more at peace today." She appeared surprised but said nothing. *I shouldn't have said that but it's true.*

Wanting to bring our conversation back to a more light-hearted, less serious mood, I responded to her original question about being a mother. "From the time our children enter the world, and all through their childhood and youth, our children will thrive on your love and care."

"*Our* love and care." She leaned down towards me, laughed when a free strand of her hair fell upon my face, and brushed it away. She kissed me. "You're going to be an amazing father." She sat up straight and looked out to sea. "We're going to have a home that's filled with love and peace."

What would I ever do without this tender and caring woman?
"Michael, look at all of the birds up here."

Sitting up, I enjoyed them with her. We marveled at their ability to manage their flight as they maneuvered in the wind along the cliff edge and the open space above.

The birds of the headland were enjoying the onshore breeze from the sea. The black guillemots, playful upon the updraft, often seemed to hover as they rested upon it, allowing themselves to be held steady in the updraft. The Fulmars and Kittiwakes soared a bit higher.

"Michael, do birds like to fly? It looks like they do."

"You've asked me that question before. I think they do." I pointed overhead. "Look at those three kittiwakes soaring and diving."

"If I were a bird," she said. "Gliding about in the breeze, it would be a great joy."

She removed her sterling silver comb, with its long tines, from her hair and put it in her pocket. Her red hair, shining in the sun revealing some blonde highlights, fell about her shoulders. She gathered it up and tied it at the back of her head with a green satin ribbon that she had brought with her.

I was struck once again with her beauty, especially when she smiled radiantly. *She has a perfectly shaped mouth. I love her sweet little nose and her big bright eyes.*

"The sun is so hot, even with this strong breeze." She unbuttoned her waist length jacket, removed it, folded it up, and laid it on the bare stone beside her. "It doesn't seem like October. It's hot here in the sun." She fanned herself with her hand.

Several birds hovered above us and then, one after another in sequence swooped back towards the precipice. "The birds here are wonderful to watch."

"If I were a bird," she said. "I know that I'd love to soar up high, dart down towards the cliff, and then suddenly ascend and soar up to the clouds again."

Throughout her description of flight, she gestured each of the maneuvers.

"Madelyn my love, you'd be an exciting bird to watch."

"Would you try and catch me and tame me, Michael?" She feigned a serious look.

"No, sweetheart. You'd never be happy in a cage."

"These dried out flowers all along the crest are so very delicate. They're not big, but they are beautiful."

"When I was here a few years ago with my grandfather, it was early summer and they were all in full bloom." I remembered the advice that I had been given from one of the older gentlemen at the Royal Stag. "Even then, fair as they may have been, they were not so beautiful as thee, my love."

She poked me in my ribs, smiled, and pointed out the little delicate sea campion flowers with their pinkish white petals and the deep purple sea lavenders. "Although they're dried out, let's collect some of these gorgeous flowers for Brynne and Meiling. The flowers have kept much of their color, even though it's been weeks since they were in bloom."

"Don't forget Aunt Muriel and Louisa," I added. "I'm sure they'd like some too."

"That's for sure." She sat up cross-legged, reached skyward, and stretched. "I'm still a bit warm on this rock."

She removed the green ribbon from the back of her head and let her hair fall around her shoulders as it had a few minutes earlier. The breeze tugged at the long auburn strands and she ran the fingers of both hands through them several times. She looked like a mysterious princess in some ancient myth. I was awestruck with her beauty. She then pulled her hair towards one side of her head in a unique way and retied the ribbon.

How is it possible that any woman could be so beautiful, and how is it possible that such a woman would love me?

Madelyn laid down beside me, finding comfort and security with her head on my shoulder, nestled in the embrace of my arm. We looked up into the bright blue sky with its little fluffy clouds racing towards the mountains in the distance behind us.

◊◊◊◊◊◊

Michael was aware of the fascinating scenic wonders here at the most westerly headland of Cumberland. The birds and puffy clouds above, the flowers beyond the picnic blanket, and the dolphins in the sea far below. Each had held his attention for a time. He was also tenderly attentive to his sweet Madelyn and couldn't help but envision the life they would share—their happiness and peace, their hopes and dreams, their home and their children.

What Michael didn't see was the loathsome man in the lighthouse. The tall man who had been watching their every move from a distance. The cruel man with two bodies at his feet: Tommy's father had served his purposes well and the lighthouse keeper had been merely an inconvenience. The vicious man with evil intent strung his bow.

◊◊◊◊◊◊

The meal had been delicious, our time with Carolyn and Tommy had been full of joy, and the view from the top of the cliff had been uplifting. I was content.

Most importantly, here I was spending time with my precious Madelyn. She was beside me and embraced by her love, I took her hand.

Madelyn, still laying on the terrace-like stone, dreamily looked up into the clouds racing through the sky. "Michael, my love, how does Saturday, the seventh of November, sound to you?"

"I suppose you're talking about our wedding date."

She looked at me with joy in her eyes. "That gives you three weeks. I can hardly wait to decorate and furnish our lovely home. We'll have beautifully upholstered and comfortably padded chairs. In our main sitting room we'll have beautiful silver-colored satin curtains. They'll look like the silver lining of clouds at the end of a stormy day." She stopped and her brow furrowed. "Will our house be completed by the seventh of November?"

"Edwyn has started the finishing work long ago and he has me helping him. I would think that all or at least most of the finishing work will be done. It will be sealed off from the weather in just a few days and the fireplaces are already functioning. It's interesting that you picked the seventh of November."

"Why? What's so interesting about that date?"

"It's Saint Bega's Day," I responded.

"Hmm, I wonder what I'll cook for you. Our first meal as husband and wife needs to be special."

"With you across from me at our table, anything would be supremely satisfying." I leaned up on my elbow and looked down at this lovely woman. The subtle emerald sparkles in her green eyes were hidden gems and the tiny lines that formed at their outside corners when she laughed were invitations to enjoy her wit. The curve of her full and sensuous lips beckoned me.

I kissed her and the sensation of her warm wet lips on mine filled my heart with passion. We kissed again, my hand at her waist, her arms reaching up around my neck and shoulders. "Madelyn, my love for you hasn't merely grown since I met you. My love for you has consumed me as fire consumes the driest tinder—"

"That's a grand idea, Sterling!" growled Caine. "After I kill you, I'll have her as my plunder."

I twisted around and we scrambled to our feet. Caine was only thirty feet away, standing over us on a slightly elevated stone terrace. Stepping in front of Madelyn, I shielded her. "Let her go! This is between us!"

"Maybe I'll kill her in front of you."

The arrow in Caine's bow was fully pulled back and aimed at my chest. "No." Caine laughed. "That would be a waste of good female flesh." He winced. "You're responsible for the death of my father, the hangings of Gavin and Victor, and my youngest brother's jail sentence."

He kept the arrow on the bowstring but relaxed his pull slightly, and his targeting drifted from a true aim as he prattled on. "Killing you two is merely the beginning of my revenge."

"Caine, let the others go." My pleading felt purposeless. His eyes burned with revenge.

He eased off on the bowstring almost entirely and the arrow was aimed near our feet, as his big mouth jabbered away. "Tommy will be next, and I should've killed Carolyn when I finished her brother."

Tommy's moving behind him. I mustn't look right at him. If I glance his way, Caine will know. Does Madelyn see Tommy? She mustn't look directly at him.

"Then, I'll put an arrow through Edwyn's daughter, like I put an arrow through his dog."

"You've got us, Caine. Let me say goodbye to this woman." I swung her around in front of me so she wouldn't look towards Tommy.

Madelyn whispered, "What are you doing?"

My right hand slid down her back and smoothed over her bottom. I kissed her ear and whispered, "Tommy is moving up behind him with his little knife." I stroked her waist slowly and caressed the back of her neck. "We need to distract him."

Madelyn unfastened her wide belt and dropped it to the ground behind her. With a loud voice, Madelyn distracted Caine. "Michael, I want your body next to mine." She reached up provocatively with both hands, pulled out her hair ribbon, and let the wind at the precipice carry it away. She ran the fingers of both of her hands upwards through her glistening hair.

Caine moaned. "That's the female flesh I'll be having. It'll be a chance for her to—"

Like a young tiger, Tommy had leapt onto Caine's back. He was poking his little knife downwards at the miscreant's upper body. Bewildered, cursing, and turning in circles, Caine hardly knew what was happening. The arrow he had at the ready in his bow was released, missed me, and harmlessly pierced the air, falling into the Irish Sea far below. Caine was able to grab the wrist of Tommy's knife-wielding hand.

"Get off!" shouted Caine. He fumbled for his own blade but dropped it down a deep, narrow crack.

Tommy grabbed his little knife with his other hand. In one final attempt to overcome the miscreant, he slashed at Caine's neck but missed, slicing along the jawbone. The follow through of the stroke cut Caine's bowstring. *Twang*, the bow straightened.

"Curse you, you little dog." Caine, having dropped his useless bow, tore Tommy from himself. He tried to throw him over the cliff but ended up throwing him into the crevice beside the terrace.

"Thomas!" screamed Carolyn. She rushed over to where he'd been thrown.

I burst upon Caine. We punched, parried, and blocked but were on the ground wrestling within minutes. In the struggle his remaining arrows broke when I flipped him and he landed on the quiver that hung from his belt. His sliced jaw gushed blood. Our relentless combat continued, but fatigue slowed us.

For a moment, to my surprise, I had the advantage, straddling him with my knees. Our struggle continued. Punches opened his wound further. I became certain I would not only overcome him but fully subdue him. *I mustn't let him get the advantage again.*

"Give up, Caine. There's no use."

He got hold of a fist-sized rock with his big hand and swung it, striking me in the head. A mere glancing blow, but it knocked me off him. Having come apart, we were both down on all fours, eyeing each other, panting and planning.

"Surrender or run. If you kill us." I tried to catch my breath. "The authorities will pursue you 'til they capture you."

He charged me and we were grappling again. He pressed the fight towards the edge of the precipice. His intentions were obvious: I'd be going over. A moment later, he was straddling me with his knees and pinning one of my arms as he choked me.

Madelyn, clutching the same rock that Caine had used on me, was now repeatedly striking him about his head and shoulders with it. "Let him go. Get off him!"

Breaking away, I scrambled to my feet. She was now in his grip. His back was to the sea.

"Stop! Don't hurt her!"

He stood at the edge of the cliff, threatening and gesturing to throw her over. He held her from behind in front of himself and one of his huge hands had a firm hold of her hair and neck. She couldn't breath. His other arm around her waist had a wrist. He was squeezing her, crushing her into himself.

"Caine, I'll do anything. Stop!"

The terror in her eyes, the crazed satisfaction in his, filled me with rage. Again, he mockingly motioned to cast her over the cliff. She was crying, struggling to breathe, and flailing with her one free arm. With his vice-like grip, she was simply a wounded dove in a fox's jaws. Her free hand slipped into her pocket. A moment later, clutching her silver comb, she was stabbing at the monstrous hand around her neck. He released his grip, grabbed the comb, and threw it over the edge. She unsuccessfully tried to break free.

My darling Madelyn must be released from this terror. I know what I need to do. I will take him over the edge.

Rushing him, tackling him with all my strength would be her only hope. It would be the only way she'd be safe. I need to infuriate him beyond his own self-control for her to fully break free. He must be enraged towards me.

"You were too frightened to help Gavin and Victor. You hid in the forest."

He gritted his teeth, snarling like a beast. "Sterling, I'm going to kill you."

"You watched me mash your brother Joseph's face. You ran away."

His eyes were aflame with anger. "I'll kill you, Sterling."

"You need to face me, man to man, instead, you're cowering behind a woman's skirts."

He lifted my sweet Madelyn off her feet and threw her to the side like a rag doll. She struck her head with a thud on the stone terrace and lay there motionless.

"Ahhg!" I charged him full force.

He thought I'd want to fight. He was mistaken. I would take him over the cliff. My arms were locked around him but I only had one of his arms. Realizing what I intended to do, he immediately collapsed to the ground.

"Sterling, you don't have the strength."

With his one free hand and his feet, he unsuccessfully tried to stop my push towards the edge. He was frantic. "Stop. Stop! I'll let you all go." He punched me in the face. I turned away. Mere inches at a time, I struggled. We slid closer to the edge.

Courageously, I clung to my resolve. "Caine, you rabid dog. I'm not letting you go." *Lord, help me. I'll not let him go. He must be stopped.*

"Stop! We'll both die," he growled through gritted teeth.

"That's what I intend."

We were at the edge. His feet were in the air. Sweating like a hog, I continued my aggressive push. My arms slipped to his head and shoulders. His legs were over. The fingertips of his free hand found a tiny crack. I wrestled them out. Our faces were inches apart.

Terror filled his eyes. "Stop, I beg you." He punched my face. I turned my head. He punched the back of my head. My grip tightened.

Tommy flopped down across the back of my legs to keep me from going over with Caine.

"Tommy, get off me. I'm not pushing him over, I'm taking him over."

"Sterling stop!" begged Caine.

He was hanging over the smooth stone edge. One of his sweaty hands held mine. The other frantically searched the smooth cliff face for a grip.

Carolyn grabbed my belt with both of her hands. The toes of one of my shoes had found a deep and narrow crack.

Tommy was still laying across the back of my knees. Caine helplessly tried to find a ledge with his feet.

Madelyn was behind us, laying on the smooth stone terrace where she'd been thrown. "Michael, don't let him fall," she moaned.

Let him fall? That's a laugh. I want him over the edge.

"Sterling stop!" His pleading was incessant. He was struggling less. We were face to face at arm's length. Carolyn, now laying beside me and holding my neck, peered over the edge. One of her hands crept along my sweaty arm and was inching down towards our locked grip.

What's she doing?

Caine's free hand, sliding repeatedly on the smooth cliff face, searched for a grip. Frustrated, his anger boiled over. "Wait 'til I get up there, I'll kill you all." We made eye contact and he realized he shouldn't have threatened us.

Instantly everything changed. His scream rose as his body fell. Carolyn's eyes met mine. She and I alone knew the truth of that moment.

Tommy looked down. "There 'e be, sprawled on the rocks far below."

Laying down, alongside Tommy, we peered over. Caine, the source of suffering and torment for so many people, was at the water's edge. A great wave crashed. His body lifted from the rocks, and he was carried away by the waves.

His threats faded as his limp body, sinking, disappeared from sight.

We crept backwards from the precipice. I rolled over onto my back, panting, being refreshed by the sea breeze.

Carolyn rushed over to Madelyn, who was sitting and leaning on one arm. She yelled, "Madelyn's badly hurt. I'll get the carriage." Off she ran towards the lighthouse and minutes later, she was back with it.

Tommy yanked the blanket from beneath the picnic basket. Plates, glasses, and leftover food went flying. "Cover 'er up with this."

Laying her down on the padded carriage seat and covering her with the blanket, we tried to make her comfortable. I held her, cradling her head in my lap. She had an abrasion at her hairline above her left ear. Blood trickled down past her beautiful eye. I was struck with my memory of the soldier who had died in my arms. I was frantic. "We need to take her to Aunt Muriel!"

In The Midst Of Loved Ones

When we arrived back at the parsonage, Aunt Muriel was working in the front garden. She saw our distress, rushed up the steps ahead of us, and swung open the door. We stepped in and I supported Madelyn as she staggered along the hallway. Tommy went to the kitchen, stoked the wood stove, and set the water on it to boil for tea.

Aunt Muriel, as always, was both comforting and reassuring. "Madelyn, you're in no condition to climb the steps to your room. Let's go down the hall to the guest room."

Madelyn, a bit dizzy, stumbled. "I'm fine. No one needs to make any fuss." She sat on the edge of the bed.

"Have a sip of water, dearie." Aunt Muriel held a glass to her dear niece's lips, giving me a worried look. "Michael, step into the hall for a few minutes? I'd like to get her into bed."

I left the room and went into the kitchen. Tommy was preparing the cups and spoons for the tea while he waited for the water to boil. He told me that Carolyn was unharnessing and caring for the horses in the stable, having driven them to their limit on the wild ride back from St. Bega's Headland.

A moment later, Aunt Muriel joined us in the kitchen. Distressed, she asked, "What happened?"

I closed my eyes and grimaced. "Robert Caine attacked us."

"Caine?" questioned Aunt Muriel. "We all thought he was long gone. Where's Caine now?"

Tommy responded, "Over the cliff 'e went. The waves took 'im away, an' 'bout now 'es standin' in front o' the Lord and waitin'—"

"Shhh." Muriel touched his arm and gently faced the palm of her other hand towards him.

At length, I told Muriel all that had happened at the precipice. She was seriously concerned about Madelyn's head injury.

"Did she lose consciousness?"

"I don't know," I responded. "I was fighting Caine."

"What are you meanin'?" asked Tommy. "Lose what?"

Muriel reworded her question. "Was she knocked out?"

"I don't know," answered Tommy. "Caine threw me down a deep crack in the rocks. I'll go and get Carolyn. She's in the stable brushin' and waterin' the 'orses. She saw everything."

Tommy quickly dashed out the door and returned with her. Aunt Muriel repeated the question. "Was Madelyn knocked out?"

"Yes, she was," answered Carolyn, nodding. "For about five minutes I think. May I see Madelyn?"

"Yes dear, go ahead. Please keep your visit short and say nothing that would upset her."

Carolyn went in and came back out a few minutes later. She closed the door to the room, winced, and staggered towards the front door, sliding her hand on the wall for support. She said nothing but went back out to the stable.

Aunt Muriel bit her lip. "Michael, come back in with me. It will be comforting for her to be near you."

When we reentered the room, Madelyn's clothes were on a desk and she was in bed wearing one of her cotton night gowns.

Muriel asked her a few questions.

"Where did you go for the picnic today?"

Madelyn blinked slowly several times. "Up, up the road. Saint... Saint Begas."

"Who was with you on your trip?"

"Them," Was all she said. She looked at me and gestured off into the distance.

"What's my name?"

Madelyn hesitated and grinned. "Auntie."

Muriel must be trying to determine Madelyn's ability to think clearly.

"Madelyn, open your eyes wide and look at me."

She raised her eyebrows and giggled. Under her breath, Muriel whispered to me, "Her pupils, the black centers of her eyes, aren't the same. One is quite a bit larger than the other."

"What's all the fuss?" asked Madelyn. "Where's, where's..." She was unable to remember Jester's name and made a petting gesture down towards the floor. "My doggie? Where's my doggie?"

Aunt Muriel spoke slowly and distinctly. "Jester is walking with Uncle Martin. He'll be back soon. I want you to rest for a while."

"Okay, Auntie."

I followed Aunt Muriel out into the hall. "She's going to be fine, isn't she?"

Aunt Muriel, with a worried grimace, responded, "She must've hit her head quite hard on the rock. We need to keep her quiet." She bit her lip. "We need to pray."

"Can I go back in and see her?"

"Encourage her and give her strength. Don't upset her."

Stepping inside, I gave her a sweet smile and sliding a chair closer, sat down beside the bed. Gently, I took her delicate little hand, and wanting to get her mind off the torment of the headland, I spoke tenderly. "Aunt Muriel said I could sit with

455

you." I leaned in towards her. "Tommy made some tea. Would you like some?"

"Maybe a little," she whimpered.

Going to the door, I stuck my head out. "Madelyn would like some tea."

I seated myself again and took her hand.

"What's all the fuss about, Michael? I'll be fine by tomorrow. Can we go and look at our house tomorrow?"

"Of course, darling, and a fine house it is," I said.

"We can stop and pet Eutychus as we walk by."

She's forgotten that Eutychus has passed away.

Tommy entered with the tea on a tray. "'ere it be. I think," his voice cracked with emotion, "I think you'll be likin' it." With that, he stepped back out into the hall.

"Why was Tommy crying?" asked Madelyn.

"He's upset that you aren't well." I lifted the cup to her sweet lips and she took a sip. "Was that tasty, my love?"

"Auntie always makes good tea."

"Tommy made the tea, sweetheart." I felt odd correcting her.

"Why was Tommy crying?"

I repeated myself. "He's upset that you aren't well."

Almost immediately, Madelyn, with a dazed look in her eyes, vomited all over the bed covers and herself. She started to cry. "I'm not well. Where's Auntie?" Her lips trembled.

I fetched Aunt Muriel, told her what had happened, and she asked me to wait in the hall.

When her clean up work was done, Muriel came out with the soiled blankets and nightgown. "You can go in now, Michael. The time you're spending with her is a comfort. Talk with her about all of the wonderful times you've had."

Once again, I sat beside the bed. "Hello, darling."

"I'm not doing well. Why was Aunt Muriel crying?"

"She loves you so much and she's worried about you being so sick."

"I'm not doing well."

I took her petite hand and wanted to get her mind off the immediate stress. "The concert that we played at Warrington Hall was wonderful. You're a great flautist."

She nodded. "Uncle Martin sang so well. I didn't know he could sing like that."

"That was Reverend Ashcroft, dear." *Should I be correcting her mistakes? I'll ignore them.*

"Was it? He sings well."

"Would you like another sip of tea?"

I lifted her cup from the night table, brought it to her lips, and gave her a sip. "One of my favorite memories is when we hiked down from Warrington Hall together. We sat on the high pedestal stone and later we saw the standing stones."

"Yes, my love. It was a wonderful hike."

"You..." She gestured towards me. "You made me a crown of vines. You wound 'round and 'round the circle of vines."

I wiped my eyes with the back of my hand. "I then added in the flowers: blue bells, primrose, and marigolds."

"Marigolds," she repeated, closing her eyes. "Why are you crying?"

"I love you so much and you're not feeling well."

"What happened?"

"You bumped your head."

"I'm not doing well. I'll be better by tomorrow. We'll look at our, our..." She couldn't find the word.

"Our home, dear."

"I'll be fine tomorrow," she mumbled. "We'll look at our home."

"Yes sweetheart, tomorrow will be a new day."

"Tomorrow's a new day," she repeated with her heavy eyes. "A new day."

Again, Madelyn vomited all over the bed covers and herself. "I'm not doing well." She started to cry.

I fetched Aunt Muriel and waited in the hall. She came out a short time later with tears streaming down her cheeks. She carried an armful of Madelyn's soiled bedding and nightgown. She couldn't speak. She merely gestured towards the door and I went back inside.

"Hello again, my sweetie," I said with a lighthearted voice.

"Why was Aunt Muriel crying? Is she mad about me being sick?"

"No, no. She's not mad at all. She loves you so much, and she's worried about you."

"I'm not doing well. I hear my doggie."

"Let me check." I looked in the hall and Uncle Martin, with worry on his face, was holding Jester. He took a deep breath and came in with me, carrying the playful little puppy.

"Here's your precious Jester," he said, gently putting him on Madelyn's stomach.

Jester, with his tail wagging wildly, rushed up to Madelyn's face and started licking it, making a whimpering sound. He sensed that something was wrong with her.

"You're so cute, Jester." Madelyn giggled.

A few minutes later, Uncle Martin said, "Your dear little doggie needs to go out now." I carried Jester out to Tommy, who was standing in the hall, quietly wincing and shaking his head. I gave him a firm hug and reentered the room. Aunt Muriel followed me back in.

"Let's have a time of prayer, Madelyn," said Uncle Martin.

As gentle as a downy feather falling on a pillow, he placed his hand on Madelyn's soft hair.

"I'll wait in the hall." Thinking I should leave, I stepped towards the door, but Uncle Martin, with his other hand, firmly took hold of my wrist and whispered in my ear, "Our dear Madelyn is in the midst of loved ones now. Let's join our hearts in prayer."

Speechless, I bit my lower lip and nodded.

"Michael," Uncle Martin continued. "This is the most serious and solemn situation that you may ever find yourself in. You need to join with us here in prayer." He gently drew me towards the bed and placed my hand tenderly with his own on Madelyn's head.

I closed my eyes.

Aunt Muriel, stepping closer, gently placed her hand on Madelyn's shoulder.

A tear ran down Uncle Martin's cheek. "Let's pray," he said with a trembling voice. "Oh Lord, your sweet Madelyn has need of you now. We all have need of you now. Spare her please, Lord, from suffering and may she know your love and presence. Heal our sweet sister, Lord, but only if that be in thy will. We seek your blessing for her. We pray that thy will be done in this dark valley, Lord. We fear no evil because you are with us in every shadowed valley. Hallowed be your name, Lord. May thy will be done, in Jesus' name. Amen."

"Amen," said Muriel.

I wiped the tears from my eyes, and whispered, "Amen."

Uncle Martin rose from the chair as Aunt Muriel quietly took her husband's hand. Each of them, in turn, leaned over Madelyn and gave her a gentle kiss on her cheek.

He tenderly cupped her chin. "We love you so much, Madelyn. You are the daughter we never had." He straightened up. "We need to go and speak with Carolyn and Tommy now, okay dear?"

"Yes Uncle. Say hello to them for me."

Looking many years older for the sorrow they were now carrying, they passed from the room.

Madelyn shared with me a crooked grin. "I'm feeling a bit better," she murmured.

Looking for strength and hope, I sat beside her and took her hand. "You're so precious to me, Madelyn. I love you as I've never loved anyone." I leaned in towards her.

She sat up with some difficulty, raised her chin, and as the covers fell upon her lap, we kissed.

Bound in our sorrow, we were closer than we'd ever been. Our kiss made time stand still, but only for those few minutes. I didn't want it to end. *Lord, she needs you now. Bless her. Keep her in your care.* My arms encircled her. She felt so delicate. So frail.

"I'm not doing well." Again, she gave me a crooked grin. "I need to lie down. I, I'm dizzy." She laid her sweet head on the pillow and I brushed the hair aside that had fallen across her face. We both laughed.

"I love your long auburn hair. It looks like a glistening sunset." I started to pull the covers back up.

"Don't cover me. I'm overheated. My nightgown is enough."

I put the blanket back at her waist. She blinked slowly a few times, as someone would waking up in the morning. Then, she smiled at me from her pillow.

I hurt so much, Lord. I had dreamed of the days when we would fall asleep together and be awakened each morning as our happy children would bound into our room and climb up onto our bed. *Lord, please don't take her from me.* Quiet tears slid down my cheeks.

"It's hot in here." I removed my already loosened cravat and my open waistcoat and tossed them onto the desk. My shirt, missing most of its buttons from fighting with Caine, fell open.

"What happened to your shirt?" she asked. "I'll sew buttons on it later. I have a headache right now."

We sat there quietly for a few minutes.

"Michael, if I ask you to keep a promise..." She hesitated. "Promises, keep promises." She inhaled deeply. "Will you?"

My eyes filled with tears. "Yes, of course I will, darling."

"Will you..." She stopped mid-sentence, then continued. "Will you seek the Lord with your whole heart? Seek Him, Michael." She blinked slowly several times. "Will you do justice, Michael?"

I nodded but couldn't speak.

"Michael, the Bible says if you seek the Lord with your whole heart, you will find Him."

"Yes Madelyn, I will. I want to seek Him. I will do justice, but don't leave me. I want to seek Him with you, not alone." My eyes overflowed with tears.

"That's the next... the next promise." She smiled. "I know..." She paused to catch her breath. Tears, like the dew of morning at sunrise, trickled slowly down her cheeks. "I know that you will always remember me, but you're a young man."

All I could do was nod and tremble. I whispered her name. "Madelyn."

"You're a young man, with much love to give. Promise me," she inhaled, "promise me you will love again."

"Madelyn, no. Please don't leave me. I can never love anyone else. Only you."

"Promise me." She slowly tapped her palm to her chest. "Easier for me." Her voice trembled. "If you promise me."

I was sobbing quietly. "Madelyn." *Why is she asking this of me? Stop, don't ask this of me. You mustn't leave me.* I was quiet on the outside, so tender and compassionate, but screaming on the inside.

She was blinking and had trouble seeing me. "Be brave, my love. The Lord Jesus gives strength... I've asked the Lord... to deepen your faith, Michael. Be brave."

"Madelyn, my love." Drawing a deep breath, I tried to regain some composure to help her be strong, though she was much stronger than I.

A question staggered into my troubled mind. "Madelyn, my darling, you kissed my ears sometimes and whispered something." I held her damp hand. "What did you whisper to me?"

"I whispered?" She looked puzzled. "I don't remember."

"I love you, Madelyn."

"I love you too. Help me sit up. I can't see you... too blurry... I need to feel you."

I leaned forward, lifted her up to a sitting position, and put an extra pillow behind her.

"Hold me, Michael." She took a deep breath and trembled. "I know the Lord is with me."

"I'm so afraid for you, my love." I leaned towards her and held her. She raised her face to meet mine and I kissed her forehead.

She smiled slyly, as she often would, when a humorous idea blossomed in her imagination. "Are you joking? A forehead kiss? Michael, we're far past that."

We laughed together. It was wonderful.

My tears trickled down. "Madelyn, my love."

I sat back in the chair.

She put her palm on her forehead. "I have a headache."

"Let's try again," I whispered.

"Try what?" she asked. "I'm so dizzy."

"The kiss."

With her hands, she reached out towards me and searched for me. Her hands, though delicate, were always so full of life.

We Both Shall Row, My Love And I

I leaned in towards her and her hands found their way inside my opened shirt. *Her hands on my body, now but never again.*

"Ahh, Michael, I love you," she whispered.

I embraced her and we kissed. *If I hold her tightly, death can't take her from me.*

I kissed her sweet lips. "Madelyn, I love you." I kissed her salty, tear-stained cheeks. She kissed the edge of my mouth. Memories of her first kisses came to mind. We struggled against her mortality.

Her lips, moving almost imperceptibly, formed two simple words, but without a sound, "My love."

One of my arms was around her shoulders and my lower arm was at her waist. *She's so frail. A delicate cherry blossom at the end of spring, ready to fall.* Still in my embrace, she exhaled deeply. Life left her, and she went limp in my arms. Her hands fell to her side.

"Madelyn." Holding her for a while, refusing to admit her absence, I clung to her more tightly. After a time, I tenderly laid my love down on her pillow. I leaned over her and held her hand. Her lifeless hand, which no longer firmly closed upon my own. My tears fell upon her nightgown. "Madelyn."

A few minutes later, Aunt Muriel looked in and stepped over towards her dear niece. She touched Madelyn's wrist and neck, and then held a tiny mirror below Madelyn's nose. She closed her lifeless eyes, sniffled, and respectfully left the room.

I sat in the chair, holding my darling's hand for a long time. Aunt Muriel returned. "Come into the sitting room, dear." She took my hand and led me to a comfortable padded chair. "Martin will take you to the Brixtons' in a little while."

"Can I go and sit with Madelyn for a few minutes?" I had never noticed, until now, how loud the old mantel clock ticked.

"Maybe in a little while."

"Where are Tommy and Carolyn?" I asked.

"They went over to the church."

She went down the hall and a few minutes later, I heard her in the kitchen. Needing to be with Madelyn, I found my way back to her. I rapped lightly on the door, stepped in, slid the chair nearer to the bed, and set myself down. My love had been completely covered with a sheet, so I pulled it from over her head, down to her neck. I sought her hand, and finding it, held it. *She's cold. So very cold.* I pulled the heavy blanket from the foot of the bed up to her shoulders and returned to her hand. *Smile at me one more time. Please Madelyn, just one more time.*

Aunt Muriel stepped in. "Come into the sitting room, Michael." She led me to the same comfortable chair. "Martin will take you back to the Brixton home in a few minutes."

She went out of the front of the house as I sat down.

She's must be looking for Uncle Martin.

I went back down the hall to be with my Madelyn. I entered, sat in the chair, and affectionately took hold of her cold hand. I adjusted her blanket, pulling it up to her neck, and with my trembling fingers, I swept a strand of her beautiful hair from where it had fallen across her forehead.

A long while later, Aunt Muriel returned. "Michael, come with me." She led me back to the comfortable chair and went into the kitchen.

Bringing me a cup of tea, she sat beside me, and resting her hand on my arm, we sat together silently for quite a while. The mantel clock, ticking loudly, was a distraction.

"Aunt Muriel, can I go and see Madelyn?"

She was about to answer but I heard someone at the front door. Uncle Martin entered with Edwyn trailing behind him.

The four of us sat together quietly for a long time. The clock on the mantel, with its loud ticking, measured off my memories of Madelyn.

Edwyn stepped over to me, leaned down, and gave me a warm fatherly hug. "I'm taking you home now. I'd like you to have a long rest."

Numb and speechless, I couldn't respond. *I want to say goodbye to Madelyn. Don't take me from her. Madelyn, don't let them take me away.*

I wouldn't answer and slowly shook my head, refusing to stand. Edwyn, such a tenderhearted gentleman, returned to his seat. The clock continued its hollow, empty ticking, measuring off the saddest day of my life.

I closed my eyes for a moment and then slowly cracked them open. Standing, I glanced down the hall and followed Edwyn out through the front door.

The Place of Remembrance

Church the next day would have been described by many as uplifting. The joyous singing, with the pump organ accompaniment, was buoyant—but not for me. I was sinking in a slew of despondency and floundering alone, out on the dismal grey rain-swept moors of my own sorrow.

As we exited the church at the end of the service, I overheard several people talking about Uncle Martin's authoritative handling of the scriptures, his optimistic outlook, and his confident faith. My outlook wasn't optimistic, and my faith was anything but confident.

The funeral service was to take place later in the afternoon. Numb is how I would describe myself on the inside. Detached is how I would describe myself relating to others on the outside. *That's me, numb and detached.*

The service in the church and at the graveyard later in the day would have nothing to do with me and certainly nothing to do with my sweet Madelyn and our lives together. I couldn't escape a despondent set of words that was forming in my mind. Pessimistic conflicting words, scrawled across a beautiful painting.

My sweetheart is vibrant, funerals are morose.
My darling is warmly affectionate, funerals are cold and detached.
My Madelyn, my love, is living sunshine, funerals are dark, dead things.

~~~~~~

Time had rolled along its course. That was time's main characteristic. It can't be stilled or held back. Time incessantly moves along.

It was late afternoon. The people of Oak Harbor that wanted to be in the service had arrived. The others, much like the sense I had in my own heart, were somewhere else. They could escape. They could share their excuses if asked. I could not. The organ started playing as the last few stragglers entered.

Not wanting to approach the front of the church, I quickly took a seat just within the door. Sitting there quietly, I saw Edwyn, Louisa, and Brynne near the front.

Numb and detached, I sat silently, waiting for the next moment, the next speaker, the next song.

Edwyn looked tired. I had heard him working late into the night and there before me, up at the front of the church, was the result of his craftsmanship. Sturdy joinery in the corners, smooth pumice work on the flat surfaces, and excellent linseed oil application, bringing out the lustrous quality of the oak. *It's a shame that such fine craftsmanship would be put into the cold wet ground.*

I'm numb and detached. I'm not connected with what's going on in the church.

Tommy approached me, bent down, and leaned in towards me. He was so close our foreheads almost touched and he hooked the back of my neck with his trembling hand. "Mr. Sterlin', sir," he shuddered. "I mean Michael." He bit his lip. "Would you walk with me to the front to see 'er, I can't face 'er alone."

He was trying to hold back his tears but one solitary tear spilled out and dribbled down his cheek. Without saying a word, I stood. He linked my arm with his own, and we took the few paces needed to arrive at the front.

There she lay before me. The most beautiful woman that I had ever seen. The most vibrant lady that had ever embraced me. The sweet fragrance of her rose petal perfume surrounded me. My lips silently formed her name. *Madelyn.*

She wore her concert dress of dark blue with the wide sash belt of dazzling silver. The words that I had said to her on the evening of the concert echoed in my aching heart: "Whenever you wear this dress in the future, it will be the most special of occasions."

A special occasion. Oh, this is so very special. Michael, you stupid fool.

Her hair, in the upswept style of the concert, was decorated with the same tiny silk bows, and each of these was mated with a dangling pearl. Her sweet shoulders were draped with a soft woolen shawl of sky blue.

Madelyn, I'm sorry that I didn't protect you from Caine. I am no Saint Michael protecting you from that evil dragon.

My Madelyn was at rest. She lay their cushioned by the padded interior of the casket, lined with silver-colored satin. I grimaced and closed my eyes. *Like the silver lining of clouds at the end of a stormy day.*

Tommy, with his voice shaking, drew my attention. "I was strugglin' with my great wool bags comin' down from Lord Warrington's sheep pens." He paused and breathed deeply. "Then the Lord sent you an' sweet Madelyn along to be givin' me a ride."

"I remember." My arm was around his shoulders. He had difficulty breathing as he held back his sobbing.

"Do you like the shawl?" Tommy's voice trembled. "It be 'ers for Christmas. I be makin' it for quite a few weeks."

"I love the shawl. It looks warm."

Tommy sniffled. "She's a charmer, you know."

I was fighting to hold back my tears. "I found that out."

We returned to our pews, Tommy across the aisle with Carolyn, me alone near the door, well behind the Brixton family. The sound of the pump organ struggled to gain my attention. I waited.

The service began and the tributes were many. I was awestruck how influential her life had been. This was my darling Madelyn's place of remembrance. She showed her love to so many people and so many people loved her in return. Elizabeth Harcourt spoke of the many times that Madelyn, with Uncle Martin, visited during her periods of intense grief.

Is he still my uncle?

A couple of the older youngsters said that she was the best teacher of Bible stories in the world. Aunt Muriel talked about how much Madelyn had helped with Carolyn.

Is she still my aunt?

Brynne talked about how Madelyn had helped her to be a better teacher.

Tommy stepped up to the podium, looking mature with Carolyn on his arm. He lifted his chin, opened his mouth to speak, but found himself speechless. He bowed his head, took a few deep breaths, and silently started to weep.

Carolyn was much stronger and looked out into the congregation. "I thank the Lord for

Madelyn." Tommy nudged her with his elbow. She smiled and reworded what she had said. "*Tommy and I* thank the Lord for Madelyn. She was not only a faithful friend, but she taught Tommy and me to read. We don't read perfectly yet, but Brynne is helping us now."

My eyes met Carolyn's.

I wonder if anyone has asked her exactly how Caine and I happened to lose our grip on each other's hands.

Tommy lifted his head and started to speak. "An' more than the readin'." He hesitated. "Madelyn taught us about the Lord." Gently but deliberately, he tapped his palm on the podium several times. "An' now, we be believin' Christians."

"Amen," said Deacon Scott.

"That's the truth!" said Uncle Martin.

Tommy looked around those gathered. "With the believin' and the readin'," his voice wavered and slowed, "Madelyn changed our lives."

Tommy and Carolyn returned to their seats.

A few others from Oak Harbor stood and shared the positive influence that Madelyn had on their children and on the community. I began to grasp that the funeral of a Christian need not be, in fact should not be, morose or cold, but that it can be a celebration of the life of the one so sorely missed.

The service continued; a hymn was sung, Aunt Muriel shared from her heart that Madelyn was like the daughter they never had, and then Uncle Martin preached about the resurrection. To most of those gathered, I'm sure that it was an encouraging service.

He closed his talk by reading from the eleventh chapter of John verses twenty-five through twenty-seven. "'I am the resurrection and the life!' That is what Jesus declared." Uncle Martin with his booming voice provided the confident assurance by his tone and manner that was needed.

> . . . he that believeth in me, though he were dead, yet shall he live: And whosoever liveth and believeth in me shall never die. Believest

thou this? She saith unto him, Yea, Lord: I believe that thou art the Christ, the Son of God, which should come into the world.

As Uncle Martin returned to his seat, Deacon Scott stood and ambled towards the pulpit in preparation to lead the final hymn. He clutched his open Bible, and with his index finger, he stabbed at a verse within it. He declared, "'Precious in the sight of the Lord is the death of his saints.' That's what God's Word says in Psalm 116, the fifteenth verse, and this is what we are seeing here today." He looked about those present. "The passing of our young sister Madelyn is precious to the Lord and so very precious to us as well. She knew her Savior." He paused and placed his Bible on the pulpit. "She knew her Savior, oh so well."

That's true. She knew her Savior and Lord.

Several in the congregation whispered, "Amen."

Then, with a sense of confidence, he announced the final hymn. "Please stand and turn in your hymnals to Saint Bega's hymn, "Hark My Soul." It was written by William Cowper to memorialize the godly devotion of Saint Bega. It is a favorite of the hymn writer and Pastor Daniel Turner of the Abingdon congregation on the Thames."

> Hark, my soul, it is the Lord;
> 'tis thy Savior, hear his word;
> Jesus speaks, and speaks to thee,
> 'Say, poor sinner, lov'st thou me?

Madelyn would've loved that first stanza.

As the final hymn ended, the casket was closed and carried by Edwyn, Tommy, John Lyon, David, George, and Albert Kline.

We Both Shall Row, My Love And I

"Brothers and sisters in the Lord, we shall now assemble for interment," said Deacon Scott with confident deliberation.

Aunt Muriel, Uncle Martin, and I exited the church, passed through the graveyard gate, and assembled around the casket beside my grandfather's stone. I observed that the Spaniard and his wife stood off to the side. *Why are they here like that, standing across the little cemetery?*

Uncle Martin cleared his throat. "Yesterday, when Muriel was alone with Madelyn for a few minutes, our dear sweet sister, knowing that she would soon leave us, made several requests."

He paused, licked his lips, and held up his index finger. "First, she asked that Michael have her Bible." We made eye contact and he passed me Madelyn's well-worn Bible. I thought back to the first time I had seen her with it. I thought it was her uncle's.

"Thank you, Uncle Martin."

Then briefly, Reverend Ekland spoke of Madelyn's love of the Lord and the Scriptures.

"Second." He held up two fingers. "She requested that Tommy and Carolyn be given Jester." He looked at them, exchanging smiles with one another. Tommy and Carolyn took each other's hands. Tommy sniffled.

"And finally," his voice trembled. "This might be difficult to hear, but these are her wishes and we will carry them out. The departed trust us to fulfill their wishes." He paused, pressed his lips together, and inhaled deeply through his nose. "Madelyn, several weeks ago, had asked Shannon to sing, 'The River Is Wide' for her wedding to Michael. At Madelyn's request, Shannon will sing that now."

The Spaniard softly played through a progression of four chords as a simple introduction. Shannon, barely above a whisper, began to sing tenderly.

> The water is wide, I can't cross o'er.
> And neither have, I wings to fly.
> Give me a boat, that can carry two,
> We both shall row, my love and I.
>
> Now love is sweet, and love is kind.
> The sweetest flow'r, when first it's new,
> But love grows old, and waxes cold,
> And fades away, like morning dew.
>
> There is a ship, she sails the seas.
> She's loaded deep, as deep can be;
> But not as deep, as the love I'm in.
> I know not how, I sink or swim.

Then Shannon, with a single tear resting on her cheek, made eye contact with me and repeated the first stanza. I blinked several times. My eyes brimmed with tears.

> The water is wide, I can't cross o'er.
> And neither have, I wings to fly.
> Give me a boat, that can carry two,
> We both shall row, my love and I.

Closing my eyes, I was taken back to that concert in May when Madelyn had sung this ballad. I remember her looking at me several times as she sang. I can hear her. Her voice is perfect and so warm. I can see her lips forming the words. She's so beautiful. So filled with love—love for me.

Shannon repeated the final line of the stanza. Her voice faded. My recollection trailed off like a strand of foggy mist being touched by the warm morning sun. I could no longer see my sweet Madelyn, but her voice remained with me.

We Both Shall Row, My Love And I

We both shall row, my love and I.

Uncle Martin proceeded with the formal service of interment and as he did so, I could still hear the voice of my true love as she sang.

Lifting my chin, and through my tears, I gazed across the harbor. High atop the ridge I could see our pedestal stone. My heart was filled with love for her. She and I, vivid in my memory, sitting upon it, looking at this exact spot.

We both shall row, my love and I.

Far below the pedestal stone, I could see our home beside the harbor. My heart was swelling up with our dreams for the future.

We both shall row, my love and I.

To my left, next to Madelyn's place of rest, was my grandfather's stone. I remembered the day that she came and sat beside me on the low wall and comforted me. I closed my eyes. I could feel her warm hand holding mine. I could smell the fragrance of her rose petal perfume. I could hear her sweet comforting voice, speaking about my grandfather. *'He is with his Lord. Grandfather Sterling is in the midst of those who loved him and those who loved his Lord.'* I could feel a wisp of her long auburn hair, as the wind swept it up against my cheek. She held my arm and leaned in against me. I remembered what she had said, *'I will meet him in heaven.'* I nodded in agreement. *They never met on earth, but they will meet in heaven.*

She had passed from this world to the next in the same room where my grandfather had passed, their mortal remains side by side, their spirits with the Lord.

I repeated to myself what she had said, but this time about my dear Madelyn, *She is with her Lord. Madelyn is in the midst of those who loved her and those who loved her Lord.* I hesitated, painfully. *Except for the living. We're still here. I miss her so much. Madelyn, I miss you desperately.*

~~~~~~

Days later, the body of Tommy's father had been found in the lighthouse at Saint Bees headland, along with that of the lighthouse keeper. People wondered how Mr. Atwater had known him. Some questions in life might never be answered. A modest service had been held in Sandwith, but only a few from Oak Harbor had attended.

Edwyn returned my grandmother's engagement ring to me. I suppose, with us being so close, it was decided that he would take responsibility for such a painful task.

In the days following, my grief for Madelyn was intense, as if I were in the grips of a terrible disease. I went through the motions of each day with neither purpose nor plan. I plodded, simply putting one foot in front of the other. The food placed before me was tasteless. The sky above me was grey. The people around me were strangers.

~~~~~~

One night a week or so later and long past midnight, I was unable to sleep and decided to go for a walk. The cool breeze drifted through the empty streets, moonlight flooded the harbor, and my singular shadow emphasized my loneliness. It was the brightest moonlit night I could remember, and my misty breath clouded about me when I exhaled. For a long time all that could be heard was the sound of my own shoes on the cobbles until a lonesome dog barked in the distance.

We Both Shall Row, My Love And I

I've often enjoyed quiet places and serene evenings, but not tonight. The seaport was at rest, but not me. People were nestled in their cozy beds with their loved ones. I was alone, cold and alone.

After walking through much of the seaport, I found myself sitting on one of the benches in front of the Royal Stag. It had closed hours earlier.

Far across the harbor, near the cemetery of Fair Havens Church where my Madelyn lay in the cold ground, a lonely candle flickered in a window. Its singularity penetrated me.

A short distance from my bench, an untethered horse strangely stood alone. Lacking a halter, I didn't concern myself with it. Searching for an unknown owner in the middle of the night would have been an impossibility. The strangeness of its presence intrigued me.

Above me, a lonely nightbird, perched on a high branch bathed in moonlight, lamented mournfully for its mate. Its grief touched me.

The atmosphere of the quiet harbor toyed with my mind, my loneliness, my loss. I found myself in an evening sorrow.

The breeze, cool—
    drifted, through the quiet harbor.
The horse, riderless—
    walked pensively, along the cobbled street.
The nightbird, lonely—
    sought its mate, its lament filling the empty seaport.
The candle, solitary—
    flickered and went out, in the window, far across the water.

The Eleutheran Quest

One frosty afternoon a week later, Edwyn and I, bundled against the cold, were sitting on his porch enjoying a pot of hot tea. The *Eleutheran Quest* drifted in on a light breeze, and as it approached us, a great beam of sunlight broke through the grey clouds and illuminated the exquisite craft.

"Michael, look at that. See how the sun is striking her sails and timbers." Lifting his chin and raising his eyebrows in admiration, he was for a moment awestruck. "It's such a splendid ship. One hundred forty feet of utilitarian grace and…"

"Yes, it is. It's marvelous. So different now than when we first saw her limp into the harbor several months ago."

"There's Mr. Chen standing beside the captain." He gestured towards them with his teacup. "Chen's a good man." He sipped his tea. "I've heard he's a near perfect navigator."

They both saw us from the deck of the ship and waving, Captain Henderson shouted, "Ahoy there, Michael, I have a letter for you from Liverpool." He pulled an envelope from his jacket pocket and waved it. Standing, I returned his wave.

"I have no idea what that might be," I said. "What were they doing in Liverpool? They usually sail to Bristol with Lord Warrington's lumber."

"And so they did," replied Edwyn. "But this time they were to stop at Liverpool on their return. They've finished with their lumber runs and will be leaving for the West Indies in a few days."

I acknowledged what he had said. "I'll go and get the letter and find out what it's about."

On the dock, I met Captain Henderson at the foot of the gangplank. He pulled the letter from his jacket pocket and passed it to me. "If you have a reply, we'll be making several stops on our way to the warmer climate of the West Indies, and Liverpool is one of them."

"Thank you, Captain. Did you have a good sail from Bristol and then from Liverpool?"

"I miss the warmth of the West Indies." He grimaced. "It's too cold for a pleasurable sail and what's worse, the wind was poor. It's been a powerless breeze for almost a week. This is a working ship. We must cover many sea miles every day to make it worthwhile."

Raising my eyebrows, I nodded. "I've never been to the West Indies—"

A busy captain, he held up his hand to cut me short. "Let me know if there's a reply," he responded brusquely. He walked off to deal with his many responsibilities.

"Thank you, Captain."

A familiar voice beckoned me from above. "Michael, it's good to see you."

Recognizing Meiling's unique accent and friendly voice, I shoved the letter in my coat pocket and looked up on the deck of the ship but couldn't find her.

"You might see me but I don't see you. Where are you, Meiling?"

"Up here, you landlubber." I heard her chuckle. "Look aloft. I'm a topman now." She laughed again.

I looked higher, shielding my eyes from the sun. There she was high above me, trousered like a man but wearing a feminine jacket.

My jaw dropped. "How did you get up there?"

"Have you never seen a cat on a high and narrow fence?" She giggled.

"Not as high as you are. Not until now."

She was up the mainmast and out on the mainsail footrope. Flanked by a couple other topmen, they were securing the sail to the yard. Smiling with her hair wound up into a knot, she was quite a dramatic sight to behold. A few long strands of hair had fallen free of the topknot and were framing her exotic face. She glanced down at me, smiled radiantly, and continued her work. I felt guilty that I was speaking to her, having noticed her attractiveness. Madelyn, so it seemed to me, was at my shoulder.

"What are you doing way up there? You're going to fall."

She laughed. "I'm picking apples. What does it look like I'm doing?" She shook her head. "I've got a book for Madelyn. Walk me over to the parsonage; I'd like to give it to her."

A few of Kline's warehouse men, moving crates on the dock, stopped what they were doing. They looked up at Meiling, then over at me, and then they returned to their work.

Not wanting to face Meiling, make explanations, and receive her condolences, I sauntered away. When I arrived back at the Brixton home, I went straight through to my room at the back of the house and sat upon my bed.

Thinking that I would try to read the Bible that Madelyn had lovingly left for me, I opened it, and when I did, a sealed, pale blue envelope fell out. My name was printed across the front.

It must be a letter from my dear Madelyn. I have no intention of reading a letter from her quite yet. Slipping it back into the pages of her well-worn Bible and sliding it under my pillow, I shook my head and sighed. I pulled on a heavy sweater, went out to Edwyn's shop, and plodded through the events of another unremarkable afternoon.

The following cold morning as I awoke, I remembered the letter I had received from Captain Henderson, and retrieving it from my coat, I hurried back to my warm bed.

Barely able to see in the dim grey of early morning, I lit an oil lamp and examined the outside of the envelope. It was addressed to me in an artistic script and the same attractive script was used for the return address of the Heywood Bank across the back. I opened it carefully. It was dated about two weeks earlier and was actually a letter forwarded from the Bank of England in London about my investments. I began reading it and what I read, after the first few paragraphs of greetings and pleasantries, shocked me to my core.

> *We are pleased to inform you that the plantation on the island of Eleuthera, of which you are a twenty percent owner, is prospering fortuitously. We would also like to make you aware that Mr. Ryan Pinder, like yourself a twenty percent owner, has passed away. His son, William, being a dedicated abolitionist, and not in support of the slavery practiced on the plantation, has sold his bequest of twenty percent to one Jason Ardel Ravenswood, who has recently moved into the mansion on the plantation.*
>
> *This selfsame Mr. Ravenswood would like to purchase an additional twenty percent interest in the property and is therefore*

highly motivated to communicate with you in this regard.

This is disgusting. I refuse to believe it. I'm a slave owner? I crumpled the letter and threw it to the floor, only to pick it up and read it again, and then a third time. *This isn't possible. It's detestable. I was told that the farm only had paid workers.*

I quickly got dressed, went into the kitchen, started a fire in the stove, and seated myself dejectedly at the table. I was utterly frustrated and dismayed.

Brynne, hearing me in the kitchen, I suppose I'd been a bit noisy, stepped through the doorway rubbing her eyes. She blinked several times, stretched, and ran her fingers through her hair. "I'll make you some tea?"

She busied herself about the kitchen and a few minutes later stood behind me with her warm hands on my shoulders. "I'll cook you up a man's breakfast."

After twenty minutes had passed, I had before me a delicious feast of bacon, eggs, cheese wedges, and buttered rye bread. A large pot of tea stood beside my cup, and I was looking forward to enjoying the "man's breakfast" she had prepared for me.

Louisa entered the kitchen and stood beside her daughter. "Brynne," she whispered. "You're a shapely woman now and your childhood days are long passed. It's not fitting to wander about the kitchen in your nightgown."

She left the kitchen only to return a few minutes later dressed for the day, and followed by her father.

"You've forgotten your top button, Brynne." Louisa tapped her own top button.

With the four of us together at the table, I decided to share the upsetting letter from the bank. Edwyn and Louisa were sitting beside one another. I moved the large teapot and set the letter down between them. When they had finished reading, they were shocked and unable to speak.

I grimaced. "I'm appalled by this." I shook my head in disgust. "Do you see the third and fourth paragraphs?"

"Let me look," demanded Brynne. She went around to her parent's side of the table, crowded in between them, and within minutes, the horror on her face heightened my sense of responsibility.

"You couldn't have been aware of this!" exclaimed Louisa. "You're a strict abolitionist."

"That's right. I knew nothing of this." I glanced at Edwyn's aghast expression. "I was told that those who worked on the farm were all paid workers. Some of the other owners must've made a decision that I knew nothing about and purchased slaves to pick fruit, tend the fields, and care for their livestock."

"What will you do?" asked Edwyn, wincing.

"I'll go there." I paused. "I'll go there and bring this to an end!" Disgusted, I shook my head. "It won't be easy."

Ringing in my ears was the promise that I had made to Madelyn to seek God and do justice. *I will my love. I will do justice.*

I excused myself and went down to the dock, needing to speak to Captain Henderson. I found him leaning against some crates examining an inventory list.

"Captain, when will you set sail? I'm seeking passage for the Bahamas."

"We'll leave port on Saturday morning, with the tide."

"Do you have a berth that I might make arrangements for?"

"Better than a berth. I can offer you a modest private cabin for £16. It has a solid cot with a substantial storage cabinet beneath it and even a modest porthole. We're picking up a few

We Both Shall Row, My Love And I

other paying passengers in Bristol and I'm saving space for them, but one little cabin is still available."

"That's what I'm looking for." I shook his hand. "Saturday then, with the tide."

He looked me in the eye. "We've been loading some of our cargo on these lumber runs. The remaining crates, barrels, and boxes are waiting at Liverpool, Swansea, and Bristol. We'll be several days in each of the ports."

"What's your cargo?" I asked.

"Finished goods from England's finest companies: copperware, carriage parts, six Newsham fire fighting pumps, furniture, clothing, bolts of cotton, newsprint, and much more. Interestingly enough, we also have twelve small swivel cannons with shot and powder. They'll be mounted on the quarter decks aboard his majesty's ships in Jamaica."

"This will be my first long voyage at sea. I'm sure it will be interesting."

"That it will." The captain gestured to a few of his men to move a crate. One of them was the big brutish man that I had often observed staring at Meiling. "When our stops in England are complete, we'll sail for Gibraltar, and then when our business there is done, and the weather's favorable, we'll set out for the West Indies; Governor's Harbor on Eleuthera; Kingston of Jamaica; and finally, George Town on Grand Cayman. See you Saturday. Don't forget the £16." He touched the brow of his cap and started to walk away, but stopped. "By the way, I'm still wanting some hardworking men for the ship. I have all the experienced hands that I need but I still need some landsmen at £1 a month. Inexperienced laborers. Are you aware of any?"

"No, sorry, no one comes to mind." I bid him farewell and strode away, saying that I'd see him on Saturday.

Only two more nights here. Then I'll begin to be free of my painful memories. From the dock, I looked down along the harbor's edge and could see our home. I quickly looked away. *I can't go there. I'm not going there.*

My grief called out to me. *You should've protected Madelyn. Move along, be free of Oak Harbor.*

When I had returned to the Brixton home, I made myself comfortable in the sitting room and almost immediately, Brynne joined me from the kitchen. She carried a tray with a large teapot, half a dozen cups, some spoons, sugar, and milk. Her arm was hooked through a smallish basket of delicious smelling biscuits.

"A few people will be stopping by to say hello," she said.

Nodding, I responded. "Thanks for the tea and biscuits."

Five or ten minutes later, Meiling, Tommy, and Carolyn arrived with Jester, but as soon as the boisterous pup was taken off the leash at the door, he turned about, bounded off the porch, and ran up the street. Carolyn dashed after him calling his name and pleading with him to come back. Meiling, more calmly, followed along behind in the direction that they had run, but Brynne, Tommy, and I remained in the front room.

"Carolyn be trainin' 'im but it's not goin' well," said Tommy, as he sat down beside me.

He gave a little chuckle. "'ave you seen me mum lately? She's full o' life. She said 'er grief, what little there was for my father, 'as passed."

"That's good that she is getting over losing your father."

Tommy enthusiastically continued. "John Lyon, 'es been a great comfort, visitin' me mum each day. 'e's a kind 'earted man."

"Yes, he is."

We sat quietly for a time as Tommy looked about the room. Eventually, he broke the silence. "I've been 'earin' that you be leavin' us, Michael. Is that the truth?"

"That's right."

"And I've 'eard about your farm situation in the West Indies."

"I need to be on my way." I leaned forward, lifted the teapot, and poured Tommy a cup of tea.

"Why would you be in an 'urry to be leavin' us?"

"I'm not leaving the many people I've grown to respect and appreciate here." I snapped off a piece of biscuit with my teeth and took a sip of tea. "I'm leaving my painful memories and going to carry out a task that mustn't be made to wait. The slaves on my farm must be freed. No man should own another."

"Michael, I'm older now and I understand what you be sayin'. I'm wonderin' if you might be needin' some 'elp gettin' justice for them there slaves in the Bahamas."

"I've been thinking along those lines as well, Thomas. You'd be a big help and I'll pay you and cover your passage if need be. I've heard the *Eleutheran Quest* is still looking for novice seamen at £1 a month. You could receive pay from them and a bit from me as well. Would you be able to join me aboard ship when she leaves harbor on Saturday with the morning tide? We'll return here in the spring."

He raised his eyebrows. "That'd be a chance to be earnin' some good coin." He slapped his thigh. "You don't be needin' to ask me twice. I'm off to be packin', but don't be tellin' Carolyn. I'll be wantin' to do that."

"Alright, I'll not mention it to her. You should go and talk to Captain Henderson about work aboard ship. Tell him I recommend you."

"Blimey, adventure and coin are comin' my way, sure enough." His demeanor changed, he broke eye contact with me, and he took on a sheepish appearance. "One more thing, Michael."

"Yes, Thomas."

"Might I be 'avin' a few shillings in advance? I'd be likin' to give them to me mum, for the family. My family, it be stony broke for sure. We be lackin' even two pennies to be rubbin' together."

"Certainly. I reached into my pocket and gave him six shillings."

He expressed thanks for the advance, headed out the door, and was on his way. Brynne, who hadn't said a word, looked as if she was ready to cry. I wasn't sure why. Carolyn, along with Meiling, returned with Jester on his leash, and after scolding him not to run away again, she removed it.

"Where's Tommy?" Carolyn asked.

"He headed off to his home but he wants to talk to you."

"What about?"

"I think you better talk to him about it," I responded.

At that point, and much to my relief, she was distracted from her questioning. Jester walked over to me, smelled my feet, walked over to Brynne, and likewise smelled hers. He then looked at Carolyn and scratched at the door. She opened it, but when she didn't get the leash on him quick enough, he capriciously bolted through the door and off the porch. Carolyn once again chased after him up the street.

Brynne laughed. "He's nothing like my Eutychus. I'll go and get some more biscuits," she said with a trembling voice as she stepped into the kitchen. She was still upset about something. Glancing at the table, I saw that there were still lots of biscuits in the basket. *That's odd. Why would she say that?*

Meiling changed chairs and seating herself close beside me, offered me a biscuit. "Michael, I'm sorry for what I said when we docked yesterday." She held her teacup in both hands, and lifting the cup to her lips, took a sip. "I didn't know about Madelyn. You have my deepest sympathy."

Brynne, still appearing quite upset, re-entered the room but without the additional biscuits she had mentioned. She had instead the book I had given her about the coastal cities of China and began flipping pages, with an intensity I've seldom seen.

Meiling, trying to lighten the atmosphere, spoke of our upcoming journey. "I've been to Eleuthera several times." She offered me a biscuit, which I silently refused. "You will find our voyage to the south, then off to the West Indies, quite fascinating."

"I have no doubt of that," I said.

"Your cabin is beside mine. I'll be able to show you the ropes, as we say aboard ship." She laughed and touched my arm. "You won't be a land lubber for much longer." She giggled, which she often did, and offered me another biscuit. Smiling, I accepted it from her hand.

Her laughter and exotic femininity held my interest. "I suppose I'll learn a few things. I love to learn new things."

Brynne hurried back into the kitchen and I think I heard her stub her toe against something, followed by an angry complaint.

Our pleasant conversation continued for a short time, we exchanged our goodbyes and I went to my room thinking that I might read.

Later in the evening, I met with Edwyn long after Louisa and Brynne had gone to bed. We shared a pot of tea and some cake in the front room.

"You're leaving for Eleuthera." Edwyn spoke hesitantly. "What would you like done with your property and house?" He paused again. "I would like to help."

"I've given it some thought," I stammered, thinking of Madelyn's home. "Please ensure that the house is completed and then..." My voice caught and I couldn't finish the sentence. My mind was flooded with memories of Madelyn and our dreams for our life together.

Edwyn sensed my distress. "Take your time, Michael."

I regained my composure and continued. "If you'd be willing to manage the property, it would be a great help. I will pay you, of course."

His mouth dropped open and angrily his eyes narrowed. "Absolutely not, young man. You will not be paying me. Expenses only when you return and not a penny more."

Clearing my throat, I leaned back in my chair, withdrawing a thick envelope from my pocket. "Thank you, Edwyn. You're a good man. Here's the money I owe you for the cabinetry and finishing work on the house." I added some more sugar to my tea. "Minus my pay and the agreed on sum for the selected trees on the woodlot."

Edwyn's eyes opened wide. "That's a great sum of money. Are you able to provide me with that? Are you sure?"

"I'm able."

Edwyn said nothing but took a forkful of his cake, followed by a long drink of tea.

"Please find someone to rent the house and use the rent money to pay the mortgage. It should be enough to cover the monthly payments. It's a substantial home." I stirred my tea. "Of course, go ahead and harvest the selected trees as we agreed."

"I'll be glad to do all of that for you. Helping you is my pleasure. You are as a son to me." He leaned forward and gripped my shoulder. "Assisting you is also an opportunity to play a limited part in helping you obtain freedom for the slaves." Edwyn observed that I was having difficulty talking about the house, Madelyn's house, so he didn't say another word. We simply sat there and enjoyed the quiet evening, the cake, and the hot pot of tea.

~~~~~~

Early the next morning, Friday, although I was not quite fully awake, I became aware of a heated conversation between Brynne and someone in the kitchen.

"You mustn't!" Followed by indistinct, muffled voices, and then silence.

"You can't tell me what to do," said Brynne with a raised voice.

Then, the person that Brynne was having a disagreement with, it sounded like Carolyn, muttered almost unintelligibly, "... time to heal..."

Carolyn might be talking about her wound or some help that Aunt Muriel is giving someone.

More muffled voices. I couldn't quite hear everything that was being said and I was still quite tired. My eyes were too heavy to remain open.

"Have you discussed this with your mother?" asked Carolyn.

Strange question. What does Brynne need to discuss with her mother? Then the conversation ended. I heard the front door close.

Nestling in my cozy blankets, I fell back asleep.

Some time later, I don't know how long, I awoke to the sound of someone working in the kitchen. *Something is being cooked. It smells wonderful. Bacon and eggs.*

As I lay there, not quite ready to begin the day, Brynne stepped into my room wearing that same pale green gingham dress that had caught my attention on several occasions.

When she saw that I was stirring, she left and a moment later, returned with a cup of tea. "Mother and father have gone to the shops." She went to the window near the foot of my bed and flung open the curtains to let in the morning light. "When I've finished making you a man's breakfast, would you be willing to take me for a walk?" She stepped towards me, sat on the edge of my bed, and touched my arm. "It's warmed up a lot this morning compared to the last few days." She grinned and adjusted the dark green ribbon in her hair.

"I suppose that would be alright. Sure, I'd enjoy going for a walk with you."

When we had finished eating, we headed through the front door, and Brynne, walking ahead of me, stepped off the porch. She turned to the right, towards Madelyn's home beside the harbor.

I froze on the top step. "Brynne, I'd rather not go that way." I gripped the porch railing.

"That's alright. I understand." She motioned in the opposite direction. "Let's walk up the road by the river instead."

I shared a crooked grin. "Okay."

She waited for me at the edge of the street and unexpectedly took my arm in a very affectionate manner. I was a bit uncomfortable as I usually saw her as a younger sister. We passed all of the familiar places and when we had walked along the river for half an hour, she led me into the forest, along an overgrown path beside a small rustic stream.

Twenty minutes more and we came to a picturesque clearing. It was bordered by several prodigious pines and a low stony ridge. A quaint tumbling brook passed along one side of it and beams of sunlight shone through the forest canopy overhead. We set ourselves down, a few feet apart, on a large flat stone, overlooking a tranquil pool.

Brynne looked excited or worried, I couldn't tell which. "Eutychus and I loved this spot but I haven't been here since..." She hesitated, looked away, and licked her lips. "Since he passed away, but I'm comfortable and safe here with you, Michael."

"It's a peaceful place."

"I like the pool," she said. "It's deep enough to swim in on a hot summer day. I'd often go in for a swim and then stretch out and read for a while before returning home."

"It's serene." I tossed a pebble into the water. "A good place to relax and think." I tossed a second pebble into the water.

She leaned back and relaxed against a tree, growing tight up against the flat stone upon which we sat. A ray of sunlight rested on her head. She removed the ribbon from her long chestnut hair, which fell passed her shoulders. "Michael, I brought you here for a reason." She smiled, the corners of her eyes wrinkled up, and she blinked slowly.

I was nervous in the way she had taken my arm when we were walking, and now for the way in which she spoke. "A reason? What might it be?" My brows furrowed. "I don't understand."

She shifted herself a little closer to me on the large flat stone and looked deeply into my eyes. "I need to talk to you about something." She trembled, broke eye contact with me, and wet her lips. "I need to ask you a question." Again, she looked at me with a penetrating gaze. "Michael, would you ever be willing to—"

Abruptly, Louisa entered the clearing. "Brynne." She stood at the edge of the path with her hands on her hips. "Carolyn has spoken to me, and now, I need to speak to you." She glanced at me and then back at her daughter. "Alone." She gestured towards Brynne, inviting her onto the path.

I felt out of place, awkward in fact. "Good morning, Louisa. Don't mind me. I'd like to remain here with my thoughts and enjoy the warm morning."

Brynne and Louisa headed back down the path away from me, disappearing from my sight.

~~~~~~

On Saturday morning, I sat down to breakfast with Louisa and Edwyn.

"Where's Brynne?" I asked.

After some unusual looks between Edwyn and his wife, Louisa responded, "She's gone for a walk." Louisa, almost in tears and breathing deeply, continued. "She'll be missing you quite a bit, Michael. She's grown quite fond of you and said that she couldn't bear to say goodbye."

We ate our breakfast, engaging in trivial conversation, each of us uncomfortable with my imminent departure.

"Brynne's very special to me as well. I'd like to bid her farewell. The tide will be easing out shortly."

Edwyn, when he had finished eating, pushed his chair back from the table and put his arm around his wife's waist as she stood beside his chair. "Thank you so much, my love. It was a wonderful breakfast."

"You're welcome, dear. I'm glad you enjoyed it." Louisa then busied herself with clearing the table.

Edwyn, looking at me, cleared his throat. "Brynne decided not to eat with us this morning because she truly wants to be alone." Edwyn's brow wrinkled. "She'll be missing you. We'll all miss you." He reached over onto a small side table near to where we were sitting, and grasping a canvas bag, rested it on the table in front of him.

"When I think of being away from you and your contented home, I have something of an empty feeling. I'm missing each of you so much already." I rested my elbows on the table. "It might seem a long time but I'm planning on returning in the spring. Without your fine cooking, Louisa, I'll be losing weight."

"And Brynne's cooking as well," she responded.

"Yes, of course, Brynne's delicious cooking as well."

"I've got something for you," said Edwyn. He pulled his telescope from the bag and passed it to me in its sturdy leather case. "I'd like you to have this. You'll get some practical use out of it, I'm sure."

"No doubt about that, Edwyn. Thank you. I'll take good care of it."

"I know you will," he responded. "Take a look in the little compartment within the case. I put the teal, teardrop amethyst necklace in there. Lord Warrington wanted you to have it. No one knows where it originated and even the Caine and Smythe families said they had no knowledge of it. Lord Warrington thought that it would serve you well as a remembrance of your help in obtaining Myra's freedom."

"Thank him for me. His pursuit of justice and the way in which the entire community stood together to secure her freedom was commendable."

"I will extend your appreciation to him." Edwyn leaned towards me and whispered, "I'd also like you to have my..." He hesitated and looked over at his wife. "My new walking stick." He whispered, "My fearsome blackthorn cudgel."

"Thank you, Edwyn." I winked and scratched my chin. "It will be useful to have on long walks."

"Safety and security," Edwyn added, "are always an important consideration."

I realized that time was passing and that the tide would soon begin to flow out to sea. "I must be going over to the main dock. My destiny, at least for the next few months, lies aboard the *Eleutheran Quest* and then on Eleuthera." I rose to my feet.

Edwyn stood without speaking.

"Tell Brynne goodbye. We've become quite close. She means a lot to me."

"I surely will," responded Edwyn, as Louisa looked away.

The three of us stepped out onto the porch together.

"Goodbye, Louisa." I leaned in towards her and gave her a hug. "The baking and cooking that you and Brynne have done for me has been marvelous."

"Take care of yourself," she responded. She then stepped back inside.

"My dear Louisa doesn't like long goodbyes."

I turned towards Edwyn. "I'll miss you like no other. I'm looking forward to seeing you and working with you again. You've taught me so much." I bit my lip. "Not merely about woodworking but about life." We shook hands, pulled each other in, and with our other hands, slapped each other's backs. "I appreciate you deeply."

"And I you," he said, as he seated himself in his chair. "I think I'll watch from here as you pass by aboard the ship. I'll be praying for you." It almost seemed to me that his hand dropped down beside his chair as if to stroke Eutychus.

Less than an hour later, after some sentimental goodbyes and a tearful embrace between Carolyn and Tommy, we were aboard the ship.

Tommy, having been shown his hammock crowded in amongst the other inexperienced landsmen, and I, having been shown to my cabin, were now back on deck. Standing together more like brothers than friends, we looked down into the groups of people on the dock beside our ship, I was faced with the memories of each of these dear friends.

John Lyon, clenching his pipe in his teeth, sat on a crate beside Belinda. He had her smallest child on his lap, and the older one clutched his arm affectionately. George, standing with his father, was looking at his hand, opening and closing his fist. He looked up, and when he saw me, he touched the brim of his tricorn hat.

My eyes met Carolyn's, and close beside her stood the magistrate from Warrington Hall. *Why is he here? I wonder if he's asked Carolyn about Caine's fall. I refuse to think about the miscreant's death.*

Uncle Martin, with one arm around Aunt Muriel, raised his other, clutching his Bible in a victorious gesture. A memory assailed me: *"There is a stain on the heart of man and a chain about his soul."* I glanced back at Carolyn standing with the magistrate.

Captain Henderson, enjoying his position of authority and the drama of the departure, stood at the front of the quarter-deck looking like a captain of His Majesty's grandest warship. He was deep in conversation with Sailing Master Powell as they gestured and pointed towards various sails and other parts of the ship.

The captain stood silently for a moment and then his voice boomed, **"Make ready to leave port, Master Powell."**

Master Powell immediately shouted out the subset of orders required and men instantly obeyed.

The gangplank, handrail, helm, mooring lines, and fenders were each dealt with expertly. Their procedure and expertise was much like that of the *Serene Breeze,* which had impressed me months earlier. A gentle breeze, assisting the tide, eased the *Eleutheran Quest* ever so slightly away from the dock.

"**Set sail for harbor passage, Master Powell,**" commanded the captain.

Again, Powell shouted out the subset of orders needed to move the ship further away from the dock and out into the open water of the harbor. The seamen expertly raised, freed, and adjusted the several sails required, specifically as Master Powell had directed.

Shielding my eyes, I looked aloft. There was Meiling on the footrope of the mainsail, working as one of the topmen, trousered but wearing her feminine jacket. The unfurled mainsail billowed out in the breeze.

"**Take her to sea, Master Powell,**" directed Captain Henderson with the full authority of his position.

Master Powell, as before, shouted out the numerous additional orders required. The men worked, knowing exactly where they should be and what they should be doing, and it resulted in the exact and powerful movement of the ship. The remaining sails were unfurled, set, and filled with the northeast breeze. Like a great mythic beast inhaling and filling its chest with life-giving spirit, the great ship arose, eager to be free of the confines of the little harbor.

A few minutes later, we gracefully sailed by the Brixton home. Edwyn and Louisa were on the porch waving. Edwyn stood, and raising both of his hands, waved with even more vigor. He pointed at his chest, then at me, and then bowed his head for a moment, and in a prayer-like fashion, clasped his hands together. I imagined it to be a gesture that he would be praying for me. I returned his wave vigorously as our ship moved through the harbor. *If he knew the depths of my need and the emptiness in my heart, he would know more fully how to pray for me. He sees me as a confident pure-hearted man. He doesn't see my stain, nor does he hear my chain.* I swept the worrisome consideration from my mind.

WE BOTH SHALL ROW, MY LOVE AND I

Crossing to the south side and looking across the water, I saw Fair Havens Church and the graveyard beside it. I breathed deeply several times and clenched my eyes shut. My heart filled with memories of Madelyn. *I need to be strong to say goodbye. Madelyn, my love, I am a different man having met you. Love is so much more than romance.* My mouth dropped open. I inhaled deeply. A painful tenderness formed in my heart. *My darling Madelyn, I will do justice on Eleuthera. I will seek the Lord but I'm not sure what that means.*

Needing to take a final look at our home, Madelyn's home, I crossed back to the north side of our ship. There, on the top step of the front porch, sat Brynne. Her elbows rested on her knees, and her head was bowed and covered with a dark blue shawl. She looked despondent. Glancing up as the *Eleutheran Quest* sailed by and searching the deck of the ship, she found me. Realizing that our eyes had met, she stood and raised her hand to bid me farewell. Walking along the porch, as if trying to remain near me, she gently waved. Returning her wave, I knew that I'd miss her, and my many friends of Oak Harbor. Brynne waved one last time and then leaned against and embraced the final post of the porch.

As we gained more headway and neared the mouth of the harbor, she could no longer be clearly seen. The *Eleutheran Quest* adjusted course, farther to the south, and as we entered the passage between the long rocky point and the barrier island, the shoreline view of Madelyn's home was blocked entirely from my sight.

Mark G. Turner

The Eleutheran Quest

A Closing Pastoral

Although there is ultimately no home or place of peace within which one may find complete security and freedom, apart from the loving presence of our Lord, I offer this pastoral poem.

On countless occasions, seeking a retreat from city stress, I have found myself at rest and enjoying the Lord of Creation in the midst of His wilderness, with my Bible, His Word, in my hands and a prayer in my heart.

God's Quiet Ink

This is my home of rock and tree,
Secure beneath this canopy,
Of leafy green and sky of blue,
This quiet valley wet with dew.

Is this my home embracing me?
As it surrounds, it sets me free,
From city stress and worldly care,
This quiet place this fox's lair.

My heart is home, this truth I see,
The scent of pine, the sound of bee,
The playful squirrel, the gentle deer,
I quietly watch, so far from fear.

Home is this place you've given me,
These hills and streams, my destiny.
Upon this rock, I sit and think,
God has used some quiet ink.
                    Mark G. Turner

About the Author

Mark G. Turner and his wife, Emma Marie, are active participants in a local church in Canada and have served as Bible teachers, counselors, and leaders in a variety of settings. They have served in Canada, the United States, the Philippines, Great Britain, the Bahamas, and recently the People's Republic of China. Mr. Turner has been a worship leader, elder, and Bible teacher for international students and Chinese Christians.

Mr. Turner has taught Bible at the college level, English at the university level, has been a public school teacher, and a social worker. He is a graduate of Briercrest College and Seminary, the University of Waterloo, York University, and the University of Leeds (MMU, music composition).

If you have found this novel interesting and would like to arrange a speaking opportunity please contact the author.

His previous book, *The Lord Is My Song*, is a series of music devotionals for worship leaders, Christian musicians, and all who love to worship our Lord. It is available on Amazon in both hardcopy and electronic form, and in some bookstores.

Mr. Turner, as an orchestral composer, has had his music premiered in the United States, Canada, Great Britain, and the People's Republic of China. A limited sampling of some of his smaller ensemble compositions can be heard and purchased through sheetmusicplus.com by simply entering his name,

Mark G. Turner

Mark G. Turner, into the search box. Contact him directly and request a sampling of his works for full symphony orchestra.

To contact him personally regarding his music or to arrange opportunities to teach or speak, he may be reached by email at mjacksonturner2017@gmail.com . If he is out of the country or if you are having difficulty reaching him, he may be contacted through his daughter, Anna Marie Dueck by email at annamariedueck@gmail.com .

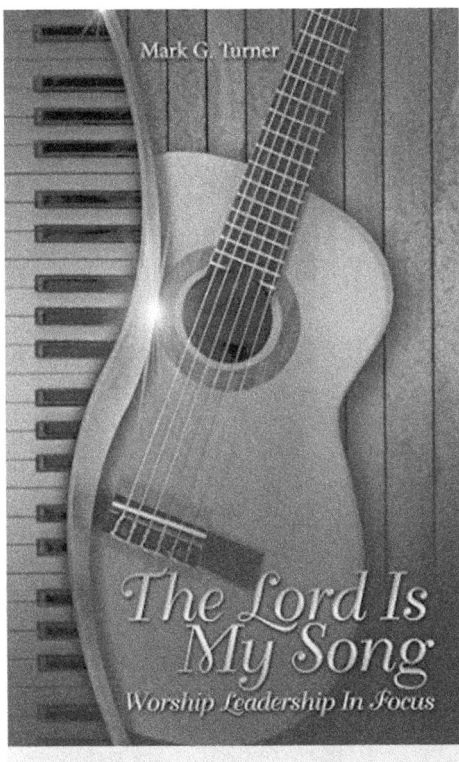

> Music is an alluring art form, but the glory of our Almighty God must be restored as the singular purpose of our worship and song.
>
> Mark G. Turner

Available on Amazon

- A Devotional Book published in 2016 -
A marvelous resource for inspiring worship leaders, their teams, choir directors, and anyone who thrives on worshipping the Lord. This is a comprehensive set of devotionals based on music-focused Scriptures to be meditated on and to be used to encourage all involved in preparing for corporate or personal worship.

Brass Exultancy

O' Kestrel Music
Mark G. Turner

This original work for brass quintet is mentioned in the third chapter of the novel.

- This march, with its stimulating dynamics, powerful melodies, and exuberant counterpoint will hold the attention of any audience.
- With dramatic modulations to other keys it carries the performers and listeners on a journey they will never forget. Playing time - 3:52.

Listen to this brass quintet and purchase the sheet music.

www.sheetmusicplus.com

Type my name, Mark G. Turner into the search box.